THE BARTIMAEUS TRILOGY

BOOK TWO

The Golem's Eye

BARTIMÆUS

The Golem's Eye

JONATHAN STROUD

DISNEP • HYPERION

LOS ANGELES   NEW YORK

Copyright © 2004 by Jonathan Stroud

First Disney • Hyperion Paperback Edition, January 2006

7 9 10 8

Printed in the United States of America

ISBN 0-7868-3654-7

Library of Congress Cataloging-in-Publication Control Number: 2004054232

FAC-25438-17132

Visit www.DisneyBooks.com

SUSTAINABLE
FORESTRY
INITIATIVE

Certified Chain of Custody
Promoting Sustainable Forestry

www.sfiprogram.org
SFI-01054

The SFI label applies to the text stock

For Philippa

The Main Characters

THE MAGICIANS

Mr. Rupert Devereaux	Prime Minister of Great Britain and the Empire
Mr. Carl Mortensen	Home Secretary
Ms. Jessica Whitwell	Security Minister
Mr. Henry Duvall	Chief of Police
Mr. Marmaduke Fry	Foreign Secretary
Ms. Helen Malbindi	Information Minister
Mr. Julius Tallow	Head of Internal Affairs
Mr. John Mandrake	Assistant to the Head of Internal Affairs
Mr. George Ffoukes	Magician Fourth Level; Department of Internal Affairs
Ms. Jane Farrar	Assistant to the Chief of Police
Mr. Sholto Pinn	A merchant; proprietor of Pinn's Accoutrements of Piccadilly
Mr. Quentin Makepeace	A playwright; author of *Swans of Araby* and other works

And various other magicians, policemen, and spies

THE COMMONERS

Kitty Jones

Jakob Hyrnek

Mr. T. E. Pennyfeather

Anne Stephens

Frederick Weaver

Stanley Hake

Nicholas Drew

Clem Hopkins

And other members of the Resistance

THE SPIRITS

Bartimaeus	A djinni—in service to Mr. Mandrake
Queezle	A djinni—in service to Mr. Ffoukes
Shubit	A djinni—in service to Ms. Whitwell
Nemaides	A djinni—in service to Mr. Tallow
Simpkin	A foliot—in service to Mr. Pinn

And numerous other afrits, djinn, foliots, and imps

THE
BARTIMAEUS
TRILOGY
BOOK TWO

The Golem's Eye

Prologue:
Prague, 1868

At dusk, the enemy lit their campfires one by one, in greater profusion than on any night before. The lights sparkled like fiery jewels out in the grayness of the plains, so numerous it seemed an enchanted city had sprung up from the earth. By contrast, within our walls the houses had their shutters closed, their lights blacked out. A strange reversal had taken place— Prague itself was dark and dead, while the countryside around it flared with life.

Soon afterward, the wind began to drop. It had been blowing strongly from the west for hours, carrying word of the invaders' movements—the rattling of the siege engines, the calling of the troops and animals, the sighing of the captive spirits, the odors of the incantations. Now, with unnatural speed, it died away and the air was steeped in silence.

I was floating high above the Strahov Monastery, just inside the magnificent city walls I'd built three hundred years before.

My leathery wings moved in strong, slow beats; my eyes scanned the seven planes to the horizon.[1] It did not make for happy viewing. The mass of the British army was cloaked behind Concealments, but its ripples of power already lapped at the base of Castle Hill. The auras of a vast contingent of spirits were dimly visible in the gloom; with every minute further brief trembles on the planes signaled the arrival of new battalions. Groups of human soldiers moved purposefully over the dark ground. In their midst stood a cluster of great white tents, domed like rocs' eggs, about which Shields and other spells hung cobweb-thick.[2]

I raised my gaze to the darkened sky. It was an angry black mess of clouds, smeared with streaks of yellow to the west. At a high altitude and scarcely visible in the dying light, I spied six faint dots circling well out of Detonation range. They progressed steadily widdershins, mapping out the walls a final time, checking the strength of our defenses.

Speaking of which . . . I had to do the same.

At Strahov Gate, farthest flung and most vulnerable outpost of the walls, the tower had been raised and strengthened. The

---

[1] *The Seven Planes*: The seven accessible planes are superimposed upon each other, and each reveals certain aspects of reality. The first includes ordinary material things (trees, buildings, humans, animals, etc.), which are visible to all; the other six contain spirits of various kinds going quietly about their business. Higher beings (such as me) can use inner eyes to observe all seven planes at once, but more lowly creatures have to make do with seeing fewer. Humans are remarkably lowly. Magicians use contact lenses to see planes two to three, but most people only see the first plane, and this makes them ignorant about all kinds of magical activity. For example, there's probably something invisible with lots of tentacles hovering behind your back right NOW.

[2] Doubtless, this was where the British magicians were skulking, at a safe distance from the action. My Czech masters were just the same. In war, magicians always like to reserve the most dangerous jobs for themselves, such as fearlessly guarding large quantities of food and drink a few miles behind the lines.

ancient doors were sealed with triple hexes and a wealth of trigger mechanisms, and the lowering battlements at the crest of the tower bristled with watchful sentries.

That at least was the idea.

To the tower I flew, hawk-headed, leather-winged, hidden behind my shroud of wisps. I alighted barefoot, without a sound, on a prominent crest of stone. I waited for the swift, sharp challenge, the vigorous display of instant readiness.

Nothing happened. I dropped my Concealment and waited for some moderate, belated evidence of alertness. I coughed loudly. Still no joy.

A glimmering Shield protected part of the battlements, and behind this crouched five sentries.[3] The Shield was a narrow affair, designed for one human soldier or three djinn at most. As such, there was a good deal of fidgeting going on.

"Will you *stop* pushing?"

"Ow! Mind those claws, you idiot!"

"Just shove over. I tell you, my backside's in plain view now. They might spot it."

"That could win us the battle on its own."

"Keep that wing under control! You nearly had my eye out."

"Change into something smaller, then. I suggest a nematode worm."

"If you elbow me one more time . . ."

"It's not *my* fault. It's that Bartimaeus who put us here. He's such a pomp—"

---

[3] Each sentry was a minor djinni, scarcely better than a common foliot. Times were hard in Prague; the magicians were strapped for slaves and quality control was not what it should have been. The chosen semblances of my sentries proved as much. Instead of fearsome, warlike guises, I was presented with two shifty vampire bats, a weasel, a pop-eyed lizard, and a small and rather mournful frog.

It was a painful display of laxity and incompetence, in short, and I refrain from recording it in full. The hawk-headed warrior folded its wings, stepped forward, and roused the sentries' attention by banging their heads together smartly.[4]

"And what kind of sentry duty do you call *this*?" I snapped. I was in no mood to mess about here; six months of continual service had worn my essence thin. "Cowering behind a Shield, bickering like fishwives . . . I ordered you to *keep watch*."

Amid the pathetic mumbling and shuffling and staring at feet that followed, the frog put up its hand.

"Please, Mr. Bartimaeus, sir," it said, "what's the good of watching? The British are everywhere—sky *and* land. And we've heard they've got a whole cohort of afrits down there. Is that true?"

I pointed my beak at the horizon, narrow-eyed. "Maybe."

The frog gave a moan. "But we ain't got a single one, have we? Not since Phoebus bought it. And there's marids down there, too, we've heard, more than one. *And* the leader's got this Staff—real powerful, it is. Tore up Paris and Cologne on the way here, they say. Is *that* true?"

My crest feathers ruffled gently in the breeze. "Maybe."

The frog gave a yelp. "Ohh, but that's just dreadful, ain't it? We've no hope now. All afternoon the summonings have been coming thick and fast, and that means only one thing. They'll attack tonight. We'll all be dead by morning."

Well, he wasn't going to do our morale much good with that kind of talk.[5] I put a hand on his warty shoulder. "Listen, son . . . what's your name?"

---

[4] Five heads knocking into one another in quick succession. It was like an unusual executive toy.

[5] i.e., accurate.

"Nubbin, sir."

"Nubbin. Well, don't go believing everything you hear, Nubbin. The British army's strong, sure. In fact, I've rarely seen stronger. But let's say it is. Let's say it's got marids, whole legions of afrits, and horlas by the bucket-load. Let's say they're all going to come pouring at us tonight, right here at the Strahov Gate. Well, let them come. We've got tricks to send them packing."

"Such as what, sir?"

"Tricks that'll blow those afrits and marids right out of the air. Tricks we've all learned in the heat of a dozen battles. Tricks that mean one sweet word: *survival*."

The frog's bulbous eyes blinked at me. "This is my first battle, sir."

I made an impatient gesture. "Failing that, the Emperor's djinn say his magicians are working on something or other. A last line of defense. Some hare-brained scheme, no doubt." I patted his shoulder in a manly way. "Feel better now, son?"

"No, sir. I feel worse."

Fair enough. I was never much cop at those pep talks. "All right," I growled. "My advice is to duck fast and when possible run away. With luck, your masters will get killed before you are. Personally, that's what *I'm* banking on."

I hope this rousing speech did them some good, for it was at that moment that the attack came. Far off, there was a reverberation on all seven planes. We all felt it: it was a single note of imperious command. I spun around to look out into the dark, and one by one, the five sentries' heads popped up above the battlements.

Out on the plains, the great army surged into action.

At their head, soaring on the updrafts of a sudden ferocious wind, came the djinn, armored in red and white, carrying slender pikes with silver tips. Their wings hummed; their screams made the tower shake. Below, on foot, a ghostly multitude: the horlas with their carved bone tridents, skipping into the huts and houses outside the walls in search of prey.[6] Beside them, vague shadows flitted, ghuls and fetches, wraiths of cold and misery, insubstantial on every plane. And then, with a great chattering and champing of jaws, a thousand imps and foliots rose from the earth like a dust storm or a monstrous swarm of bees. All these and many others came a-hurrying toward the Strahov Gate.

The frog tapped my elbow. "Good job you had a word with us, sir," he said. "I'm overwhelmingly confident now, thanks to you."

I scarcely heard him. I was staring far off beyond the terrible host, to a low rise near the domed white tents. A man was standing on it, holding up a stick or a staff. He was too remote for me to take in many details, but I could sense his power all right. His aura lit up the hill about him. As I watched, several lightning bolts speared from the boiling clouds, impaling themselves upon the tip of the outstretched staff. The hill, the tents, the waiting soldiers, were briefly lit, as if by day. The light went out, the energy absorbed into the staff. Thunder rolled about the beleaguered city.

"So *that's* him, is it?" I muttered. "The famous Gladstone."

---

[6] They found no one, as their disappointed keening soon attested. The suburbs were deserted. Almost as soon as the British army crossed the Channel, the Czech authorities had begun preparing for the inevitable attack on Prague. As a first precaution, the population of the city was removed to within the walls—which, incidentally, were the strongest in Europe at the time, a marvel of magical engineering. Did I mention I had a hand in their construction?

The djinn were nearing the walls now, passing over waste ground and the wrecks of newly dismantled buildings. As they did so, a buried hex was triggered; jets of blue-green fire erupted upward, incinerating the leaders where they flew. But the fire died back, and the rest came on.

This was the trigger for the defenders to act: a hundred imps and foliots rose from the walls, uttering tinny cries and sending Detonations toward the flying horde. The invaders replied in kind. Infernos and Fluxes met and mingled in the half dark; shadows looped and spun against the flares of light. Beyond, Prague's fringes were aflame; the first of the horlas thronged below us, trying to snap the sturdy Binding spells that I'd used to secure the walls' foundations.

I unfurled my wings, ready to enter the fray; at my side, the frog swelled out its throat and uttered a defiant croak. The next instant a looping bolt of energy stabbed from the magician's staff far off on the hill, arced through the sky and smashed into the Strahov Gate tower, just below the battlements. Our Shield was ruptured like tissue paper. Mortar and stone shattered, the roof of the tower gave way. I was blown spinning into the air—and fell, almost to earth, colliding heavily with a cartload of hay bales that had been drawn inside the gates before the siege began. Above me, the wooden structure of the tower was on fire. I could not see any of the sentries. Imps and djinn milled about confusedly in the sky above, exchanging bursts of magic. Bodies dropped from the sky, igniting roofs. From nearby houses, women and children ran screaming. The Strahov Gate shook with the scratching of the horlas' tridents. It would not hold for long.

The defenders needed my help. I extricated myself from the hay with my usual haste.

"When you've picked the last bit of straw from your loin-cloth, Bartimaeus," a voice said, "you're wanted up at the castle."

The hawk-headed warrior glanced up. "Oh—hullo, Queezle."

An elegant she-leopard was sitting in the middle of the street, staring at me with lime-green eyes. As I watched, she negligently rose, walked a few paces to the side, sat down again. A gout of burning pitch slammed into the cobblestones where she'd been, leaving a smoldering crater. "Bit busy," she remarked.

"Yes. We're done for here." I jumped down from the cart.

"Looks like the Binding spells in the walls are breaking," the leopard said, glancing at the trembling gate. "There's shoddy workmanship for you. Wonder which djinni built that?"

"Can't think," I said. "So, then—our master calls?"

The leopard nodded. "Better hurry, or he'll stipple us. Let's go on foot. Sky's too crowded."

"Lead on." I changed, became a panther, black as midnight. We ran up through the narrow streets toward Hradčany Square. The roads we took were empty; we avoided the places where the panic-stricken people surged like livestock. More and more buildings were burning now, gables collapsing, side walls falling in. Around the roofs small imps were dancing, waving embers in their hands.

At the castle, imperial servants stood in the square under flickering lanterns, gathering random pieces of furniture into carts; beside them ostlers were struggling to tether horses to the struts. The sky above the city was peppered with bursts of colored light; behind, back toward Strahov and the monastery, came the dull thump of explosions. We slipped through the main entrance unopposed.

"The Emperor's getting out, is he?" I panted. Frantic imps were passing us, balancing cloth bundles on their heads.

"He's more concerned about his beloved birds," Queezle said. "Wants our afrits to airlift them to safety." The green eyes flicked at me in rueful amusement.

"But all the afrits are dead."

"Exactly. Well, almost there."

We had arrived in the northern wing of the castle, where the magicians had their quarters. The taint of magic hung thick about the stones. Down a long flight of stairs the leopard and panther ran, out along a balcony overlooking the Stag Moat, and in through the arch that led to the Lower Workroom. This was a broad, circular room that took up almost the entire ground floor of the White Tower. I had been summoned here often over the centuries, but now the usual magical paraphernalia—the books, the incense pots, the candelabra—had been swept aside, to make way for a row of ten chairs and tables. On each table was a crystal orb, flickering with light; on each chair, a hunched magician peering into his or her respective orb. There was absolute silence in the room.

Our master was standing at a window, staring through a telescope into the dark sky.[7] He noticed us, made a gesture for silence, then beckoned us into a side room. His gray hair had turned white with the strain of the last few weeks; his hooked nose hung thin and pinched, and his eyes were as red as an

---

[7] The telescope contained an imp whose gaze allowed humans to see by night. These are useful devices, although capricious imps sometimes distort the view, or add perverse elements of their own: streams of golden dust, strange dreamlike visions, or ghostly figures from the user's past.

imp's.[8] He scratched at the back of his neck. "You don't need to tell me," he said. "I know. How long have we got?"

The panther flicked its tail. "I'd give us an hour, no more."

Queezle looked back toward the main room, where the silent magicians toiled. "You're bringing out the golems, I see," she said.

The magician nodded curtly. "They will cause great damage to the enemy."

"It won't be enough," I said. "Even with ten. Have you seen the *size* of the army out there?"

"As ever, Bartimaeus, your opinion is ill considered and unlooked for. This is a diversion only. We plan to get His Highness away down the eastern steps. A boat is waiting at the river. The golems will ring the castle and cover our retreat."

Queezle was still staring at the magicians; they stooped low over their crystals, mouthing continuous silent instructions to their creatures. Faint moving images in the crystals showed each one what his or her golem saw. "The British won't bother with the monsters," Queezle said. "They'll find these operators and kill *them*."

My master bared his teeth. "By then the Emperor will be gone. And that, incidentally, is my new charge for both of you—to guard His Highness during his escape. Understood?"

I held up a paw. The magician gave a heartfelt sigh. "Yes, Bartimaeus?"

"Well, sir," I said, "if I might make a suggestion. Prague's

---

[8] Comparing masters is rather like comparing facial spots: some are worse than others, but even the best don't exactly tickle your fancy. This one was the twelfth Czech magician I'd served. He wasn't overly cruel, but he was a bit sour, as if lemon juice ran in his veins. He was also thin-lipped and pedantic, obsessed with his duty to the Empire.

surrounded. If we try to escape the city with the Emperor, we'll all die horribly. So why don't we just forget the old fool and slip away instead? There's a little beer cellar on Karlova Street with a dried-up well. Not deep. The entrance is a bit small, but—"

He frowned. "You expect me to hide in there?"

"Well, it would be tight, but I reckon we could squeeze you in. Your pot belly might give us trouble, but it's nothing a good shove wouldn't fix—Ow!" My fur crackled; I broke off sharpish. As always, the Red-hot Stipples made me lose my train of thought.

"Unlike you," the magician snarled, "I know the meaning of loyalty! I do not need to be compelled to act honorably toward my master. I repeat: you are both to guard his life with your own. Do you understand?"

We nodded reluctantly; as we did so, the floor shook with a nearby explosion.

"Then follow me," he said. "We don't have much time."

Back up the stairs we went, and through the echoing corridors of the castle. Bright flashes illuminated the windows; fearsome cries echoed all around. My master ran on his spindly legs, wheezing with each step; Queezle and I loped alongside.

At last we came out onto the terrace where for years the Emperor had maintained his aviary. It was a large affair, delicately constructed from ornate bronze, with domes and minarets and feeding ledges, and doors for the Emperor to stroll between. The interior was filled with trees and potted shrubs, and a remarkable variety of parrots, whose ancestors had been brought to Prague from distant lands. The Emperor was besotted with these birds; in recent times, as London's power grew and the

Empire slipped from his hands, he had taken to sitting for long periods within the aviary, communing with his friends. Now, with the night sky rent by magical confrontation, the birds were in panic, swirling around the cage in a flurry of feathers, squawking fit to burst. The Emperor, a small plump gentleman in satin breeches and a crumpled white chemise, was little better off, remonstrating with his bird handlers and ignoring the advisors who massed about him.

The Chief Minister, Meyrink, pale, sad-eyed, was plucking at his sleeve. "Your Highness, *please*. The British are pouring up Castle Hill. We must get you to safety—"

"I *cannot* leave my aviary! Where are my magicians? Summon them here!"

"Sir, they are engaged in battle—"

"My afrits, then? My faithful Phoebus . . ."

"Sir, as I have already informed you several times—"

My master shouldered his way through. "Sir: I present Queezle and Bartimaeus, who will assist us in our departure, then save your wondrous birds as well."

"Two cats, man? Two *cats*?" The Emperor's mouth went all white and pursed.[9]

Queezle and I rolled our eyes. She became a girl of unusual beauty; I took Ptolemy's form. "Now, Your Highness," my master said, "the eastern steps . . ."

Great concussions in the city; half the suburbs were now alight. A small imp came bowling over the parapet at the end of the terrace, its tail aflame. It skidded to a halt beside us. "Permission to report, sir. A number of savage afrits are fighting their way up to the castle. The charge is led by Honorius

---

[9] It was rather catlike in itself, if you get my meaning.

and Patterknife, Gladstone's personal servants. They are very terrible, sir. Our troops have broken before them." It paused, looked at its smoldering tail. "Permission to find water, sir?"

"And the golems?" Meyrink demanded.

The imp shuddered. "Yessir. They have just engaged with the enemy. I kept well away from the cloud, of course, but I believe the British afrits have fallen back a little, in disarray. Now, about the water—"

The Emperor gave a warbling cry. "Good, good! Victory is ours!"

"The advantage is only temporary," Meyrink said. "Come sir, we must go."

Despite his protests, the Emperor was bundled away from the cage, toward a wicket gate. Meyrink and my master were at the head of the group, the Emperor behind, his short frame hidden among the courtiers. Queezle and I brought up the rear.

A flash of light. Over the parapet behind us two black figures came leaping. Tattered cloaks whipped about them, yellow eyes burned in the depths of their cowls. They moved across the terrace in great drifting bounds, touching ground only rarely. In the aviary, the birds fell into sudden silence.

I looked at Queezle. "Yours or mine?"

The beautiful girl smiled at me, showing her sharp teeth. "Mine." She fell back to meet the advancing ghuls. I ran on after the Emperor's entourage.

Beyond the gate, a narrow path followed the moat north, under the castle wall. Down below, the Old Town was on fire; I could see the British troops running through the streets, and Prague's people fleeing, fighting, falling before them. It all seemed far away; the only sound that came to us was a distant sighing. Flocks of imps drifted here and there like birds.

The Emperor ceased his loud complaints. The group hurried in silence through the night. So far, so good. We were at the Black Tower now, at the top of the eastern steps, and the way ahead was clear.

A flutter of wings; Queezle landed beside me, ashen-faced. She was wounded in the side. "Trouble?" I said.

"Not the ghuls. An afrit. But a golem came, destroyed it. I'm fine."

Onward down the stairs in the side of the hill. Light from the burning castle was reflected in the waters of the Vltava below, giving it a melancholy beauty. We met no one, no one pursued us, and soon the worst of the conflict was left behind.

As the river neared, Queezle and I gave each other hopeful looks. The city was lost, as was the Empire, but escape here would allow us some small restoration of personal pride. Although we loathed our servitude, we also thoroughly disliked being beaten. It looked as if we were going to get away.

The ambush came when we were nearly at the bottom of the hill.

With a scuttle and a rush, six djinn and a band of imps hopped out onto the steps below. The Emperor and his courtiers cried out and fell back in disarray. Queezle and I tensed, ready to spring.

A light cough behind us. As one, we turned.

A slim young man stood five steps above. He had tight blond curls, big blue eyes, and wore sandals and a toga in the late Roman style. He had a rather sappy, coy expression on his face, as if he couldn't hurt a fly. However, as an extra detail that I couldn't help but notice, he also carried a monstrous scythe with a silver blade.

I checked him out on the other planes, in the faint hope that he might actually be an eccentric human on his way to a fancy-dress party. No such luck. It was an afrit of some potency. I swallowed. This wasn't good at all.[10]

"Mr. Gladstone's compliments to the Emperor," the young man said. "He requests the pleasure of his company. The rest of you rabble can make yourselves scarce."

That sounded reasonable. I looked at my master beseechingly, but he furiously motioned me forward. I sighed, took a reluctant step toward the afrit.

The young man tsked loudly. "Oh, hop it, small-timer. You haven't a chance."

His derision stoked my fury. I pulled myself up. "Beware," I said coldly. "You underestimate me at your peril."

The afrit batted his eyelashes with an ostentatious lack of concern. "Indeed? Have you a name?"

"A name?" I cried. "I have *many* names! I am Bartimaeus! I am Sakhr al-Jinni! I am N'gorso the Mighty and the Serpent of Silver Plumes!"

I paused dramatically. The young man looked blank. "Nope. Never heard of you. Now if you'll just—"

"I have spoken with Solomon—"

"Oh, please!" The afrit made a dismissive gesture. "Haven't we all? Let's face it, he got around."

"I have rebuilt the walls of Uruk, Karnak, and Prague—"

The young man smirked. "Prague? What, these ones here? The ones it took Gladstone five minutes to break down? Sure you didn't work on Jericho, too?"

---

[10] The measliest afrit is worth avoiding, and this one was formidable indeed. On the higher planes, his forms were vast and terrifying, so presumably appearing in such a weedy first-plane guise appealed to his twisted sense of humor. I can't say I was laughing, though.

"Yes, he did," Queezle put in. "One of his first jobs. He keeps quiet about it, but—"

"Look, Queezle—"

The afrit fingered his scythe. "Last chance, djinni," he said. "Vamoose. You can't win this one."

I shrugged in a resigned sort of way. "We'll see."

And so, sad to say, we did. Very quickly, too. My first four Detonations were deflected by the twirling scythe. The fifth, which I'd made a real humdinger, rebounded directly at me, sending me crashing off the path and down the hill in a shower of essence. I tried to rise, but fell back in pain. My wound was too great; I could not recover in time.

Up on the path, the imps were pouring onto the courtiers. I saw Queezle and a burly djinni spin past, hands at each other's throats.

With insulting nonchalance, the afrit ambled down the slope toward me. He winked and raised the silver scythe.

And at that moment, my master acted.

He'd not been a particularly good one, all told—he'd been too fond of the Stipples for starters—but from my point of view his last deed was the best thing he ever did.

The imps were all around him, vaulting over his head, ducking between his legs, reaching for the Emperor. He gave a cry of fury and from a pocket in his jacket produced a Detonation stick, one of the new ones made by the alchemists of Golden Lane in response to the British threat. They were shoddy, mass-produced rubbish, inclined to explode too fast, or often not at all. Either way, it was best, when using them, to throw them speedily in the general direction of the enemy. But my master was a typical magician. He wasn't used to personal combat. He gabbled the Word of Command all right, but then proceeded to hesitate, holding the stick above his head and feinting at the imps, as if undecided which one to choose.

He hesitated a fraction too long.

The explosion tore half the stairs away. Imps, Emperor, and courtiers were blown into the air like dandelion seeds. My master himself vanished utterly, as if he had never been.

And with his death, the bonds that tethered me withered into nothing.

The afrit brought the scythe blade down, exactly where my head had lain. It drove uselessly into the ground.

Thus, after several hundred years and a dozen masters, my ties to Prague were broken. But as my grateful essence fled in all directions, and I looked down upon the burning city and the marching troops, on the wailing children and the whooping imps, on the death throes of one empire and the bloody baptism of the next, I must say I didn't feel particularly triumphant.

I had a feeling it was all going to get a whole lot worse.

Part One

I

London: a great and prosperous capital, two thousand years old, which in the hands of the magicians aspired to be the center of the world. In size at least it had succeeded. It had grown vast and ungainly on the rich feasts of empire.

The city sprawled for several miles on either side of the Thames, a smoke-bound crust of housing, dotted with palaces, towers, churches, and bazaars. At all times and in all places, it thrummed with activity. The streets were clogged and crowded with tourists, workers, and other human traffic, while the air buzzed invisibly with the passage of imps busy about their masters' errands.

On the crowded quays extending into the gray waters of the Thames, battalions of soldiers and bureaucrats waited to set sail on journeys across the globe. In the shadows of their iron-clad sailing ships, colorful merchant vessels of every size and shape negotiated the cluttered river. Bustling carracks from Europe; sharp-sailed Arab dhows, laden with spices; snub-nosed junks from China; elegant, slim-masted clippers from America—all were surrounded and impeded by the tiny river-boats of the Thames watermen, who competed loudly for the custom of guiding them into dock.

Two hearts powered the metropolis. To the east was the City district, where traders from distant lands gathered to exchange their wares; to the west, hugging a sharp bend in the river, lay the political mile of Westminster, where the magicians worked ceaselessly to extend and protect their territories abroad.

The boy had been in central London on business; now he was returning to Westminster on foot. He walked at an easy pace, for though it was still early morning, it was already warm, and he could feel the sweat beading beneath his collar. A slight breeze caught the edges of his long black coat and whipped it up behind him as he went. He was aware of the effect, which pleased him. Darkly impressive, it was; he could sense heads turning as he passed. On *really* windy days, with his coat flapping out horizontally, he had the feeling he didn't look quite so stylish.

He cut across Regent Street and down between the whitewashed Regency buildings to Haymarket, where the street sweepers were busy with broom and brush outside the theater fronts and young fruit sellers were already beginning to parade their wares. One woman supported a tray piled high with fine, ripe, colonial oranges, which had been scarce in London since the southern European wars began. The boy approached; as he passed, he flipped a coin dexterously into the small pewter bowl hanging from her neck and, with an extension of the same movement, plucked an orange from the top of the tray. Ignoring her thanks, he went his way. He did not break stride. His coat trailed impressively behind him.

At Trafalgar Square, a series of tall poles, each striped with a dozen spiraling colors, had recently been erected; gangs of workmen were at that moment winching ropes into place between them. Each rope was heavily laden with jaunty red, white, and blue flags. The boy stopped to peel his orange and consider the work.

A laborer passed, sweating under the weight of a mass of bunting.

The boy hailed him. "You, fellow. What's all this in aid of?"

The man glanced sideways, noticed the boy's long black

coat, and immediately attempted a clumsy salute. Half the bunting slipped out of his hands onto the pavement. "It's for tomorrow, sir," he said. "Founder's Day. National holiday, sir."

"Ah yes. Of course. Gladstone's birthday. I forgot." The boy tossed a coil of peel into the gutter and departed, leaving the workman grappling with the bunting and swearing under his breath.

And so down to Whitehall, a region of massive gray-clad buildings, heavy with the odor of long-established power. Here, the architecture alone was enough to browbeat any casual observer into submission: great marble pillars; vast bronze doors; hundreds upon hundreds of windows with lights burning at every hour; granite statues of Gladstone and other notables, their grim, lined faces promising the rigors of justice for all enemies of State. But the boy tripped with light steps past it all, peeling his orange with the unconcern of one born to it. He nodded to a policeman, flashed his pass to a guard, and stepped through a side gate into the courtyard of the Department of Internal Affairs, under the shade of a spreading walnut tree. Only now did he pause, gulp down the remainder of his orange, wipe his hands on his handkerchief, and adjust his collar, cuffs, and tie. He smoothed back his hair a final time. Good. He was ready now. It was time to go to work.

More than two years had passed since the time of Lovelace's rebellion, and the sudden emergence of Nathaniel into the elite. By now, he was fourteen years old, taller by a head than when he had returned the Amulet of Samarkand to the protective custody of a grateful government; bulkier, too, but still lean-framed, with his dark hair hanging long and shaggy around his face after the fashion of the day. His face was thin and pale with long hours of study, but his eyes burned hot and bright; all his movements were characterized by a barely suppressed energy.

Being a keen observer, Nathaniel had soon perceived that among working magicians, appearance was an important factor in maintaining status. Shabby attire was frowned upon; indeed it was a sure-fire mark of mediocre talent. He did not intend to give this impression. With the stipend that he received from his department, he had bought a tight-fitting black drainpipe suit and a long Italian coat, both of which he considered dangerously fashionable. He wore slim, slightly pointed shoes and a succession of garish handkerchiefs, which provided an explosion of color across his breast. With this outfit carefully in place, he would walk around the Whitehall cloisters with a lanky, purposeful stride, reminiscent of some wading bird, clutching sheaves of paper in his arms.

His birth name he kept well hidden. To his colleagues and associates, he was known by his adult name, John Mandrake.

Two other magicians had borne this name, neither of great renown. The first, an alchemist in the days of Queen Elizabeth, had turned lead to gold in a celebrated experiment before the court. It was afterward discovered that he had managed this by coating gold pellets with thin films of lead, which vanished when gently heated. His ingenuity was applauded, but he was beheaded nonetheless. The second John Mandrake was a furniture-maker's son who had spent his life researching the many variants of demonic mite. He had amassed a list of 1,703 increasingly irrelevant subtypes before one of them, a Lesser Frilled Green Hornetwing, stung him in an unguarded area; he swelled to the size of a chaise lounge and so died.

The inglorious careers of his predecessors did not concern

Nathaniel. In fact, they gave him quiet satisfaction. He intended to make the name famous for himself alone.

Nathaniel's master was Ms. Jessica Whitwell, a magician of indeterminate age, with cropped white hair and a frame that was slender, tending to the skeletal. She was reckoned one of the four most potent magicians in the government, and her influence was long. She recognized her apprentice's talent and set about developing it fully.

Living in a spacious apartment in his master's riverside town-house, Nathaniel led an ordered, well-directed existence. The house was modern and sparsely furnished, its carpets lynx-gray and the walls stark white. The furniture was made of glass and silvered metal, and of pale wood felled in Nordic forests. The whole place had a cool, businesslike, almost antiseptic feel, which Nathaniel came to admire strongly: it signaled control, clarity, and efficiency, all hallmarks of the contemporary magician.

Ms. Whitwell's style even extended to her library. In most magical households, libraries were dark, brooding places—their books bound in exotic animal skins, with embroidered pentacles or curse runes on the spines. But this look, Nathaniel now learned, was *very* last century. Ms. Whitwell had requested Jaroslav's, the printers and bookbinders, to provide uniform bindings of white leather for all her tomes, which were then indexed and stamped with identifying numbers in black ink.

In the center of this white-walled room of neat white books was a rectangular glass table, and here Nathaniel would sit two days every week, working on the higher mysteries.

In the early months of his tenure with Ms. Whitwell, he had embarked on a period of intensive study and, to her surprise and approval, mastered successive grades of summoning in record time. He had progressed from the lowest level of demon (mites, moulers, and goblin-imps), to medium (the full range of foliots), to advanced (djinn of various castes) in a matter of days.

After watching him dismiss a brawny djinni with an improvisation that administered a slap on its blue rump, his master expressed her admiration. "You're a natural, John," she said. "A natural. You displayed bravery and good memory at Heddleham Hall in dismissing the demon there, but I little realized how adept you'd be at general summonings. Work hard and you'll go far."

Nathaniel thanked her demurely. He did not tell her that most of this was nothing new to him, that he had already raised a middle-ranking djinni by the age of twelve. He kept his association with Bartimaeus strictly to himself.

Ms. Whitwell had rewarded his precocity with new secrets and tuition, which was exactly what Nathaniel had long desired. Under her guidance, he learned the arts of constraining demons to multiple or semipermanent tasks, without recourse to cumbersome tools such as Adelbrand's Pentacle. He discovered how to protect himself from enemy spies by weaving sensor webs around himself; how to dispel surprise attacks by invoking rapid Fluxes that engulfed the aggressive magic and carried it away. In a very short space of time, Nathaniel had absorbed as much new knowledge as many of his fellow magicians who were five or six years older. He was now ready for his first job.

It was the custom for all promising magicians to be given work in lowly departmental positions as a way of instructing them in the practical use of power. The age at which this occurred depended on the talent of the apprentice and the influence of the master. In Nathaniel's case, there was another factor, too, for it was well known about the coffee bars of

Whitehall that the Prime Minister himself was following his career with a keen and benevolent eye. This ensured that, from the outset, he was the object of much attention.

His master had warned him of this. "Keep your secrets to yourself," she said, "especially your birth name, if you know it. Keep your mouth shut like a clam. They'll pry it all out of you otherwise."

"Who will?" he asked her.

"Enemies you haven't yet made. They like to plan ahead."

A magician's birth name was certainly a source of great weakness if uncovered by another, and Nathaniel guarded his with great care. At first, however, he was considered something of a soft touch. Pretty female magicians approached him at parties, lulling him with compliments before inquiring closely into his background. Nathaniel fended off these crude enticements fairly easily, but more dangerous methods followed. An imp once visited him while he slept, cooing gentle words into his ear and asking for his name. Perhaps only the loud tolling of Big Ben across the river prevented an unguarded revelation. As the hour struck, Nathaniel stirred, woke, and observed the imp squatting on the bedpost; in an instant, he summoned a tame foliot, which seized the imp and compressed it to a stone.

In its new condition, the imp was sadly unable to reveal anything about the magician who had sent it on its errand. After this episode, Nathaniel employed the foliot to guard his bedroom conscientiously throughout each night.

It soon became clear that John Mandrake's identity was not going to be compromised easily, and no further attempts occurred. Soon afterward, when he was still scarcely fourteen, the expected appointment was made and the young magician joined the Department of Internal Affairs.

2

In his office, Nathaniel was welcomed by a glare from the secretary and a teetering pile of new papers in his in-box.

The secretary, a trim, well-kempt young man with oiled ginger hair, paused in the act of leaving the room. "You're *late*, Mandrake," he said, pushing his glasses higher with a swift, nervous gesture. "What's the excuse this time? You've got responsibilities, too, you know, just the same as us *full-timers*." He hovered by the door and frowned fiercely down his little nose.

The magician threw himself back into his chair. He was tempted to put his feet up on the desk, but rejected this as being too showy. He restricted himself to a lazy smile. "I've been at an incident scene with Mr. Tallow," he said. "Been working there since six. Ask him if you like, when he gets in; he might tell you a few details—if they're not *too* secret, that is. What have *you* been up to, Jenkins? Photocopying hard, I hope."

The secretary made a sharp noise between his teeth and pushed his glasses higher up his nose. "Keep it up, Mandrake," he said. "Just keep it up. You may be the Prime Minister's blue-eyed boy now, but how long's *that* going to last if you don't deliver? Another incident? The second this week? You'll soon be back scrubbing teacups again, and then—we'll see." With something between a scuttle and a flounce, he departed.

The boy made a face at the closing door and for a few seconds sat staring at nothing. He rubbed his eyes wearily and glanced at his watch. Only nine forty-five. Already it had been a long day.

A teetering pile of papers on his desk awaited his attention. He took a deep breath, adjusted his cuffs and reached out for the topmost file.

For reasons of his own, Nathaniel had long been interested in Internal Affairs, a subdepartment of the sprawling Security apparatus headed by Jessica Whitwell. Internal Affairs conducted investigations into various kinds of criminal activity, notably foreign insurgency and domestic terrorism directed against the State. When he first joined the department, Nathaniel had merely undertaken humble activities such as filing, photocopying, and tea-making. But he did not carry out these tasks for long.

His rapid promotion was not (as his enemies whispered) simply the product of raw nepotism. It was true that he benefited from the goodwill of the Prime Minister and from the long reach of his master, Ms. Whitwell, whom none of the magicians in Internal Affairs wanted to displease. Yet this would have availed him nothing if he had been incompetent or merely average in his craft. But Nathaniel was gifted, and more than that, he worked hard. His elevation was swift. Within months he had maneuvered his way through a succession of humdrum clerical jobs, until—not yet fifteen—he had become assistant to the Internal Affairs Minister himself, Mr. Julius Tallow.

A short, burly man of bullish build and temperament, Mr. Tallow was abrupt and abrasive at the best of times, and inclined to sudden outbursts of incandescent rage, which sent his minions scurrying for cover. Aside from his temper, he was additionally distinguished by an unusual yellowish complexion, bright as daffodils at noonday. It was not known among his staff what had caused this affliction; some claimed it was hereditary, that he was the offspring of a union between magician and succubus. Others rejected this on biological grounds, and suspected he was the victim of malignant magic. Nathaniel subscribed to the latter view. Whatever the cause, Mr. Tallow concealed his problem as best he could. His collars were high, his hair hung long. He wore a broad-brimmed hat at all times and kept a keen ear open for levity on the subject among his staff.

Eighteen people worked in the office with Nathaniel and Mr. Tallow; they ranged from two commoners, who performed administrative duties that did not impinge on magical matters, to Mr. Ffoukes, a magician of the fourth level. Nathaniel adopted a policy of bland politeness to everyone, with the single exception of Clive Jenkins, the secretary. Jenkins's resentment of his youth and standing had been clear from the outset; in turn, Nathaniel treated him with a cheery impudence. It was perfectly safe to do so. Jenkins had neither connections nor ability.

Mr. Tallow had soon realized the extent of his assistant's talents, and directed him to an important and taxing task: the pursuit of the shadowy group known as the Resistance.

The motives of these zealots were transparent, if bizarre. They were opposed to the benevolent leadership of the magicians and eager to return to the anarchy of Commoners' Rule. Over the years, their activities had become increasingly annoying. They stole magical artifacts of all descriptions from careless or unlucky magicians, and later used them in random assaults on government persons and property. Several buildings had been badly affected, and a number of people killed. In the most audacious attack of all, the Resistance had even attempted to assassinate the Prime Minister. The government's response was draconian: many commoners had been arrested on suspicion, a few were executed and others deported by prison hulk to the colonies. Yet despite these sensible acts of deterrence, the incidents continued, and Mr. Tallow was beginning to feel the displeasure of his superiors.

Nathaniel accepted his challenge with great eagerness. Years before, he had crossed paths with the Resistance in a way that made him feel he understood something of its nature. One dark night, he had encountered three child commoners operating a black market of magical objects. It was an experience Nathaniel had not enjoyed. The three had promptly stolen his own precious scrying glass, then very nearly killed him. Now he was keen for a measure of revenge.

But the task had not proved easy.

He knew nothing of the three commoners beyond their names: Fred, Stanley, and Kitty. Fred and Stanley were paperboys, and Nathaniel's first act had been to send minute search orbs to trail all newspaper sellers in the city. But this surveillance had thrown up no new leads: evidently, the duo had changed their occupation.

Next, Nathaniel had encouraged his chief to send a few handpicked adult agents out to work undercover in London. Over several months, they immersed themselves in the capital's underworld. Once they had been accepted by the other commoners, they were instructed to offer "stolen artifacts" to anyone who seemed interested in them. Nathaniel hoped this ploy might encourage agents of the Resistance to break cover.

It was a forlorn hope. Most of the stool pigeons failed to rouse any interest in their magical trinkets, and the only man who *was* successful vanished without making his report. To Nathaniel's frustration, his body was later found floating in the Thames.

Nathaniel's most recent strategy, for which he initially had high hopes, was to command two foliots to adopt the semblance of orphan waifs and to send them out to roam the city by day. Nathaniel strongly suspected that the Resistance was largely composed of child street gangs, and he reasoned that, sooner or later, they might try to recruit the newcomers. But so far, the bait had not been taken.

The office that morning was hot and drowsy. Flies buzzed against the windowpanes. Nathaniel went so far as to remove his coat and roll up his extensive sleeves. Suppressing his yawns, he plowed through a mass of paperwork, most of which was concerned with the latest Resistance outrage: an attack on a shop in a Whitehall backstreet. At dawn that day, an explosive device, probably a small sphere, had been tossed through a skylight, grievously wounding the manager. The shop supplied tobacco and incense to magicians; presumably this was why it had been targeted.

There were no witnesses, and surveillance spheres had not been in the area. Nathaniel cursed under his breath. It was hopeless. He had no leads at all. He tossed the papers aside and picked up another report. Rude slogans at the expense of the Prime Minister had again been daubed on lonely walls throughout the city. He sighed and signed a paper ordering an immediate cleanup operation, knowing full well the graffiti would reappear as fast as the whitewash men could work.

Lunchtime came at last, and Nathaniel attended a party in the garden of the Byzantine embassy, held to mark the forth-coming Founder's Day. He drifted among the guests, feeling listless and out of sorts. The problem of the Resistance was preying on his mind.

As he ladled strong fruit punch from a silver tureen in a corner of the garden, he noticed a young woman standing close by. After eyeing her warily for a moment, Nathaniel made what he hoped was an elegant gesture. "I understand you had some success recently, Ms. Farrar. Please accept my congratulations."

Jane Farrar murmured her thanks. "It was only a *small* nest of Czech spies. We believe they had come in by fishing boat from the Low Countries. They were clumsy amateurs, easily spotted. Some loyal commoners raised the alarm."

Nathaniel smiled. "You are far too modest. I heard that the spies led the police on a merry dance around half of England, killing several magicians in the process."

"There were a few small incidents."

"It is a notable victory, even so." Nathaniel took a small sip of punch, pleased with the backhanded nature of his compli-ment. Jane Farrar's master was the police chief Mr. Henry Duvall, a great rival of Jessica Whitwell. At functions such as this, Ms. Farrar and Nathaniel often exchanged feline conver-sation, all purred compliments and carefully sheathed claws, testing each other's mettle.

"But what of *you*, John Mandrake?" Jane Farrar said, sweetly. "Is it true that you've been assigned responsibility for uncovering this irritating Resistance? That is no small matter either!"

"I am only amassing information; we have a network of

informers to keep busy. It is nothing too exciting."

Jane Farrar reached for the silver ladle and stirred the punch gently. "Perhaps not, but unheard of for someone as inexperienced as you. Well *done*. Would you care for another tot?"

"Thank you, no." With annoyance, Nathaniel felt the color rush to his cheeks. It was true, of course: he *was* young, he *was* inexperienced; everyone was watching to see whether he failed. He fought back a strong desire to scowl. "I believe we will see the Resistance broken within six months," he said thickly.

Jane Farrar poured punch into a glass and raised her eyebrows at him with an expression that might have been amusement. "You impress me," she said. "Three years they've been hunted, without anything like a breakthrough. And you will break them within six months! But you know, I believe you can do it, John. You are quite a little man already."

Another flush! Nathaniel tried to master his emotions. Jane Farrar was three or four years older than he was, and just as tall, perhaps taller, with long, straight, light brown hair hanging to her shoulders. Her eyes were a disconcerting green, alive with wry intelligence. He could not help feeling gawky and inelegant beside her, despite the splendors of his ruffed red handkerchief. He found himself trying to justify his statement, where he should have kept silent.

"We know the group consists mainly of youths," he said. "That fact has been repeatedly observed by victims, and the one or two individuals we have managed to kill have never been older than *us*." (He placed a light stress on this last word.) "So the solution is clear. We send agents out to join the organization. Once they have won the traitors' trust, and gained access to their leader . . . well, the matter will be over swiftly."

Again the amused smile. "Are you *sure* it will be so simple?"

Nathaniel shrugged. "I nearly gained access to the leader myself, years ago. It can be done."

"Really?" Her eyes widened, showing genuine interest. "Tell me more." But Nathaniel had regained control of himself. *Safe, secret, secure.* The fewer tidbits of information he divulged the better. He cast his eyes across the lawns.

"I see Ms. Whitwell has arrived unattended," he said. "As her loyal apprentice I should make myself useful. If you would excuse me, Ms. Farrar?"

Nathaniel left the party early and returned to his office in a rage. He promptly retired to a private summoning chamber and blurted out the incantation. The two foliots, still in orphan guise, appeared. They looked disconsolate and shifty.

"Well?" he snapped.

"It's no good, master," the blond orphan said. "The street kids just ignore us."

"If we're lucky," the tousled orphan agreed. "Those that *don't* tend to throw things at us."

"What?" Nathaniel was outraged.

"Oh, cans, bottles, small rocks and things."

"I don't mean that! I mean what's happened to a spot of common humanity? Those children should be deported in chains! What's the matter with them? You're both sweet, you're both thin, you're both faintly pathetic—*surely* they'd take you under their wings."

The two orphans shook their pretty little heads. "Nope. They treat us with revulsion. It's almost as if they can see us as we really are."

"Impossible. They don't have lenses, do they? You must be

doing it wrong. Are you sure you're not giving the game away somehow? You're not floating or growing horns or doing something else stupid when you see them, are you?"

"No, sir, honest we're not."

"No, sir. Although Clovis *did* once forget to remove his tail."

"You sneak! Sir—that's a lie."

Nathaniel clapped a hand to his head. "I don't care! I don't care. But it'll be the Stipples for you both if you don't succeed soon. Try different ages, try going about separately, try giving yourself small disabilities to raise their sympathy—but no infectious diseases, as I told you before. For now, you're dismissed. Get out of my sight."

Back at his desk, Nathaniel grimly took stock. It was clear the foliots were unlikely to succeed. They were a lowly demonic rank . . . perhaps *that* was the problem—they weren't clever enough to fully impersonate a human's character. Certainly the notion that the children could *see through* their semblance was absurd; he dismissed it out of hand.

But if they failed, what next? Each week, new Resistance crimes took place. Magicians' houses were burgled, cars robbed, shops and offices attacked. The pattern was obvious enough: opportunistic crimes, carried out by small, fast-moving units who somehow managed to stay clear of patrolling vigilance spheres and other demons. All very well. But still no breakthrough came.

Nathaniel knew that Mr. Tallow's patience was running out. Little teasing comments, such as those from Clive Jenkins and Jane Farrar, suggested that other people knew this, too. He tapped his pencil on his notepad, his thoughts drifting to the three members of the Resistance he had seen. Fred and

Stanley . . . the memory of them made him grind his teeth and tap the pencil ever harder. He *would* catch them one day, see if he didn't. And there was the girl, too. Kitty. Dark-haired, fierce, a face glimpsed in the shadows. The leader of the trio. Were they in London still? Or had they fled somewhere far off, to lurk beyond the reaches of the law? All he needed was a clue, a single measly clue. Then he'd pounce on them, faster than thought.

But he had nothing whatsoever to go on.

"Who *are* you?" he said to himself. "Where are you hiding?"

His pencil broke in his hand.

3

It was a night ripe for enchantment. A huge full moon, resplendent with the tinctures of apricots and wheat, and surrounded by a pulsing halo, held sovereignty over the desert sky. A few wispy clouds fled before its majestic face, leaving the heavens naked, glistening blue-black, like the belly of some cosmic whale. In the distance, the moonlight lapped the dunes; down in the secret valley, the golden haze penetrated the contours of the cliffs to bathe the sandstone floor.

But the wadi was deep and narrow, and to one side an outcrop of rock sheathed an area in inky darkness. In this sheltered place a small fire had been lit. The flames were red and meager; they cast little light. A starveling trail of smoke rose up from the fire and drifted away into the cold night air.

At the edge of the well of moonlight, a figure sat crosslegged before the fire. A man, muscular and bald, with glistening, oiled skin. A heavy gold ring hung from his ear; his face was blank, impassive. He stirred; from a pouch looped around his waist, he took a bottle, fixed with a metal stopper. With a series of languid movements that nevertheless suggested the feral, easy strength of a desert lion, he uncorked the bottle and drank. Tossing it aside, he stared into the flames.

After a few moments, an odd scent extended out across the valley, accompanied by distant zither music. The man's head nodded, drooped. Now only the whites of his eyes showed; he slept where he sat. The music grew louder; it seemed to come from the bowels of the earth.

Out from the darkness someone stepped, past the fire, past the sleeper, into the lit ground at the center of the valley. The music swelled; the very moonlight seemed to brighten in homage to her beauty. A slave girl: young, exquisite, too poor to afford adequate clothing. Her hair hung in long, dark ringlets that bounced with every tripping step. Her face was pale and smooth as porcelain, her eyes wide and studded with tears. At first tentatively, then with a sudden loosening of emotion, she danced. Her body dipped and spun, her flimsy drape struggled vainly to keep up with her. Her slender arms wove enticements in the air, while from her mouth issued a strange chanting, heavy with loneliness and desire.

The girl finished her dance. She tossed her head in proud despair and gazed up into the darkness, toward the moon. The music died away. Silence.

Then, a distant voice, as if borne on the wind: "Amaryllis . . ."

The girl started; she looked this way and that. Nothing but the rocks and the sky and the amber moon. She gave a pretty sigh.

"My Amaryllis . . ."

In a husky, tremulous voice, she answered: "Sir Bertilak? Is that you?"

"It is I."

"Where are you? Why do you taunt me so?"

"I hide behind the moon, my Amaryllis, lest your beauty burn my essence. Shield your face with the gauze that presently lies so uselessly upon your breast, that I might venture near to you."

"Oh, Bertilak! With all my heart!" The girl did as she was bid. From the darkness came several low mutterings of approval. Somebody coughed.

"Darling Amaryllis! Stand away! I descend to earth."

Giving a little gasp, the girl pressed her back against the contours of a nearby rock. She tossed her head in proud expectation. A crack of thunder sounded, fit to disturb the slumbers of the dead. Open-mouthed, the girl looked up. At a stately pace, a figure descended from the sky. He wore a silvered jerkin across his bare torso, a long flowing cape, puffed pantaloons, and a pair of elegant curled slippers. An impressive scimitar was tucked into his jeweled belt. Down he came, head back, dark eyes flashing, chin jutting forward proudly beneath his aquiline nose. A pair of curving bone-white horns rose from the edges of his forehead.

He landed gently near where the girl was draped against the rock and, with a casual flourish, flashed a gleaming smile. Faint female sighs sounded all around.

"What, Amaryllis—are you struck dumb? Do you forget so soon the face of your beloved genie?"

"No, Bertilak! Were it seventy years, not seven, I could never forget a single oiled hair upon your head. But my tongue falters and my heart pounds with fear, lest the magician wake and catch us! Then he will bind my slender white legs in chains once more, and immure you in his bottle!"

At this, the genie gave a booming laugh. "The magician sleeps. My magic is greater than his, and ever shall be. But the night is growing old, and by dawn I must be away with my brothers, the afrits, riding on the currents of the air. Come to my arms, my darling. In these short hours, while I still have human form, let the moon be witness to our love, which shall defy the hatred of our peoples even unto the ending of the world."

"Oh, Bertilak!"

"Oh, Amaryllis, my Swan of Araby!"

The genie strode forward and enfolded the slave girl in a muscular embrace. At this point the ache in Kitty's bottom became too much to bear. She shifted in her seat.

Genie and girl now began an intricate dance, involving much swirling of clothing and extending of limbs. There was a smattering of applause from the audience. The orchestra set to with renewed gusto. Kitty yawned like a cat, slumped lower and rubbed an eye with the palm of one hand. She felt for the paper bag, tipped out the last few salted peanuts and, cupping them to her mouth, crunched unenthusiastically.

The anticipation that always came before a job was upon her, digging like a knife into her side. That was normal, she expected it. But layered on top of this was the boredom of sitting through the endless play. No doubt, as Anne had said, it would provide a perfect alibi—but Kitty would rather have been working out her tension on the streets, keeping moving, dodging the patrols, not witnessing such awful pap.

On stage, Amaryllis, the Chiswick missionary lass turned slave girl, was now singing a song in which (once again) she expressed her unremitting passion for the genie lover in her arms. She did so with such force on the high notes that the hair rippled on Bertilak's head and his earrings spun. Kitty winced and glanced along the shrouded silhouettes in front until she came to the outlines of Fred and Stanley. Both looked highly attentive, eyes trained on the stage. Kitty curled her lip. Presumably they were admiring Amaryllis.

Just so long as they remained alert.

Kitty's gaze wandered down into the well of darkness by her side. At her feet was the leather bag. The sight made her stomach lurch; she closed her eyes, instinctively patting her coat to feel the reassuring hardness of the knife. Relax . . . all would be fine.

Would the interval *never* come? She raised her head and surveyed the dusky reaches of the auditorium, where, on either side of the stage, the magicians' boxes hung, heavy with gold fretwork and thick red curtains to shield the occupants from the commoners' eyes. But every magician in town had seen this play years ago, long before it had opened to the sensation-hungry masses. Today the curtains were drawn back, the boxes empty.

Kitty glanced at her wrist, but it was too dark to make out the time. Doubtless there were many forlorn partings, cruel ravishments, and joyful reunions left to endure before the interval. And the audience would love every minute of them. Like sheep, they thronged here night after night, year after year. Surely all of London had seen *Swans of Araby* by now, many people more than once. But still the buses puttered in from the provinces, bringing new customers to gasp at all the shabby glamour.

"Darling! Be silent!" Kitty nodded with approval. Nice one, Bertilak. He'd cut her off in the middle of her aria.

"What is it? What do you sense that I cannot?"

"Hist! Do not speak. We are in peril . . ." Bertilak rotated his noble profile. He looked high, he looked low. He seemed to sniff the air. All was still. The fire had burned right down; the magician slumbered; the moon had been obscured behind a cloud and cold stars twinkled in the sky. Not a sound came from the audience. To her great disgust, Kitty found she was holding her breath.

Suddenly, with a ringing oath and a rasp of iron, the genie drew his scimitar and clutched the trembling girl to his chest. "Amaryllis! They come! I see them with my powers."

"What, Bertilak? What do you see?"

"Seven savage imps, my darling, sent by the queen of the afrits to capture me! Our dalliance displeases her: they will bind us both and drag us naked before her throne to await her awful pleasure. You must flee! No—we have no time for soft words, though your limpid eyes implore me! Go!"

With many a tragic gesture, the girl disentangled herself from his arms and crept to the left of the stage. The genie tossed aside his cape and jerkin in bare-chested readiness for battle.

From the orchestral pit came a dramatic discord. Seven terrifying imps leaped out from behind the rocks. Each was played by a midget wearing a leather loincloth and a skin-coat of luminous green paint. With horrid whoops and grimaces, they drew stiletto daggers and fell upon the genie. A battle ensued, accompanied by a frenzy of screeching violins.

Vicious imps . . . a wicked magician . . . It was a subtle job, this *Swans of Araby*, Kitty could see that. Ideal propaganda, gently acknowledging popular anxieties rather than denying them flat out. Show us a little of what we fear, she thought, only take away its teeth. Add music, fight scenes, lashings of star-crossed love. Make the demons frighten us, then let us watch them die. We are in control. At the end of the show, all would no doubt be made well. The wicked sorcerer would be destroyed by the good magicians. The wicked afrits would be cast down, too. As for Bertilak, the rugged genie, doubtless he'd be a man after all, an eastern princeling transformed into a monster by some cruel enchantment. And he and Amaryllis would live happily ever after, watched over by the wise council of benevolent magicians. . . .

A sudden sick feeling swelled in Kitty. It was not the tension of the job, this time; it came from deeper down, from the reservoir of fury that bubbled away perpetually inside. It was born of knowing that everything they did was utterly forlorn and useless. It would never change anything. The crowd's response told her this. Watch! Amaryllis has been seized: an imp has her under his arm, kicking and weeping. Hear the crowd gasp! But see! Bertilak the heroic genie has tossed one imp over his shoulder into the smoldering fire! Now he pursues the captor and—one, two—makes short work of him with his scimitar. Hoorah! Hear the crowd cheer!

It didn't matter what they did in the end; it didn't matter what they stole, what daring attacks they made. It would make no difference. Tomorrow the queues would still be forming in the streets outside the Metropolitan, the spheres would still be watching from above, the magicians would still be elsewhere, enjoying the trappings of their power.

So it had always been. Nothing she had ever done had made any difference, right from the beginning.

4

The noise on the stage receded; in its place she heard bird-song, the hum of distant traffic. In her mind's eye, the darkness of the theater was replaced by remembered light.

Three years ago. The park. The ball. Their laughter. Disaster on its way, like lightning from a blue sky.

Jakob grinning as he ran toward her; the bat's weight, dry and wooden in her hand.

The strike! The triumph of it! Dancing with delight.

The distant crash.

How they ran, hearts thudding. And then—the creature on the bridge . . .

She rubbed her fingers into her eyes. But even that terrible day—was it truly the beginning? For the first thirteen years of her life, Kitty had remained unaware of the exact nature of the magicians' rule. Or perhaps she was not *consciously* aware of it, for looking back she realized that doubts and intuitions *had* managed to negotiate their way into her mind.

The magicians had long been at the zenith of their power and no one could remember a time when this wasn't so. For the most part, they kept themselves removed from the experience of the ordinary commoner, remaining in the center of the city and in the suburbs, where broad, leafy boulevards idled between secretive villas. What lay between was left to everyone else, streets clogged with small shops, waste ground, the facto-ries and brickworks. Magicians passed through occasionally in their great black cars, but otherwise their presence was mainly felt in the vigilance spheres floating randomly above the streets.

"The spheres keep us safe," Kitty's father told her one evening, after a large red orb had silently accompanied her home from school. "Don't be frightened of them. If you're a good girl, they'll do you no harm. It's only bad men, thieves and spies, who need to be afraid." But Kitty *had* been frightened; after that, livid, glowing spheres often pursued her in her dreams.

Her parents were visited by no such fears. Neither of them was overly imaginative, but they were robustly conscious of the greatness of London and of their own small place in it. They took for granted the superiority of the magicians and fully accepted the unchanging nature of their rule. Indeed, they found it reassuring.

"I'd lay down my life for the Prime Minister," her father used to say. "He's a great man."

"He keeps the Czechs where they belong," her mother said. "Without him, we'd have the hussars marching down Clapham High Road, and you wouldn't want *that*, dear, would you?"

Kitty supposed not.

They had lived, the three of them, in a terrace house in the south London suburb of Balham. It was a small home, with a sitting room and a kitchen downstairs and a tiny bathroom out back. Upstairs was a little landing and two bedrooms—Kitty's parents' and her own. A long, thin mirror stood on the landing, before which, on weekday mornings, the whole family stood in turn, brushing hair and arranging their clothes. Her father in particular fiddled endlessly with his tie. Kitty could never understand why he kept on tying and untying it, kept on weaving the strip of fabric in, up, around and out, since the variations between each attempt were practically microscopic.

"Appearances are very important, Kitty," he would say, surveying the umpteenth knot with furrowed brow. "In my job you've got only one chance to impress."

Kitty's father was a tall, wiry man, stubborn of outlook and blunt of speech. He was shop-floor manager in a large department store in central London and very proud of this responsibility. He supervised the Leathers section: a broad, low-ceilinged hall, dimly lit by orange lights and filled with expensive bags and briefcases made from cured animal skin. The leather goods were luxury items, which meant that the vast majority of customers were magicians.

Kitty had visited the shop once or twice, and the darkly overpowering smell of the processed leather always made her head spin.

"Stay out of the magicians' way," her father said. "They're very important people, and they don't like anyone getting under their feet, even pretty little girls like you."

"How do I know who's a magician?" Kitty asked. She was seven at the time, and wasn't sure.

"They're always well dressed, their faces are stern and wise, and sometimes they have fine walking sticks. They wear expensive scents, but sometimes you can still catch hints of their magic: strange incenses, odd chemicals. . . . But if you smell that, the chances are you'll be too close! Stay out of their way."

Kitty had promised faithfully. She scampered to far corners whenever customers entered the Leather hall and watched them with wide, curious eyes. Her father's tips did not help much. Everyone visiting the store seemed well dressed, many carried sticks, and the stench of leather masked any unusual scents. But she soon began to pick out the magicians by other clues: a certain hardness in the visitors' eyes, their air of cool command and, above all, a sudden stiffening in her father's manner. He always seemed awkward when talking with them, his suit newly wrinkled with anxiety, his tie nervously askew. He gave little bobs and bows of agreement as they spoke. These signs were very subtle, but they were enough for Kitty, and they disconcerted and even distressed her, though she hardly knew the reason why.

Kitty's mother worked as a receptionist at Palmer's Quill Bureau, a long-established firm hidden among the many book-binders and parchment makers of South London. The Bureau provided special quill pens for the magicians to use in their con-jurations. Quills were messy, slow, and difficult to write with, and fewer magicians than ever bothered to use them. The staff of Palmer's used ballpoints instead.

The job allowed Kitty's mother glimpses of the magicians themselves, since occasionally one would visit the Bureau to inspect a new consignment of pens. She found their proximity thrilling.

"She was so *glamorous*," she would say. "Her clothes were the finest red-gold taffeta—I'm sure they came from Byzantium itself! And she was so *imperious,* too! When she snapped her fingers, everyone jumped like crickets to do her bidding."

"Sounds rather rude to me," Kitty said.

"You're so *very* young, love," her mother said. "No, she was a great woman."

One day, when Kitty was ten years old, she came home from school to find her mother sitting tearfully in the kitchen.

"Mum! What's the matter?"

"It's nothing. Well, what am I saying?—I *am* hurt a little. Kitty, I am afraid . . . I am afraid that I have been made redundant. Oh dear, *what* are we going to tell your father?"

Kitty sat her mother down, made her a pot of tea, and brought her a biscuit. Over much snuffling, sipping, and sighing, the truth came out. Old Mr. Palmer had retired. His firm had been acquired by a trio of magicians, who disliked having ordinary commoners on their staff; they had brought in new personnel and sacked half the original employees, including Kitty's mother.

"But they can't *do* that," Kitty had protested.

"Of course they can. It's their right. They protect the country, make us the greatest nation in the world; they have many privileges"—her mother dabbed at her eyes and took another slurp of tea—"but even so, it *is* a little hurtful, after so many years. . . ."

Hurtful or not, that was the last day that Kitty's mother worked at Palmer's. A few weeks later, her friend Mrs. Hyrnek, who had also been dismissed, got her a job as a cleaner in a printing works, and life resumed its structured course.

But Kitty didn't forget.

Kitty's parents were avid readers of *The Times*, which brought daily news of the army's latest victories. For years, it seemed, the wars had been going well; the Empire's territories expanded by the season, and the world's wealth was flowing back into the capital. But this success came at a price, and the paper continually advised all readers to be on the lookout for spies and saboteurs from enemy states, who might be living in ordinary neighborhoods, while all the time quietly working on wicked plots to destabilize the nation.

"You keep your eyes open, Kitty," her mother advised. "No one takes heed of a girl like you. You never know, you might see something."

"Especially around here," her father added, sourly. "In Balham."

The area where Kitty lived was famous for its Czech community, which was long established. The high street had several little borscht cafes, marked by their thick net curtains and colorful flowerpots on the sills. Tanned old gentlemen with drooping white mustaches played chess and skittles in the streets outside the bars, and many of the local firms were owned by the grandchildren of the émigrés who had come to England back in Gladstone's time.

Flourishing though the area was (it contained several important printing firms, including the noted Hyrnek and Sons), its strong European identity drew the constant attention of the Night Police. As she grew older, Kitty became used to witnessing daytime raids, with patrols of gray-uniformed officers breaking down doors and throwing belongings into the street. Sometimes young men were taken away in vans; on other occasions the families were left intact, to piece together the wreckage of their homes. Kitty always found these scenes upsetting, despite her father's reassurances.

"The police must maintain a presence," he insisted. "Keep troublemakers on their toes. Believe me, Kitty, they wouldn't act without good intelligence on the matter."

"But, Dad, those were friends of Mr. Hyrnek."

A grunt. "He should pick his pals more carefully then, shouldn't he?"

Kitty's father was in fact always civil to Mr. Hyrnek, whose wife had, after all, gotten Kitty's mother a new job. The

Hyrneks were a prominent local family, whose business was patronized by many magicians. Their printing works occupied a large site close to Kitty's house, and provided employment for many people of the area. Despite this, the Hyrneks never seemed especially well-off; they lived in a big, sprawling, run-down house set a little back from the road, behind an over-grown garden of long grass and laurel bushes. In time, Kitty came to know it well, thanks to her friendship with Jakob, the youngest of the Hyrnek sons.

Kitty was tall for her age and growing taller, slender beneath her baggy school jersey and wide-legged trousers, stronger than she looked, too. More than one boy had regretted a facetious comment to her face; Kitty did not waste words when a punch would do. Her hair was dark brown, veering to black, and straight, except at the ends, where it had a tendency to curl in an unruly fashion. She wore it shorter than the other girls, mid-way down her neck.

Kitty had dark eyes and heavy black brows. Her face openly reflected her opinions, and since opinions came thick and fast to Kitty, her eyebrows and mouth were in constant motion.

"Your face is never the same twice," Jakob had said. "Er—that's a compliment!" he added hastily, when Kitty glowered at him.

They sat together in the same classrooms for several years, learning what they could from the mixed bag of disciplines on offer to the common children. Crafts were encouraged, since their futures lay in the factories and workshops of the city; they learned pottery, woodcutting, metalwork, and simple mathematics. Technical drawing, needlepoint, and cookery were also taught, and for those like Kitty, who enjoyed words, reading and writing were on offer, too, with the proviso that this skill would one day be properly employed, perhaps in a secretarial career.

History was another important subject; daily, they received instruction in the glorious development of the British State. Kitty enjoyed these lessons, which featured many stories of magic and far-off lands, but couldn't help sensing certain limitations in what they were being taught. Often she would put up her hand.

"*Yes*, Kitty, what is it *this* time?" Her teachers' tones often displayed a slight weariness, which they did their best to disguise.

"Please, sir, tell us more about the government that Mr. Gladstone overthrew. You say it had a parliament already. We've got a parliament now. So why was the old one so wicked?"

"Well, Kitty, *if* you'd been listening properly, you'd have heard me say that the Old Parliament was not wicked so much as weak. It was run by ordinary people, like you and me, who did not have *any* magical powers. Imagine that! Of course, that meant that they were constantly getting harassed by other, stronger countries, and there was nothing they could do to stop it. Now, which was the most dangerous foreign nation in those days . . . let me see now . . . Jakob?"

"Don't know, sir."

"Speak up, boy, don't mumble! Well, I'm surprised to hear you say that, Jakob, you of all people. It was the Holy Roman Empire, of course. Your ancestors! The Czech Emperor ruled most of Europe from his castle in Prague; he was so fat he sat on a wheeled throne of steel and gold and was pulled about the corridors by a single bone-white ox. When he wished to leave the castle, they had to lower him out by reinforced pulley. He kept an aviary of parakeets and shot a different colored one each night for his supper. Yes, you may well be disgusted, children. *That* was the kind of man who ruled Europe in those days, and our Old Parliament was helpless against him. He governed a terrible assembly of magicians, who were wicked and corrupt and whose leader, Hans Meyrink, is said to have been a vampire. Their soldiers rampaged—*yes*, Kitty, what is it *now?*"

"Well, sir, if the Old Parliament was so incompetent, how come the fat Emperor never invaded Britain, because he didn't, did he, sir? And why—"

"I can answer only one question at a time, Kitty, I'm not a magician! Britain was lucky, that's all. Prague was always slow to act; the Emperor spent much of his time drinking beer and engaging in terrible debauchery. But he would have turned his evil gaze to London eventually, believe you me. Fortunately for us, there *were* a few magicians in London in those days, to whom the poor powerless ministers sometimes came for advice. And one of them was Mr. Gladstone. He saw the dangers of our situation and decided on a preemptive strike. Can you remember what he did, children? Yes—Sylvester?"

"He persuaded the ministers to hand over control to him, sir. He went in to see them one evening and talked so cleverly that they elected him Prime Minister there and then."

"That's right, good boy, Sylvester, you'll get a star. Yes, it was the Night of the Long Counsel. After a lengthy debate in Parliament, Gladstone's eloquence won the day and the ministers unanimously resigned in his favor. He organized a defensive attack on Prague the following year, and overthrew the Emperor. Yes, Abigail?"

"Did he free the parakeets, sir?"

"I'm sure he did. Gladstone was a very kind man. He was sober and moderate in all his tastes and wore the same starched shirt each day, except on Sundays, when his mother cleaned it for him. After that, London's power increased, while Prague's diminished. And as Jakob might realize, if he weren't slumped so rudely in his seat, that was when many Czech citizens, like his family, immigrated to Britain. Many of Prague's best magicians came, too, and helped us create the modern State. Now, perhaps—"

"But I thought you said the Czech magicians were all wicked and corrupt, sir."

"Well, I expect all the wicked ones were killed, don't you, Kitty? The others were just misguided and saw the error of their ways. Now there's the bell! Lunchtime! And no, Kitty, I'm not going to answer any more questions just now. Everyone stand up, put your chairs under your desks, and please leave *quietly*!"

After such discussions in school, Jakob was frequently morose, but his moodiness rarely lasted long. He was a cheerful and energetic soul, slight and dark-haired, with an open, impudent face. He liked games, and from an early age spent many hours with Kitty, playing in the long grass of his parents' garden. They kicked footballs, practiced archery, improvised cricket, and generally kept out of the way of his large and boisterous family.

Nominally, Mr. Hyrnek was the head of the household, but in practice, he, like everyone else, was dominated by his wife, Mrs. Hyrnek. A bustling bundle of maternal energy, all broad shoulders and capacious bosom, she sailed around the house like a galleon blown by an erratic wind, forever uttering raucous whoops of laughter, or calling out Czech curses after her four unruly sons. Jakob's elder brothers, Karel, Robert, and Alfred, had all inherited their mother's imposing physique, and their size, strength, and deep, resounding voices always awed Kitty into silence whenever they came near. Mr. Hyrnek was like Jakob, small and slight, but with leathery skin that reminded Kitty of a shriveled apple's. He smoked a curved, rowan-wood pipe that left wreaths of sweet smoke hanging around the house and garden.

Jakob was very proud of his father.

"He's brilliant," he told Kitty, as they rested under a tree after a game of fives against the side wall of the house. "No one else can do what he does with parchment and leather. You should see the miniature spell-pamphlets he's been working on lately— they're embossed in gold filigree in the old Prague style, but reduced to the tiniest scale! He works in little outlines of animals and flowers, in perfect detail, then embeds tiny pieces of ivory and precious stones inside. Only Dad can do stuff like that."

"They must cost a fortune when he's finished," Kitty said.

Jakob spat out a grass shoot he was chewing. "You're joking, of course," he said flatly. "The magicians don't pay him what they should. Never do. He can barely keep the factory working. Look at all that—" He nodded up at the body of the house, with its slates skew-whiff on the roof, the shutters crooked and ingrained with dirt, the paint peeling on the veranda door. "Think we should be living in a place like this? Come off it!"

"It's a lot bigger than my house," Kitty observed.

"Hyrnek's is the second biggest printer in London," Jakob said. "Only Jaroslav's is bigger. And *they* just churn stuff out, ordinary leather bindings, annual almanacs, and indexes, nothing special. It's we who deal in the delicate work, the real *craft*. That's why so many magicians come to us when they want their best books bound and personalized; they love the unique, luxurious touch. Last week, Dad finished a cover that had a pentacle fashioned in tiny diamonds on the front. Ludicrous, but there you go; that's what the woman wanted."

"Why don't the magicians pay your dad properly? You'd think they'd worry he'd stop doing everything so well, make it lousy quality."

"My dad's too proud for that. But the real point is they've got him over a barrel. He's got to behave, or they'll close us down, give the business to someone else. We're Czechs, remember; suspicious customers. Can't be trusted, even though the Hyrneks have been in London for a hundred and fifty years."

"What?" Kitty was outraged. "That's ridiculous! Of course they trust you—they'd throw you out of the country, otherwise."

"They tolerate us because they need our skill. But what with all the trouble on the Continent, they watch us all the time, in case we're in league with spies. There's a permanent search sphere operating in Dad's factory, for instance; and Karel and Robert are always being followed. We've had four police raids in the last two years. The last time, they turned the house upside down. Grandmama was taking a bath; they dumped her out in the street in her old tin tub."

"How *awful*." Kitty threw the cricket ball high into the air and caught it in an outstretched palm.

"Well. That's magicians for you. We hate them, but what can you do? What's the matter? You're twisting your lip. That means something's bothering you."

Kitty untwisted her lip hurriedly. "I was just thinking. You hate the magicians, but your whole family supports them:

your dad, your brothers working in his workshop. Everything you make goes to them, one way or another. And yet they treat you so badly. It doesn't seem right. Why doesn't your family do something else?"

Jakob grinned ruefully. "My dad's got a saying: 'The safest place to swim is right behind the shark.' We make the magicians beautiful things and that makes them happy. It means they keep off our backs—just about. If we didn't do that, what would happen? They'd be on us in a flash. You're frowning again."

Kitty was not sure she approved. "But if you don't like the magicians, you shouldn't cooperate with them," she persisted. "It's morally wrong."

"What?" Jakob kicked out at her leg with genuine irritation. "Don't give me that! *Your* parents cooperate with them. *Everyone* does. There's no alternative, is there? If you don't, the police—or something worse—pays a visit in the night and spirits you away. There's no alternative to cooperation—is there? *Is there?*"

"S'pose not."

"No, there isn't. Not unless you want to end up dead."

5

The tragedy had occurred when Kitty was thirteen years old.

It was high summer. There was no school. The sun shone on the terrace tops; birds trilled, light spilled into the house. Her father hummed as he stood before the mirror, adjusting his tie. Her mother left her an iced bun for her breakfast, waiting in the fridge.

Jakob had called on Kitty early. She opened the door to find him flourishing his bat.

"Cricket," he said. "It's perfect for it. We can go to the posh park. Everyone will be at work, so there'll be no one there to clear us out."

"All right," Kitty said. "But I'm batting. Wait till I get my shoes."

The park stretched to the west of Balham, away from the factories and shops. It began as a rough area of waste ground, covered with bricks, thistles, and old rusted sections of barbed wire. Jakob and Kitty, and many other children, played there regularly. But if you followed the ground west, and clambered over an old metal bridge above a railway, you found the park becoming increasingly pleasant, with spreading beech trees, shady walks and lakes where wild ducks swam, all dotted across a great sward of smooth green grass. Beyond was a wide road, where a row of large houses, hidden by high walls, marked the presence of magicians.

Commoners were not encouraged to enter the pleasant side

of the park; stories were told in the playgrounds of children who had gone there for a dare, and never come back. Kitty did not exactly believe these tales, and she and Jakob had once or twice crossed the metal bridge and ventured out as far as the lakes. On one occasion a well-dressed gentleman with a long black beard had shouted at them across the water, to which Jakob responded with an eloquent gesture. The gentleman himself did not appear to respond, but his companion, whom they had not previously observed—a person very short and indistinct—had set off running around the side of the lake toward them with surprising haste. Kitty and Jakob had only just made good their escape.

But usually, when they looked across the railway line, the forbidden side of the park was empty. It was a shame to let it go to waste, especially on such a delightful day when all magicians would be at work. Kitty and Jakob made their way there at good speed.

Their heels drummed on the tarmac surface of the metal bridge.

"No one about," Jakob said. "Told you."

"Is that someone?" Kitty shielded her eyes and peered out toward a circle of beeches, partly obscured by the bright sun. "By that tree? I can't quite make it out."

"Where? No. . . . It's just shadows. If you're chicken, we'll go over by that wall. It'll hide us from the houses across the road."

He ran across the path and on to the thick green grass, bouncing the ball skillfully on the flat surface of the bat as he went. Kitty followed with more caution. A high brick wall bounded the opposite side of the park; beyond it lay the broad avenue, studded with magicians' mansions. It was true that the center of the grass was uncomfortably exposed, overlooked by the black windows of the houses' upper stories; it was also true that if they hugged close to the wall it would shield them from this view. But this meant crossing the whole breadth of the park, far from the metal bridge, which Kitty thought unwise. But it was a lovely day and there was no one about, and she let herself run after Jakob, feeling the breeze drift against her limbs, enjoying the expanse of blue sky.

Jakob came to a halt a few meters from the wall beside a silvered drinking fountain. He tossed the ball into the air and thwacked it straight up to an almighty height. "Here'll do," he said, as he waited for the ball to return. "This is the stumps. I'm in bat."

"You promised me!"

"Whose bat is it? Whose ball?"

Despite Kitty's protests, natural law prevailed, and Jakob took up position in front of the drinking fountain. Kitty walked a little way off, rubbing the ball against her shorts in the way that bowlers did. She turned and looked toward Jakob with narrow, appraising eyes. He tapped the bat against the grass, grinned inanely, and wiggled his bottom in an insulting manner.

Kitty began the run-up. Slowly at first, then building up pace, ball cupped in hand. Jakob tapped the ground.

Kitty swung her arm up and over and loosed the delivery at demonic speed. It bounced against the tarmac of the path, shot up toward the drinking fountain.

Jakob swung the bat. Made perfect contact. The ball disappeared over Kitty's head, high, high into the air, so that it became nothing but a dot against the sky . . . and finally fell to earth halfway back across the park.

Jakob did a dance of triumph. Kitty considered him grimly.

With a heavy, heartfelt sigh, she began the long trudge to retrieve the ball.

Ten minutes later, Kitty had bowled five balls and made five excursions to the other side of the park. The sun beat down. She was hot, sweaty, and irate. Returning at last with dragging steps, she pointedly tossed the ball on the grass and flopped herself down after it.

"Bit knackered?" Jakob asked considerately. "You almost got the last one."

A sarcastic grunt was the only reply. He proffered the bat. "Your go, then."

"In a minute." For a time, they sat in silence watching the leaves moving on the trees, listening to the sound of occasional cars from beyond the wall. A large flock of crows flew raucously across the park and settled in a distant oak.

"Good job my grandmama's not here," Jakob observed. "She wouldn't like that."

"What?"

"Those crows."

"Why not?" Kitty had always been a little scared of Jakob's grandmama, a tiny, wizened creature with little black eyes in an impossibly wrinkled face. She never left her chair in the warm spot of the kitchen, and smelled heavily of paprika and pickled cabbage. Jakob claimed she was 102 years old.

He flicked a beetle off a grass stalk. "She'd reckon they were spirits. Servants of the magicians. That's one of their preferred forms, according to her. It's all stuff she learned from *her* mum, who came over from Prague. She hates windows being left open at night, no matter how hot it gets." He put on an aged, quivering voice. " 'Close it up, boy! It lets the demons in.' She's full of things like that."

Kitty frowned. "You don't believe in demons, then?"

"Of course I do! How else d'you think the magicians get their power? It's all in the spell books they send over to get bound or printed. That's what magic is all about. The magicians sell their souls and the demons help them in return—*if* they get the spells right. If they don't, the demons kill 'em dead. Who'd be a magician? I wouldn't, for all their jewels."

For a few minutes, Kitty lay silently on her back, watching the clouds. A thought occurred to her. "So, let me get this right . . ." she began. "If your dad, and his dad before him, have always worked on spell books for magicians, they must have read a lot of the spells, right? So that means—"

"I can see where you're going with this. Yeah, they must have seen stuff, enough to know to keep well clear of it, anyway. But a lot of it's written in weird languages, and you need more than just the words; I think there are things to draw, and potions and all sorts of horrid extras to learn, if you're going to master demons. It's not something anybody decent wants to be part of; my dad just keeps his head down and makes the books." He sighed. "Mind you, people have always assumed my family is in on it all. After the magicians fell from power in Prague, one of my grandpapa's uncles was chased by a mob and thrown from a high window. Landed on a roof and died. Grandpapa came to England soon after and started the business again. It was safer for him here. Anyway . . ." He sat up, stretched. "Whether those crows are demons, I very much doubt. What would they be doing sitting in a tree? Come on—" He tossed her the bat. "Your turn, and I bet I get you out first ball."

To Kitty's vast frustration, this was exactly what he did. And the next time, and the next. The park rang with the metallic *bong* of cricket ball on drinking fountain. Jakob's whoops resounded high and low. At last, Kitty threw down the bat.

"This isn't *fair*!" she cried. "You've weighted the ball, or something."

"It's called sheer skill. My turn."

"One more go."

"All right." Jakob tossed the ball with an ostentatiously gentle underarm throw. Kitty swung the bat with savage desperation, and to her vast surprise made contact so firmly that she jarred her arm up to her elbow.

"Yes! A hit! Catch that one if you can!" She began a dance of victory, expecting to see Jakob pelting off across the lawn . . . but he was quite stationary, standing in an uncertain posture and gazing up into the sky somewhere up behind her head.

Kitty turned and looked. The ball, which she had contrived to swipe high up over her shoulder, plummeted serenely out of the sky, down, down, down, behind the wall, out of the park, into the road.

There followed a terrible smash of breaking glass, a squeal of tires, a loud, metallic crump.

Silence. A faint hissing sound from behind the wall, as of steam escaping from a broken machine.

Kitty looked at Jakob. He looked at her.

Then they ran.

Hard across the grass they went, making for the distant bridge. They ran side by side, heads down, fists pumping, not looking back. Kitty was still holding the bat. It weighed her down; with a gasp she tossed it from her grip. At this, Jakob gave a gulping cry and skidded to a halt.

"You idiot! My name's on it—" He darted back; Kitty slowed, turned to watch him pick it up. As she did so, she saw, in the middle distance, an open gate in the wall, leading to the road. A figure in black limped into view; it stood in the center of the gateway, looking into the park.

Jakob had seized the bat and was coming on again. "Hurry *up!*" she panted, as he fell in alongside. "There's someone . . ." She gave up, hadn't the breath to speak more.

"Almost there—" Jakob led the way past the edge of the lake, where flocks of wild fowl squawked and plumed out in fear across the water; under the shadows of the beech trees, and up a slight rise toward the metal bridge. "We'll be safe . . . once we're over . . . hide in the craters . . . aren't far now . . ."

Kitty had a strong desire to look behind her; in her mind's eye she saw the figure in black running after them across the grass. The image gave her a crawling sensation down the skin on her spine. But they were going too fast for it to catch them; it would be all right, they were going to get away.

Jakob ran up onto the bridge, Kitty following. Their feet pounded like jackhammers, sending up a hollow clatter and the hum of vibrating metal. Up to the top, down the other side . . .

Something stepped from nowhere onto the end of the bridge.

Jakob and Kitty both cried out. Their headlong rush came to an abrupt halt; they stopped dead, crashing hard against each other in their supreme, instinctive effort to avoid colliding with the thing.

It stood as tall as a man, and indeed carried itself as if this were so, standing upright on two long legs, with arms outstretched, and fingers clasping. But it was not a man; if anything, it looked more like a horribly distorted kind of *monkey*, oversized and very stretched. It had pale green fur across its body, except around its head and muzzle, where the fur grew dark green, almost black. The malevolent eyes were yellow. It cocked its head and smiled at them, flexing its tapering hands. A slender ribbed tail thrashed behind it like a whip, making the air sing.

For a brief moment, neither Jakob nor Kitty could speak or move. Then . . .

"Back, back, back!" This was Kitty; Jakob was dumbstruck, rooted to the spot. She grasped the collar of his shirt and pulled him, turning as she did so.

Hands in pockets, tie tucked neatly into a moleskin waist-coat, a gentleman in a black suit stood blocking the other exit from the bridge. He was not the slightest bit out of breath.

Kitty's hand remained clawed in Jakob's collar. She could not let him go. She faced one way, he the other. She felt his hand reach out and, scrabbling at the fabric of her T-shirt, clutch it fast. There was no sound but their terrified breathing and the swishing of the monster's tail through the air. A crow passed overhead, cawing loudly. Kitty heard blood pounding in her ears.

The gentleman did not seem in a hurry to speak. He was fairly short, but stocky and of powerful build. His round face had, at its center, an uncommonly long, sharp nose and, even in those moments of abject terror, suggested to Kitty something of a sundial. The face seemed without expression.

Jakob was trembling at her side. Kitty knew he would not speak.

"Please sir—" she began hoarsely. "W-what do you want?"

There was a long pause; it appeared as if the gentleman was loath to address her. When he did, it was with terrifying soft-ness. "Some years ago," he said, "I purchased my Rolls-Royce at auction. It was in much need of repair, but even so, it cost me a considerable sum. Since then I have spent a great deal more on it, fitting new bodywork, tires, engine, and above all an original front windscreen of tinted crystal, to make my machine perhaps the finest example in London. Call it a hobby for me, a small diversion from my work. Only yesterday, after many months of searching, I located an original porcelain number-plate and affixed it to the bonnet. At last, my vehicle was complete. Today I took it out for a spin. What happens? I am attacked, from nowhere, by two commoners' brats. You smash my windscreen, you make me lose control; I collide with a lamppost, destroying bodywork, tires, and engine, and shattering my number-plate in a dozen places. My car is ruined. It will never run again . . ." He paused for breath; a fat pink tongue flicked across his lips. "What do I want? Well, first I am curious to know what you have to say."

Kitty looked from side to side in search of inspiration. "Erm . . . would 'Sorry' be a start?"

"'Sorry'?"

"Yes, sir. It was an accident, you see, and we didn't—"

"After what you've done? After the damage you've caused? Two vicious little commoners—"

Tears studded Kitty's eyes. "That's not so!" she said desperately. "We didn't mean to hit your car. We were just playing! We couldn't even see the road!"

"Playing? In this private park?"

"It's not private. Well, if it is, it shouldn't be!" Against her better judgment, Kitty found herself almost shouting. "There's no one *else* enjoying it, is there? We weren't doing any harm. Why *shouldn't* we come here?"

"Kitty," Jakob croaked. "Shut up."

"Nemaides—" the gentleman addressed the monkey-thing on the opposite side of the bridge—"come a step or two closer, would you? I have some business I wish you to take care of."

Kitty heard the gentle tapping of claws on metal; felt Jakob cringing at her side.

"Sir," she said quietly, "we're sorry about your car. Truly we are."

"Then *why*," said the magician, "did you run away and not stay to admit responsibility?"

A small, small sound: "Please, sir . . . we were scared."

"How very wise. Nemaides . . . I think the Black Tumbler, don't you?"

Kitty heard a cracking of giant knuckles, and a deep, thoughtful voice. "Of what velocity? They are of under average size."

"I think rather severe, don't you? It was an expensive car. Take care of it." The magician seemed to feel his part in the matter was concluded; he turned, hands still in pockets, and began to limp off back toward the distant gate.

Perhaps if they could run . . . Kitty dragged at Jakob's collar "Come on—!"

His face was a deathly white; she could scarcely catch the words. "There's no point. We can't—" He had loosened his grip on her now; his hands hung hapless at his side.

A *tap-tap-tap*ping of claws on metal. "Face me, child."

For a moment, Kitty considered letting Jakob go and running, herself alone, down off the bridge and away into the park. Then she despised the thought, and herself for thinking it, and turned deliberately to face the thing.

"That's better. Direct frontal contact is preferable for the

Tumbler." The monkey face did not seem particularly full of malice; if anything, its expression was slightly bored.

Mastering her fear, Kitty held up a small, pleading hand. "Please . . . don't hurt us!"

The yellow eyes widened, the black lips made a rueful pout. "I am afraid that is impossible. I have been given my orders—namely to effect the Black Tumbler upon your persons—and I cannot reject this charge without great danger to myself. Would you have me become subject to the Shriveling Fire?"

"In all honesty, I *would* prefer that."

The demon's tail twitched back and forth like that of an irritated cat; it bent a leg and scratched the back of the opposite knee with an articulated claw. "No doubt. Well, the situation is unpleasant. I suggest we get it over with as rapidly as possible."

It raised one hand.

Kitty put her arm around Jakob's waist. Through flesh and fabric, she felt the jerking of his heart.

A circle of billowing gray smoke expanded from a point just in front of the demon's outstretched fingers and shot toward them. Kitty heard Jakob scream. She had just enough time to see red and orange flames flickering in the heart of the smoke before it hit her in the face with a burst of heat, and everything went dark.

6

"Kitty . . . Kitty!"

"Mmm?"

"Wake up. It's time."

She raised her head, blinked, and with a rush awoke to the roar of the theater interval. The lights in the auditorium had come on, the great purple curtain had descended across the stage; the audience had fragmented into hundreds of red-faced individuals filing slowly from the stalls. Kitty was awash in a lake of sound that beat against her temples like a tide. She shook her head to clear it, and looked at Stanley, who was leaning over the stall in front, a sardonic expression on his face.

"Oh," she said, confusedly. "Yes. Yes, I'm ready."

"The bag. Don't forget it."

"I'm hardly likely to, am I?"

"You were hardly likely to fall asleep."

Breathing hard and brushing a loop of hair from her eyes, Kitty snatched up the bag and stood to allow a man to squeeze in front of her. She turned to follow him out along the row of stalls. As she did so, she caught sight of Fred for a moment: his dull eyes were, as always, hard to decipher, but Kitty thought she detected a trace of derision. She compressed her lips and shuffled her way into the aisle.

Every inch of space between the stalls was crowded with people thronging variously toward the bars, the toilets, the ice-cream girl standing in a pool of light against a wall. Movement in any direction was difficult; it reminded Kitty of a cattle market, with the beasts being shepherded slowly through a maze of concrete and metal fencing. She took a deep breath and, with a succession of muttered apologies and judiciously applied elbows, joined the herd. She inched her way between assorted backs and bellies toward a set of double doors.

Midway across, a tap on her shoulder. Stanley's grinning face. "Didn't think much of the show, I take it?"

"Of course not. Dire."

"I thought it had a couple of good points."

"You would."

He tutted in mock surprise. "At least *I* wasn't sleeping on the job."

"The job," Kitty snapped, "comes now."

With set face and hair disheveled, she spilled out through the doors into the side corridor that looped around the edge of the auditorium. She was angry with herself now, angry for dozing, angry for allowing Stanley to get under her skin so easily. He was always looking for any sign of weakness, trying to exploit it with the others; this would only give him more ammunition. She shook her head impatiently. Forget it: this was not the time.

She weaved her way into the theater foyer, where a good many members of the audience were spilling out into the street to sip iced drinks and enjoy the summer evening. Kitty spilled with them. The sky was deep blue; the light was slowly fading. Colorful flags and banners hung from the houses opposite, ready for the public holiday. Glasses clinked, people laughed; with silent watchfulness, the three of them passed among the happy crowd.

At the corner of the building, Kitty checked her watch. "We have fifteen minutes."

Stanley said: "There's a few magicians out tonight. See that old woman swilling gin, the one in green? Something in her bag. Powerful aura. We could snatch it."

"No. We stick to the plan. Go on, Fred."

Fred gave a nod. From the pocket of his leather jacket he produced a cigarette and lighter. He dawdled forward to a point that gave a view along a side road and, while lighting the cigarette, scanned along it. Seemingly satisfied, he set off down it without a backward glance. Kitty and Stanley followed. The street contained shops, bars, and restaurants; a fair number of people strolled past, taking the air. At the next corner, Fred's cigarette appeared to go out. He paused to relight it, again peering closely in all directions. This time, his eyes narrowed; casually he strolled back the way he had come. Kitty and Stanley were busy window-shopping, a happy couple holding hands. Fred passed them. "Demon coming," he said softly. "Keep the bag hidden."

A minute passed. Kitty and Stanley cooed and clucked over the Persian carpets in the window. Fred inspected the flower displays in the next shop along. From the edge of her eye, Kitty watched the corner of the road. A little old gentleman, well dressed and white-haired, came around it, humming a military air. He crossed the road out of sight. Kitty glanced at Fred. Almost imperceptibly, he shook his head. Kitty and Stanley remained where they were. A middle-aged lady wearing a large flowery hat appeared around the corner; she walked slowly, as if contemplating the ills of the world. Sighing heavily, she turned toward them. Kitty smelled her perfume as she passed, a strong, rather vulgar scent. Her footfalls died away.

"Okay," Fred said. He returned to the corner, made a quick reconnaissance, nodded and disappeared around it. Kitty and

Stanley peeled themselves away from the window and followed, dropping each other's hands as if they had sprouted plague. The leather bag, which had been held under Kitty's coat, reappeared in her grasp.

The next road was narrower and there were no pedestrians nearby. On the left, dark and empty behind a black railing, lay the delivery yard for the carpet shop. Fred was slouching against the railing, looking up and down the street. "Search Sphere's just passed down the end," he said. "But we're clear. Your turn, Stan."

The gate to the yard was padlocked. Stanley approached and examined it closely. From an obscure portion of his clothing he drew a pair of steel pincers. A squeeze, a twist, and the chain snapped open. They entered the yard, Stanley in the lead. He was staring hard at the ground in front of them.

"Anything?" Kitty said.

"Not here. The back door's got a fuzz over it: some kind of spell. We should avoid it. But that window's safe." He pointed.

"Okay." Kitty stole to the window, scanned inside. From what little she could see, the room beyond was a storeroom; it was piled with carpets, each rolled and tightly wrapped in linen. She looked at the others. "Well?" she hissed. "See anything?"

"Of course, *this*," Stanley said lightly, "is why it's so stupid *you* being in charge. You're helpless without us. Blind. Nope—there's no traps."

"No demons," Fred said.

"Okay." Kitty now had black gloves on her hands. She tensed a fist, drove it into the lowest pane of glass. A crack, a brief tinkling of glass upon the sill. Kitty reached through, flipped the latch, raised the window. She vaulted up and into the room, landing silently, eyes flicking side to side. Without waiting for the others, she passed among the pyramids of linen, breathing the rich fustiness of the shrouded carpets, arriving swiftly at a half-open door. From the bag, a torch: the beam of light illuminated a large, richly appointed office, with desks, chairs, paintings on the wall. In a corner, low and dark, a safe.

"Hold it." Stanley caught Kitty's arm. "There's a little glowing thread at foot-level—runs between the desks. Trip-spell. Avoid."

Angrily, she pulled herself free from his grip. "I wasn't just going to go blundering in. I'm not stupid."

He shrugged. "Sure, sure."

Stepping high above the invisible thread, Kitty reached the safe, opened the bag, produced a small white sphere and laid it on the ground. Carefully, she retreated. Back at the door, she spoke a word; with a soft sigh and a rush of air, the sphere imploded into nothing. Its suction pulled nearby pictures off the walls, the carpet off the floor, the safe door off its hinges. Calmly, stepping over the invisible thread, Kitty returned to kneel by the safe. Her hands moved quickly, piling objects into her bag.

Stanley was hopping with impatience. "What have we got?"

"Mouler glasses, couple of elemental spheres . . . documents . . . and money. Lots of it."

"Good. Hurry up. We've got five minutes."

"I know."

Kitty shut the bag and left the office without haste. Fred and Stanley had already departed through the window, and were hovering impatiently outside. Kitty crossed the room, jumped out into the yard, and set off toward the gate. A moment later, with an odd intuition, she glanced over her shoulder—just in time to see Fred tossing something back into the storeroom.

She stopped dead. "What the hell was that?"

"No time to chat, Kitty." Fred and Stanley hurried past her. "Play's starting."

"What did you just do?"

Stanley winked as they trotted out onto the road. "Inferno stick. Little present for them." At his side, Fred was chuckling.

"That wasn't the plan! This was a raid only!" She could smell the smoke already, drifting on the air. They rounded the corner past the front of the shop.

"We can't take the carpets, can we? So why leave them to be sold to the magicians? Can't have pity for collaborators, Kitty. They deserve it."

"We could get caught . . ."

"We won't. Relax. Besides, a little boring break-in won't make the headlines, will it? But a break-in and fire *will*."

White with rage, fingers clenched on the handles of the bag, Kitty strolled beside them up the road. This wasn't about publicity—this was Stanley challenging her authority again, more seriously than before. It was *her* plan, her strategy, and he'd deliberately undercut it. She'd have to take action now, no question. Sooner or later, he'd get them all killed.

At the front of the Metropolitan Theatre, an intermittent bell was ringing, and the dregs of the audience were slipping back inside its doors. Kitty, Stanley, and Fred joined them without breaking pace, and a few moments later subsided in their seats once more. The orchestra was warming up again; onstage, the safety curtain had been raised.

Still shaking with fury, Kitty placed her bag between her feet. As she did so, Stanley turned his head and grinned. "Trust me," he whispered. "We'll be front-page news now. There won't be anything bigger than us tomorrow morning."

7

Half a mile north of the dark waters of the Thames, the merchants of the world gathered daily in the City District to barter, buy, and sell. As far as the eye could see the market stalls stretched, huddled under the eaves of the ancient houses like chicks beneath their mother's wing. There was no end to the richness on display: gold from southern Africa, silver nuggets from the Urals, Polynesian pearls, flakes of Baltic amber, precious stones of every hue, iridescent silks from Asia, and a thousand other wonders. But most valuable of all were the magical artifacts that had been looted from old empires and brought to London to be sold.

At the heart of the City, at the junction of Cornhill and Poultry Streets, the supplicating cries of traders fell harshly on the ear. Only magicians were allowed into this central zone, and gray-uniformed police guarded the entrances to the fair.

Each stall here was crammed with items that claimed to be extraordinary. A cursory survey might reveal enchanted flutes and lyres from Greece; pots containing burial dirt from the royal cemeteries of Ur and Nimrud; frail gold artifacts from Tashkent, Samarkand, and other Silk Road towns; tribal totems from the North American wastes; Polynesian masks and effigies; peculiar skulls with crystals embedded in their mouths; stone daggers, heavy with the taint of sacrifice, salvaged from the ruined temples of Tenochtitlán.

It was to this place that, once a week, late on Monday evenings, the eminent magician Sholto Pinn would make his stately way, to survey the competition, such as it was, and purchase any trifles that took his fancy.

Mid-June, and the sun was lowering behind the gables. Although the market itself, wedged between the buildings, was firmly encased in blue shadow, the street still reflected sufficient warmth for it to be a pleasant stroll for Mr. Pinn. He wore a white linen jacket and trousers, and a broad-brimmed straw hat upon his head. An ivory cane swung loosely in one hand; the other dabbed occasionally at his neck with an extensive yellow handkerchief.

Mr. Pinn's smart attire extended even to his polished shoes. This was despite the filth of the pavements, which were thick with evidence of a hundred hurried meals—discarded fruit, falafel wraps, nut and oyster shells, and scraps of fat and gristle. Mr. Pinn minded it not: wherever he chose to walk, the debris was swept away by an invisible hand.

As he progressed, he inspected the stalls on either side through his thick glass monocle. He wore a habitual expression of bored amusement—protection against the approaches of the merchants, who knew him well.

"Señor Pinn! I have here an embalmed hand of mysterious provenance! It was found in the Sahara—I suspect it to be the relic of a saint. I have resisted all comers, waiting for you . . ."

"Please halt a moment, Monsieur; see what I have in this strange obsidian box . . ."

"Observe this scrap of parchment, these runic symbols . . ."

"Mr. Pinn, sir, do not listen to these bandits! Your exquisite taste will tell you . . ."

". . . this voluptuous statue . . ."

". . . these dragons' teeth . . ."

". . . this gourd . . ."

Mr. Pinn smiled blandly, scanned the items, ignored the merchants' cries, moved slowly on. He never purchased much; most of his supplies were flown directly to him from his agents working across the Empire. But even so, one could never tell. The fair was always worth a look.

The row ended with a stall piled high with glass and earthenware. Most of the samples were quite obviously recent forgeries, but a tiny blue-green pot with a sealed stopper caught Mr. Pinn's eye. He addressed the attendant casually. "This item. What is it?"

The seller was a young woman wearing a colorful headscarf. "Sir! It is a faience pot from Ombos in Old Egypt. It was found in a deep grave, under a heavy stone, next to the bones of a tall, winged man."

Mr. Pinn raised an eyebrow. "Indeed. Do you have this marvelous skeleton?"

"Alas, no. The bones were dispersed by an excitable crowd."

"How convenient. But the pot: it has not been opened?"

"No, sir. I believe it contains a djinni, or possibly a Pestilence. Buy it, open it, and see for yourself!"

Mr. Pinn picked up the pot and turned it over in his fat white fingers. "Hmm," he murmured. "It seems oddly heavy for its size. Perhaps a compressed spell. . . . Yes, the item is of some small interest. What is your price?"

"For you, sir—a hundred pounds."

Mr. Pinn gave a hearty chuckle. "I am indeed wealthy, my dear; I am also not to be trifled with." He snapped a finger, and with a rattling of pottery and a scrabbling of cloth, an unseen person clambered swiftly up one of the poles that supported the stall, skittered across the tarpaulin, and dropped lightly down upon the woman's back. She screamed. Mr. Pinn did not look up from the pot in his hand. "Bartering is all very well, my dear, but one should always begin at a sensible level. Now, why don't you suggest another figure? My assistant, Mr. Simpkin, will readily confirm if your price is worth considering."

A few minutes later the woman, blue-faced and choking from the grip of invisible fingers around her neck, finally stammered out a nominal sum. Mr. Pinn flipped a few coins onto the counter and departed in good humor, carrying his prize securely in his pocket. He left the fair and strode away down Poultry Street to where his car was waiting. Anyone blocking his path was brushed aside cursorily by the invisible hand.

Mr. Pinn heaved his bulk into the car and signaled the chauffeur to move off. Then, settling back into his seat, he spoke into thin air. "Simpkin."

"Yes, master?"

"I shall not be working late tonight. Tomorrow is Gladstone's Day, and Mr. Duvall is giving a dinner in our founder's honor. Regretfully, I must attend this dollop of tedium."

"Very good, master. Several crates arrived from Persepolis shortly after lunch. Do you wish me to start unpacking them?"

"I do. Sort and label anything of lesser importance. Leave unopened any parcel stamped with a red flame; that mark indicates a major treasure. You will also find a crate of stacked sandalwood slabs—take care with that; it contains a hidden box with a child mummy from the days of Sargon. Persian customs are increasingly vigilant and my agent must become ever more inventive in his smuggling. Is that all clear?"

"Master, it is. I shall obey with zeal."

The car drew up before the golden pillars and bright displays of Pinn's Accoutrements. A rear door opened and closed, but

Mr. Pinn remained inside. The car drew away into the Piccadilly traffic. A short while later, a key rattled in the lock of the shop's front door; it opened, then drew softly shut again.

Minutes later, an extensive system of blue warning nodes extended up around the building on the fourth and fifth planes, coiled together at the top of the house and sealed itself. Pinn's Accoutrements was secured for the night.

Evening drew on. Traffic lessened on Piccadilly and few pedestrians passed the shop. Simpkin the foliot picked up a hooked rod in his tail and drew hinged wooden shutters down across the windows. One of them squeaked a little as it descended. With a tut of annoyance, Simpkin removed his semblance of invisibility, revealing himself to be small and lime green, with bow legs and a fussy expression. He located a can behind the counter and extended his tail up to oil the hinge. Then he swept the floor, emptied the bins, adjusted the mannequin display and, with the shop tidied to his satisfaction, dragged several large crates in from the backroom.

Before settling down to his task, Simpkin double-checked the magical alarm system with great care. Two years previously a vicious djinni had succeeded in getting in under his watch and many precious items had been destroyed. He had been lucky that the master had forgiven him, far luckier than he deserved. Even so, the memory of his punishments still made his essence tremble. It must never happen again.

The nodes were intact and vibrated warningly whenever he stepped near the walls. All was well.

Simpkin gained entry to the first crate, and began removing the wool-and-sawdust packing. The first item he came to was small and wrapped in tarry gauze; with expert fingers he removed the gauze and surveyed the object dubiously. It was a doll of sorts, made of bone, straw, and shell. Simpkin scratched a note in the accounts with a long goose quill. *Mediterranean Basin, 4,000 years old approx. Curiosity value only. Of insignificant worth.* He placed it on the counter and continued delving.

Time passed. Simpkin was on the penultimate crate. It was the one stuffed with sandalwood, and he was carefully picking through it in search of the smuggled mummy when he first heard the rumbling sounds. What were they? Car traffic? No— they stopped and started too abruptly. Perhaps rolls of distant thunder?

The noises grew louder and more disquieting. Simpkin laid down his quill and listened, his round head slightly to one side. Strange, disjointed crashes . . . punctuated by heavy thudding. Where did they come from? Somewhere beyond the shop, that was obvious, but from which direction?

He hopped to his feet and cautiously approaching the nearest window, raised the shutters briefly. Beyond the blue security nodes, Piccadilly was dark and empty. There were few lights on in the houses opposite and little traffic. He could see nothing to explain the sounds.

He listened again. They were stronger now; in fact, they seemed to be coming from somewhere *behind* him, back within the recesses of the building. . . . Simpkin lowered the shutter, his tail swishing uneasily. Retreating a little, he stretched behind the counter and retrieved a large and knobbly club. With this in hand, he padded to the storeroom door and peered inside.

The room was as normal: filled with stacks of crates and cardboard boxes and shelves of artifacts being prepared for show or sale. The electric light in the ceiling hummed gently.

Simpkin returned to the shop floor, frowning in puzzlement. The noises were quite loud now—something, somewhere, was being smashed. Should he perhaps alert the master? No. An unwise thought. Mr. Pinn disliked being bothered unnecessarily. It was best not to disturb him.

Another reverberating crash and the sound of breaking glass; for the first time, Simpkin's attention was drawn to the right-hand wall of Pinn's, which joined on directly to a delicatessen and wine merchant's. Very strange. He stepped forward to investigate. At that moment three things happened.

Half the wall exploded inward.

Something large stepped into the room.

All light in the shop went out.

Transfixed in the center of the floor, Simpkin could see nothing—neither on the first plane, nor on any of the other four to which he had access. A swath of ice-cold darkness had engulfed the shop, and deep within it, something moved. He heard a footstep, then a horrendous crashing noise from the direction of Mr. Pinn's antique porcelain. Another step followed, then a ripping and a rending that could come only from the racks of suits that Simpkin had so carefully hung that very morning.

Professional distress overcame his fear: he let out a groan of fury and, flexing the club, scraped it accidentally against the counter.

The footsteps stopped. He sensed something peering in his direction. Simpkin froze. Darkness coiled about him.

He flicked his eyes back and forth. From memory, he knew he was only a few meters away from the nearest shuttered window. If he stepped backward now, perhaps he could reach it before—

Something stepped across the room toward him. It came with a heavy tread.

Simpkin tiptoed backward.

There was a sudden splintering noise midway across the room. He halted, wincing. That was the mahogany cabinet that Mr. Pinn was so fond of! Regency period, with ebony handles and lapis lazuli inlays! What a terrible disaster!

He forced himself to concentrate. Only a couple of yards more to the window. Keep going . . . he was almost there. The heavy tread came after him, each step a ringing concussion against the floor.

A sudden clatter and screeching of torn metal. Oh—now that was *too* much! Those racks of protective silver necklaces had taken him an age to sort!

In his outrage, he paused again. The footsteps were closer now. Simpkin hurriedly tottered a little farther and his searching fingers touched the metal shutters. He felt the warning nodes vibrating beyond it. All he had to do was break his way through.

But Mr. Pinn had instructed him to remain within the shop at all times, to protect it with his life. True, it was not an official charge, made in a pentacle. He hadn't had one of those for years. So he *could* disobey it, if he chose. . . . But what would Mr. Pinn say if he left his post? The idea didn't bear thinking about.

A shuffling step beside him. A cold taint of earth and worms and clay.

If Simpkin had obeyed his instincts and turned tail and fled, he might yet have saved himself. The shutters could have been broken through, the alarm nodes torn open, he could have fallen out into the road. But years of willing subjugation to Mr. Pinn had robbed him of his initiative. He had forgotten how to do anything under his own volition. So he could do nothing but stand and tremble and utter hoarse squeaks of ever escalating pitch as the air about him grew grave-cold and slowly filled with an unseen presence.

He shrank back against the wall.

Right above him, glass shattered; he felt it cascading to the floor.

Mr. Pinn's Phoenician incense jars! Priceless!

He gave a cry of rage and, in his final moment, remembered the club held in his hand. Now, blindly, with all his strength, he swung it at last, lashing out at the looming dark that bent down to receive him.

8

When dawn broke on the morning of Founder's Day, investigators from the Department of Internal Affairs had long been busy in Piccadilly. Ignoring the conventions of the holiday, which prescribed casual wear for all citizens, the officials were dressed in dark gray suits. From a distance, as they clambered ceaselessly over the rubble of the ruined shops, they resembled ants toiling on a mound. In every direction men and women were at work, bending to the floor, straightening, placing fragments of debris in plastic bags with tweezers or inspecting minute stains upon the walls. They wrote in notebooks and scribbled diagrams on parchment strips. More peculiarly, or so it seemed to the crowd loitering beyond the yellow warning flags, they uttered orders and made curt signals into the empty air. These directions were often accompanied by little unexpected air currents, or faint rushing noises that suggested swift and certain movement—sensations that nagged uncomfortably at the imaginations of the onlookers until they suddenly remebered other engagements and went elsewhere.

Standing atop the pile of masonry that spread from Pinn's Accoutrements, Nathaniel watched the commoners depart. He did not blame them for their curiosity.

Piccadilly was in turmoil. All the way from Grebe's to Pinn's, each shop had been disemboweled, its contents scrambled and disgorged out into the road through broken doors and windows. Foodstuffs, books, suits, and artifacts lay sad and ruined amid a mess of glass, wood, and broken stone. Inside the buildings the scene was even worse. Each of these shops had an ancient, noble pedigree; each had been ravaged beyond repair. Shelves and counters, stands and draperies lay bludgeoned into fragments, the valuable produce smashed and crushed and ground into the dust.

The scene was overwhelming, but it was also very odd. Something appeared to have passed through the partition walls between the shops, in a roughly straight line. Standing indoors at one end of the devastation zone, it was possible to gaze right down the length of the block, through the shells of all five shops, and see workers moving in the rubble at the other end. Also, only the ground floors of the buildings had suffered. The upper reaches were untouched.

Nathaniel tapped his pen against his teeth. Strange. . . . It was unlike any Resistance attack he had ever seen. Far more devastating, for one thing. And its exact cause was quite unclear.

A young woman appeared amid the debris of a nearby window. "Hey, Mandrake!"

"Yes, Fennel?"

"Tallow wants to speak with you. He's just inside."

The boy frowned slightly, but turned, and treading delicately to avoid getting too much brick dust on his patent leather shoes, descended the rubble into the murk of the ruined building. A short, burly figure, wearing a dark suit and a hat with a wide brim, stood in what had once been the center of the shop. Nathaniel approached.

"You wanted me, Mr. Tallow?"

The minister gestured brusquely all around. "I want your opinion. What would you say happened here?"

"No idea, sir," Nathaniel said brightly. "But it's very interesting."

"I don't care how *interesting* it is," the minister snapped. "I don't pay you to be *interested*. I want a solution. What do you think it means?"

"I can't say yet, sir."

"What good is that to me? It's not worth a farthing! People are going to want answers, Mandrake, and we have to supply them."

"Yes, sir. Perhaps if I could continue looking around, sir, I might—"

"Answer me this," Tallow said. "What do you think did it?"

Nathaniel sighed. He did not miss the desperation in the minister's voice. Tallow was feeling the pressure now; such a brazen attack on Gladstone's Day would not go down well with their superiors. "Demon, sir," he said. "An afrit could wreak such destruction. Or a marid."

Mr. Tallow ran a yellowish hand wearily across his face. "No such entity was involved. Our boys sent spheres into the block while the enemy was still within. Shortly before they vanished, they reported no sign of demon activity."

"Forgive me, Mr. Tallow, but that can't be true. Human agencies couldn't do this."

The minister cursed. "So *you* say, Mandrake. But in all honesty, how much have you yet discovered about how the Resistance operates? The answer is not very much." There was an unpleasant edge to his tone.

"What makes you think this was the Resistance, sir?" Nathaniel kept his voice calm. He could see the way this was going: Tallow would do his best to foist as much blame as possible onto his assistant's shoulders. "It's very different from their known attacks," he continued. "A completely different scale."

"Until we get evidence otherwise, Mandrake, they are the

most likely suspects. They're the ones who go in for random destruction like this."

"Yes, but just with mouler glasses, small-time stuff. They couldn't wreck a whole block, especially without demons' magic."

"Perhaps they had other methods, Mandrake. Now, run me again through the events of last night."

"Yes, sir; it would be a pleasure." And a complete waste of time. Inwardly fuming, Nathaniel consulted his vellum notebook for a few moments. "Well, sir, at some time around midnight, witnesses living in the apartments across Piccadilly summoned the Night Police, describing disturbing noises coming from Grebe's Luxuries at one end of the block. The police arrived, to find a large hole blown in the end wall, and Mr. Grebe's best caviar and champagne scattered all over the pavement. A terrible waste, if I may say so, sir. By this time, tremendous crashes were coming from Dashell's Silk Emporium two doors down; the officers peered through the windows, but all the lights had been extinguished inside and the source was not clear. It might be worth mentioning here, sir," the boy added, looking up from the notebook, "that today all electric lights are fully functioning in the buildings."

The minister made an irritable gesture and kicked at the remnants of a small doll made of bone and shell, lying in the debris of the floor. "The significance being?"

"That whatever entered here had the effect of blocking out all light. It's another oddity, sir. Be that as it may. . . . the Night Police commander sent his men inside. Six of them, sir. Highly trained and savage. They entered through the window of Coot's Delicatessen, one after the other, close to where the crashing noise was sounding. After that, it all went quiet. . . .

Then there were six small flashes of blue light from inside the shop. One after the other. No big noise, nothing. All was dark again. The commander waited, but his men didn't come back. A little later, he heard the crashing again, somewhere up near Pinn's. By this time, about 1:25 A.M., magicians from Security had arrived and had sealed the whole block in a nexus. Search spheres were sent in, as you mentioned, sir. They promptly vanished . . . Not long afterward, at 1:45, something broke through the nexus at the rear of the building. We don't know what, because the demons stationed there have disappeared, too."

The boy closed the notebook. "And that's all we know, sir. Six police casualties, plus eight Security demons gone. . . . Oh, and Mr. Pinn's assistant." He glanced over at the far wall of the building, where a small heap of charcoal gently smoldered. "The financial costs are of course far greater."

It was not clear that Mr. Tallow had gained much from the account; he grunted irritably and turned away. A black-suited magician with a gaunt, sallow face passed through the rubble, carrying a small golden cage with an imp sitting in it. Every now and then the imp shook the bars furiously with its claws.

Mr. Tallow addressed the man as he passed. "Ffoukes, has there been any word back yet from Ms. Whitwell?"

"Yes, sir. She requests results in double-quick time. Her words, sir."

"I see. Does the imp's condition suggest any pestilence or poison remaining in the next shop?"

"No sir. He is as limber as a ferret, and twice as evil. There is no danger."

"Very well. Thank you, Ffoukes."

As Ffoukes moved off, he spoke sidelong to Nathaniel. "You're going to have to work overtime on this one, Mandrake.

The P.M.'s not at all happy, from what I hear." He grinned, departed; the rattle of the imp's cage faded slowly into the distance.

Stony-faced, Nathaniel swept his hair back behind one ear, and turned to follow Tallow, who was picking his way among the rubble of the room. "Mandrake, we will inspect the remains of the police officers. Have you eaten breakfast?"

"No, sir."

"Just as well. We must go next door, to Coot's Delicatessen." He sighed. "I used to get good caviar there."

They came to the partition wall leading to the next establishment. It had been staved clean through. Here, the minister paused.

"Now, Mandrake," he said. "Use that brain of yours that we've heard so much about, and tell me what you deduce from this hole."

Despite himself, Nathaniel enjoyed tests such as this. He adjusted his cuffs and pursed his lips thoughtfully. "It gives us some idea of the perpetrator's size and shape," he began. "The ceiling's thirteen feet high here, but the hole's only ten feet tall: so whatever made it is unlikely to be larger than that. Breadth of hole three and a half feet, so judging by the relative dimensions of height and width, I'd say it could be man-shaped, although obviously much bigger. But more interesting than that is the way the hole was made—" He broke off, rubbing his chin in what he hoped was a clever, mulling sort of way.

"Obvious enough so far. Go on."

Nathaniel did not believe Mr. Tallow had already made such calculations. "Well sir, if the enemy had used a Detonation or some similar explosive magic, the bricks in the way would have been vaporized, or shattered into small fragments. Yet here they are, snapped and broken at the edges certainly, but many of them still mortared together in solid chunks. I'd say whatever broke in here simply pushed its way through, sir, swiped the wall aside as if it didn't exist."

He waited, but the minister just nodded, as if with unutterable boredom. "So . . . ?"

"*So,* sir . . ." The boy gritted his teeth; he knew he was being made to do his leader's thinking for him, and resented it with a passion. "So . . . that makes an afrit or marid less likely. They'd blast their way through. It's not a conventional demon we're dealing with." That was it; Tallow wasn't getting a word more out of him.

But the minister seemed satisfied for the moment. "My thoughts exactly, Mandrake, my thoughts exactly. Well, well, so many questions. . . . And over here is another." He levered himself up and over the space in the wall into the next shop. Glowering, the boy followed. Julius Tallow was a fool. He appeared complacent, but like a weak swimmer out of his depth, his legs were kicking frantically under the surface, trying to keep him afloat. Whatever happened, Nathaniel did not intend to sink with him.

The air in Coot's Delicatessen carried a strong taint, sharp and unpleasant. Nathaniel reached into his breast pocket for his voluminous colored handkerchief and held it under his nose. He stepped gingerly into the dim interior. Vats of olives and pickled anchovies had been broached and the contents spilled; their smell combined nastily with something denser, more acidic. A trace of burning. Nathaniel's eyes stung a little. He coughed into his handkerchief.

"So here they are: Duvall's best men." Tallow's voice was heavy with sarcasm.

Six conical piles of jet-black ash and bones were dotted here and there across the shop floor. In the nearest, a couple of sharp canine teeth were clearly visible; also the end of a long thin bone, perhaps the policeman's tibia. Most of the body had been completely consumed. The boy bit his lip and swallowed.

"Got to get used to this kind of thing in Internal Affairs," the magician said heartily. "Feel free to step outside if you're feeling faint, John."

The boy's eyes glittered. "No, thank you. I'm quite all right. This is very—"

"Interesting? Isn't it, though? Reduced to pure carbon—or near as makes no odds; just the odd tooth escaped. And yet each little mound tells a story. Look at that one near the door, for instance, spread out more than the others. Implies he was moving fast, leaping for safety, maybe. But he wasn't fast enough, I fancy."

Nathaniel said nothing. He found the minister's callousness harder to stomach than the remains, which were, after all, very neatly piled.

"So, Mandrake," Tallow said. "Any ideas?"

The boy took a deep, grim breath and leafed swiftly through his well-stocked memory. "It's not a Detonation," he began, "nor a Miasma; nor a Pestilence—they're all much too messy. Might have been an Inferno—"

"Do you think so, Mandrake? Why?"

"—I was going to say, sir, it *might* have been an Inferno, except that there's no damage anywhere around the remains. They're all that's burned, nothing else."

"Oh. So what then?"

The boy looked at him. "I really have no idea, sir. What do *you* think?"

Whether Mr. Tallow would have managed a reply, the boy doubted; the minister was saved from responding by the faint tinkling of an unseen bell and a shimmering in the air beside him. These signs announced the arrival of a servant. Mr. Tallow spoke a command and the demon materialized fully. For unknown reasons, it wore the semblance of a small green monkey, which sat cross-legged on a luminous cloud. Mr. Tallow regarded it. "Your report?"

"As you requested, we have scanned the rubble and all levels of the buildings on each plane at the most minute dimension of scale," the monkey said. "We can find no traces of magical activity remaining, except the following, which I shall enumerate:

"One: Faint glimmerings of the nexus boundary, which the Security team erected around the perimeter.

"Two: Residual traces of the three demi-afrits that were sent inside the boundary. It seems their essences were destroyed in Mr. Pinn's establishment.

"Three: Numerous auras from the artifacts of Pinn's Accoutrements. Most of these remain scattered in the road, although several small items of value have been appropriated by your assistant, Mr. Ffoukes, when you weren't looking.

"That is the sum total of our researches." The monkey twirled its tail in a relaxed fashion. "Do you require any further information at this stage, master?"

The magician waved a hand. "That will be all, Nemaides. You may go."

The monkey inclined its head. It stuck its tail straight up

into the air, clasped it with all four feet as if it were a rope, and clambering up at speed, vanished from view.

The minister and his assistant remained silent for a moment. At last Mr. Tallow broke the silence. "You see, Mandrake?" he said. "It is a mystery. This is not magicians' work: any higher demon would have left traces of its passing. Afrits' auras remain detectable for days, for example. Yet there is no trace, none! Until we find evidence otherwise, we must assume that Resistance traitors have found some non-magical means of attack. Well, we must apply ourselves, before they strike again!"

"Yes, sir."

"Yes . . . Well, I think you have seen enough for one day. Go and do some research, consider the problem." Mr. Tallow gave him a side glance; his voice held thinly concealed implications. "You are, after all, officially in *charge* of this case, this being a Resistance matter."

The boy bowed stiffly. "Yes, sir."

The minister waved his hand. "You have my leave to depart. Oh, and on your way out, would you mind asking Mr. Ffoukes to step inside for a moment?"

A thin smile briefly flickered on Nathaniel's face. "Certainly, sir. It would be a pleasure."

9

That evening, Nathaniel set off for home in a mood of black despondency. The day had not gone well. A barrage of messages throughout the afternoon had proclaimed the agitation of the senior ministers. What was the latest on the Piccadilly outrage? Had any suspects been arrested? Was a curfew to be enforced on this, a day of national rejoicing? Who exactly was in charge of the investigation? When were the police to be given more powers to deal with the traitors in our midst?

While he toiled, Nathaniel had sensed the side glances of his colleagues and the sniggering of Jenkins behind his back. He trusted none of them; all were eager to see him fail. Isolated, without allies, he didn't even have a servant he could rely on. The two foliots, for instance, had been useless. He had dismissed them for good that afternoon, too dispirited even to give them the stippling they deserved.

What I need, he thought, as he departed his office without a backward glance, is a *proper* servant. Something with power. Something I know will obey me. Something like Tallow's Nemaides, or my master's Shubit.

But this was easier said than done.

All magicians required one or more demonic entities as their personal slaves, and the nature of these slaves was a sure indicator of status. Great magicians, such as Jessica Whitwell, commanded the services of potent djinn, which they summoned fast as a finger snap. The Prime Minister himself was served by no less than a blue-green afrit—although the word-bonds necessary to snare it had been wrought by several of his aides. For everyday, most magicians made use of foliots, or imps of greater or lesser power, who generally attended their masters on the second plane.

Nathaniel had long been eager to employ a servant of his own. He had first summoned a goblin-imp, which appeared in a yellow guff of brimstone; it was secured to his service, but Nathaniel soon found its tics and grimaces unendurable and dismissed it from his sight.

Next he had tried a foliot: although it maintained a discreet appearance, it was compulsively mendacious, trying to twist every one of Nathaniel's commands to its advantage. Nathaniel had been forced to frame even the simplest orders in complex legal language that the creature could not pretend to misconstrue. It was when he found himself taking fifteen minutes to order his servant to run a bath that Nathaniel's patience expired; he blasted the foliot with hot Palpitations and banished it for good.

Several more attempts followed, with Nathaniel recklessly summoning ever more powerful demons in his search for the ideal slave. He had the necessary energy and skill, but lacked the experience to judge the character of his choices before it was too late. In one of his master's white-bound books, he had located a djinni named Castor, last summoned during the Italian Renaissance. It duly appeared, was courteous and efficient and (Nathaniel was pleased to note) effortlessly more elegant than the ungainly imps of his colleagues in the office. However, Castor possessed a fiery pride.

One day, an important social function had been held at the Persian Consulate; it was an opportunity for everyone to display their servants, and thus their aptitude. At first all went well. Castor accompanied Nathaniel at his shoulder in the form of a fat, pink-faced cherub, even going so far as to wear a drape that matched its master's tie. But its coy appearance aroused the distaste of the other imps, which whispered insults as they passed. Castor could not ignore such provocation; in a flash it bounded from Nathaniel's side, seized a shish kebab from a platter and, without even pausing to remove the vegetables from the skewer, hurled it like a javelin through the chest of the worst offender. In the ensuing pandemonium, several other imps leaped into the fray; the second plane became awash with whirling limbs, brandished silverware, and contorted bog-eyed faces. It took the magicians many minutes to regain control.

Fortunately Nathaniel had dismissed Castor on the instant, and despite an investigation, it was never satisfactorily resolved which demon had begun the fight. Nathaniel would have dearly liked to punish Castor for its actions, but summoning it again was far too risky. He reverted to less ambitious slaves.

However, try as he might, nothing Nathaniel summoned had the combination of initiative, power, and obedience that he required. More than once, in fact, he was surprised to find himself thinking almost wistfully of his first servant . . .

But he had resolved not to summon Bartimaeus again.

Whitehall was filled with flocks of excitable commoners, straggling down to the river for the evening's naval sail-past and fireworks display. Nathaniel made a face; all afternoon, while he had been hunched at his desk, the sounds of marching bands and happy crowds had filtered through the open window, breaking his concentration. But it was an officially sanctioned nuisance and he could do nothing about it. On Founder's Day, ordinary people were encouraged to celebrate; the magicians, who were not expected to swallow propaganda so wholeheartedly, worked as usual.

All around him were red and shiny faces, happy smiles. The commoners had already enjoyed hours of free eating and drinking at the special stalls set up throughout the capital, and had been captivated by the free shows arranged by the Ministry of Entertainment. Every park in central London contained wonders: stilt-walkers; fire-eaters from the Punjab; rows of cages—some with exotic beasts, some containing sullen rebels captured in the North American campaigns; piles of treasures collected from around the Empire; military displays; fetes and carousels.

A few of the Night Police were in evidence along the street, although even they were doing their best to fit in with the general frivolity. Nathaniel saw several holding sticks of bright pink candy floss and one, teeth bared in an unconvincing smile, posing with an elderly lady for her husband's tourist snap. The mood of the crowd seemed relaxed, which was a relief—the events in Piccadilly had not overly agitated them.

The bright sun was still high over the sparkling waters of the Thames as Nathaniel crossed Westminster Bridge. He squinted up; through his contact lenses, among the wheeling gulls, he saw the demons hovering, scanning the crowds for possible attack. He bit his lip, kicked savagely at a discarded falafel wrap. It was exactly the kind of day the Resistance would choose for one of their little stunts: maximum publicity, maximum embarrassment for the government. . . . Was it *possible* the Piccadilly raid had been one of theirs?

No, he couldn't accept it. It was too different from their

normal crimes, far more savage and destructive in its scale. And it wasn't the work of humans, whatever that fool Tallow might say.

He arrived on the south bank and turned left, away from the crowds, into a restricted residential area. Below the quay, the magicians' pleasure yachts lay bobbing unattended, Ms. Whitwell's *Firestorm* the largest and most streamlined of the lot.

As he approached the apartment block, the blaring of a horn made him start. Ms. Whitwell's limousine was parked against the curb, its motor ticking. A stolid chauffeur stared out in front. From a rear window, his master's angular head protruded. She beckoned him.

"At *last*. I sent an imp, but you'd left already. Get in. We're going to Richmond."

"The Prime Minister—?"

"Wants to see us directly. Hurry up."

Nathaniel trotted to the car at speed, heart hammering in his chest. A sudden demand for an audience like this did not bode well.

Almost before he'd slammed the door, Ms. Whitwell signaled to the chauffeur. The car set off abruptly along the Thames embankment, jerking Nathaniel back in his seat. He composed himself as best he could, aware of his master's eyes upon him.

"You know what this is about, I suppose?" she said, dryly.

"Yes, ma'am. This morning's incident in Piccadilly?"

"Naturally. Mr. Devereaux wants to know what we are doing about it. Notice I said 'we,' John. As Security Minister, I'm responsible for Internal Affairs. I will be under some pressure over this. My enemies will seek to gain advantage over me. What will I tell them about this disaster? Have you made arrests?"

Nathaniel cleared his throat. "No, ma'am."

"Who is to blame?"

"We . . . are not altogether certain, ma'am."

"Indeed. I spoke to Mr. Tallow this afternoon. He blamed the Resistance quite clearly."

"Oh. Is . . . erm, is Mr. Tallow coming to Richmond, too, ma'am?"

"He is not. I am bringing you because Mr. Devereaux has a liking for you, which may stand in our favor. Mr. Tallow is less presentable. I find him bumptious and incompetent. Hah, he cannot even be trusted to work a spell correctly, as his skin color attests." She snorted down her pale, thin nose. "You are a bright boy, John," she went on. "You understand that if the Prime Minister loses patience with me, I will lose patience with those below. Mr. Tallow is consequently a worried man. He trembles as he goes to bed. He knows that worse things than nightmares can come to a man as he sleeps. For the moment, he shields you from the full glare of my displeasure, but do not be complacent. Young as you are, you can be blamed for things quite easily. Already, Mr. Tallow seeks to displace responsibility onto you."

Nathaniel said nothing. Ms. Whitwell considered him for a while in silence, then turned to glare out at the river, where a flotilla of small naval vessels had begun to pass seaward with much fanfare. Some were ironclads bound for the far colonies, their wooden hulls encased with metal sheeting, others were smaller patrol boats, designed for European waters, but all had sails unfurled, flags waving. On the banks, crowds cheered, streamers were shot high above to fall into the river like rain.

* * *

At that time, Mr. Rupert Devereaux had been Prime Minister for almost twenty years. He was a magician of secondary abilities, but a consummate politician, who had succeeded in remaining in power through his ability to play his colleagues off one another. Several attempts had been made to overthrow him, but his efficient spy network had succeeded in almost every case in snaring the conspirators before they struck.

Recognizing from the first that his rule depended, to some degree, on maintaining a lofty detachment from his lesser ministers in London, Mr. Devereaux had established his court at Richmond, some ten miles from the heart of the capital. Senior ministers were invited out to consult with him on a weekly basis; supernatural messengers maintained a constant flow of orders and reports, and so the Prime Minister kept himself informed. Meanwhile, he was able to indulge his inclination toward fine living, a habit for which the secluded nature of the Richmond estate was admirably suited. Among his other pleasures, Mr. Devereaux had developed a passion for the stage. For some years he had cultivated the acquaintance of the leading playwright of the day, Quentin Makepeace, a gentleman of boundless enthusiasm, who regularly attended Richmond to give the Prime Minister private one-man shows.

As he grew older and his energies lessened, Mr. Devereaux rarely ventured forth from Richmond at all. When he did so—perhaps to review troops departing for the Continent, or to attend a first night theatrical performance—he was accompanied at all times by a bodyguard of ninth-level magicians and a battalion of horlas on the second plane. This caution had become more marked since the days of the Lovelace conspiracy, when Mr. Devereaux had very nearly died. His paranoia had grown up like a weed in good muck, twisting and twining itself tightly around all those who served him. None of his ministers could feel entirely secure with either their employment or their lives.

The gravel road passed through a succession of villages made prosperous by Mr. Devereaux's bounty, before ending at Richmond itself—a cluster of well-appointed cottages set about a broad green dotted with oaks and chestnut trees. At one side of the green was a tall brick wall, punctured by a wrought-iron gate that had been reinforced with the usual magical securities. Beyond this, a short drive between rows of box yew ended at the redbrick courtyard of Richmond House.

The limousine hummed to a standstill before the entrance steps, and four scarlet-coated servants hurried forth in attendance. Although it was still daylight, bright lanterns hung above the porch and shone merrily in several of the tall windows. Somewhere far off, a string quartet played with melancholic elegance.

Ms. Whitwell did not immediately signal for the car door to be opened.

"It will be a full council," she said, "so I needn't tell you how to behave. No doubt Mr. Duvall will be at his most aggressive. He sees last night as a great opportunity to gain a decisive advantage. We must both be suitably composed."

"Yes, ma'am."

"Don't let me down, John."

She tapped on the window; a servant leaped forward to open the car door. They passed together up shallow sandstone steps and into the foyer of the house. The music was stronger here, drifting lazily among the heavy drapes and Eastern furnishings, swelling occasionally, dying back again. The sound seemed quite close, but there was no sign of the musicians. Nathaniel did not expect to see them. On previous occasions when he had visited Richmond, similar music had always been playing; it followed you wherever you went, a permanent backdrop to the beauty of house and grounds.

A manservant ushered them through a series of luxurious chambers, until they passed under a high white arch and into a long, open, sunlit room, evidently a conservatory appended to the house. On either side stretched brown flowerbeds, neat and empty and decorous, and studded with ornamental rosebushes. Here and there, invisible persons tilled the earth with rakes.

Inside the conservatory, the air was warm, stirred only by a sluggish fan hanging from the ceiling. Below, on a semicircle of low couches and divans, reclined the Prime Minister and his retinue, drinking coffee from small, white Byzantine cups and listening to the complaints of an immense man in a white suit. Nathaniel's stomach churned to see him there: this was Sholto Pinn, whose business had been ruined.

"I regard it as the most despicable outrage," Mr. Pinn was saying. "A gross affront. I have sustained such losses . . ."

The couch nearest to the door was empty. Ms. Whitwell sat here, and Nathaniel, after a hesitation, did likewise. His quick eyes scanned the occupants of the room.

First: Pinn. Ordinarily, Nathaniel regarded the merchant with suspicion and dislike, since he had been a close friend of the traitor Lovelace. But nothing had ever been proved, and clearly he was the injured party here. His lament rumbled on.

". . . that I fear I may never recover. My collection of irreplaceable relics is gone. All I have left is a faience pot containing a useless dried paste! I can scarcely . . ."

Rupert Devereaux himself lounged on a high-backed couch. He was of average height and build, originally handsome, but now, thanks to his many and varied indulgences, slightly heavier around the jowls and belly. Expressions of boredom and annoyance flitted perpetually across his face as he listened to Mr. Pinn.

Mr. Henry Duvall, the Chief of Police, sat nearby, arms folded, his gray cap resting squarely on his knees. He wore the distinctive uniform of the Graybacks, the elite cadre of the Night Police of which he was commander: a ruffed white shirt; a smog-gray jacket, squared, crisply pressed and decorated with bright red buttons; gray trousers tucked into long black boots. Bright brass epaulettes like claws gripped his shoulders. In such an outfit, his hulking frame appeared even bigger and broader than it was; silent and seated, he dominated the room.

Three other ministers were present. A bland, middle-aged man with lank blond hair sat studying his nails—this was Carl Mortensen of the Home Office. Beside him, yawning ostentatiously, sat Helen Malbindi, the soft-spoken Information Minister. The Foreign Secretary, Marmaduke Fry, a man of capacious appetites, was not even pretending to listen to Mr. Pinn; he was engaged in loudly ordering an extra luncheon from a deferential servant.

". . . six croquette potatoes, green beans, sliced lengthways . . ."

". . . for thirty-five years I've built up my supplies. Each one of you has benefited from my experience . . ."

". . . and another cod roe omelette, with a judicious sprinkling of black pepper."

On the same couch as Mr. Devereaux, separated from him by a teetering pile of Persian cushions, sat a short, red-haired gentleman. He wore an emerald-green waistcoat, tight black trousers with sequins sewn into the fabric, and an enormous smile. He appeared to be enjoying the debate hugely. Nathaniel's eyes lingered on him for a moment. Quentin Makepeace was the author of more than twenty successful plays, the latest of which, *Swans of Araby*, had broken box office records across the Empire. His presence in the company was somewhat incongruous, but not entirely unexpected. He was known to be the Prime Minister's closest confidante, and the other ministers tolerated him with wary courtesy.

Mr. Devereaux noted Ms. Whitwell's arrival and raised an acknowledging hand. He coughed discreetly; instantly Mr. Pinn's flow of grievances ceased.

"Thank you, Sholto," the Prime Minister said. "You are most articulate. We are all deeply moved by your predicament. Perhaps now we may get some answers. Jessica Whitwell is here, together with young Mandrake, whom I'm sure you all remember."

Mr. Duvall grunted, his voice heavy with irony. "Who does not know the great John Mandrake? We follow his career with interest, particularly his efforts against the troublesome Resistance. I hope he brings news of a breakthrough in this case."

All eyes fixed upon Nathaniel. He gave a brief, stiff bow as courtesy required. "Good evening, sirs, madams. Erm, I have no firm news as yet. We have been carefully investigating the scene, and—"

"I knew it!" The medals on the Police Chief's chest swung and clicked with the force of his interruption. "You hear that, Sholto? 'No firm news.' Hopeless."

Mr. Pinn regarded Nathaniel through his monocle. "Indeed. Most disappointing."

"It is about time Internal Affairs was taken off this case,"

Duvall continued. "We at the police could do a better job. It's time the Resistance was crushed."

"Hear, hear." Mr. Fry looked up briefly, then returned to the servant. "And a strawberry roulade for dessert . . ."

"It certainly is," Helen Malbindi said gravely. "I have myself suffered some losses—a valuable collection of African spirit masks was taken recently."

"Some of my associates," Carl Mortensen added, "were burgled, too. And the backroom of my Persian carpet supplier was set on fire last night."

From his corner, Mr. Makepeace smiled equably. "In truth, most of these crimes are terribly small scale, are they not? They do not truly hurt us. The Resistance are fools: they alienate the commoners with their explosions—people are frightened of them."

"Small scale? How can you say that," Mr. Duvall cried, "when one of the most prestigious streets in London has been devastated? Our enemies around the world will be rushing home to communicate the good news—that the British Empire is too weak to prevent attacks on its own doorstep. That'll go down well in the backwoods of America, I can tell you. And on Gladstone's Day, above all."

"Which is a ridiculous extravagance, incidentally," Mortensen said. "A waste of valuable resources. I don't know why we honor the old fool."

There was a chuckle from Mr. Makepeace. "You wouldn't have said that to his face, Mortensen."

"Gentlemen, gentlemen . . ." The Prime Minister stirred himself. "We should not bicker. In one respect, Carl is correct. Founder's Day is a serious business and must be done well. We befuddle the population with gaudy trivialities. Millions are taken from the Treasury to finance the free food and games. Even the Fourth Fleet has delayed embarking for America to provide a little extra spectacle. Anything that spoils the effect—and wounds Mr. Pinn into the bargain—needs to be quickly addressed. Currently, it is the job of Internal Affairs to investigate crimes of this nature. Now, Jessica, if you would care to report . . ."

Ms. Whitwell gestured at Nathaniel. "Mr. Mandrake has been conducting the case with Mr. Tallow. He has not yet had time to report to me. I suggest we hear him out."

The Prime Minister smiled benignly at Nathaniel. "Go ahead, John."

Nathaniel swallowed. His master was leaving him to fend for himself. Very well, then. "It's too early to tell what caused this morning's disruption," he said. "Maybe—"

Sholto Pinn's monocle popped out of his eye. "*'Disruption'?*" he roared. "This is a catastrophe! How *dare* you, boy?"

Nathaniel persevered doggedly. "It's too early, sir," he said, "to tell whether this was in fact the Resistance at all. It might well not be. It might be agents from a foreign power, or the pique of a homegrown renegade. There are odd aspects about the case—"

Mr. Duvall held up a hairy hand. "Ridiculous! It's a Resistance attack for sure. It has all the hallmarks of their crimes."

"No, sir." Nathaniel forced himself to meet the police chief's gaze. He was not going to kowtow any further. "Resistance attacks are small-scale, generally involving low-level magical attack—mouler glasses, Elemental Spheres. They are always conducted against political targets—against magicians, or the businesses that supply us—and have a whiff of opportunism about them. They are always hit-and-run. The Piccadilly incident was different. It was ferocious in its intensity and was sustained for many minutes. The buildings were wrecked from the *inside out*—the outer walls remaining largely intact. In short, I believe something was exerting high-level magical control over the destruction."

Ms. Whitwell spoke then. "But there was no evidence of imps or djinn."

"No, ma'am. We methodically combed the area, looked for clues, and found nothing. There were no *conventional* magical traces, which seems to rule out the presence of demons; nor was there any sign of human involvement. Those persons present during the attack were killed by strong magic of a sort, but we have been unable to identify its source. If I might speak freely—Mr. Tallow is ploddingly meticulous, but his methods throw up no new leads. Should our enemy strike again, I believe that we will continue to stumble along in his wake, unless we change our tactics."

"We need more power to the Graybacks," Mr. Duvall said.

"With respect," Nathaniel said, "six of your wolves were not enough last night."

There was a short silence. Mr. Duvall's small black eyes appraised Nathaniel up and down. His nose was short, but unusually broad, his chin blue with stubble, protuberant as a snowplow. He said nothing, but the look in the eyes was clear.

"Well, that is plainly spoken," Mr. Devereaux said finally. "So, what is *your* suggestion, John?"

This was it. He had to seize the chance. They were all waiting for him to fail. "I think there is every reason to believe last night's assailant will strike again," he said. "It has just attacked

Piccadilly—one of the most popular tourist destinations in London. Perhaps it seeks to humiliate us, to spread uncertainty among visitors from abroad, to undermine our international standing. Whatever the reason, we need high-level djinn on patrol across the capital. I would station them near other prominent shopping areas, and tourist sites such as museums and galleries. Then, if anything happens, we will be in a position to act quickly."

There were snorts of disapproval from the assembled ministers and a general outcry. The suggestion was ridiculous: vigilance spheres were already on patrol; the police were out in force, too; high-level djinn required much expenditure of energy. . . . Only the Prime Minister remained quiet—along with Mr. Makepeace, who sat back in his seat wearing an expression of great merriment.

Mr. Devereaux called for silence. "It seems to me the evidence is inconclusive. Is this outrage the work of the Resistance? Perhaps, perhaps not. Would more surveillance be useful? Who knows? Well, I have come to a decision. Mandrake, you have proved yourself more than capable in the past. Now do so again. Organize this surveillance and track down the perpetrator. Hunt out the Resistance, too. I want results. If Internal Affairs fails"—here he eyed Nathaniel and Ms. Whitwell meaningfully—"we will have to let other departments take over. I suggest you head off now and pick your demons with due care. For the rest of us—it is Founder's Day, and we should be celebrating. Let us go to dinner!"

Ms. Whitwell did not speak until the purring car had left Richmond village far behind them. "You have made an enemy in Duvall," she said at last. "And I don't think the others care for you much either. But that is now the least of your worries." She looked out at the dark trees, the rushing countryside at dusk. "I have faith in you, John," she went on. "This idea of yours may bear some fruit. Talk to Tallow, get your department working, send out your demons." She ran a long, thin hand through her hair. "I cannot concentrate on this problem myself. I have too much to do preparing for the American campaigns. But *if* you succeed in discovering our enemy, *if* you bring some pride back to Internal Affairs, you will be well rewarded . . ." The statement held the implication of its opposite. She left it hanging; she did not need to say the rest.

Nathaniel felt impelled to respond. "Yes, ma'am," he said huskily. "Thank you."

Ms. Whitwell nodded slowly. She glanced at Nathaniel and despite his admiration and respect for his master, despite his years living in her house, he suddenly felt that she was eyeing him dispassionately, as if from a great distance. It was the look that an airborne hawk might give a scrawny rabbit, while considering whether it was worth the plunge. Nathaniel was suddenly overly conscious of his youth and frailty, of his raw vulnerability beside her power.

"We do not have much time," his master said. "For your sake, I hope you have a competent demon readily to hand."

10

As always, of course, I tried to resist.

I exerted all my energies to counteract the pull, but the wrenching words were just too strong; each syllable was a harpoon spearing my substance, drawing it together, dragging me off. For three short seconds, the gentle gravity of the Other Place helped me hang back . . . then, all at once, its support weakened and I was torn away like a child from its mother's breast.

With extreme suddenness, my essence was compacted, extended to an infinite length and, a moment later, expelled out into the world and the familiar, hated confinements of a pentacle.

Where, following the immemorial laws, I materialized instantly.

Choices, choices. What should I be? The summons was a powerful one—the unknown magician was certainly experienced, and thus unlikely to be cowed by a roaring buggane or a cobweb-eyed specter. So I decided upon a delicate, fastidious guise to impress upon my captor my formidable sophistication.

It was a snappy piece of work, if I say so myself. A large iridescent bubble, glimmering all over with a pearly sheen, rotated in midair. Soft fragrances of aromatic woods drifted forth, with—faintly, as if borne from a great distance—the ethereal music of harps and violins. Inside the bubble, with little round spectacles perched upon her shapely nose, sat a beautiful maiden.[1] She peered calmly out.

And let off a cry of astonished fury.

"You!"

"Now, hold on, Bartimaeus—"

"You!" The ethereal music cut off with an unpleasant squelch; the soft aromatic fragrances turned rank and sour. The beautiful maiden's face grew crimson, her eyes bulged like a pair of poached eggs, the glass in the spectacles cracked. Her rosebud mouth opened to reveal sharp yellow teeth champing up and down with rage. Flames danced inside the bubble and its surface swelled dangerously, as if about to burst. It spun so fast, the air began to hum.

"Just listen for a minute—"

"We had an agreement! We each made a vow!"

"Now, strictly speaking, that's not quite true—"

"No? Have you forgotten so soon? And it *is* soon, isn't it? I lose track in the Other Place, but you look barely different from before. You're still a kid!"

He drew himself up. "I am an important member of the government—"

"You're not even shaving. What is it?—two years later, maybe three?"

"Two years, eight months."

"So you're fourteen now. And already you're summoning me again."

"Yes, but wait a minute—I never made a vow back then. I just let you go. I never said—"

---

[1] Her face was based on a vestal virgin I'd met in Rome, a woman of admirably independent outlook. Julia used to sneak away from the Sacred Flame by night to bet on the chariots at the Circus Maximus. She didn't really wear spectacles, of course. I added them here to give the face a bit more gravitas. Call it artistic license.

"That you'd not call me back? That was the firm implication: I'd forget your true name, you'd forget mine. Deal. But
now . . ." Inside the whirling bubble, the beautiful maiden's
face was fast regressing down an evolutionary slope—a
prominent beetling brow had appeared, a jagged nose, red
feral eyes . . . the little round glasses were somewhat out of
place, and a claw reached up within the bubble, seized the
glasses, and shoved them into the mouth, where sharp teeth
crunched them into powder.

The boy raised a hand. "Just stop messing around and listen
to me for a moment."

"*Listen* to you? Why should I do that, when the ache from
last time has barely gone? I can tell you I was anticipating rather
longer than two years—"

"Two years, eight months."

"Two measly human years to get over the trauma of meeting you. Sure, I knew some idiot with a pointy hat would one
day call me up again, but I hardly thought it would be the same
idiot as last time!"

He pursed his lips. "I *don't have* a pointy hat."

"You're a fool! I know your birth name and you bring me
back into the world against my will. Well, that's fine, because
I'm going to crow it from the rooftops before I'm done!"

"No—you vowed—"

"My vow is over, finished, void, annulled, returned to
sender marked unopened. Two can play at your game, boy."
The maiden's face was gone. Instead, a bestial shape, all teeth
and spiny hair, snapped at the bubble's surface as if trying to
break free.

"If you'll just give me a minute to explain! I'm doing you a
favor!"

"A favor? Oh boy, this is going to be priceless! This I've *got* to hear."

"In that case keep quiet for half a second and let me speak."

"All right! Fine! I'll be quiet."

"Good."

"I'll be silent as the grave. Your grave, incidentally."

"In that case—"

"And we'll see if you can even remotely come up with an excuse worth hearing, because I doubt—"

"Will you shut up!" The magician raised a sudden hand and I felt a corresponding pressure on the outside of the bubble. I stopped ranting sharpish.

He took a deep breath, smoothed back his hair and adjusted his cuffs unnecessarily. "Right," he said. "I'm two years older, as you so correctly guessed. But I'm two years *wiser* as well. And I should warn you I won't be using the Systemic Vise, if you misbehave. No. Have you ever experienced the Inverted Skin? Or the Essence Rack? Of course you have. With a personality like yours, it's guaranteed.[2] Well, then. Don't try my patience now."

"We've been through all this before," I said. "Remember? You know my name, I know yours. You fire a punishment at me, I fire it right back. Nobody wins. We both get hurt."

The boy sighed, nodded. "True. Perhaps we should both calm down." He crossed his arms and gave himself over to a few moments' grim contemplation of my bubble.[3]

---

[2] He was right, sadly. I'd suffered both in my time. The Inverted Skin is particularly vexing. It makes motion difficult and conversation almost impossible. Plays hell with your soft furnishings, too.

[3] Which now hung dead still a few feet off the floor. The surface was opaque, the monster inside having vanished in a huff.

I regarded him bleakly in my turn. His face still had the old pale and hungry look, or at least the bit I could see did, since half of it was curtained by a veritable mane of hair. I swear he hadn't been within a mile of a pair of scissors since I'd last set eyes on him; his locks cascaded around his neck like a greasy black Niagra.

As for the rest, he was less weedy than before, true, but he hadn't so much gotten bulkier as been clumsily *stretched*. He looked as if some giant had grabbed his head and feet, yanked once, then gone off in disgust: his torso was narrow as a spindle, his arms and legs gangly and ill-fitting, his feet and hands quietly reminiscent of an ape's.

The gangly effect was heightened by his choice of clothes: a swanky suit, so tight it looked as if it had been painted on, a ridiculous long black coat, dagger-sharp shoes, and a flouncy handkerchief the size of a small tent hanging from his breast pocket. You could tell he thought he looked terribly dashing.

There were some cast-iron insult opportunities here, but I bided my time. I took a quick look around the room, which appeared to be some formal summoning chamber, probably in a government building. The floor was laid with a kind of artificial wood, entirely smooth, without knots or defects, evidently perfect for pentacle construction. A glass-fronted cupboard in one corner held an array of chalks, rulers, compasses, and papers. Another beside it was filled with jars and bottles of several dozen incenses. Aside from these, the chamber was completely bare. The walls were painted white. A square window high in one wall looked onto a black night sky; a drab cluster of bare bulbs dangling from the ceiling illuminated the room. The only door was made of iron and was bolted on the inside.

The boy came to the end of his musing, adjusted his cuffs

again, and furrowed his brow. He put on a slightly pained expression: he was either attempting to be solemn or had bad indigestion—exactly which was hard to say. "Bartimaeus," he said ponderously, "listen well. Believe me, I profoundly regret summoning you again, but I had little choice. Circumstances have changed here, and we will both benefit from renewing our acquaintance."

He paused, seeming to think I might have a constructive remark to make. Not a chance. The bubble remained dull and motionless.

"In essentials, the situation is simple," he went on. "The government, of which I am now a part,[4] is planning a major land offensive in the American colonies this winter. The fighting is likely to be costly to both sides, but since the colonies are refusing to bow to London's will, there sadly seems little choice but to authorize bloodshed. The rebels are well organized and have magicians of their own, some with power. To defeat them, we are sending out a large force of magician warriors, with their djinn and lesser demons in tow."

I stirred at this. A mouth opened in the side of the bubble. "You will lose the war. Have you been to America? I dwelled there, off and on, for two hundred years. The whole continent is a wilderness—it goes on seemingly forever. The rebels will retreat, draw you into an endless guerrilla campaign, and bleed you dry."

"We will not lose, but you are right that it will be difficult. Many men and many djinn will perish."

"Many men, certainly."

---

[4] Here he smoothed back his hair once more. This act of pompous preening reminded me vaguely of someone, but I couldn't quite think who.

"The djinn fall just as fast. Has it not always been so? You've been in enough battles in your time. You know how it goes. And this is why I'm doing you a favor.

"The Senior Archivist has been through the records and has tabulated a list of demons that might be useful for the American campaign. Your name is among them."

A great campaign? Lists of demons? Sounded unlikely to me. But I trod carefully, tried to draw more out of him. The bubble twitched, an action not unlike a shrug. "Good," it said. "I liked America. Better than this hog-pit of London you call home. No foul urban mess—just great tracts of sky and grass-land, with white-peaked mountains rising up forever . . ." To emphasize my satisfaction, I made a happy buffalo face appear inside the bubble.

The boy gave that old familiar thin-lipped smile that I'd known and disliked so heartily two years before. "Ah. You've not been to America for a while, have you?"

The buffalo eyed him askance. "Why?"

"There are cities there too now, ranged along the eastern seaboard. A couple even approach London in size. That's where the trouble is. Beyond the cultivated strip is the wilderness you refer to, but we're not interested in that. You'll be fighting in the cities."

The buffalo studied a hoof with feigned indifference. "Doesn't bother me none."

"No? Wouldn't you rather work here for me? I can get you off the war list. It would be a fixed term, just a few weeks. Bit of surveillance duty. Far less dangerous than open warfare."

"Surveillance?" I was scathing. "Ask an imp."

"The Americans have afrits, you know."

This had gone far enough. "Oh please," I said. "I can handle myself. I managed to get through the battle of Al-Arish and the Siege of Prague without you there to hold my hand. Let's face it, you must be in big trouble, or you'd never have brought me back. Especially given what I know—eh, *Nat*?"

It seemed for an instant as if the boy was going to explode with fury, but he mastered himself in time. He blew wearily through his cheeks. "All right," he said. "I admit it. I haven't summoned you here just to do you a favor."

The buffalo rolled its eyes. "Well now, there's a shock."

"I'm under pressure here at home," the boy went on. "I need results fast. If not"—he clenched his teeth hard together—"I may be . . . disposed of. Believe me, I'd love to have summoned a de—a djinni with better manners than you, but there's no time for me to research one properly."

"Now, *that* has the ring of truth," I said. "That American story is complete cobblers, isn't it? Trying to earn my gratitude in advance. Well, tough. I'm not falling for it. I've got your birth name and I intend to use it. If you've got half a brain, you'll dismiss me pronto. Our conversation is at an end." To emphasize this, the buffalo head raised its muzzle skyward and swiveled haughtily inside the bubble.

The boy was hopping with agitation. "Oh, come *on*, Bartimaeus . . ."

"No! Beg all you like, this buffalo's not listening."

"I'll *never* beg you!" Now his anger was unleashed in all its fury. Boy, it was an awesome torrent of petulance. "Listen closely," he snarled. "If I don't get help, I'll not survive. That may not mean anything to you—"

The buffalo looked over its shoulder, eyes wide. "Such powers! You read my mind!"

"But *this* just might. The American campaign *does* exist.

There's no list, I admit, but if you don't help me and I lose my life, I'll make sure before I go that your name is recommended to the troops out there. Then you can blab my birth name far and wide for all the good it'll do you. I won't be around to suffer. So those are your options," he concluded, folding his arms once more, "a simple bit of surveillance or exposure to battle. Up to you."

"Is that so?" I said.

He was breathing hard; his hair had flopped down in front of his face. "Yes. You betray me at your peril."

The buffalo turned around and gave him a long, hard stare. In truth, a bit of surveillance *was* infinitely preferable to joining a war—battles have a nasty habit of getting out of control. And furious though I was with the youth, I had always found him a marginally more sympathetic master than most of them. Whether he was so still was far from clear. As little time had passed, it was possible he had not been wholly corrupted. I unzipped the front of the bubble and leaned out of it, hoof on chin. "Well, seems like you've won again," I said quietly. "Seems like I've got no choice."

He shrugged. "Not much, no."

"In that case," I went on, "the least you can do is fill me in a little. I can see you've gone up in the world. What's your posting?"

"I work for Internal Affairs."

"Internal Affairs? Wasn't that Underwood's department?" The buffalo raised an eyebrow. "Aha. . . . *Someone's* following in his old master's footsteps."

The boy bit his lip. "I'm not. That's got nothing to do with it."

"Maybe *someone's* still a little bit guilty about his death. . . ."[5]

The boy flushed. "Rubbish! It's a complete coincidence. My new master suggested I take the job."

"Ah yes, of course. The fragrant Ms. Whitwell. A delightful creature."[6] I appraised him closely, warming to my task. "Did she advise you on your fashion sense as well? What's with those comical skin-tight trousers, anyway? I can read the label on your underpants right through them. As for those cuffs—"

He bristled. "This shirt was very expensive. Milanese silk. Big cuffs are the latest fashion."

"They look like lacy toilet plungers. It's a wonder you don't get blown backward in a draft. Why don't you cut them off and make them into a second suit? It couldn't be worse than the one you're wearing. Or they'd make a pretty Alice band for your hair."

It was notable that these jibes about his clothes seemed to annoy him more than the Underwood one. His priorities had certainly shifted over the years. He struggled to master his fury, picking restlessly at his cuffs, repeatedly smoothing back his hair.

"Look at you," I said. "So many new little habits. I bet you're copying them off one of your precious magicians."

His hand shot down from his hair. "No, I'm not."

"You probably pick your nose the way Ms. Whitwell does, you're so desperate to be like her."

Bad though it was to be back, it was nice to see him writhe

---

[5] Owing to a complex series of thefts and deceptions, Nathaniel had (more or less) inadvertently brought about his master's demise two years before. At the time, it had preyed on his conscience. I was intrigued to see whether it did so still.

[6] This is called irony. Whitwell was in fact a thoroughly unpleasant specimen. Tall and bone-thin, her limbs were like long dry sticks. I was surprised she didn't catch fire when she crossed her legs.

with fury once again. I let him hop about inside his pentacle for a moment or two. "Surely you hadn't forgotten," I said cheerily. "You summon me, the backchat comes free. It's part of the package."

He groaned into his hands. "Suddenly death doesn't seem quite so terrifying."

I felt a bit better now. At least our ground rules were firmly reestablished. "So tell me about this surveillance job," I said. "You say it's simple?"

He composed himself. "Yes."

"And yet your job, your very life, hangs in the balance over it."

"That's right."

"So there's nothing remotely dangerous or complex about it?"

"No. Well . . ." He paused. "Not much."

The buffalo tapped its hoof grimly. "Go on . . ."

The boy sighed. "There's something out there in London that's highly destructive. Not a marid, not an afrit, not a djinni. It leaves no magical traces. It tore up half of Piccadilly last night, causing terrible devastation. Pinn's Accoutrements was destroyed."

"Really? What happened to Simpkin?"

"The foliot? Oh, he perished."

"Tsk. That's a shame."[7]

The boy shrugged. "I share some responsibility for security in the capital, and blame has come my way. The Prime Minister is furious, and my master refuses to protect me."

"Are you surprised? I warned you about Whitwell."

---

[7] I meant this wholeheartedly. I'd been robbed of my revenge.

He looked sullen. "She'll come to regret her disloyalty, Bartimaeus. Anyhow, we're wasting time. I need you to keep watch and track down the aggressor. I am organizing other magicians to send their djinn out, too. What do you say?"

"Let's get it over with," I said. "What is the charge and what are your terms?"

He glowered at me from between his luscious locks. "I propose a similar contract to last time. You agree to serve me, without revealing my birth name. If you are zealous and keep abusive remarks to a minimum, your duration of service will be relatively short."

"I want a definite duration. No vagaries."

"All right. Six weeks. That's a mere heartbeat to you."

"And my exact duties?"

"General multipurpose protection of your master (me). Surveillance of certain sites in London. Pursuit and identification of an unknown enemy of considerable power. How's that?"

"Surveillance, okay. The protection clause is a bit of a drag. Why don't we leave that out?"

"Because then I won't be able to trust you to keep me safe. No magician would ever take a chance on that.[8] You'd stab me in the back first chance you got. So—do you accept?"

"I do."

"Then prepare to accept your charge!" He raised his arms and jutted out his chin, a pose that failed to be as impressive as intended because his hair kept falling in front of his eyes. He looked every one of his fourteen years.

---

[8] He was wrong there: one magician *had* dispensed with all protective clauses and put his trust in me. That was Ptolemy, of course. But he was unique. Nothing like that would ever happen again.

"Hold on. Let me help. It's late, you should be tucked up in bed." The buffalo was now wearing the maiden's spectacles perched upon its muzzle. "How about this . . . ?" I intoned it in a bored, official voice: "'I shall serve you once again for six full weeks. Under sufferance, I promise not to reveal your name during that time—'"

"My *birth* name."

"Oh, all right—'your birth name during that time to any human who comes my way.' How about that?"

"Not quite enough, Bartimaeus. It's not a question of trust, more one of completeness. I suggest: '. . . during that time to any human, imp, djinni, or other sentient spirit, whether in this world or another, on any plane; nor to let slip the syllables of the name in such a way that an echo might be overheard; nor to whisper them into a bottle, cavity, or other secret place where their traces might be detected by magical means; nor to write them down or otherwise inscribe them, in any known language, so that their meaning can be descried.'"

Fair enough. I repeated the words grimly. Six long weeks. At least he'd missed one implication of the phrasing I had chosen: once the weeks were up, I'd be free to talk. And talk I would, if I got the slightest chance.

"Very well," I said. "It is done. Tell me more about this unknown enemy of yours."

Part Two

II

On the morning after Founder's Day, the weather took a marked turn for the worse. Drab gray clouds piled over London and a thin rain began to fall. The streets quickly emptied of all but essential traffic, and members of the Resistance, who would ordinarily have been abroad seeking out new targets, congregated at their base.

Their meeting point was a small but well-stocked shop in the heart of Southwark. It sold paints and brushes and other such supplies, and was popular among artistically minded commoners. A few hundred yards north, beyond a row of decrepit stores, the great Thames flowed; beyond *that* was central London, where magicians thronged. But Southwark was relatively poor, filled with small-time industry and commerce, and magicians rarely set foot in it.

Which suited the inhabitants of the art shop very well.

Kitty was standing behind the glass counter, sorting reams of paper by size and weight. On the counter to one side of her was a pile of parchment rolls, tied up with string, a small rack of scalpels, and six large glass jars, bristling with horsehair brushes. To the other side, rather too close for comfort, was Stanley's bottom. He was sitting cross-legged on the counter, head buried in the morning paper.

"They blame us, you know," he said.

"For what?" Kitty said. She knew quite well.

"For that nasty business up in town." Stanley bent the paper in half and folded it neatly on his knee. "And I quote:

'Following the Piccadilly outrage, Internal Affairs spokesman Mr. John Mandrake has advised all loyal citizens to be alert. The traitors responsible for the carnage are still at large in London. Suspicion has fallen on the same group that carried out a series of earlier attacks in Westminster, Chelsea, and Shaftesbury Avenue.' Shaftesbury Avenue . . . Hey, that's us, Fred!"

Fred only grunted. He was sitting in a wicker chair between two easels, leaning back against the wall so that it teetered and wobbled on two legs. He had been in the same position for almost an hour, staring into space.

"'The so-called Resistance is thought to be made up of disaffected youths,'" Stanley went on, "'highly dangerous, fanatical and addicted to violence'—Blimey, Fred, is it your mother writing this? They seem to know you so well—'they should not be approached. Please inform the Night Police' . . . blah de blah . . . 'Mr. Mandrake will be organizing new night-time patrol . . . curfew after 9 P.M. for public safety'. . . . The usual story." He tossed the paper down upon the counter. "Sickening, I call it. Our last job barely gets a mention. The Piccadilly thing's totally stolen our thunder. It's not good enough. We need to take action."

He looked across at Kitty, who was busily counting sheets of paper. "Don't you reckon, boss? We should load up with some of those goodies in the cellar; pay a visit to Covent Garden or somewhere. Cause a proper stir."

She raised her eyes, glowered at him under her brows. "No need, is there? Someone's done it for us."

"Someone, yes. . . . Wonder who?" He lifted the back of his cap, scratched with precison. "I blame the Czechs, me." He looked at her out of the corner of his eye.

He was goading her again, rubbing up against her authority,

testing for weaknesses. Kitty yawned. He'd have to try a bit harder than that. "Maybe," she said lazily. "Or it might be the Magyars or the Americans . . . or a hundred other groups. No shortage of contenders. Whoever it was, they hit a public place and that isn't our way, *as you well know*."

Stanley groaned. "You're not *still* sore about the carpet fire, are you? Bor-ring. We wouldn't have gotten a mention at all if it wasn't for that."

"People were hurt, Stanley. Commoners."

"Collaborators, more like. Running to save their masters' rugs."

"Why can't you just—" She subsided; the door had opened. A middle-aged woman, dark-haired, with a lined face, entered the shop, shaking droplets off her umbrella. "Hello, Anne," Kitty said.

"Hello, all." The newcomer glanced around, sensing the tension. "Nasty weather having an effect? Bit of an atmosphere here. What's wrong?"

"Nothing. We're fine." Kitty attempted a relaxed smile. It wouldn't do to spread the dispute further. "How did you get on yesterday?"

"Oh, rich pickings." Anne said. She hung her umbrella on an easel and strolled to the counter, ruffling Fred's hair en route. She was dowdy of frame, a little rolling in her gait, but her eyes were quick and bright as a bird's. "Every magician ever spawned was out at the river last night, watching the sail-past. Remarkable how few of them guarded their pockets." She raised a hand and made a quick snatching motion with her fingers. "Nicked a couple of jewels with strong auras. The Chief will be interested. He can show them to Mr. Hopkins."

Stanley stirred. "Got 'em here?" he asked.

Anne made a face. "I stopped at the mews on the way down and left them in the cellar. Think I'd bring them *here*? Go and make me a cup of tea, you stupid boy."

"It might be the last stuff we get for a while, though," Anne continued, as Stanley hopped down from the counter and disappeared into the back of the shop. "That Piccadilly hit was sensational, whoever did it. Like lobbing a rock into a wasps' nest. Did you see the skies last night? Swarming with demons."

From his chair, Fred growled in agreement. "Swarming," he said.

"It's that Mandrake again," Kitty said. "The paper says."

Anne nodded grimly. "He's nothing if not persistent. Those fake kids—"

"Hold it." Kitty nodded at the door. A thin, bearded man entered from the rain. He browsed awhile among the pencils and notebooks; Kitty and Anne busied themselves about the shop, and even Fred exerted himself to some menial task. Finally the man made his purchases and left.

Kitty looked at Anne, who shook her head. "He was okay."

"When's the Chief coming back?" Fred said, discarding the box he was carrying.

"Soon, I hope," Anne said. "He and Hopkins are researching something big."

"Good. We're just stewing here."

Stanley returned, bearing a tray of cups of tea. With him was a thickset young man with tow-colored hair, one arm supported by a sling. He grinned at Anne, patted Kitty on the back, and took a cup from the tray.

Anne was frowning at the sling. "How?" she said simply.

"Got into a fight." He took a swig of tea. "Last night, at the

128

meeting house behind the Black Dog Pub. Commoners' action group, *so called*. I was trying to get them interested in some real positive action. They were scared; refused point-blank. I got a bit angry, told them what I thought of them. Bit of a scrap." He made a face. "It's nothing."

"You idiot, Nick," Kitty said. "You're hardly going to recruit anyone that way."

He scowled. "You should have heard them. They're terri-fied."

"Cowards," Stanley slurped loudly from his cup.

"Of what?" Anne asked.

"You name it: demons, magicians, spies, spheres, magic of any kind, police, reprisals. . . . Useless."

"Well, it's no wonder," Kitty said. "They don't have our advantages, do they?"

Nick shook his head. "Who knows? They won't take risks to find out. I dropped hints about the kinds of thing we did—mentioned that carpet shop the other night, for instance—but they just went all quiet, drank their beers, and refused to answer. There's no *commitment* anywhere." He plunked his cup down angrily on the counter.

"We need the Chief back," Fred said. "He'll tell us what to do."

Kitty's anger rose to the surface once more. "No one wants to get involved in stuff like the carpet job—it's messy and dangerous and above all it affects commoners more than magicians. That's the point, Nick: we've got to show them we're doing more than just blowing stuff up. Show them we're leading them somewhere—"

"*Listen* to her," Stanley crowed. "Kitty's getting soft."

"Look, you little creep—"

Anne clinked the edge of her cup twice against the glass counter, so hard it cracked. She was looking toward the shop door. Slowly, without following her gaze, everyone dispersed around the room. Kitty went behind the counter; Nick returned to the backroom; Fred picked up his box again.

The shop door opened and a young thin man in a buttoned raincoat slipped around it. He removed his hood, revealing a shock of dark hair. With a slightly timid smile, he approached the counter, where Kitty was inspecting the receipts in the till. "Morning," she said. "Can I help you?"

"Good morning, miss." The man scratched his nose. "I work for the Security Ministry. I wonder if I might ask you a couple of questions."

Kitty put the receipts down and rewarded him with her full attention. "Fire away."

The smile broadened. "Thank you. You may have read about some unpleasant incidents in the news recently. Explosions and other acts of terror not far from here."

The newspaper was beside her on the counter. "Yes," Kitty agreed. "I did."

"These wicked acts have injured many ordinary decent people, as well as damaged the property of our noble leaders," the man said. "It is imperative we find the perpetrators before they strike again."

Kitty nodded. "Absolutely."

"We are asking honest citizens to look out for anything suspicious—strangers in your area, odd activities, that sort of thing. Have you noticed anything untoward, miss?"

Kitty considered. "It's tricky. There are always strangers around here. We're near the quays, of course. Foreign sailors, merchants . . . it's hard to keep track."

"You haven't seen anything specific that you can bring to mind?"

Kitty thought hard. "I'm afraid not."

The man's smile turned rueful. "Well, come to us if you *do* see anything. There are great rewards for informants."

"I most certainly shall."

His eyes studied her face; he turned away. A moment later, he had slipped out and was walking across the street to the next shop. Kitty noticed he had forgotten to pull his hood back over his head, despite the pouring rain.

One by one, the others emerged from aisles and recesses. Kitty gave Anne and Fred questioning looks. They were both white-faced and perspiring. "I take it he wasn't a man," she said dryly. Fred shook his head.

Anne said: "A thing with a beetle's head, all black, with red mouth parts. Its feelers were right out, almost touching you. Ugh, how could you not tell?"

"That's not one of my talents," Kitty said shortly.

"They're closing in," Nick muttered. His eyes were wide; he spoke almost to himself. "We need to do something definite soon, or they'll get us. Just one mistake is all it'll take. . . ."

"Hopkins has a plan, I think." Anne was trying to be reassuring. "He'll get us the breakthrough. You'll see."

"I hope so," Stanley said. He cursed. "I wish I could *see* like you, Anne."

She pursed her lips. "It's not a pleasant gift. Now then, demon or no demon, I want to itemize the stuff I stole. Who wants to come to the cellar? I know it's wet, but it's only a couple of streets away. . . ." She looked around.

"Red feelers . . ." Fred gave a shudder. "You should have seen 'em. Covered with little brown hairs. . . ."

"That was *too* close," Stanley said. "If it had overheard us talking . . ."

"Just one mistake is all it'll take. Just one, and we'll be—"

"Oh, shut up, Nick." Kitty slammed the counter hatch back and stomped off across the shop. She knew she was only feeling what they all felt: the claustrophobia of the hunted. On a day like this, with the rain drumming endlessly down, they were all reduced to loitering helplessly indoors, a state that exacerbated their permanent sense of fear and isolation. They were cut off from the rest of the teeming city, with wicked, clever powers set against them.

This was no new sensation for Kitty. She'd never been clear of it, not once, for three long years. Not since the attack in the park, when her world turned upside down.

12

Perhaps an hour had passed before a gentleman walking his dog had found the bodies on the bridge, and contacted the authorities. An ambulance had arrived soon afterward, and Kitty and Jakob were removed from public view.

She had woken in the ambulance. A small window of light switched on far away, and for a time she watched it approaching on a long slow curve through the darkness. Little forms moved inside the light, but she couldn't make them out. Her ears felt as if they were stuffed with cork. The light grew steadily, then with a sudden rush, and her eyes were open. Sound returned to her ears with a painful pop.

A woman's face peered down at her. "Try not to move. You'll be all right."

"What—what—?"

"Try not to speak."

With sudden panic, memory returned: "That monster! That monkey!" She struggled, but found her arms pinned to the trolley.

"Please, dear. Don't. You'll be all right."

She lay back, every muscle rigid. "Jakob . . ."

"Your friend? He's here, too."

"He's all right?"

"Just try to rest."

And whether it was the motion of the ambulance or the weariness deep inside her, she had soon slept, waking in the hospital to find nurses cutting her clothes away. The front of her T-shirt and shorts were charred and crispy, flaking into the air like wisps of burned newspaper. Once attired in a flimsy white shift, she was, for a short while, the focus of attention: doctors swarmed around her like wasps around jam, checking her pulse, respiration, and temperature. Then they suddenly drew back, and Kitty was left lying isolated in the empty ward.

After a long while, a nurse passed by. "We've informed your parents," she said. "They're coming to take you home." Kitty looked at her with incomprehension. The woman halted. "You're quite well," she said. "The Black Tumbler must have just missed you, caught you only with its aftershock. You're a very lucky girl."

This took a moment to sink in. "Then Jakob's all right, too?"

"He wasn't so lucky, I'm afraid."

Terror welled up inside her. "What do you mean? Where is he?"

"He's nearby. He's being cared for."

She began to cry. "But he was standing beside me. He's *got* to be all right."

"I'll bring you something to eat, dear. That'll make you feel better. Why don't you try reading something to take your mind off it? There are magazines on the table."

Kitty did not read the magazines. When the nurse had gone, she slipped out of the bed and stood, unsteadily, on the cool wooden floor. Then, step by step, but growing in confidence in her own strength, she crossed the quiet ward, walking through bright patches of sunlight under the tall, arched windows, till she came to the corridor outside.

On the opposite side of the corridor was a closed door. A curtain had been drawn across the inside of its window.

Checking quickly left and right, Kitty flitted forward like a ghost, until she stood with her fingers on the handle. She listened, but the room beyond was silent. Kitty turned the handle and went in.

It was an airy room, small, with a single bed in it, and a large window that overlooked the roofscapes of South London. The sunlight blazed a yellow diagonal across the bed, snipping it neatly in two. The upper half of the bed was in shade, the figure lying asleep there likewise.

The room was heavy with normal hospital smells—medicine, iodine, antiseptics—but underlying them all was another scent, a smoky one.

Kitty shut the door, stole on the balls of her feet across the floor, hovered by the bed. She looked down at Jakob, her eyes filling with tears.

Her first thought was anger at the doctors for shaving off his hair. Why did they have to make him bald? It would take an age to regrow it, and Mrs. Hyrnek doted on his long black curls. He looked so strange, particularly with the odd shadows thrown upon his face. . . . Only then did she realize what the shadows were.

Where his hair had protected him, Jakob's skin was its normal swarthy color. Everywhere else, from the base of his neck right up to his hairline, it was seared or stained with roughly vertical wavy streaks of black and gray, the color of ash and burned wood. There wasn't an inch of his ordinary skin color left on his face, except faintly at the eyebrows. These had been shaved away: two little pink-brown crescents showed there. But his lips, his eyelids, the lobes of his ears were all discolored. It was more like a tribal mask, an effigy made for a carnival parade, than a living face.

Under the bedclothes, his chest rose and fell raggedly. A little wheezing sound came from between his lips.

Kitty reached out and touched a hand lying on the blanket. His palms, which he had raised to ward off the smoke, were the same streaked color as his face.

Her touch aroused a response: the head turned from side to side; discomfort flickered across the livid face. The gray lips parted; they moved as if they were trying to speak. Kitty took her hand away, but bent closer.

"Jakob?"

The eyes flicked open with such suddenness that she could not prevent herself from jerking back in shock, colliding painfully with a corner of the bedside table. She leaned forward again, though instantly aware he was not conscious. The eyes gazed straight ahead, wide and sightless. Against the black–gray skin, they stood out pale and clear like two milky-white opal stones. It was then she wondered if he were blind.

When the doctors arrived, bringing with them Mr. and Mrs. Hyrnek, and Kitty's mother clamoring behind, they found her kneeling by the bedside, hands clasping Jakob's, her head resting against the blanket. It was only with difficulty that they pried her free.

At home, Kitty pried herself in turn from the anguished questioning of her parents and climbed the stairs to the landing of the little house. For many minutes she stood in front of the mirror, looking at herself, at her ordinary, unblemished face. She saw the smooth skin, the thick dark hair, the lips and eyebrows, the freckles on her hands, the mole on the side of her nose. It was all exactly the same as always, as it simply had no right to be.

* * *

The mechanism of the Law, such as it was, swung laboriously into action. Even while Jakob still lay unconscious in the hospital bed, the police called on Kitty's family to take a statement, much to her parents' anxiety. Kitty recounted what she knew tersely and without elaboration, a young policewoman taking notes all the while.

"We hope there'll be no trouble, officer," Kitty's father said, as she finished.

"We wouldn't want that," her mother added. "Really we wouldn't."

"There will be an investigation," the policewoman said, still scribbling.

"How will you find him?" Kitty asked. "I don't know his name, and I've forgotten the name of the . . . *thing*."

"We can trace him by his car. If he crashed as you say, the vehicle will have been picked up by some garage or other, taken to be serviced. Then we can establish the truth of the matter."

"You've *got* the truth," Kitty said flatly.

"We don't want any trouble," her father said again.

"We'll be in touch," the policewoman said. She snapped her notebook shut.

The car, a Rolls-Royce Silver Thruster, was quickly located; the identity of its owner followed. He was a Mr. Julius Tallow, a magician working for Mr. Underwood at the Ministry of Internal Affairs. While not particularly senior, he was well connected and a familiar figure around the city. He cheerfully admitted that it had been he who had unleashed the Black Tumbler on the two children in Wandsworth Park; indeed, he wanted it known that he was proud to have done so. He had been peacefully driving past when he had been attacked by the individuals concerned. They had smashed his windscreen with a missile so that he lost control, then approached him aggressively, wielding two long staves of wood. It was evident that they intended to rob him. He had acted in self-defense there and then, striking them down before they had a chance to attack. He considered his response a restrained one, given the circumstances.

"Well, he's obviously lying," Kitty said. "We were nowhere near the road to start with—and if he acted in self-defense at the roadside, how does he explain our being found up at the bridge? Did you arrest him?"

The policewoman looked surprised. "He's a magician. It isn't that simple. He denies your charges. The case will be heard at the Courts of Justice next month. If you wish to take the matter further, you must attend and speak against Mr. Tallow then."

"Good," Kitty said. "I can't wait."

"She won't be attending," her father said. "She's done enough damage already."

Kitty snorted, but said nothing. Her parents abhorred the idea of confrontation with the magicians and strongly disapproved of her act of trespass in the park. On her safe return from hospital, they had seemed almost angrier with her than with Tallow—a state of affairs that had awoken her strong resentment.

"Well, it's up to you," the policewoman said. "I'll send the details anyway."

For a week or more there was little word on Jakob's condition in the hospital. Visits were forbidden. In an effort to get news, Kitty finally plucked up the courage to trudge down the road to the Hyrnek house for the first time since the incident. She walked up the familiar pathway diffidently, unsure of her reception; guilt weighed heavily on her mind.

But Mrs. Hyrnek was polite enough; indeed, she clasped Kitty to her ample bosom and hugged her tightly before ushering her indoors. She led her into the kitchen, over which, as always, the smell of cooking hung strong and pungent. Bowls of half-chopped vegetables sat in the center of the trestle table; across the wall stretched the great oak dresser, laden with gaudily decorated plates. Odd utensils of every description hung from the dark walls. Jakob's grandmama sat in her high chair beside the great black stove, stirring a saucepan of soup with a long-handled spoon. All was as normal, down to the last familiar crack in the ceiling.

Except that Jakob was not there.

Kitty sat at the table and accepted a mug of strongly scented tea. With a heavy sigh and a creak of protesting wood, Mrs. Hyrnek sat opposite her. For some minutes, she did not speak—in itself a unique occurrence. Kitty, for her part, did not feel she could start the conversation. Up by the stove, Jakob's grandmama continued stirring the steaming soup.

At last, Mrs. Hyrnek took a loud slurp of tea, swallowed, spoke abruptly. "He woke up today," she said.

"Oh! Is he—?"

"He's as well as could be expected. Which isn't well."

"No. But if he's woken, that's good, isn't it? He'll be okay?"

Mrs. Hyrnek made an expressive face. "Hah! It was the Black Tumbler. His face will not recover."

Kitty felt the tears welling. "Not at all?"

"The scorching is too fierce. You should know this. You have seen it."

"But why should he—?" Kitty furrowed her brows. "I mean—*I'm* all right, and I was hit, too. We were both—"

"You? *You* were not hit!" Mrs. Hyrnek tapped her fingers against her face and looked at Kitty with such ferocious condemnation that Kitty shrank back against the kitchen wall and did not dare continue. Mrs. Hyrnek eyed her for a long moment with a basilisk's gaze, then resumed sipping her tea.

Kitty spoke in a small voice. "I–I'm so sorry, Mrs. Hyrnek."

"Do not be sorry. *You* did not hurt my son."

"But is there no way of changing it back?" Kitty said. "I mean, surely if the doctors don't have treatments, the magicians could do something?"

A shake of the head. "The effects are permanent. Even if they weren't, they would not choose to help us."

Kitty scowled. "They *must* help us! How can they not? What we did was an accident. What Mr. Tallow did was a calculated crime." Her anger rose within her. "He wanted to kill us, Mrs. Hyrnek! The Courts *must* see that. Jakob and I can tell them, next month at the hearing—he'll be better by then, won't he? We'll shoot Tallow's story full of holes and they can take him to the Tower. Then they'll find some way of helping Jakob's face, Mrs. Hyrnek, you'll see."

Even amid the passion of her speech, she was aware of how hollow her words sounded. But Mrs. Hyrnek's next words were unexpected, nevertheless.

"Jakob will not be going to the hearing, dear. And neither should you. Your parents do not want you to, and they are quite right. It is not wise."

"But we *have* to, if we're to tell them—"

Mrs. Hyrnek reached across the table and laid her great pink hand upon Kitty's own. "What do you think will happen to Hyrnek and Sons if Jakob engages in a lawsuit with a magician? Well? Mr. Hyrnek would lose everything in twenty-four hours. They'd close us down, or transfer their trade to Jaroslav's or another of our competitors. Besides . . ." She smiled sadly. "Why bother? We wouldn't have any chance of *winning*."

For a moment, Kitty was too stunned to reply. "But I've been requested to appear," she said. "And so has Jakob."

Mrs. Hyrnek shrugged. "Such an invitation can be easily declined. The authorities would prefer not to be troubled by such a trifling matter. Two common children? It is a waste of their precious time. Take my advice, dear. Do not go to the Courts. No good can come of it."

Kitty stared at the callused tabletop. "But that means letting him—Mr. Tallow—off, scot-free," she said quietly. "I can't—it wouldn't be right."

Mrs. Hyrnek stood suddenly, her chair screeching against the tiles on the floor. "It is not a question of 'right,' girl," she said. "It is a question of common sense. And anyway"— she seized a bowl of chopped cabbage in one hand and advanced to the stove—"it is not entirely certain Mr. Tallow is going to get off quite as freely as you think." With a jerk of the wrists, she tipped the cabbage hissing and bubbling into a vat of boiling water. By the side of the stove Jakob's grandmama nodded and grinned through the steam like a goblin, stirring, stirring, stirring the soup with her knotted, bony hands.

13

There weeks passed, in which, through a combination of stubbornness and pride, Kitty resisted all efforts to dissuade her from the path she had chosen. The harder her parents tried to threaten or cajole her, the more entrenched she became: she was determined to attend the Courts on the scheduled day to see that justice was done.

Her resolve was strengthened by word of Jakob's condition: he remained in the hospital, conscious, lucid, but unable to see. His family hoped that his sight would return in time. The thought of the alternative made Kitty tremble with grief and rage.

If her parents had had the power, they would have declined the summons when it arrived. But Kitty was the plaintiff: her signature was needed to halt the case, and this she would not give. The process of Law continued, and on the appropriate morning, Kitty arrived at the Great Gate of the Courts at 8:30 sharp, dressed in her smartest jacket and best suede trousers. Her parents were not with her; they had refused to come.

All about her was a motley throng, jostling and elbowing her as they waited for the doors to open. At the lowest end of the spectrum, a few guttersnipes barged back and forth, selling hot pastries and pies from large wooden trays. Kitty kept tight hold of her shoulder bag whenever they passed near. She noticed several tradesmen too, ordinary people like her, decked out in their best suits, all pale-faced and sickly with nerves. By far the largest group consisted of worried-looking magicians, resplendent in their Piccadilly suits and formal capes and gowns. Kitty scanned their faces, looking for Mr. Tallow, but he was nowhere to be seen. Burly Night Police kept watch on the fringes of the crowd.

The doors opened, a whistle blew; the crowd streamed in.

Each visitor was funneled past an official in a uniform of red and gold. Kitty gave her name; the man scanned a piece of paper.

"Courtroom twenty-seven," he said. "Stairs on the left, hard right at the top. Fourth door along. Hurry along there."

He pushed her forward and she was past him, under a high stone arch and out into the cool marble halls of the Judicial Courts. Stone busts of great men and women gazed down dispassionately from niches in the walls; silent people hurried to and fro. The air hummed with seriousness and hush and a distinct smell of carbolic soap. Kitty climbed the stairs and made her way along a busy corridor until she arrived at the door of Courtroom 27. Outside it was a wooden bench. A sign above instructed all claimants to sit and wait to be called.

Kitty sat and waited.

For the next fifteen minutes, a small, pensive group of people gathered one by one outside the courtroom. They stood or sat in silence, absorbed in their own thoughts. Most were magicians: they immersed themselves in sheaves of legalistic documents, written on paper headed with complex stars and signs. They did their best to avoid one another's eyes.

The door to Courtroom 27 opened. A young man wearing a smart green cap and an eager expression poked his head around it.

"Kathleen Jones!" he said. "Is she here? She's next up."

"That's me." Kitty's heart was pounding; her wrists tingled with fear.

"Right. Julius Tallow. Is he here? We need him, too."

Silence in the corridor. Mr. Tallow had not arrived.

The young man made a face. "Well, we can't hang around. If he isn't here, he isn't. Miss Jones, if you would be so kind . . ."

He ushered Kitty ahead of him through the door and closed it softly behind them.

"That's your seat over there, Miss Jones. The court's ready to begin."

The courtroom was of intimate size, square, and filled with a stained, melancholy light that filtered in through two giant arched windows of colored glass. The pictures in the windows both depicted heroic knight-magicians. One, encased in armor, was in the process of running a sword through the belly of a great demonic beast, all claws and knobbly teeth. The other, wearing a helmet and what looked like a long white shift, was exorcising a hideous goblin, which was falling through a square black hole that had opened in the ground. The other walls in the room were lined with dark wooden panels. The ceiling was wood, too, carved to resemble the stone vaults of a church. The room was fearsomely old-fashioned. As was perhaps the intention, Kitty felt awed and terribly out of place.

Against one wall ran a high platform, upon which was a huge wooden throne resting behind a long table. At one end of the table was a small desk, where three black-suited clerks sat, busily tapping at computers and leafing through piles of paper. Kitty passed in front of this platform, following the direction of the young man's outstretched arm, toward a solitary high-backed chair silhouetted in front of the windows. Here, she sat. Another similar chair faced her from the opposite wall.

Across from the platform, a couple of public benches were separated from the court by a brass railing. To Kitty's surprise, a few spectators were already gathering there.

The young man consulted his watch, took a deep breath, then yelled so loudly that Kitty jumped where she sat. "All rise!" he roared. "All rise for Ms. Fitzwilliam, Magician Fourth Level and Judge of this Court! All rise!"

A grinding of chairs, a scuffling of shoes. Kitty, clerks, and spectators got to their feet. As they did so, a door opened in the paneling behind the throne and a woman entered, black-robed and hooded. She sat herself on the throne and threw back her hood, revealing herself to be young, with brown bobbed hair and too much lipstick.

"Thangyoo, ladies and gennlemen, thangyoo! All sit, please!" The young man saluted toward the throne and marched off to sit in a discreet corner.

The judge presented a small cold smile to the assembled court. "Good morning, everyone. We start, I believe, with the case of Julius Tallow, Magician Third Level, and Kathleen Jones, a commoner from Balham. Miss Jones has chosen to attend, I see; where is Mr. Tallow?"

The young man leaped to his feet like a jack-in-the-box. "He's not here, ma'am!" He saluted smartly and sat down.

"I can see that. Where is he?"

The young man leaped to his feet. "Haven't the foggiest idea, ma'am!"

"Well, too bad. Clerks, put Mr. Tallow down for contempt of court, pending. We shall begin . . ." The judge put on a pair of spectacles and studied her papers for a few moments. Kitty sat straight-backed, rigid with nerves.

The judge removed her spectacles and looked across at her. "Kathleen Jones?"

Kitty leaped up. "Yes, ma'am."

"Sit down, sit down. We like to keep it as informal as we can. Now, being young—how old *are* you, Miss Jones?"

"Thirteen, ma'am."

"I see. Being young, and of common stock as you undoubtedly are—I see here your father is a *sales assistant* and your mother a *cleaner*"—she spoke these words with slight distaste—"you might very well be overawed by these august surroundings." The judge gestured at the court. "But I must tell you not to fear. This is a house of justice, where even the less equal among us are welcome, provided they speak truthfully. Do you understand?"

Kitty had a frog in her throat; she found it hard to answer clearly. "Yes, ma'am."

"Very well. Then we shall hear your side of the case. Please proceed."

For the next few minutes, in a rather raspy voice, Kitty outlined her side of events. She began awkwardly, but warmed to her theme, going into as much detail as she could. The court listened in silence, including the judge, who stared at her impassively over her spectacles. The clerks tapped away at their keyboards.

She concluded with an impassioned description of Jakob's condition under the spell of the Black Tumbler. As she finished, a heavy silence filled the courtroom. Someone somewhere coughed. During the speech, it had begun to rain outside. Drops tapped gently at the windows; the light in the room was watery and smudged.

The judge sat back in her chair. "Clerks of the Court, do you have all that down?"

One of the three men in black raised his head. "We do, ma'am."

"Very well." The judge frowned, as if dissatisfied. "In the absence of Mr. Tallow, I must reluctantly accept this version of events. The verdict of the court—"

A sudden ferocious knocking sounded on the courtroom door. Kitty's heart, which had leaped sky-high at the judge's words, descended to her boots in a heap of foreboding. The young man in the green cap sprang across to open the door; as he did so, he was almost bowled off his feet by the muscular entrance of Julius Tallow. Dressed in a gray suit with thin pink pinstripes and with his chin thrust forward, he strode across to the vacant chair and sat decisively upon it.

Kitty gazed at him with loathing. He returned the look with a veiled smirk and turned to face the judge.

"Mr. Tallow, I assume," she said.

"Indeed, ma'am." His eyes were downcast. "I humbly—"

"You're *late*, Mr. Tallow."

"Yes ma'am. I humbly extend my apologies to the Court. I was kept busy at the Ministry of Internal Affairs this morning, ma'am. Emergency situation—small matter of three bull-headed foliots loose in Wapping. Possible terrorist action. I had to help brief the Night Police on the best methods for dealing with 'em, ma'am." He adopted an expansive posture, winked at the crowd. "A pile of fruit, lathered with honey—that's what does the trick. The sweetness draws them near, you see, then—"

The judge banged her gavel down upon the bench. "If you don't mind, Mr. Tallow, that is quite beside the point! Punctuality is vital for the smooth running of justice. I find you guilty of contempt of court and hereby fine you five hundred pounds."

He hung his head, the picture of bulky contrition. "Yes, ma'am."

"However . . ." The judge's voice lightened somewhat. "You have arrived just in time to state your side of the matter. We have heard Miss Jones's version already. You know the charges. How do you respond?"

"Not guilty, ma'am!" He was suddenly bolt upright again, swelling with aggressive confidence. The pinstripes on his chest expanded like plucked harp strings. "I'm sorry to say, ma'am, that I have to recount an incident of almost incredible savagery, in which two thugs—including, I am sorry to say, that prim young madam sitting yonder—waylaid my car with intent to rob and injure. It was only pure chance that, with the power I am fortunate enough to wield, I was able to fend them off and make good my escape."

He continued to develop his lie for almost twenty minutes, providing harrowing accounts of the chilling threats made by his two assailants. Frequently he digressed into little anecdotes that reminded the court of his important role in government. Kitty sat white-faced with fury throughout, clenching her fingernails into her palms. Once or twice she noticed the judge shake her head at some unpleasant detail; two of the clerks were heard to gasp in outrage when Mr. Tallow described the cricket ball hitting his windscreen, and the spectators in the gallery oohed and aahed with increasing regularity. She could tell which way the case was going.

At last, when with sickening self-effacement Mr. Tallow described how he had ordered the Black Tumbler to be fired only at the ringleader—Jakob—through his desire to keep casualties to a minimum, Kitty could no longer restrain herself.

"That's another lie!" she cried. "It came straight at me, too!"

The judge rapped the bench with her gavel. "Order in the Court!"

"But it's so obviously untrue!" Kitty said. "We were standing together. The monkey-thing fired at us both, as Tallow ordered. I was knocked out by it. The ambulance took me to hospital."

"Silence, Miss Jones!"

Kitty subsided. "I'm . . . sorry, ma'am."

"Mr. Tallow, if you would be so good as to continue?"

The magician wound it up soon afterward, leaving the spectators whispering excitedly among themselves. Ms. Fitzwilliam brooded a while on her throne, occasionally bending down to exchange whispered asides with the Clerks of the Court. Finally, she tapped the table. The room fell silent.

"This is a difficult and distressing case," the judge began, "and we are hampered in it by the lack of witnesses. We have only one person's word against the other. *Yes*, Miss Jones, what is it?"

Kitty had put up her hand politely. "There is another witness, ma'am. Jakob."

"If so, why isn't he here?"

"He's not well, ma'am."

"His family could have made a submission on his behalf. They have chosen not to do so. Perhaps they feel their case is weak?"

"No, ma'am," Kitty said. "They're scared."

"Scared?" The judge's eyebrows arched. "Ridiculous! Of what?"

Kitty hesitated, but there was no help for it now. "Reprisals, ma'am. If they speak out against a magician in court."

At this, the room erupted with a barrage of noise from the spectators' benches. The three clerks ceased typing in amazement. The young man in the green cap was gawping in his corner. Ms. Fitzwilliam's eyes narrowed. She had to bang the table repeatedly to quiet things down.

"*Miss Jones,*" she said, "if you dare utter such nonsense I shall have you up on a charge myself! Do not speak out of turn again." Kitty saw Julius Tallow grinning openly. She fought to hold back the tears.

The judge stared at Kitty sternly. "Your wild accusation only increases the weight of evidence that has already built up so heavily against you. *Do not speak!*" Overcome with shock, Kitty had automatically opened her mouth again.

"Each time you speak you further damn your case," the judge went on. "Quite patently, if your friend was confident with your story, he would be here in person. Equally patently, you were not hit by the Black Tumbler as you have just claimed, otherwise you could hardly—how shall I put it?—be so well turned out today."

The judge paused to take a sip of water.

"I almost admire your audacity in taking your claim to the court," she said, "together with your temerity in challenging such a prominent citizen as Mr. Tallow." She gestured across at the magician, who wore the complacent expression of a stroked cat. "However, such considerations cannot carry the day in a court of law. Mr. Tallow's case rests on his good reputation and the expensive garage bill required to pay for the damage that you caused. Your case rests on nothing except wild accusations, which I believe to be fabricated." (Gasps from the crowd.) "Why? Simply because if you are mendacious with regard to the Tumbler—which you say hit you, when clearly it did not—there is no reason for the court to accept the rest of your story. Moreover, you can produce no witnesses, not even your friend, the other 'injured party.' As your outbursts have proved, you are clearly of a passionate and turbulent nature, liable to erupt in a rage at the slightest opportunity. When I consider these points, it can only lead me to a glaring fact that I have done my best to ignore. It is this: when all is said and done, you are both a minor and a commoner, whose word can hardly stand against that of a trusted servant of the State."

The judge at this point took a deep breath and a subdued cry of "Hear, hear," rose from the public benches. One of the clerks looked up, muttered, "Well said, ma'am," and buried his nose in his computer again. Kitty slumped in her chair, weighed down by leaden despair. She could not look at the judge, the clerks or, least of all, the odious Mr. Tallow. She stared instead at the shadows of the raindrops trickling across the floor. All she wished for now was to escape.

"In conclusion"—the judge assumed an expression of the utmost dignity— "the court finds against you, Miss Jones, and rejects your charge. If you were older, you would certainly not escape a custodial sentence. As it is, and since Mr. Tallow has already applied his own appropriate punishment to your gang-land group, I will restrict myself to fining you for wasting the court's time."

Kitty swallowed. *Please* let it not be much, please let it not be—

"You are hereby fined one hundred pounds."

Not too bad. She could cope with that. She had almost seventy-five pounds in her bank account.

"In addition, it is customary to transfer the winner's costs across to the losing side. Mr. Tallow owes five hundred pounds for his late arrival. You must pay this, too. The total due to the court is therefore six hundred pounds."

Kitty reeled in shock, feeling the tears coming strongly now. Furiously she fought them back. She would not cry. She *would* not. Not here.

She managed to turn the first sob into a loud, rumbling cough. At that moment the judge banged the gavel twice.

"Court dismissed."

Kitty ran from the room.

14

Kitty had her cry in one of the little cobbled side roads running off the Strand. Then she wiped her face, bought a reviving bun from a Persian café on the corner opposite the Judicial Courts, and tried to work out what to do. She certainly could not pay the fine and doubted her parents could either. That meant she had a month in which to find six hundred pounds, or she—and perhaps her parents, too—would be bound for the debtors' prison. She knew this, because before she had managed to exit the echoing courtrooms, one of the black-suited clerks had appeared, tugged respectfully at her elbow, and thrust an order for payment, with the ink still wet upon it, into her trembling fingers. It spelled out exactly what the penalties were.

The thought of informing her parents gave Kitty sharp pains in her chest. She couldn't face going home; she would walk beside the river first.

The cobbled lane ran down from the Strand to the Embankment, a pleasant pedestrianized walkway following the bank of the Thames. It had stopped raining, but the cobbles were dark and flecked with water. On either side the usual shops stretched: Middle Eastern fast-food joints, tourist boutiques stuffed with kitsch memorabilia, herbalists whose cut-price baskets of dogwood and rosemary bulged halfway out into the street.

Kitty had nearly reached the Embankment when a rapid tapping behind her heralded the sudden appearance of a stick, followed by an ancient man, half hobbling, half stumbling out of control down the cobbled slope. She jumped back out of his way. To her surprise, instead of careering onward and ending up in the river, the man halted, with much scuffling and gasping, directly beside her.

"Ms. Jones?" The words wheezed out between each gasp of breath.

She spoke heavily. "Yes." Some other clerk with a new demand.

"Good, good. Let—let me get my voice back."

This took a few seconds, during which time Kitty observed him closely. He was a thin, bony, and aged gentleman, bald on top, with a semicircle of dirty-white hair acting as a ruff to the back of his skull. His face was painfully thin, but his eyes were bright. He wore a neat suit and a pair of green leather gloves; his hands wobbled as he leaned upon his stick.

At last: "Sorry about that. Afraid I'd lost you. Started along the Strand first. Turned back. Intuition."

"What do you want?" Kitty had no time for intuitive old men.

"Yes. Getting to the point. Good. Well. I was in the gallery just now. Courtroom twenty-seven. Saw you in action." He regarded her closely.

"So?"

"Wanted to ask. One question. Simple one. If you don't mind."

"I don't want to talk about it, thank you." Kitty made to move off, but the stick shot out with surprising speed and gently barred the way. Her anger fizzed inside her; in the mood she was in, kicking an old man down the street did not seem beyond possibility. "*Excuse* me," she said. "I've got nothing to say."

"Understand that. Really. Might be to your advantage, though. Listen, then decide. The Black Tumbler. Sitting at the back of the court. Bit deaf. Thought you said the Tumbler hit you."

"I did. It did."

"Ah. Knocked you out, you said."

"Yes."

"Flames and smoke all around you. Searing heat?"

"Yes. Now I—"

"But, Court didn't accept it."

"No. Now I really must go." Kitty sidestepped the outstretched stick and trotted the last few yards down to the Embankment. But to her surprise and fury the old man kept up with her, continually jabbing his stick out at an angle so that it became entangled with her legs, or tripped her feet, or forced her to take outsize steps to avoid it. At last she could take it no longer; seizing the end of the stick, she yanked hard, jerking the gentleman off balance so that he collapsed against the river wall. Then she set off at a brisk pace, but once more heard the frantic tapping close behind her.

She wheeled around. "Now, *look*—"

He was hard on her heels, whey-faced, gasping. "Ms. Jones, please. I understand your anger. Truly. But I am on your side. What if I said—? What if I said that I could pay the fine? That the Court has levied? All six hundred pounds. Would that help?"

She looked at him.

"Ah. That interests you. I get a result."

Kitty felt her heart beating wildly in confusion and anger. "What are you talking about? You're trying to set me up. Get me arrested for conspiracy or—or something. . . ."

He smiled; his skin stretched tight against his skull. "Ms. Jones. That is not the idea at all. I am not rushing you into anything. Listen. My name is Pennyfeather. Here is my card." He reached into the pocket of his coat and handed a small business card to Kitty with a flourish. It was decorated with two crossed paint-brushes above the words *T. E. Pennyfeather, Artists' Materials*. There was a telephone number in the corner. Uncertainly, Kitty took it.

"Good. I'm going now. Leave you to your walk. Good day for it. Sun coming out. Ring if interested. Within a week."

For the first time, Kitty made an attempt at being polite, without quite knowing why. "But, Mr. Pennyfeather," she said. "Why should you help me? It doesn't make sense."

"No, but it will. Ahh! What—?" His cry was occasioned by two young men—evidently magicians from the expense of their clothes—who, in striding down the street, laughing loudly and tucking into lentil takeaways from the Persian café, had barged right past him, knocking him almost into the gut-ter. They proceeded merrily, without a backward glance. Kitty stretched out a hand to steady the old man, but drew back at the flash of anger in his eyes. He righted himself slowly, lean-ing heavily on his stick and muttering under his breath.

"Forgive me," he said. "Ah, those—they think they own the place. As—as perhaps they do. For the moment." He looked along the Embankment; away into the blue distance people went about their business, visiting stalls or passing up into the cluttered side streets. On the river, four tethered coal barges drifted downstream, the bargees reclining and smoking on the side. The old man bared his teeth. "Few of these fools suspect what flies above them in the open air," he said. "Or guess what hops behind them in the street. And if they guess, they dare not challenge it. They let the magicians strut among them; let them build their palaces upon the broken backs of the people; let them tread all notions of justice into the mud. But you and I—we have seen what the magicians do. And what they do it *with*. Perhaps we are not as passive as our fellows, eh?"

He smoothed down his jacket and grinned suddenly. "You must think for yourself. I will say no more. Only this: I believe your story. The whole of it—of course I do—but most particularly about the Black Tumbler. Who, after all, would be so stupid as to make that point up if they had no injury? Ah, this is what is so interesting. I will await your call, Ms. Jones."

With that, the old man turned on his heel and made off at a brisk pace back up the side street, stick *tap-tap-tap*ping on the cobbles, ignoring the sharp entreaties of an herbalist standing in the doorway of his shop. Kitty watched him until he turned onto the Strand and out of sight.

Waiting in the darkness of the cellar, Kitty drifted through the events of long ago. How distant it all seemed; how naïve she had been, standing in the courtroom demanding justice. She flushed angrily: the memory was painful even now. Justice from the magicians? The very idea was laughable. Clearly, direct action was the only feasible alternative. At least they were doing *something* now, showing their defiance.

She glanced at her watch. Anne had been gone in the secret chamber some time. In total, eleven new magical artifacts had been stolen on Founder's Day—nine minor weapons and two jewels of unknown purpose. Now Anne was storing them away. Outside, the rain had intensified. During the short walk from the art shop to the deserted courtyard, they had all gotten soaked. Even in the cellar they were not safe from the water:

a steady stream of drips was falling from a deep crack in the plaster ceiling. Directly below sat a black bucket of extreme age. It was almost brim-full.

"Empty it out, would you, Stanley?" Kitty said.

Stanley was sitting on the coal bin, shoulders hunched, head pressed on his knees. He hesitated just a moment longer than necessary; finally he jumped down, picked up the bucket and steered it, with some difficulty, to a grille beside the wall. He sluiced the water away.

"I don't know why he doesn't get that pipe fixed," he growled, returning the bucket to its position. The maneuver had taken only a few seconds, but already a small puddle had gathered between the worn bricks of the cellar floor.

"Because we want the cellar to appear unused," Kitty said. "That's obvious."

Stanley grunted. "The stuff's sitting useless in there. It's no place for it."

From his station near the entrance arch, Fred nodded. He was fingering an open flick-knife in his hand. "Should let us go in," he said.

At the far end of the little room, which was only dimly lit by a single bulb, a pile of logs had been precariously stacked. The wall behind it appeared solid, if a little crumbling, but they all knew how the mechanism worked: how a metal lever could be depressed into the floor; how, at the same time, the brick-work above the logs could be made to swing open at a touch. They knew the dull grating noise, the cold, chemical smell emanating from inside. But they didn't know exactly what the secret recess contained, as only Anne, who was the quartermaster of the group, was allowed into their leader's chamber. The others always remained outside, on guard.

Kitty shifted her back against the wall. "There's no point using it all yet," she said. "We need to save as much as possible, wait till we have more support."

"Like that's *ever* going to happen." Stanley had not returned to the coal bin, but was pacing fretfully around the cellar. "Nick's right. The commoners are like oxen. They'll never do anything."

"All those weapons in there," Fred said wistfully. "We should be doing more with them. Like Mart did."

"Didn't do *him* much good," Kitty remarked. "Prime Minister's still alive, isn't he? And where's Mart? Food for the fishes."

She'd intended it to wound, and it did. Stanley had been close friends with Martin. His voice rose a pitch, harsh and resentful: "He was unlucky. The sphere wasn't strong enough, that's all. He could have had Devereaux and half the cabinet. Where's Anne? Why can't she hurry up?"

"You're kidding yourself." Kitty pursued the point bitterly. "Their defenses were too strong. Mart never had a chance. How many magicians have we killed in all these years? Four? Five? And none of them any good. I'm telling you, weapons or not, we need a better strategy."

"I'll tell him you said that," Stanley said. "When he gets back."

"You *would*, you little sneak." Kitty's voice was scathing. Even so, the thought of it made her shiver.

"I'm hungry," Fred said. He pressed the button on the hasp of his knife, flicked out the blade again.

Kitty looked at him. "You had a massive lunch. I saw you."

"I'm hungry again."

"Tough."

"I can't fight if I've not et." Fred suddenly leaned forward; his fingers twisted, blurred; there was a whizzing noise in the air, and the flick-knife buried itself in the cement between two bricks, three inches above Stanley's head. Stanley slowly raised his head and considered the quivering handle; his face was a little green.

"See?" Fred said. "Lousy shot." He folded his arms. "That's because I'm hungry."

"It seemed pretty good to me," Kitty said.

"Good? I missed him."

"Give him his knife back, Stanley." Kitty suddenly felt very tired.

Stanley was struggling unsuccessfully to pull the knife free of the wall when the hidden door opened above the log pile and Anne emerged. The small bag she had taken in with her was nowhere to be seen.

"Squabbling again?" she said tartly. "Come along, children."

The walk back to the shop was just as wet as the outward journey, and the spirits of the group were lower than ever by the time they arrived. As they entered in a gout of spray and steam, Nick ran forward, his face shining with excitement.

"What is it?" Kitty asked. "What's happened?"

"Just got word," he said breathlessly. "From Hopkins. They're coming back within the week. Going to tell us something of the first importance. A new job. Bigger than anything we've ever done."

"Bigger than Westminster Hall?" Stanley sounded skeptical.

Nick grinned. "Saving Mart's memory, bigger even than that. Hopkins's letter doesn't say what, but it's going to shake everything up, he says. It's what we've always wanted, every one of us. We're going to do something that'll transform our fortunes at a stroke. It's dangerous, but if we do it right, he says, we'll knock the magicians off their perch. London will never be the same again."

"About time," Anne said. "Stanley, go and put the kettle on."

15

Picture the scene. London in the rain. Gray sheets of water tumbled from the sky, breaking upon the pavements with a roar louder than cannon fire. A strong wind buffeted the rain this way and that, blowing it under porches and eaves, cornices and capstones, drowning each possible refuge with a freezing spray. There was water everywhere, bouncing off the tarmac, swilling along the gutters, congregating in basement corners and above the drains. It overflowed the city's cisterns. It cascaded horizontally through pipes, diagonally across roof slates, vertically down walls, staining the brickwork like sweeping washes of blood. It dripped between joists and through cracks in ceilings. It hung in the air in the form of a chill white mist, and above, invisibly, in the black reaches of the sky. It seeped into the fabric of buildings and the bones of their cowering inhabitants.

In dark places underground, rats huddled in their lairs, listening to the echoes of the drumming overhead. In humble houses, ordinary men and women closed the shutters, turned lights on and clustered about their hearth fires with steaming cups of tea. Even in their lonely villas, the magicians fled the endless rain. They skulked to their workrooms, bolted fast the iron doors and, conjuring clouds of warming incense, lost themselves in dreams of distant lands.

Rats, commoners, magicians: all safely undercover. And who could blame them? The streets were deserted, all London was shut down. It was close to midnight and the storm was getting worse.

No one in their right mind would be out on a night like this.

Ho hum.

Somewhere amid the driving rain was a place where seven roads met. In the center of the crossroads stood a granite plinth, topped by a statue of a large man on a horse. The man waved a sword, his face frozen in the midst of a heroic cry. The horse was rearing up, back legs splayed, front legs out. Perhaps it was signaling dramatic defiance, perhaps it was preparing to hurl itself into battle. Perhaps it was simply trying to dislodge the fat bloke on its back. We'll never know. But see: under the belly of the horse, sitting right at the center of the plinth, its tail tucked elegantly against its paws—a large gray cat.

The cat affected not to notice the bitter wind that rippled its sodden fur. Its handsome yellow eyes gazed out steadily into the murk, as if piercing the rain. Only the slight downward tilt of its tufted ears signaled dissatisfaction with its circumstances. One ear flicked occasionally; otherwise, the cat might have been carved from stone.

The night darkened. The rain intensified. I tucked my tail in grimly and watched the roads.

Time trickled on.

Four nights is not a particularly long time even for humans, let alone for us higher beings from the Other Place.[1] Yet the last four nights had really *dragged*. For each one of them I had been

---

[1] Where time, strictly speaking, doesn't exist. Or, if it does, only in a circuitous, nonlinear sort of way. . . . Look, it's a complicated concept and I'd love to discuss it with you, but perhaps now's not quite the best moment. Remind me about it later.

patrolling the central regions of London, hunting for the unknown marauder. I'd not been alone, admittedly; I had the company of a few other unlucky djinn and a barrel-load of foliots. The foliots in particular had caused incessant trouble, forever trying to bunk off by hiding under bridges or slipping down chimneys, or getting startled out of their skins[2] by thunderclaps or one another's shadows. It was all one could do to keep them in line. And all the while it had rained continually, hard enough to cause a canker in one's essence.

Nathaniel, needless to say, had not been sympathetic. He was under pressure himself, he said, and he needed results soon. In his turn he was having difficulty marshaling the small group of magicians from his department who were providing the other djinn for the patrols. Reading between the lines, they were openly mutinous, disliking being ordered around by an upstart of a youth. And let's face it, who could blame them? Nevertheless, each night djinn and foliots alike assembled glumly on the gray slate roofs of Whitehall and were directed out on our patrols.

Our aim was to protect certain prominent tourist regions of the city, which Nathaniel and his immediate superior, a certain Mr. Tallow, considered under threat. A list of possible sites was given to us: museums, galleries, swanky restaurants, the aerodrome, shopping arcades, statues, arches, and other landmarks. . . . Taken in toto, it pretty much accounted for most of London. This meant we had to work our interlocking circuits continuously all night to have any chance of keeping check.

Not only was this tedious and tiring (and very wet), it was also an unnerving business, since the nature of our opponent

---

[2] Literally so, I'm afraid. All rather messy and inconvenient.

was both mysterious and malign. Several of the more nervy foliots began a whispering campaign straightaway: our enemy was a rogue afrit; itself was—worse—a marid; it wrapped a cloak of darkness around it at all times, so its victims could not see their deaths approaching; no, it destroyed buildings with its breath;[3] it carried with it the odor of the grave which paralyzed human and spirit alike. To improve morale I tried starting a counterrumor that it was nothing but a small imp with a grouchy personality, but this, sadly, didn't stick; the foliots (and a couple of the djinn) went out into the night wide-eyed and tentative of wing.

One small bonus for me was the appearance, among the djinn, of none other than my old associate from my days in Prague—Queezle. She was newly enslaved to one of the other magicians in Nathaniel's department, a sour and desiccated individual named Ffoukes. Despite his strict regime however, Queezle retained her old vigor. We made it our business to hunt together wherever possible. [4]

The first two nights of hunting, nothing happened, except for two foliots getting swept away while hiding under London Bridge. But on the third night, loud crashing sounds were heard shortly before midnight, emanating from the west wing

---

[3] I've known magicians with similar powers, especially first thing in the morning.

[4] I liked Queezle. She was fresh and youthful (a mere 1,500 years in your world) and had been lucky with her masters. Her first summoning was by a hermit living in the Jordanian desert, who ate honey and dried tubers and treated her with austere courtesy. When he died, she had escaped further service until a female French magician (1400s) uncovered her name. This master, too, was unusually clement and never so much as jabbed her with the Stimulating Compass. By the time she reached Prague, Queezle's personality was thus less embittered than that of hoary old lags like me. Released from service there by the death of our master, she had since served magicians in China and Ceylon, without great incident.

of the National Gallery. A djinni named Zeno was first on the scene, with me not far behind. Simultaneously, several magicians, including my master, arrived in a convoy; they encased the gallery in a dense nexus and ordered us into battle.

Zeno displayed admirable bravery. Without hesitation, he flew straight to the source of the disturbance and was never seen again. I was close on his heels, but owing to a dicky leg and the complex layout of the gallery corridors, lagged behind, got lost, and didn't manage to reach the west wing until much later. By this time, having wrought considerable damage, the marauder had departed.

My excuses cut no ice with my master, who would have worked some inventive punishment on me had I not had the protection of knowing his name. As it was, he vowed to encase me in an iron cube should I neglect to engage the enemy next time it appeared. I made soothing answers, perceiving he was addled with anxiety: his hair was disheveled, his cuffs hung limp, his drainpipe trousers sagged loose upon his frame as if he had lost weight. I pointed this out to him in a sympathetic sort of way.

"Eat more," I advised. "You're too thin. Currently, the only bit of you that's growing outward is your hair. If you don't watch out, you'll overbalance soon."

He rubbed his red, sleepless eyes. "Will you stop going on about my hair? Eating is for people who have nothing else to do, Bartimaeus. I'm living on borrowed time—as are *you*. If you can destroy the enemy, all well and good; if not, at least get some information about its nature. Otherwise the Night Police are likely to take charge."

"So? What's that to me?"

He spoke seriously. "It'll mean my downfall."

"So? What's that to me?"

"Everything, if I bind you into the iron cube before I go. In fact, I'll make it a silver one—even more painful. And it'll happen, unless I get results soon."

I ceased arguing then. There was little point. The boy had changed somewhat since I'd last seen him, and not for the better. His master and his career had worked an unpleasant alchemy upon him: he was harder, harsher, and altogether more brittle. He also had even less of a sense of humor than previously, which was itself a remarkable achievement. One way or another, I looked forward to the end of my six weeks.

But until then, surveillance, danger, and the rain.

From my position beneath the statue, I could see down three of the seven roads. Each one was lined with swanky shop fronts, dark and shadowy, secured by metal grilles. Frail lamps shone in alcoves above the doors, but the rain was stronger than the light, and their radiance did not travel far. Water sluiced along the pavements.

A sudden movement in the left-hand road: the cat's head turned. Something had dropped onto a first-floor window ledge. It perched there for a moment, a black smudge in the gloom—then, in a single sinewy movement, poured itself over the ledge and down the wall, zigzagging through the grooves between the bricks like a thin rope of hot treacle. At the base of the wall, it dropped onto the pavement, became a small black smudge again, grew legs, and began to splitter-splatter along the pavement in my direction.

I watched all this. I did not move an inch.

The smudge reached the crossroads, waded through the spreading puddles, and jumped onto the plinth. Here it was fully revealed as an elegant spaniel with big brown eyes. She halted in front of the cat, paused, shook herself vigorously.

A shower of water sprayed out and hit the cat directly in the face.

"Thanks for that, Queezle," I said. "You must have spotted I wasn't quite wet enough."

The spaniel blinked, stuck her head coyly on one side, and gave an apologetic bark.

"And you can drop that old routine right now," I went on. "I'm not some human dunderhead who's going to be charmed by limpid eyes and a clot of wet fur. You forget I can see you quite clearly on the seventh plane, dorsal tubes and all."

"Can't help myself, Bartimaeus." The spaniel raised a hind leg and scratched herself nonchalantly behind one ear. "It's all this undercover work. It's becoming second nature to me. You should think yourself lucky you're not sitting under a lamp-post."

I did not dignify this remark with a response. "So where've you been?" I said. "You're two hours later than agreed."

The spaniel nodded wearily. "False alarm at the silk ware-houses. Pair of foliots thought they'd seen something. Had to search the whole place thoroughly before giving the all clear. Stupid first-timers. Of course I had to reprimand them."

"Nipped their ankles, did you?"

A small crooked smile flickered across the spaniel's muzzle. "Something like that."

I shifted across to allow Queezle a bit of room on the center of the plinth. Not that it was any less damp there particu-larly, but it seemed a comradely thing to do. She shuffled up and huddled alongside.

"Can't really blame them," I said. "They're jumpy. It's all this rain. And what happened to Zeno. Being summoned night after night doesn't help either. It wears your essence down after a while."

Queezle gave me a side glance out of those big brown puppy-dog eyes. "*Your* essence, too, Bartimaeus?"

"I was speaking rhetorically. *I'm* all right." To prove it I arched my back in a big luxuriant cat stretch, the kind that runs from whisker tip to tail tuft. "Ahhh, that's better. Nope, I've seen worse than this and so have you. Just some pumped-up imp lurking in the shadows. It's nothing we can't handle, once we find him."

"That's what Zeno said, as I recall."

"I don't remember what Zeno said. Where's your master tonight? Safely under cover?"

The spaniel gave a small growl. "He claims to be within signaling distance. The Whitehall office, allegedly. In fact, he's probably holed up in some magician's bar with a bottle in one hand and a girl in the other."

I grunted. "*That* sort, is he?"

"Yup. What's yours like?"

"Oh, the same. Worse, if anything. He'd have girl and bottle in the same hand."[5]

The spaniel gave a sympathetic whimper. I got slowly to my feet.

"Well, we'd better swap circuits," I said. "I'll start by patrolling up to Soho and back. You can head between the posh shops down Gibbet Street to the Museum district behind."

---

[5] Manifestly untrue. Despite his crimped shirts and flowing mane (or perhaps because of them) I had seen no evidence as yet that Nathaniel even knew what a girl was. If he'd ever met one, chances are they'd both have run screaming in opposite directions. But in common with most djinn, I generally preferred to exaggerate my master's foibles in conversation.

"I might rest a bit," Queezle said. "I'm tired."

"Yes. Well, good luck."

"Good luck." The spaniel rested her head gloomily across her paws. I trotted out into the driving rain, to the edge of the plinth, and bent my legs, ready for the off. A little voice sounded behind me: "Bartimaeus?"

"Yes, Queezle?"

"Oh, nothing."

"What?"

"It's just . . . well, it's not *just* the foliots. I'm jumpy, too."

The cat trotted back and sat beside her for a moment, curling its tail around her affectionately. "You don't need to be," I said. "It's already past midnight and neither of us has seen anything. On every occasion when this thing has attacked, it's done so by midnight. Your only fear should be the boredom of a long, tedious vigil."

"I suppose so." The rain drummed all around, like a solid thing. We were cocooned within it. "Between ourselves," Queezle said softly, "what do you think it is?"

My tail twitched. "I don't know, and I'd rather not find out. So far it's killed everything it's come across. My advice is keep vigilant watch, and if you see something unusual coming, scamper the other way pronto."

"But we have to destroy it. That's our charge."

"Well, destroy it by running away."

"How?"

"Um . . . Make it chase you, then lure it into heavy traffic? Something like that. I don't know, do I? Just don't do what Zeno did and attack it head on."

The spaniel heaved a sigh. "I liked Zeno."

"A little too eager, that was his trouble."

There was a heavy silence. Queezle said nothing. The incessant rain beat down.

"Well," I said at last. "I'll see you."

"Yes."

I hopped down from the plinth and ran, tail out, through the rain and across the waterlogged street. A single jump took me up onto a low wall beside a deserted café. Then, in a series of leaps and bounds—wall to porch, porch to ledge, ledge to tiles—I negotiated my athletic feline way, until I had sprung up onto the guttering of the nearest, lowest roof.

I took a quick look back, down into the square. The spaniel was a forlorn and lonely speck, hunched in the shadows beneath the horse's belly. A gust of rain blocked her from my view. I turned and set off along the roof crests.

In that part of town, the ancient houses huddled close together, leaning forward like gossiping hunchbacks so that their gables almost met above the street. Even in the rain, it was thus an easy matter for an agile cat to make its way swiftly in whatever direction it fancied. And so I did. Anyone lucky enough to be peering out of their shuttered window might have glimpsed a flash of gray lightning (nothing more) leaping from chimney pot to weathervane, streaking across slates and thatch, never putting a paw wrong.

I halted for a breather in the valley between two steeply pitching roofs and scanned the skies longingly. It would have been quicker for me to get to Soho by flying, but I had orders to remain near the ground, keeping my eye out for trouble there. No one knew exactly how the enemy arrived or departed, but my master had a hunch it was somehow earthbound. He doubted it was anything like a djinni at all.

The cat rubbed some moisture from its face with a paw and prepared for another jump—a big one this time, a proper road's width. At that moment, everything was illuminated by a sudden burst of orange light—I saw the tiles and chimney pots beside me, the lowering clouds above, and even the raindrop curtains hanging all around. Then darkness fell again.

The orange Flare was the agreed emergency signal. It came from close behind.

Queezle.

She had found something. Or something had found her.

The time for rules was past. I turned; even as I did so, I made the change: an eagle with black crest and golden wingtips launching itself in haste into the sky.

I had traveled only two blocks from the place where the portly horseman guarded the seven roads. Even if she had moved, Queezle would not be far away. It would take less than ten seconds to get back. No problem. I would be in time.

Three seconds later, I heard her scream.

16

The eagle hurtled down out of the night, angling painfully into the teeth of the gale. Over the roofs to the lonely cross-roads, down to the statue, I alighted on the edge of the plinth, where rain spattered harshly against the stone. Everything was exactly as it had been a minute or two before. But the spaniel had gone.

"Queezle?" No answer. Nothing but the howling of the wind.

A moment later, perched on the horseman's hat, I scanned the seven roads on each of the seven planes. The spaniel was nowhere to be seen; nor were there any djinn, imps, hexes, or other magical effusions. The streets were deserted. I was quite alone.

In doubt, I returned to the plinth and subjected it to a minute inspection. I thought to detect a faint black mark upon the stonework, roughly where we had been sitting, but it was impossible to tell whether or not it had been there before.

All of a sudden I felt very exposed. Whichever way I turned on the plinth, my back was vulnerable to something creeping up quietly out of the rain. I took off promptly and spiraled up around the statue, the crashing of the raindrops thrumming in my ears. Up above rooftop level I rose, safely out of reach of anything lurking in the street.

It was then that I heard the crash. It wasn't a nice, restrained sort of crash—like a bottle breaking on a bald man's head, say. It sounded rather as if a large forest oak had been uprooted and tossed casually aside, or an entire building had been swatted impatiently out of the path of something very big. Unpromising, in other words.

Worse still, I could tell the direction from which it came. If the rain had been just a little louder, or the crashing just a little quieter, I might have been able to misjudge it and head off bravely to investigate in the wrong direction. But no such luck.

Anyway, there was always the small possibility that Queezle might still be alive.

So I did two things. First, I sent up another Flare, hoping against hope that it would be spotted by another watcher in our group. The nearest, if memory served, was a foliot, based somewhere down near Charing Cross. He was a meager individual, devoid of valor or initiative, but any reinforcements would be welcome now, if only as cannon fodder.

Next, I proceeded in a northerly direction, at chimney height along the road from which the sound had come. I was heading for the museum quarter. I flew about as slowly as an eagle can without falling out of the air.[1] All the while I scanned the buildings below. It was an area of luxury shops, small, dark, discreet. Old painted signs above the doors hinted at the delights within: necklaces, rolls of silk, jeweled pocket watches. Gold featured prominently in this district, diamonds likewise. It was to these establishments that magicians came to buy those little extras that emphasized their status. Rich tourists flocked here too.

The tremendous crash had not been repeated; all the shop fronts seemed healthy enough, their alcove lights burning, their wooden signs creaking in the wind.

Rain fell around me, down into the street. In places the cobbles had disappeared beneath the stippled surface of the

---

[1] If it's possible to flap your wings gingerly, that's exactly what I did.

water. There was no sign of anyone, mortal or otherwise. I might have been flying above a ghost town.

The road widened a little, to pass on either side of a small circle of grass and pretty flowers. It seemed an incongruous sight in the narrow street, perhaps a little out of place. Then you noticed the old broken post in the center of the grass, the flagstones hidden among the flowers, and realized its original purpose.[2] Tonight it was all looking very water-blown and windswept, but what interested me, and made me circle around to land upon the post, were the markings in the grass.

They were footprints, of a sort. Large ones. Vaguely spatula-shaped, with the imprint of one separate toe visible at the wider end. They crossed the grass circle from one side to the other, each print driven down deep into the earth.

I shook moisture from my head feathers and drummed my claws against the post. Perfect. Just perfect. My enemy wasn't just mysterious and powerful, he was big and heavy, too. The night was getting better and better.

I followed the direction of the footsteps with my eagle eye. For the first few steps beyond the grass they were still partially visible, as indicated by a desultory trail of deposited mud. Beyond that they disappeared, but it was clear that none of the shops on either side had suffered from the attentions of any marauder. My quarry was evidently heading elsewhere. I took off and continued on along the road.

Gibbet Street came to its end at a wide boulevard that ran from left to right into the darkness. Directly opposite was a tall,

---

[2] The name of the road, *Gibbet Street*, kind of gave the game away, too. The London authorities had always been good at setting examples for the commoners, although in recent years the bodies of felons were hung up only in the prison district, around the Tower. Elsewhere it was thought to deter tourism.

imposing fence of metal railings, each post twenty feet high, two inches thick, and of solid iron. There was a set of double gates in the fence, and these were hanging open. In fact, to be accurate, they were hanging open off a nearby lamppost, together with a substantial portion of the adjoining rails. A great twisted hole gaped in the fencing. Something had ripped it in two in its hurry to get inside. How nice to be so eager. By contrast, it was with extreme reluctance that I approached, flying slowly across the street.

I alighted on a wrenched and tortured tip of metal. Beyond the ruined gate was a broad driveway leading up to an expansive flight of steps. Above these was a giant portico of eight imposing columns, attached to a vast building, tall as a castle, dull as a bank. I recognized it of old: the fabled British Museum. It stretched outward in either direction, wing upon wing, farther than my eyes could see. It was the size of a city block.[3]

Was it me, or was *everything* fairly big around here? The eagle fluffed up its feathers vigorously, but couldn't help feeling rather small. I considered the position. No prizes for guessing

---

[3] The British Museum was home to a million antiquities, several dozen of which were legitimately come by. For two hundred years prior to the magicians' rule, London's rulers had made it their habit to filch anything interesting they could from countries where their traders called. It was something of a national addiction, based on curiosity and avarice. Lords and ladies taking the Grand Tour of Europe kept their eyes open for small treasures that could be stuffed unnoticed into handbags; soldiers on campaign filled their chests with looted gems and reliquaries; every merchant returning to the capital carried an extra crate of valuables in his hold. Most of these items made their eventual way to the ever-expanding collections of the British Museum, where they were set out on display with clear labels in many languages so that foreign tourists could come and see their lost valuables with minimum inconvenience. In due course, the magicians looted the museum of its magical items, but it remained an imposing cultural charnel house.

why the unknown, big-footed and evidently rather strong enemy had come here. The museum held enough material worth destroying to keep it busy for a week. Whoever wished to heap embarrassment upon the British government had chosen well, and it was safe to say that my master's wretched career would not continue much longer if the marauder completed an uninterrupted night's work.

Which of course meant that I had to follow it inside.[4]

The eagle glided forward, low over the driveway and up over the steps, to land between the columns of the portico. Ahead was the great bronze door of the museum; typically, my quarry had decided to ignore it and had staved its way through the solid stone wall instead. This sort of thing wasn't stylish, but had a bowel-looseningly impressive quality that made me spend a couple of extra minutes engaged in flagrant delaying tactics such as checking the rubble of the portico carefully for danger.

The hole in the building gaped wide and black. From a respectful distance, I peered inside, into a lobby of a kind. All was still. No activity on any plane. A tumble of shattered wood and masonry and a splintered sign cheerfully proclaiming WELCOME TO THE BRITI showed where something had shoveled its determined way. Dust hung thickly in the air. A wall on the left had been broken through. I listened hard. In the distance, behind the pummeling of the rain, I fancied I could hear the distinctive sound of priceless antiquities being broken.

I sent another Flare into the sky in case that shirking foliot chose to glance in my direction. Then I made my change and stepped into the building.

---

[4] Revenge was another motive for me now. I no longer held out much prospect of seeing Queezle alive again.

The ferocious minotaur[5] glanced imperiously around the ruined lobby, steam rising from its nostrils, its clawed hands flexing, its hooves pawing at the dirt. Who dared challenge it? No one! Well, because, as expected, there was nothing in the room. Right. Fine. That meant I had to try the next one. No problem. With a deep breath, the minotaur tiptoed tentatively through the debris to the splintered wall. It peeped around with great caution.

Darkness, rain drumming on the windows, amphorae and Phoenician pots lying scattered on the floor. And somewhere distant—breaking glass. The enemy was still several rooms ahead. Good. The minotaur stepped bravely through the hole.

The next few minutes saw a rather slow game of cat and mouse, with this process repeated several times. New room, empty, sounds farther on. The marauder went on its merrily destructive way; I trailed uncertainly in its wake, less keen than I strictly might have been to catch up with it. It wasn't exactly your traditional Bartimaeus panache, I'll admit. Call me overcautious, but Zeno's fate lay heavy on my mind and I was trying to think of a foolproof plan to avoid being killed.

The extent of the carnage I was passing made it seem unlikely that I was dealing with any human agency, so what would it be? An afrit? Possible, but oddly out of style. You'd expect afrits to use lots of magical attacks—high-class Detonations and Infernos, for instance—and there was no evidence of anything

---

[5] Guaranteed to strike fear into a human enemy, there's nothing better than a bull-headed minotaur if you want a bit of the old shock and awe. And after centuries of careful honing, my particular minotaur guise was a doozy. The horns had just the right amount of curl and the teeth were nicely sharpened, as if filed. The skin was blue-black ebony. I'd kept the human torso, but had gone for a satyr's goat legs and cloven hooves, which are that bit scarier than pimply knees and sandals.

here except sheer brute force. A marid? Same again, and surely I'd have sensed their magical presence before now.[6] But I was getting no familiar feedback. All the rooms were dead and cold. This was in line with what the boy had told me about the previous attacks: it did not seem that spirits were involved at all.

To be absolutely sure, I sent a small magical Pulse bubbling ahead of me through the next jagged hole, from which loud noises were emanating. I waited for the Pulse to return, either weaker (if no magic lay ahead) or stronger (if something potent lurked in wait).

To my consternation, it did not come back at all.

The minotaur rubbed its muzzle thoughtfully. Odd, and vaguely familiar. I was sure I'd seen this effect somewhere before.

I listened at the hole; once again, the only sounds were distant ones. The minotaur sneaked through—

And came out in a large gallery, double the height of the other rooms. The rain beat against tall rectangular windows high up on either side, and from somewhere in the night, perhaps some distant tower, a faint white light shone down upon the contents of the hall. It was a room filled with ancient statues of colossal size, all swathed in shadow: two Assyrian gate-keeper djinn—winged lions with the heads of men, which had once stood before the gates of Nimrud;[7] a motley assembly of Egyptian gods and spirits, carved in a dozen kinds of colored

---

[6] Marids radiate so much power that it is possible to track their recent movements by following residual magical trails: they leave them hanging in the atmosphere much as a snail deposits slime. It isn't wise to use this analogy to a marid's face, of course.

[7] These were stone representations only; in the glory days of Assyria, the djinn would have been real, asking riddles of strangers in a manner similar to the Sphinx, and devouring them if the answer was incorrect, ungrammatical, or simply spoken in a rustic accent. They were punctilious beasts.

stone and given the heads of crocodile, cat, ibis, and jackal;[8]
huge carved representations of the holy scarab beetle; sar-
cophagi of long-forgotten priests; and, above all, fragments of
the monolithic statues of the great pharaohs—shattered faces,
arms, torsos, hands, and feet, found buried in the sands and
carried by sail and steamship to the gray lands of the north.

On another occasion, I could have had a nostalgic trip here,
looking for images of distant friends and masters, but now was
not the time. A clear corridor had been driven halfway through
the hall; several smaller pharaohs had already been bunted aside
and lay like ninepins in indignant heaps on the margins, while
a couple of gods were in closer proximity to each other than
they would have cared for in life. But if these had given little
trouble, some of the larger statues seemed to be putting up
more resistance. Halfway down the hall, and directly in the path
that the enemy was taking, rose a giant seated figure of Ramses
the Great, more than thirty feet high and carved from solid
granite. The top of its headdress was gently shaking; muffled
scraping sounds came from the darkness below, suggesting that
something was trying to force Ramses from its path.[9]

Even an utukku would have figured out after a couple of
minutes that the easiest thing to do was to walk around
something so big and just head off on its travels. But my

---

[8] This last one, old Anubis, always unnerves me if I spot it out of the corner of
my eye. But gradually I'm learning to relax. Jabor is long gone.

[9] Ramses wouldn't have been surprised that his statue was proving so troublesome; he had the biggest ego of any human it's been my misfortune to serve.
This despite being small, bandy-legged, and with a face as pockmarked as a
rhino's bottom. His magicians, however, were strong and inflexible—for forty
years I labored on grandiose building projects on his behalf, along with a thousand other benighted spirits.

enemy was worrying away at the statue like a small dog trying to lift an elephant's shinbone. So perhaps (a positive thought) my adversary was very stupid. Or perhaps (less positive, this) it was simply ambitious—intent on causing maximum destruction.

Anyway, it was evidently happily occupied for the present. And this gave me the opportunity to take a closer look at what I was up against. Without a sound, the minotaur minced through the blackness of the hall until it came to a tall sarcophagus that so far remained untouched. It peered around it, toward the base of Ramses' statue. And frowned in perplexity.

Most djinn have perfect night sight; it's one of the countless ways in which we are superior to humans. Darkness has little meaning for us—even on the first plane, which you see, too. But now, though I scrolled through the other planes with the speed of thought, I found I could not penetrate a deep well of blackness centered on the statue's base. It swelled and shrank around its edges, but remained as inkily inscrutable on the seventh plane as on the first. Whatever was causing Ramses to shake was deep within the darkness, but I could see nothing of it.

However, I could certainly judge roughly where it would be, and since it was being good enough to remain stationary, it seemed the time had come for a surprise attack. I looked around me for an appropriate missile. In a glass cabinet nearby was an odd black stone, of irregular outline, small enough to lift, but large enough to brain an afrit nicely. It had a lot of scribbling down one flat side, which I didn't have time to read. It was probably a set of rules for visitors to the museum, since it seemed to be written in two or three languages. Whatever, it would do the job.

The minotaur carefully and quietly lifted the glass case off the floor and over the top of the rock, setting it down again without a sound. It checked across: the blackness still welled aggressively against Ramses' feet, but the statue remained immobile. Good.

With a bend and a lift, the rock was in the minotaur's brawny arms, and I was heading back across the gallery, looking for a suitable vantage point. A smallish pharaoh met my eye. I didn't recognize him: he can't have been one of the more memorable ones. Even his statue had a slightly apologetic expression. But he was sitting high up on a carved throne on top of a dais, and his lap looked big enough for a minotaur to stand on.

Still holding the rock, I hopped up, first onto the dais, then onto the throne, then onto the pharaoh's lap. I squinted over his shoulder; perfect—I was a stone's throw away from the pulsating blackness now, high up enough to get just the right trajectory. I tensed my goat legs, flexed my biceps, gave a snort for luck, and tossed the stone up and over, as if from a siege catapult.

For a single second, maybe two, its inscribed surface flashed in the light from the windows, then it plummeted down in front of Ramses' face, down to the base of the statue and into the center of the black smog.

Smack! A crack of stone on stone, rock on rock. Small black pieces flew out of the smog in all directions, pinging off the masonry and cracking glass.

Well, I'd hit something, and it was hard.

The black cloud boiled as if in sudden rage. Briefly, it drew back; I caught a glimpse of something very large and solid at its heart, thrashing a giant arm about in mindless fury. Then the cloud closed up again and swelled outward, lapping against the nearest statues as if blindly seeking the perpetrator of the crime.

In point of fact, the heroic minotaur had made itself scarce: I was crouching down as low as possible in the pharaoh's lap, peeping out through a crack in the marble. Even my horns had drooped a little so as not to be exposed. I watched the darkness move now, as whatever was inside it began its hunt: it shifted decisively away from Ramses' base, welling back and forth against nearby statues. A series of heavy impacts sounded: the noise of hidden footfalls.

While it is true to say that my hopes for my first attack hadn't been sky-high, given that my adversary was capable of smashing through solid walls, I was a little disappointed that the stone hadn't made more of an impact. But it *had* given me a tiny glimpse of the creature within, and since—if I couldn't destroy it—one of my charges was to get information on the marauder, this was something worth following up. A small stone had made a small dent in the darkness. . . . This being so, what would a *large* stone do?

The billowing cloud was moving off to investigate a suspicious group of statues on the opposite side of the hall. With unlikely stealth, the minotaur descended from the pharaoh's lap and proceeded, in a series of little darting movements between hiding places, across the gallery to where a large sandstone torso of another pharaoh stood beside the wall.[10]

The torso was high—about fifteen feet tall. I squeezed into the shadows behind it, on my way plucking a small burial pot off a nearby stand. Once suitably concealed, I stuck out a hairy

---

[10] The cartouche on its chest proclaimed it to be Ahmose of the 18th Dynasty, "he who unites in glory." Since he was currently lacking his own head, legs, and arms, this boast rang a little hollow.

arm and tossed the pot to the ground ten feet or so away. It broke with a satisfyingly crisp crack.

Instantly, as if it had been waiting for just such a sound, the cloud of darkness shifted position and began flowing rapidly in the direction of the noise. Eager footfalls sounded; questing tentacles of blackness extended out, whipping against the statues that they passed. The cloud drew close to the smashed pot; it paused there, billowing uncertainly.

It was in position. By this time, the minotaur had clambered halfway up the sandstone torso, braced its back against the wall behind, and was pushing at the statue with all the might of its cloven hooves. The torso began to shift immediately, rocking back and forth, and making a slight scraping sound as it did so.[11] The cloud of blackness caught the noise; it darted in my direction.

Not fast enough. With one final heave, the torso's center of balance shifted irrevocably; down it came, whistling through the dark hall, slap-bang into the cloud.

The force of the impact blew the cloud into a million ragged wisps; they shot out in all directions.

I jumped clear, landing nimbly to the side. I turned eagerly, scanning the scene.

The torso was not flat against the ground. It had cracked across the middle; its top end was several feet off the floor, as if it were resting on something large.

I walked toward it carefully. From my angle I couldn't get a view of what was lying comatose beneath. Still, it looked as if

---

[11] My adversary should have borne the principles of leverage in mind when trying to shift Ramses. As I once told Archimedes, "give me a lever long enough and I will move the world." In this case, the world was a tad ambitious, but a six-ton headless torso suited me just fine.

I'd been successful. In a few moments I could head off, signal the boy, and get ready for my dismissal.

I drew close and bent down to look beneath the statue.

A giant hand shot out, faster than thought, grabbed me by one hairy leg. It was blue-gray, possessed of three fingers and a thumb, hard and cold as buried stone. Veins ran through it as through marble, but they pulsed with life. Its grip crushed my essence like a vise. The minotaur bellowed with pain. I needed to change, to withdraw my essence from the fist, but my head was spinning—I could not concentrate long enough to do so. A terrible coldness extended outward, wrapped itself around me like a blanket. I felt my fires dwindling, my energy leaching out of me like blood dripping from a wound.

The minotaur swayed, collapsed like an empty puppet upon the floor. The chilly solitude of death was all about me.

Then, unexpectedly, the stone wrist flexed, the grip was loosed; the minotaur's body was hurled high into the air, in an ungainly arc, to be dashed hard against the nearby wall. My consciousness flickered; I fell, crashing tail over horns to the floor below.

I lay there for a moment, dazed, uncomprehending. I heard scraping sounds, as of a sandstone torso being shifted, and did nothing. I felt the floor shake, as if that torso was being summarily dropped to one side, and did nothing. I heard first one, then another, firm concussion, as of great stone feet righting themselves, and still did nothing. But all the while the hideous burning chill of the great hand's touch was slowly lessening, and my fires were being restoked. And now, as the great stone feet moved purposefully toward me and I sensed something fixing me with a cold intent, enough energy returned for action.

I opened my eyes, saw a shadow looming.

With a tortured effort of will, the minotaur became the cat once more; the cat leaped high into the air, out of the path of the descending foot, which drove deep down into the fabric of the floor. The cat landed a short way off, hackles raised, tail flared like a toilet brush; with a yowl it leaped again.

As it leaped, it looked to the side and caught a view of its adversary full on.

The black wisps were re-forming about it already, gathering like mercury globules into the creature's permanent concealing shroud. But enough remained free for me to see it there, its outline exposed in the moonlight, following my progression with a swift turn of its head.

At first glance, it was as if one of the statues in the hall had come to life: a vast figure, roughly humanoid in shape, standing three meters tall. Two arms, two legs, a hulking torso, a relatively small, smooth head sitting atop it all.

It existed only on the first plane; on the others, darkness was utter and absolute.

The cat landed on the scaly head of Sobek, the crocodile god, and perched there for a moment, hissing defiance. Everything about the figure radiated an alien otherness; I felt my energy being sapped simply by seeing it.

It stepped toward me with surprising speed. For an instant, its face—such as it was—was caught in the light from the window, and that was where the comparison with the ancient statues fell down. Those statues were exquisitely carved, without exception; that was what the Egyptians were really good at, along with organized religion and civil engineering. But aside from its scale, the most obvious thing about the creature was how crude it was, how artificial. The skin surface was covered in irregularities: with lumps, cracks, and flat areas, as if it had only roughly been patted into shape. It had no ears, no hair. Where you'd expect its eyes to be, it had two round holes that looked as if they'd simply been punched in its surface with the blunt end of a giant pencil. It had no nose, and only a great slash of a mouth, which hung slightly open in the stupid, voracious manner of a shark's. And in the center of its forehead was an oval shape that I knew I'd seen before, not very long ago.

This oval was fairly small, fashioned out of the same dark blue-gray substance as the rest of the figure, but was as intricate as the face and body were crude. It was an open eye, without lids or lashes, but complete with crosshatched iris and round pupil. And in the center of that pupil, just before the cloak of blackness swathed it from my view, I caught the flash of a dark intelligence, watching me.

The blackness made a lunge; the cat gave a bound. Behind me, I heard Sobek splintering. I landed on the floor then shot toward the nearest door. It was time to go; I had discovered what I needed. I did not flatter myself I could do anything more here.

A missile of some kind shot over my head, collided with the door, breaking it in. The cat plunged through. Jarring footsteps came behind.

I was in a small, dark room hung with fragile ethnic drapes and tapestries. A tall window at the end promised a way out. The cat ran toward it, whiskers back, ears flat against its head, claws scrabbling on the floor. It jumped, then jerked to the side at the last minute with a very uncatlike curse. It had seen the glowing white lines of a high-strength nexus beyond the window. The magicians had arrived. They'd sealed us in.

The cat wheeled around, seeking another exit. Finding none.

Bloody magicians.

A boiling cloud of darkness filled the doorway.

The cat hunched down defensively, pressing itself against the floor. Behind it, rain drummed against the windowpanes.

For a moment neither cat nor darkness moved. Then something small and white erupted from the cloud, shooting across the room: the crocodile head of Sobek, ripped from its shoulders. The cat sprang aside. The head crashed through the window, fizzing as it struck the nexus. Hot rain drove in through the hole, steaming from its contact with the barrier; with it came a sudden draught. The tapestries and sheets of fabric on the walls fluttered outward.

Footsteps. An approaching darkness that swelled to fill the room.

The cat slunk back into a corner, pressing itself as small as it would go. Any moment now, that eye would see me. . . .

Another gust of rain: the edges of the tapestries flicked up. An idea formed.

Not a very good one, but I wasn't fussy right then.

The cat leaped at the nearest hanging fabric, a fragile piece, possibly from America, showing squareish humans amid a sea of stylized corn. It scrabbled its way to the top, where careful cords attached it to the wall. A flash of claw—the fabric was free. Instantly, the wind caught it; it blew outward into the room, colliding with something in the midst of the black cloud.

The cat was already on the next tapestry, slashing it loose. Then the next. In a moment, half a dozen sheets of fabric had been whipped into the center of the room, where they danced palely like ghosts amid the wind and driving rain.

The creature in the cloud had ripped the first sheet away, but now another was blown upon it. From all sides, fragments of material dipped and spun, confusing the creature, obscuring its view. I sensed the great arms flailing, the giant legs blundering back and forth within the confines of the room.

While it was thus occupied, I aimed to creep elsewhere.

This was easier said than done, as the black cloud now seemed to fill the room, and I didn't want to bump into the death-bringing body within it. So I went cautiously, hugging the walls.

I'd made it about halfway to the door when the creature, evidently reaching a peak of frustration, lost all sense of perspective. There was a sudden pounding of feet and a great blow struck against the left-hand wall. Plaster dropped from above and a cloud of dust and debris fell into the room to join the general whirl of wind, rain, and antique fabrics.

On the second blow, the wall collapsed, and with it the entire ceiling.

For a split second, the cat was motionless, eyes wide, then it curled into a protective ball.

An instant later, a dozen tons of stone, brick, cement, steel, and assorted masonry crashed down directly upon me, burying the room.

17

The small man gave an apologetic smile. "We have removed most of the rubble, madam," he said, "and have so far found nothing."

Jessica Whitwell's voice was cold and calm. "Nothing, Shubit? You realize what you are telling me is quite impossible. I think someone is shirking."

"I humbly believe that not to be so, madam." He certainly seemed humble enough right then, standing with his bandy legs slightly bent, his head bowed, his cap scrunched tightly in his hands. Only the fact that he was standing in the center of a pentacle revealed his demonic nature. That and his left foot—a black bear's tufted paw poking out from his trousers—which from oversight or caprice he had neglected to transform.

Nathaniel regarded the djinni balefully and tapped his fingers together in what he hoped was a brooding and quizzical manner. He was sitting in a high-backed easy chair of studded green leather, one of several arranged around the pentacle in an elegant circle. He had deliberately adopted the same pose as Ms. Whitwell—straight-backed, legs crossed, elbows resting on the arms of the chair—in an attempt to replicate her air of powerful resolve. He had an uncomfortable feeling it did not begin to disguise his terror. He kept his voice as level as he could. "You must search every cranny of the ruins," he said. "My demon must be there."

The small man cast him a single look with his bright green

eyes, but otherwise ignored him. Jessica Whitwell spoke: "Your demon might well have been destroyed, John," she said.

"I think I would have felt its loss, madam," he said politely.

"Or it might have escaped its bonds." The rumbling voice of Henry Duvall rose from a black chair opposite Nathaniel. The Police Chief filled every inch of it; his fingers tapped impatiently on the arms. The black eyes glinted. "With over-ambitious apprentices, such things have been known to happen."

Nathaniel knew better than to rise to the challenge. He remained silent.

Ms. Whitwell addressed her servant once more. "My apprentice is right, Shubit," she said. "You must scan the debris again. Do so, at all speed."

"Madam, I shall." He bowed his head, vanished.

There was a moment's silence in the room. Nathaniel kept his face calm, but his mind was awhirl with emotion. His career and perhaps his life were in the balance, and Bartimaeus could not be found. He had staked everything on his servant, and judging by the expressions of the others in the room, they believed he was about to lose. He glanced around, witnessing the hungry satisfaction in Duvall's eyes, the flinty displeasure in his master's and, from the depths of a leather armchair, the furtive hope in Mr. Tallow's. The head of Internal Affairs had spent much of the night distancing himself from the whole surveillance enterprise, and pouring criticism down upon Nathaniel's head. In truth, Nathaniel could not blame him. First Pinn's, then the National Gallery, now (and worst of all) the British Museum. Internal Affairs was in desperate straits, and the ambitious police chief was preparing to make his move. No sooner had the extent of the damage to the museum become clear than Mr. Duvall had insisted on being present in the cleanup operation. He had watched everything with ill-concealed triumph.

"Well . . ." Mr. Duvall clapped his hands upon his knees and prepared to rise. "I think I have wasted enough time, Jessica. In summary, following the efforts of Internal Affairs, we have a ruined wing of the British Museum and a hundred artifacts lost within it. We have a trail of destruction across the ground floor, several priceless statues destroyed or broken, and the Rosetta stone pulverized to dust. We have no perpetrator of this crime and no prospect of finding one. The Resistance is as free as a bird. And Mr. Mandrake has lost his demon. Not a wildly impressive tally, but one I must communicate to the Prime Minister nevertheless."

"*Please remain seated*, Henry." Ms. Whitwell's voice was so venomous that Nathaniel felt his skin crawl. Even the police chief seemed transfixed by it: after a moment's hesitation, he relaxed back into the chair. "The exploration is not yet finished," she went on. "We shall wait a few minutes more."

Mr. Duvall snapped his fingers. A human servant glided forward from the shadows of the chamber, carrying a silver tray with wine upon it. Mr. Duvall took a glass, swilled the wine around it musingly. There was a long silence.

Julius Tallow ventured an opinion from beneath his wide-brimmed hat. "It is a pity *my* demon was not at the scene," he said. "Nemaides is an able creature and would have managed *some* communication with me before dying. This Bartimaeus was evidently most feeble."

Nathaniel glared at him but said nothing.

"Your demon," Duvall said, looking at Nathaniel suddenly. "What level was it?"

"Fourth-level djinni, sir."

"Slippery things." He swilled his glass. The wine danced in the neon light of the ceiling. "Guileful and hard to control. Few people of your age manage it."

The implication was clear. Nathaniel ignored it. "I do my best, sir."

"They require complex summonings. Some misquotations kill magicians, or allow the demon to run amok. Can be destructive—result in whole buildings being destroyed . . ." The black eyes glittered.

"That hasn't happened in my case," Nathaniel said evenly. He gripped his fingers together to stop their shaking.

Mr. Tallow sniffed. "Clearly the youth has been promoted beyond his ability."

"Quite so," Duvall said. "First sensible thing you've ever said, Tallow. Perhaps Ms. Whitwell, *who promoted him*, has a comment to make on that?" He grinned.

Jessica Whitwell rewarded Tallow with a look of pure malevolence. "I believe *you* are something of an expert on mis-quoted summonings, Julius," she said. "Wasn't that how your skin acquired its delightful color?"

Mr. Tallow pulled his hat brim down a little lower over his yellow face. "It was no fault of mine," he said sullenly. "There was a printing error in my book."

Duvall smiled, drew the glass to his lips. "Head of Internal Affairs, and he misreads his own book. Dear me. What hope do we have? Well, we shall see whether *my* department can shed any light on the Resistance, when it is given its extra powers." He took a short swig, emptied the glass in one. "I shall first sug-gest—"

Without sound, smell, or other theatrical device, the pentacle was occupied once more. The small, apologetic man was back again, this time with two bear's paws instead of feet. He carried an object delicately in both hands. A bedraggled cat—limp and comatose.

He opened his mouth to speak, then—remembering his affectation of humility—dropped the cat so that it swung from one hand by its tail. He used the other hand to doff his cap in appropriately servile manner. "Madam," he began, "we found this specimen in the space between two broken beams; in a small pore, it was, madam; tucked right in. We overlooked it the first time."

Ms. Whitwell frowned with distaste. "This thing . . . is it worthy of our attention?"

Nathaniel's lenses, like his master's, could shed no further light: to him, it was a cat on all three planes. Nevertheless, he guessed what he was seeing, and it seemed dead. He bit his lip.

The small man made a face; he swung the cat back and forth by its tail. "Depends on what you call 'worthy,' madam. It is a djinni of a disreputable cast, that's certain. Ugly, un-kempt; it gives off an unpleasant stench on the sixth plane. Furthermore—"

"I *assume*," Ms. Whitwell interrupted, "that it is still alive."

"Yes, madam. It requires merely an appropriate stimulus to awake."

"See to it, then you may depart."

"Gladly." The small man tossed the cat unceremoniously upward; he pointed, spoke a word. A jarring arc of green elec-tricity erupted from his finger, caught the cat head-on, and held it, jerking and dancing in midair, all its fur extended. The small man clapped his hands and descended into the floor. A moment passed. The green electricity vanished. The cat plummeted to the center of the pentacle, where in defiance of all normal laws it landed on its back. It lay there a moment, legs pointing outward in four directions from amid a ball of static fluff.

Nathaniel rose to his feet. "Bartimaeus!"

The cat's eyes opened; they bore an indignant expression. "No need to shout." It paused and blinked. "What's happened to you?"

"Nothing. You're upside down."

"Oh." With a flurry of motion, the cat righted itself. It glanced around the room, noticing Duvall, Whitwell, and Tallow sitting impassively in their high-backed chairs. It scratched itself carelessly with a hind leg. "Got company, I see."

Nathaniel nodded. Beneath his black coat he was crossing his fingers, praying that Bartimaeus did not choose to reveal anything inappropriate, such as his name. "*Be careful* how you answer me," he said. "We are among the great." He made the warning sound as portentous as possible for his superiors' sake.

The cat looked silently at the other magicians for a moment. It raised a paw, leaned forward conspiratorially. "Between you and me, I've seen greater."

"So, I imagine, have they. You look like a pompom with legs."

The cat noticed its fluffy condition for the first time. It gave a hiss of annoyance and changed instantly; a black panther sat in the pentacle, smooth-furred and gleaming of coat. It flicked its tail neatly around its paws. "So then, you wish my report?"

Nathaniel held up a hand. Everything depended on what the djinni would say. If it did not have strong insight into the nature of their adversary, his position was vulnerable indeed. The level of destruction at the British Museum paralleled that in Piccadilly the week before, and he knew that a messenger imp had already visited Ms. Whitwell, communicating the Prime Minister's wrath. That boded ill for Nathaniel. "Bartimaeus," he said, "we know this much. Your signal was seen outside the museum last night. I arrived soon afterward, along with others from my department. Disturbances were heard inside. We sealed off the museum."

The panther extended its claws and tapped the floor meaningfully. "Yes, I kind of noticed that."

"At approximately 1:44 A.M., one interior wall of the east wing was seen to collapse. Soon afterward, something unknown broke through the security cordon, killing imps in the vicinity. We have since searched the area. Nothing was found, except yourself—in an unconscious condition."

The panther shrugged. "Well, what do you expect when a building falls on me? That I'd be dancing a mazurka in the ruins?"

Nathaniel coughed loudly and drew himself up. "Be that as it may," he said sternly, "in the absence of other evidence, blame will fall on you as the cause of all this devastation, unless you can give us information to the contrary."

"What!" The panther's eyes widened in outrage. "You're blaming *me*? After what I've suffered? My essence is one big bruise, I tell you! I've got bruises where bruises don't ought to be!"

"So then . . ." Nathaniel said, "what caused it?"

"What caused the building to collapse?"

"Yes."

"You want to know what caused all the devastation last night and yet disappeared from right under your noses?"

"That's right."

"So you're asking me for the identity of the creature that

arrives as if from nowhere, departs again unseen and, while it's here, wraps a cloak of blackness around it to protect it from the vision of spirit, human or animal, on this and every other plane? That's seriously what you're asking?"

Nathaniel's heart had sunk down into his boots. ". . . Yes."

"That's easy. It's a golem."

There was a small gasp from the direction of Ms. Whitwell and snorts from Tallow and Duvall. Nathaniel sat back in shock. "A . . . a golem?"

The panther licked a paw and smoothed back the fur above one eye. "You'd better believe it, buster."

"You're sure about this?"

"A giant man of animated clay, hard as granite, invulnerable to attack, with the strength to rip down walls. Cloaks itself in darkness and carries the odor of earth in its wake. A touch that brings death to all beings of air and fire like me . . . that within seconds reduces our essences to smoldering ash. Yes, I'd say I was pretty sure."

Ms. Whitwell made a dismissive gesture. "You may be mistaken, demon."

The panther turned its yellow eyes upon her. For a horrid moment, Nathaniel thought it was going to be cheeky. But if so, it seemed to reconsider. It bowed its head. "Madam, I may. But I have seen golems before, during my time in Prague."

"In Prague, yes! Centuries ago." Mr. Duvall spoke for the first time; he appeared irritated by the turn of events. "They disappeared with the Holy Roman Empire. The last recorded use of them against our forces was in the time of Gladstone. They drove one of our battalions into the Vltava, below the ramparts of their castle. But the magicians controlling them were located and destroyed, and the golems disintegrated on the Stone Bridge. This is all in the annals of the day."

The panther bowed again. "Sir, this may well be true."

Mr. Duvall banged a heavy fist down upon the arm of his chair. "It *is* true! Since the implosion of the Czech Empire, no golems have been recorded. The magicians who defected to us did not bring the secrets of their construction, while those who remained in Prague were shadows of their predecessors, amateurs in magic. Hence the lore has been lost."

"Evidently not to everyone." The djinni swished its tail back and forth. "The golem's actions were being controlled by somebody. He or she was observing through a watch-eye in the golem's forehead. I saw the glint of his or her intelligence when the black clouds drew back."

"Pah!" Mr. Duvall was unconvinced. "This is fanciful stuff. The demon lies!"

Nathaniel glanced at his master; her face was frowning. "Bartimaeus," he said, "I charge you to speak truthfully. Can there be any doubting what you saw?"

The yellow eyes blinked slowly. "None. Four hundred years ago, I witnessed the activities of the first golem, which the great magician Loew created deep in the ghetto at Prague. He sent it out from its attic of shrouds and cobwebs to instill fear into the enemies of his people. It was itself a creature of magic, but it worked against the magic of the djinn. It wielded the essence of earth with a great weight: our spells failed in its presence, it made us blind and weak; it struck us down. The creature I fought last night was of the same kind. It killed one of my fellows. I do not lie."

Duvall snorted. "I have not lived as long as I have by believing every tale a demon told. This is a blatant fabrication to protect its master." He tossed his glass aside and, standing, glared around at the company. "But golem or not makes little difference. It is clear that Internal Affairs has lost all control of the situation. We shall see whether my department can do any better. I shall apply to the Prime Minister for an interview forthwith. Good day to you."

He strode to the door, straight-backed, the leather on his jackboots squeaking. No one said a word.

The door closed. Ms. Whitwell remained still. The strip lights in the ceiling shone down harshly upon her; her face was more cadaverous even than usual. She stroked her pointed chin thoughtfully, the long nails making a slight scratching noise upon the skin. "We must consider this with care," she said at last. "If the demon speaks truthfully, we have gained valuable insight. But Duvall is right to be skeptical, although he speaks from a desire to belittle our achievements. Creating a golem is a difficult business, considered nigh on impossible. What do you know of it, Tallow?"

The minister made a face. "Very little, madam, thank goodness. It is a primitive kind of magic that has never been practiced in our enlightened society. I have never cared to investigate."

"Mandrake, what of you?"

Nathaniel cleared his throat; he always relished questions of general knowledge. "A magician needs two powerful artifacts, ma'am," he said brightly. "Each with a different function. First, he or she requires a parchment inscribed with the spell that brings the golem to life; once the body has been formed of river clay, this parchment is inserted into the golem's mouth to animate it."

His master nodded. "Exactly. That is the spell that is considered lost. The Czech masters never wrote the secret down."

"The second artifact," Nathaniel continued, "is a special piece of clay, created by separate spells. It is placed in the monster's forehead and helps focus its power. It acts as a watch-eye for the magician, much as Bartimaeus described. He or she can then control the creature through a common crystal orb."

"Correct. So, if your demon speaks truthfully, we are looking for someone who has acquired both a golem's eye and the animating parchment. Who might that be?"

"No one." Tallow interlinked his fingers and, flexing, cracked the joints loudly, like a volley of rifle shots. "It is absurd. These objects no longer exist. Mandrake's creature should be consigned to the Shriveling Fire. As for Mandrake, madam, this disaster is *his* responsibility."

"You seem very confident about your facts," the panther remarked, yawning loudly and displaying an impressive set of teeth. "It's true that the parchments disintegrate when they are removed from the golem's mouth. And by the terms of the spell, the monster must then return to its master and subside back into clay, so the body doesn't survive either. But the golem's eye is not destroyed. It can be used many times. So there may well be one here, in modern London. Why are you so yellow?"

Tallow's jaw dropped in rage. "Mandrake—keep this thing under control, or I'll make you suffer the consequences."

Nathaniel removed his smirk promptly. "Yes, Mr. Tallow. Silence, slave!"

"Oooh, pardon me, I'm sure."

Jessica Whitwell held up a hand. "Despite its insolence, the demon is correct on one account at least. Golem's eyes *do* exist. I saw one myself, two years ago."

Julius Tallow raised an eyebrow. "Indeed, madam? Where?"

"In the collection of someone we all have reason to remember. Simon Lovelace."

Nathaniel gave a little start; a cold shiver ran between his shoulder blades. The name still had power over him. Tallow shrugged. "Lovelace is long dead."

"I know . . ." Ms. Whitwell had an air of preoccupation. She sat back in her chair and swiveled it to face another pentacle similar to the one in which the panther sat. The room contained several, each of subtly different design. She snapped her fingers and her djinni appeared, this time in full bear's guise. "Shubit," she said, "visit the Artifact Vaults beneath Security. Locate the Lovelace collection; itemize it fully. Among it, you will find a carved eye of hardened clay. Bring it to me at speed."

The bear bent its legs and vanished as it sprang.

Julius Tallow gave Nathaniel an unctuous smile. "*That's* the kind of servant you need, Mandrake," he said. "No glibness, no chatter. Obeys without question. I'd get rid of this smooth-tongued serpent, if I were you."

The panther swished its tail. "Hey, we've all got problems, chum. I'm overly talkative. You look like a field of buttercups in a suit."

"The traitor Lovelace had an interesting collection," Ms. Whitwell mused, ignoring Tallow's cries of fury. "The golem's eye was one of several noteworthy items we confiscated. It will be interesting to inspect it now."

With a clicking of hairy joints, the bear was back, landing lightly in the center of its circle. Its paws were empty, except for its cap, which it held in fully humble pose.

"Yep, that's the kind of servant you need," the panther said. "No chatter. Obedient. Absolutely useless. You wait: it'll have forgotten its charge."

Ms. Whitwell gave an impatient signal. "Shubit—you have been to the Lovelace collection?"

"Madam, I have."

"Is a clay eye among the items?"

"No, madam. It is not."

"Was it among the goods labeled in the inventory?"

"It was. Number thirty-four, madam. 'A clay eye of nine centimeters width, decorated with cabalistic symbols. Purpose: golem's watch-eye. Origin: Prague.'"

"You may depart." Ms. Whitwell spun her chair back to face the others. "So," she said. "There was such an eye. Now it is gone."

Nathaniel's face flushed with excitement. "It *can't* be a coincidence, ma'am. Someone's stolen it and put it to use."

"But did Lovelace have the animating parchment in his collection?" Tallow asked irritably. "Of course not! So where'd that come from?"

"That," Jessica Whitwell said, "is what we need to find out." She rubbed her slender white hands together. "Gentlemen, we have a new situation. After tonight's debacle, Duvall will press the Prime Minister for greater powers at my expense. I must go to Richmond now and prepare to speak against him. In my absence, I wish you, Tallow, to continue organizing surveillance. Doubtless, the golem—if that is what it is—will strike again. I now entrust this to you alone."

Mr. Tallow nodded smugly. Nathaniel cleared his throat. "You, er, you no longer wish me to be involved, ma'am?"

"No. You are walking a tightrope, John. I entrusted you with great responsibility—and what happens? The National Gallery and British Museum are ransacked. However, thanks to your demon, we do have a clue to the nature of our enemy.

Now we need to know the identity of whoever controls it. Is it a foreign power? A local renegade? The theft of the golem's eye suggests that someone has discovered the means to create the animating spell. That must be where you start. Seek out the lost knowledge, and do so quickly."

"Very well, ma'am. Whatever you say." Nathaniel's eyes were glazed in doubt. He had not the first idea how to begin this task.

"We shall attack the golem through its master," Ms. Whitwell said. "When we find the source of the knowledge, we will find the face of our enemy. And then we can act decisively." Her voice was harsh.

"Yes, ma'am."

"This djinni of yours seems useful. . . ." She contemplated the panther, which was sitting washing its paws with its back to them, studiously ignoring the conversation.

Nathaniel made a grudging face. "It's all right, I suppose."

"It survived the golem, which is more than anything else has done. Take it with you."

Nathaniel paused a moment. "Sorry, ma'am, I don't think I understand. Where do you want me to go?"

Jessica Whitwell stood, ready to depart. "Where do you think? The historic home of all golems. The place, where, if anywhere, the lore must have been preserved. I wish you to go to Prague."

18

Kitty rarely allowed considerations beyond the group to impinge upon her, but on the day after the rains ceased, she took a trip to see her parents again.

That evening, at their emergency meeting, the Resistance would to learn about the great new hope, the biggest job they had ever undertaken. The details remained to be discovered, but an air of almost painful anticipation prevailed at the shop, a weight of excitement and uncertainty that made Kitty beside herself with agitation. Bowing to her restlessness, she departed early, bought a small bunch of flowers from a kiosk, and took the crowded bus to Balham.

The street was as quiet as ever, the little house trim and neat. She knocked loudly, fumbling for her keys in her bag while supporting the flowers as best she could between shoulder and chin. Before she located them, a shadow approached behind the glass and her mother opened the door, peering around it hesitantly.

Her eyes came alive. "Kathleen! How lovely! Come in, love."

"Hi, Mum. These are for you."

An awkward ritual of kissing and hugging ensued, mingled with the flowers being inspected and Kitty's attempting to squeeze past into the hall. At last, with difficulty, the door was shut and Kitty was ushered up and along to the familiar small kitchen, where potatoes were bubbling on the cooker and her father was sitting at the table polishing his shoes. With hands still full of brush and shoe, he stood up, allowed her to kiss his cheek, then motioned her to an empty chair.

"We've got a hot pot on, love," Kitty's mother said. "It'll be ready in five minutes."

"Oh, that's great. Cheers."

"So . . ." After a moment's consideration, her father placed his brush upon the table and laid the shoe sole-down beside it. He smiled at her broadly. "How's life among the pots and paints?"

"It's fine. Nothing special, but I'm learning."

"And Mr. Pennyfeather?"

"He's getting a little frail. Doesn't walk so well now."

"Dear, dear. And the business? Most importantly, do you have the magicians' custom? Do they paint?"

"Not so much."

"*That's* where you have to direct your energies, girl. That's where the money is."

"Yes, Dad. We're directing our energies at the magicians now. How's work?"

"Oh, you know. I made a big sale at Easter."

"Easter was months ago, Dad."

"Business is slow. How about a cup of tea, Iris?"

"Not before lunch." Her mother was busying herself collecting extra cutlery and setting the place before Kitty with reverent care. "You know, Kitty," she said, "I don't see why you don't stop here with us. It's not so far. And it would be cheaper for you."

"Rent's not high, Mum."

"Yes, but food and that. You must spend so much on it, when we could cook for you. It's a waste of money."

"Mmm." Kitty picked up her fork and tapped the table with it absently. "How's Mrs. Hyrnek?" she said. "And Jakob—have you seen him lately?"

Her mother had on a large pair of oven gloves and was kneeling before the oven; a gust of red-hot air, heavy with the fragrance of spiced meats, belched from its open door. Her voice echoed strangely as she rummaged within. "Jarmilla is well enough," she said. "Jakob works for his father, as you know. I have not seen him. He does not go out. Alfred—could you fetch out the wooden mat? This is piping hot. That's it. Now drain the potatoes. You should visit him, dear. He'd be glad for company, poor boy. Especially if it's you. It's a shame you don't see him anymore."

Kitty frowned. "That wasn't what you *used* to say, Mum."

"All that business was a *long* time ago. . . . You're much steadier now. Oh, and the grandmother has died, Jarmilla says."

"What? When?"

"Last month sometime. Don't give me that look—if you came to see us more often, you'd have known about it earlier, wouldn't you? Not that I can see it matters much to you in any case. Oh—*do* ladle it out, Alfred. It'll go cold, else."

The potatoes were overcooked, but the stew was excellent. Kitty ate ravenously and, to her mother's delight, plowed through a second helping before her parents had finished their first. Then, while her mother told her news of people she had never met or didn't remember, she sat quietly, fingering a small, smooth, and heavy object in her trouser pocket, lost in thought.

The evening following her trial had been deeply unpleasant for Kitty, as first her mother, then her father, had expressed their fury at the consequences. It was in vain that Kitty reminded them of her innocence, of the wickedness of Julius Tallow. It was in vain that she swore to somehow find the £600 necessary to placate the wrath of the Courts. Her parents were unmoved. Their argument boiled down to a few eloquent points: (1) They did not have the money. (2) They would have to sell their house. (3) She was a stupid, arrogant brat to think of challenging a magician. (4a) What had everyone told her? (4b) What had *they* told her? (5) Not to do it. (6) But she was too boneheaded to listen. And (7) *now* what were they going to do?

The encounter had finished predictably, with the mother weeping, the father raging, and Kitty rushing furiously to her room. It was only when she was there, sitting on the bed, staring hot-eyed at the opposite wall, that she remembered the old man, Mr. Pennyfeather, and his strange offer of assistance. It had entirely slipped her mind during the argument, and now, in the midst of her confusion and distress, it seemed altogether unreal. She thrust it to the back of her mind.

Her mother, bringing her a conciliatory cup of tea some hours later, found a chair wedged firmly against the door from within. She spoke through the thin plywood. "I forgot to tell you something, Kathleen. Your friend Jakob is out of the hospital. He went home this morning."

"What! Why didn't you say?" The chair was feverishly removed; a flushed face glared out from under a mane of unkempt hair. "I have to see him."

"I don't think that will be possible. The doctors—" But Kitty was already gone.

He was sitting up in bed, wearing a brand-new pair of blue pajamas that still had the creases in the sleeves. His variegated hands were folded in his lap. A glass bowl of grapes sat untouched upon the counterpane. Two bright white circles of fresh gauze were strapped across his eyes, and a short fuzz of hair was growing upon his scalp. His face was as she remembered, stained by its dreadful wash of gray and black.

As she entered, he broke into a small, twisted smile.

"Kitty! That was quick."

Trembling, she approached the bed and took his hand. "How—how did you know it was me?"

"No one else comes up the stairs like a bull elephant the way you do. You all right?"

She glanced at her unblemished, pink-white hands. "Yes. Fine."

"I *heard* about that." He tried to maintain his smile, failed narrowly. "You're lucky. . . . I'm glad."

"Yes. How are you feeling?"

"Oh, knackered. Sick. Like a round of smoked bacon. My skin's painful when I move. And itchy. That'll all pass, they say. And my eyes are healing."

Kitty felt a surge of relief. "That's great! When—?"

"Sometime. I don't know. . . ." He seemed suddenly weary, irritable. "Never mind all that. Tell me what's been going on. I hear you've been to the Courts."

She told him the whole story, except her encounter with Mr. Pennyfeather. Jakob sat upright in bed, smoky-faced and somber. At the finish, he sighed.

"You are *so* stupid, Kitty," he said.

"Thanks for that." She ripped a few grapes off the bunch and stuffed them savagely into her mouth.

"My mum told you not to. She said—"

"She and everyone else. They are all *so* right and I am *so* wrong." She spat grape seeds into her palm and threw them into a bin beside the bed.

"Believe me, I'm grateful for what you tried to do. I'm

sorry you're suffering on my account now."

"It's no big deal. We'll find the money."

"Everyone knows the Courts are rigged—it's not what you've done that counts there, it's who you are and who you know."

"All right! Don't go on about it." Kitty wasn't in the mood for lectures.

"I won't." He grinned, a little more successfully than before. "I can feel your scowl through the bandages."

They sat in silence for a while. At last, Jakob said, "Anyway, you needn't think that Tallow will get off scot-free." He rubbed the side of his face.

"Don't rub. What do you mean?"

"It's just so itchy! Meaning there are ways other than the Courts. . . ."

"Such as?"

"Ahh! It's no good, I'll have to sit on my hands. Well, come in close—something might be listening. . . . Right. Tallow, being a magician, will think he's away and clear. He won't give me another thought now, if he ever has. And he certainly won't connect me with Hyrnek's."

"Your dad's firm?"

"Well, whose else is it? Of course my dad's firm. And that's going to be costly for Tallow. Like a lot of other magicians, he gets his books of magic bound at Hyrnek's. Karel told me: he's checked the accounts. Tallow places orders with us every couple of years. Likes a maroon crocodile-skin binding, does Tallow, so we can add lack of taste to his other crimes. Well, we can afford to wait. Sooner or later, he'll send in another book for us to treat, or order something up . . . Ah! I can't bear it! I've got to scratch!"

"*Don't*, Jakob—have a grape instead. Take your mind off it."

"It won't do any good. I wake up scratching my face in the night. Mum has to wrap my hands in bandages. But it's *killing* me now—you'll have to call Mum for some cream."

"I'd better leave."

"In a minute. But, I was saying—it won't just be the *binding* of Tallow's book that gets changed next time."

Kitty wrinkled her forehead. "What—the spells inside?"

Jakob gave a grim smile. "It's possible to substitute pages, doctor sentences, or alter diagrams if you know what you're doing. In fact, it's more than possible—it's downright easy for people my dad knows. We'll sabotage a few likely incantations and then . . . we'll see."

"Won't he notice?"

"He'll simply read the spell, draw the pentacle, or whatever it is he does, and then . . . who knows? Nasty things happen to magicians when spells go wrong. It's a precise art, my dad tells me." Jakob settled back against the pillows. "It may be years before Tallow falls into the trap—but so what? I'm in it for the long haul. My face'll still be ruined in four, five years' time. I can wait." He turned his face away suddenly. "You'd better get Mum now. And don't tell *anyone* what I've just told you."

Kitty located Mrs. Hyrnek in the kitchen; she was sieving an odd, oily white lotion, thick with dark-green aromatic herbs, into a medicine jar. At Kitty's news, she nodded, her eyes gray with weariness.

"I've made the lotion just in time," she said, stoppering the jar hastily and seizing a cloth from the sideboard. "You'll see yourself out, won't you?" With this, she bustled from the room.

Kitty had taken no more than two trailing steps toward the

hall when a low, short whistle halted her in her tracks. She turned: Jakob's aged grandmama was sitting in her usual chair beside the stove, a large bowl of unshelled peas wedged upon her bony lap. Her bright black eyes glittered at Kitty; the numberless crinkles on her face shifted as she smiled. Kitty smiled back uncertainly. A withered hand was raised; a shriveled finger curled and beckoned, twice. Heart pounding, Kitty approached. Never, in all her many visits, had she spoken two words to Jakob's grandmama; she had never even heard her speak. A ridiculous panic engulfed her. What should she say? She did not speak Czech. What did the old woman want? Kitty felt herself suddenly part of a fairy tale, a waif trapped in the kitchen of a cannibal witch. She—

"This," Jakob's grandmama said in a clear, crisp South London accent, "is for you." She delved a hand somewhere into the pockets of her voluminous skirts. Her eyes did not leave Kitty's face. "You should keep it close. . . . Ah, where is the beggar? Aha—yes. Here."

Her hand, when she raised it to Kitty's, was tightly clenched, and Kitty felt the weight of the object and its coldness in her palm before she saw what it was. A small metal pendant, fashioned in the shape of a teardrop. A little loop at the top showed where it could be affixed to a chain. Kitty did not know what to say.

"Thank you," she said. "It's . . . beautiful."

Jakob's grandmama grunted. "Huh. It's silver. More to the point, girl."

"It—it must be very valuable. I . . . don't think I should—"

"Take it. And wear it." Two leathery hands enclosed Kitty's, folding her fingers over the pendant. "You never know. Now, I have a hundred peas to shell. Perhaps a hundred and two—one for each year, eh? So. I must concentrate. Be off with you!"

The next few days saw repeated deliberations between Kitty and her parents, but the upshot was always the same—with all their savings pooled, they were still several hundred pounds short of the Court's fine. Selling the house, with the uncertainty that entailed, seemed the only solution.

Except, possibly, for Mr. Pennyfeather.

Ring if interested. Within a week. Kitty had not mentioned him to her parents, or to anyone else, but his words were always on her mind. He had promised to help her, and she had no problem with that in principle. The question was, Why? She did not think he was doing it out of the goodness of his heart.

But her parents were going to lose their house if she did not act.

T. E. Pennyfeather certainly existed in the telephone directory: he was listed as an "Artists' Supplier" in Southwark, alongside the same phone number that Kitty had on the card. So that much of his story appeared to be true.

But what did he want? Part of Kitty felt very strongly that she should leave him alone; another part couldn't see what she had to lose. If she didn't pay up soon, she would be arrested, and Mr. Pennyfeather's offer was the only lifeline she had to seize.

At length, she made up her mind.

There was a telephone box two streets away from where she lived. One morning, she squeezed herself into its narrow, muggy space, and rang the number.

A voice answered, dry and breathless. "Artists' Supplies. Hello."

"Mr. Pennyfeather?"

"Ms. Jones! I am delighted. I feared you would not ring."

"Here I am. Listen, I'm—I'm interested in your offer, but I must know what you want from me before I go any further."

"Of course, of course. I shall explain to you. May I suggest we meet?"

"No. Tell me now, over the phone."

"That would not be prudent."

"It would for me. I'm not putting myself at risk. I don't know who you—"

"Quite so. I will suggest something. If you disagree, well and good. Our contact will be at an end. If you agree, we shall move on. My suggestion: we meet at the Druids' Coffeehouse at Seven Dials. Do you know it? A popular spot—always busy. You can talk to me in safety there. If in doubt I suggest another thing. Seal my card in an envelope together with the information about where we are meeting. Leave it in your room, or post it to yourself. Whichever. Should anything happen to you, the police will find me. That may put your mind at rest. Another thing. Whatever the outcome of our meeting, I shall end it by giving you the money. Your debt will be paid by the end of the day."

Mr. Pennyfeather seemed worn out by this long speech. While he wheezed gently, Kitty considered the offer. It didn't take long. It was too good to resist.

"All right," she said. "Agreed. What time at the Druids'?"

Kitty prepared carefully, writing a note to her parents and slipping it with the business card inside an envelope. She placed it on her bed, propped against her pillow. Her parents would not be back till seven. The meeting was scheduled for three. If all went well, she would have plenty of time to return and remove the note before it was found.

She came out of the tube at Leicester Square and set off in the direction of Seven Dials. A couple of magicians shot past in chauffeur-driven limousines; everyone else struggled along the tourist-cluttered pavements, guarding their pockets against cut-purses. Her progress was slow.

To speed her way, she took a shortcut, an alley that curved off behind a fancy-dress shop and bisected a whole block, opening out again on a street near Seven Dials. It was dank and narrow, but there were no buskers or tourists all along its length, which in Kitty's view made it a grand highway. She ducked down it and set off at a good pace, glancing at her watch as she did so. Ten to three. Perfect timing.

Midway along the alley she had a shock. With a screech like a banshee, a brindled cat leaped off a concealed ledge in front of her face and disappeared through a grating in the opposite wall. The sound of tumbling bottles followed from within. Silence.

Taking a deep breath, Kitty walked on.

A moment later, she heard quiet footsteps stealing along behind her.

The hairs on the back of her neck rose. She speeded up. Don't panic. Someone else taking a short cut. Anyway, the alley's end was not far off. She could glimpse people moving in the main street beyond.

The footsteps behind seemed to speed up with her. Eyes wide, heart pounding, Kitty began to trot.

Then something stepped out from the shadows of a doorway. It was dressed in black and its face was covered by a smooth mask with narrow slits for eyes.

Kitty cried out and turned.

Two more masked figures, tiptoeing behind.

She opened her mouth to scream, but did not have a chance to do so. One of her pursuers made a quick motion: something left its hand—a small, dark sphere. It hit the ground just at her feet, splintering into nothing. From the place where it vanished a black vapor rose, twirling, growing thick.

Kitty was too frightened to move. She could only watch as the vapor formed itself into a small blue-black winged creature, with long, slender horns and wide red eyes. The thing hovered for an instant, tumbling head over heels in the air, as if uncertain what to do.

The figure that had thrown the sphere pointed its hand at Kitty and cried out a command.

The thing stopped twirling. A grin of wicked glee cracked its face almost in two.

Then it lowered its horns, beat its wings into a frenzy, and with a shrill cry of delight, hurled itself at Kitty's head.

19

In an instant, the thing was on her, with light glinting on its two sharp horns and its serrated mouth gaping wide. Blue-black wings beat in her face, small callused hands clawed at her eyes. She felt its foul breath on her skin; its keening cry deafened her. She beat at it madly with her fists, shouting out now, screaming. . . .

And with a loud, moist popping sound, the thing burst, leaving nothing but a shower of cold black droplets and a lingering bitter smell.

Kitty collapsed against the nearest wall, chest heaving, looking wildly about her. There was no doubt—the thing had gone, and the three masked figures had vanished too. On either side, the alley was empty. Nothing stirred.

She ran now, as fast as she could, careering out into the busy street and weaving, ducking, dodging her way among the crowd, up the gentle slope that led to Seven Dials.

Seven roads met here at a cobbled roundabout, which was surrounded on all sides by rambling medieval buildings of black wood and colored plaster. In the center of the roundabout was a statue of a general on a horse, below which a relaxed crowd was sitting, enjoying the afternoon sun. Opposite him was another statue, this one of Gladstone in his attitude of the Lawgiver. He was dressed in robes and held an open scroll, with one arm raised as if he were declaiming to the multitudes. Someone—either drunk, or of anarchistic bent—had climbed the great man and placed an orange traffic cone upon his majestic head, giving him the look of a comedy storybook sorcerer. The police had not yet noticed.

Directly behind Gladstone's back was the Druids' Coffeehouse, a meeting place for the young and thirsty. The ground floor walls of the building had been ripped out and replaced with rough stone pillars decorated with curling vines. A series of tables covered with white cloth spilled around the pillars onto the cobbled road in Continental fashion. Every table was occupied. Waiters in blue tunics hurried back and forth.

Kitty came to a halt next to the statue of the general and caught her breath. She surveyed the tables. Three o'clock precisely. Was he . . . ? There!—almost out of sight behind a pillar—the crescent of white hair, the shiny bald pate.

Mr. Pennyfeather was sipping a café latte when she approached. His stick lay flat across the table. He saw her, smiled broadly, indicated a chair.

"Ms. Jones! Right on time. Sit, if you please. What do you care for? Coffee? Tea? A cinnamon bun? They are very good."

Kitty ran a distraught hand through her hair. "Um, a tea. And chocolate. I need chocolate."

Mr. Pennyfeather clicked his fingers; a waiter drew close. "A pot of tea and an éclair. A large one. Now, Ms. Jones. You seem a little breathless. You have been running. Or am I wrong?"

His eyes twinkled, his smile widened. Kitty leaned forward furiously. "It's no laughing matter," she hissed, with a glance at the nearby tables. "I've just been attacked! On my way to see *you*," she added, to drive the point home.

Mr. Pennyfeather's amusement did not slacken. "Indeed? Indeed? That is most serious! You must tell me—ah! Here is your tea. What speed! And a most sizable éclair! Good. Have a bite, then tell me all."

"Three people trapped me in an alley. They threw something—a container, I think—and a demon appeared. It leaped at me and tried to kill me and—are you taking this seriously, Mr. Pennyfeather, or shall I get up and leave right now?" His continuing good humor was beginning to enrage Kitty, but at her words his smile vanished.

"Forgive me, Ms. Jones. It is a grave matter. Yet you managed to escape. How did you do so?"

"I don't know. I fought back—hitting the thing when it was gouging at my face, but I didn't do anything, really. It just burst like a balloon. The men disappeared, too."

She took a long drink of tea. Mr. Pennyfeather eyed her calmly, saying nothing. His face remained grave, but his eyes seemed delighted, full of life.

"It's that magician—Tallow!" Kitty went on. "I *know* it is. He's trying to do me in after what I said in court. He'll send another demon, now that one's failed. I don't know what to—"

"*Do* have a bite of that éclair," Mr. Pennyfeather said. "That is my first suggestion. Now then, when you are calm, I will tell you something."

Kitty ate the éclair in four bites, washed it down with tea and felt a little calmer. She looked about her. From where she was seated, she had a good view of most of the customers of the coffeehouse. Some were tourists, immersed in colorful maps and handbooks; the rest were young—students probably, along with a smattering of families out for the day. There seemed no immediate likelihood of another attack.

"All right, Mr. Pennyfeather," she said. "Fire away."

"Very well." He dabbed at the corners of his mouth with a neatly folded napkin. "I shall return to that . . . incident in a moment, but I have something else to say first. You will be wondering why I should be interested in your troubles. Well—in fact I am not so much interested in your troubles as interested in *you*. By the way, the six hundred pounds is safely here"—he smiled and tapped his breast pocket—"you shall have it at the end of this conversation. So. I was in the gallery at Court and heard your evidence about the Black Tumbler. No one else believed you—the judge in her arrogance, the rest in their ignorance. But I pricked up my ears. Why should you lie? I asked. No reason. Therefore it must be true."

"It *was* true," Kitty said.

"But no one who is hit by a Black Tumbler—even by its outer edge—can fail to escape its mark. I know this."

"How?" Kitty asked sharply. "Are you a magician?"

The old man winced. "Please, you may insult me in any way you please—say I am bald, ugly, an old fool who smells of cabbage, or what you will, but do not call me that. It offends my soul. I am certainly *not* a magician. But it is not only magicians who have knowledge, Ms. Jones. Others of us can read, even if we are not steeped in wickedness like them. Do you read, Ms. Jones?"

Kitty shrugged. "Of course. At school."

"No, no, that is not proper reading. The magicians write the books you see there; you cannot trust them. However, I digress. Trust me—the Black Tumbler taints everything it touches. It touched you, you say, but you were not tainted. That is a paradox."

Kitty thought of Jakob's marbled face and felt a wave of guilt. "I can't help that."

"This demon that attacked you just now. Describe it."

"Blackish wings. A big red mouth. Two thin, straight horns—"

"A broad belly, covered in fur? No tail?"

"That's right."

He nodded. "A mouler. A minor demon of no great power. Even so, it should certainly have rendered you unconscious, owing to its disgusting smell."

Kitty wrinkled her nose. "It smelled bad for sure, but not *that* bad."

"Also, moulers do not usually burst. They latch on to your hair with their hands and remain attached until their master dismisses them."

"This one just popped."

"My dear Ms. Jones, you must forgive me if I am cheerful again. You see, I am delighted with what you are telling me. It means, quite simply, that you possess something special: a *resilience* to magic."

He sat back in his chair, summoned a waiter and smilingly ordered another round of drinks and cakes, oblivious to Kitty's look of bafflement. For the entire time it took for the food to arrive he did nothing but grin across the table at her, giggling to himself every now and then. Kitty forced herself to remain polite. The cash was still out of reach, in his coat pocket.

"Mr. Pennyfeather," she said at last. "I'm sorry, but I don't understand you at all."

"It's obvious, surely? Minor magic—we can't be sure about more powerful stuff yet—has little or no effect on you."

Kitty shook her head. "Rubbish. The Black Tumbler knocked me out."

"I said *little* or no effect. You are not immune. Neither for that matter am I, but I *have* withstood the assault of three foliots at once, which I believe is quite unusual."

This meant nothing to Kitty. She looked blank. Mr.

Pennyfeather made an impatient gesture. "What I am saying is that you and I—and several others, for we are not alone—are able to resist some of the magicians' spells! We are not magicians, but neither are we powerless, unlike the rest of the *commoners*"—he spat the word out with undisguised venom—"in this poor, godforsaken country."

Kitty's head was spinning, but she was still skeptical; she did not believe him yet.

"It doesn't make any sense to me," she said. "I've never heard of this 'resilience.' All I'm interested in is avoiding jail."

"Is that so?" Mr. Pennyfeather placed his hand lightly inside his jacket. "In that case you may have the money on the instant and be on your way. Fine. But I think you want something more than this. I see it in your face. You want several things. You want revenge for your friend Jakob. You want to change the way things are done here. You want a country where men like Julius Tallow don't flourish and walk tall. Not all countries are like this—some places have no magicians! None! Think of *that* next time you visit your friend in the hospital. I'm telling you," he went on in a quieter voice, "you can make a difference. *If* you listen to me."

Kitty gazed into the mess at the bottom of her cup and saw Jakob's ruined face reflected back. She sighed. "I don't know . . ."

"Be sure of one thing—I can help you with your vengeance."

She stared up at him. Mr. Pennyfeather was smiling at her, but his eyes had the same bright, angry gleam that she had seen when he had been jostled in the street.

"The magicians have hurt you," he said softly. "Together, we can wield the sword of retribution. But only if you assist me first. You help me. I help you. Fair bargain."

For an instant Kitty saw Tallow again, smirking across the courtroom, puffed up with self-confidence and the guaranteed protection of his friends. It made her shudder with disgust.

"First tell me how you need my help," she said.

Somebody sitting two tables away coughed loudly, and, as if a heavy curtain had suddenly fallen away inside her mind, Kitty realized the danger she was in. There she was, sitting among strangers, overtly discussing treason.

"We're mad!" she hissed furiously. "Anyone might hear us! They'll summon the Night Police and carry us away."

At this the old man actually laughed. "No one will overhear," he said. "Do not fear, Ms. Jones. It is all under control."

Kitty scarcely listened. Her attention had been seized by a young, blond-haired woman sitting at a table behind Mr. Pennyfeather's left shoulder. Though her glass was empty, she remained seated, engrossed in her book. Her head was down, her eyes modestly lowered; one hand toyed with the corner of a page. Suddenly Kitty became convinced that this was all a sham. She dimly recalled noticing the woman when she first sat down, sitting in a similar pose, and though Kitty had had her in full view all this while, she did not remember her once actually turning the page.

Next moment, she was sure of it. As if Kitty's gaze had brushed against her, the woman glanced up, caught her eyes, and gave her a cool little smile before returning to her book. There could be no doubt—she had been listening to everything!

"Are you all right?" Mr. Pennyfeather's voice sounded outside her panic.

Kitty could hardly speak. "Behind you . . . " she whispered. "A woman . . . a spy, an informer. She's heard it all."

Mr. Pennyfeather did not turn around. "Blond lady?

Reading a yellow paperback? That would be Gladys. Don't worry, she is one of us."

"One of—?" The woman looked up again and gave Kitty a broad wink.

"To her left is Anne; on my right—just beyond this pillar—sits Eva. That's Frederick on my left; Nicholas and Timothy are ranged behind you. Stanley and Martin couldn't get a table, so they're in the pub opposite."

In a daze, Kitty looked around. A middle-aged, black-haired woman grinned at her from behind Mr. Pennyfeather's right shoulder; on Kitty's right, a spotty, unsmiling youth glanced up from a dog-eared copy of *Motorbike Trader*. The woman beyond the pillar was obscured except for a black jacket hanging on her chair. Risking a crick in her neck, Kitty checked behind her, catching a glimpse of two more faces—young, serious—staring at her from other tables.

"No need to worry, you see," Mr. Pennyfeather said. "You're among friends. No one beyond them could hear what we say, and there are no demons present or we'd know about it."

"How?"

"Time enough for questions later. First I must make you an apology. I'm afraid you have met Frederick, Martin, and Timothy already." Kitty looked blank again. It was fast becoming a habit. "In the alley," Mr. Pennyfeather prompted.

"The alley?" Wait a minute—

"It was they who set the mouler on you. Not so fast! Do not leave! I am sorry that we scared you, but we had to be sure, you see. Sure that you were resilient like us. We had the mouler glass handy; it was a simple matter—"

Kitty found her voice. "You swine! You're as bad as Tallow! I could have been killed."

"No. I told you—the worst a mouler can do is knock you out. Its stench—"

"And that isn't bad enough?" Kitty rose to her feet in fury.

"If you must go, don't forget this." The old man drew a thick white envelope from his jacket and tossed it contemptuously on the tabletop between the cups. "You'll find the six hundred pounds there. Used notes. I don't break my word."

"I don't want it!" Kitty was livid, incandescent; she wanted to smash something.

"Don't be a fool!" The old man's eyes flared. "Do you want to rot in the Marshalsea prison? That's where debtors go, you know. That packet completes the first part of our bargain. Consider it an apology for the mouler. But it *could* be just the beginning. . . ."

Kitty snatched up the envelope, almost knocking the cups flying as she did so. "You're crazy. You *and* your friends. Fine. I'll take it. It's what I came for anyway." She was still standing. She pushed her chair back.

"Shall I tell you how it began for me?" Mr. Pennyfeather was leaning forward now, his gnarled fingers pressing hard against the tablecloth, scrunching it up. His voice was low, urgent; he fought against his lack of breath in his eagerness to speak. "I was like you at first—the magicians meant nothing to me. I was young, happily married—what did I care? Then my dear wife, heaven rest her soul, attracted the attention of a magician. Not unlike your Mr. Tallow, he was: a cruel, strutting popinjay. He wished her for himself, tried to beguile her with jewels and fine Eastern clothes. But my wife, poor woman, refused his advances. She laughed in his face. It was a brave act, but foolish. I wish now—I have wished this for thirty years— that she had gone with him.

"We lived in a flat above my shop, Ms. Jones; each day I worked late into the evening, sorting my stock and completing my accounts, while my wife retired to our rooms to prepare our meal. One night, I was sitting at my desk as usual. A fire was burning in the grate. My pen scratched on the paper. All at once, the dogs in the street began to howl; a moment later, my fire quivered and went out, leaving the hot coals hissing like the dead. I rose to my feet. Already I feared . . . well, what it was I did not know. And then—I heard my wife scream. Just once, a shriek cut off. I have never run so fast. Up the stairs, tripping in my haste, through our door, into our little kitchen . . ."

Mr. Pennyfeather's eyes no longer saw her. They gazed at something else, far off. Mechanically, hardly knowing what she did, Kitty sat down again and waited.

"The thing that had done it," Mr. Pennyfeather said at last, "had barely gone. I smelled its presence lingering. Even as I knelt beside my wife upon our old linoleum floor, the gas hobs on the cooker burst back to life, the stew in the pot resumed its bubbling. I heard the barking of dogs, windows down the road banging in a sudden breeze . . . then silence." He ran a finger among the éclair crumbs on a plate, gathered them up and popped them in his mouth. "She was a good cook, Ms. Jones," he said. "I remember that still, though thirty long years have passed."

On the other side of the coffeehouse, a waiter spilled a drink on a customer: the resulting uproar seemed to detach Mr. Pennyfeather from his memories. He blinked, looked at Kitty again. "Well, Ms. Jones, I shall cut my story short. Suffice it to say that I located the magician; for some weeks I followed him subtly, learning his movements, giving in neither to the ravings of grief nor the urges of impatience. In due time I had my chance; I waylaid him in a lonely spot and slew him. His corpse joined the bobbing filth floating down the Thames. However, before he died, he summoned three demons: one by one, their attacks on me all failed. It was in this manner that—somewhat to my surprise, for I was resolved to die in my revenge—I discovered my resilience. I do not pretend to understand it, but it is a fact. I have it; my friends have it; you have it. It is for each of us to decide whether we take advantage of this or not."

His voice ceased. He seemed all of a sudden worn out, his face lined and old.

Kitty hesitated a few moments before replying. "All right," she said, for Jakob's sake, for Mr. Pennyfeather's sake, and for the sake of his dead wife. "I won't go yet. I'd like you to tell me more."

20

Over several weeks, Kitty met regularly with Mr. Pennyfeather and his friends, at Seven Dials, at other coffee shops scattered across central London, and at Mr. Pennyfeather's flat above his Artists' Supplies shop, in a busy street just south of the river. Each time, she learned more about the group and their objectives; each time, she found herself identifying with them more closely.

It seemed that Mr. Pennyfeather had assembled his company haphazardly, relying on word of mouth and reports in newspapers to lead him to people with unusual capabilities. Some months he haunted the courtrooms, looking for someone such as Kitty; otherwise he simply used taproom chat to single out interesting rumors of people who had survived magical disaster. His art shop was modestly successful; generally he left it in the hands of his assistants and prowled through London on his surreptitious errands.

His followers had joined him over a long period of time. Anne, a vivacious woman of forty, had met him almost fifteen years before. They were veterans of many campaigns together. Gladys, the blond woman from the café, was in her twenties; she had withstood a side blast from a magicians' duel ten years earlier, when still a girl. She and Nicholas, a stocky young man with a brooding manner, had worked for Mr. Pennyfeather since they were children. The rest of the company were younger; no one older than eighteen. Kitty and Stanley, both thirteen, were the youngest of all.

The old man dominated them all with his presence, which was at once inspiring and autocratic. His willpower was iron-strong and his mental energies untiring, but his body was gradually failing him, and this roused him to outbursts of incoherent fury. In the early days such occasions were rare, and Kitty listened intently to his impassioned accounts of the great struggle in which they were engaged.

Ordinarily, Mr. Pennyfeather argued, it was impossible to resist the magicians or their rule. They did exactly as they pleased, as all the company had discovered to their cost. They ran everything important: the government, the civil service, the biggest businesses, and the newspapers. Even the plays put on at the theaters had to be officially sanctioned in case they contained subversive messages. And while the magicians enjoyed the luxuries of their rule, everyone else—the vast majority—got on with providing the essential services the magicians required. They worked in the factories, ran the restaurants, fought in the army . . . if it involved real work, the commoners did it. And providing they did it quietly, the magicians left them alone. But if there was even the smallest hint of dissatisfaction, the magicians came down hard. Their spies were everywhere; one word out of place and you were whisked off for interrogation in the Tower. Many troublemakers disappeared for good.

The magicians' power made it impossible to rebel: they controlled dark forces that few had glimpsed but which everyone feared. But Mr. Pennyfeather's company—this small handful of souls gathered up and driven forward by his implacable hatred—was more fortunate than most. And its good fortune came in several forms.

To some degree, all of Mr. Pennyfeather's friends shared his resilience to magic, but how far this stretched was impossible to say. Because of his past, it was clear Mr. Pennyfeather could withstand a fairly strong attack; most of the others, such as Kitty, had only been gently tested so far.

Some of them—these were Anne, Eva, Martin, and the surly and pockmarked Fred—had another talent. Since early childhood, they had each regularly observed small demons traveling hither and thither through the streets of London. Some flew, others walked among the crowds. No one else noticed them, and upon investigation, it appeared that to most people the demons were either invisible or masked by disguise. According to Martin—who worked in a paint factory, and was, after Mr. Pennyfeather, the most fiery and passionate—a good many cats and pigeons were not what they seemed. Eva (brown curly hair, fifteen, still at school) said she had once seen a stickle-backed demon walk into a grocer's and buy a bunch of garlic; her mother, who was with her, had seen nothing but a bent old lady doing her shopping.

Penetrating illusions in this way was a trait that was very useful to Mr. Pennyfeather. Another ability that he highly prized was that of Stanley, a chipper, rather cocksure boy who, despite being Kitty's age, had already left school. He worked delivering newspapers. Stanley could not see demons; instead, he was able to perceive a faint, flickering radiance given off by any object containing magical force. As a small boy, he had so delighted in these auras that he had taken to stealing the objects concerned; by the time Mr. Pennyfeather caught up with him (at the Judicial Courts) he was already an accomplished pickpocket. Anne and Gladys had a similar ability, but it was not nearly so marked as that of Stanley, who could sense magical items through clothes and even behind thin wooden partitions. As a result, Stanley was one of the key figures of Mr. Pennyfeather's company.

Instead of *seeing* magical activity, the gentle, quiet Timothy seemed able to *hear* it. As far as he could describe it, he sensed a kind of humming in the air. "Like a bell ringing," he said, when pressed. "Or the sound you get when you tap an empty glass." If he concentrated, and if there wasn't too much other noise around, he could actually trace the hum to its source, perhaps a demon or a magical object of some kind.

When all these abilities were set together, Mr. Pennyfeather said, they formed a small but effective force to set against the might of the magicians. It could not declare itself openly, of course, but it could work to undercut their enemies. Magical objects could be traced, hidden dangers could be avoided and—most important of all—attacks could be made on the magicians and their wicked servants.

From the first, these revelations enthralled Kitty. She observed Stanley as, on a training day, he picked out a magical knife from six ordinary specimens, each one concealed from him in a separate cardboard box. She followed Timothy as he walked back and forth through Mr. Pennyfeather's shop, locating the resonance of a jeweled necklace that had been hidden in a pot of brushes.

Magical objects were at the center of the company's strategy. Kitty regularly observed members of the group arriving at the shop with small parcels or bags that they passed to Anne, Mr. Pennyfeather's second-in-command, to be stowed quietly away. These contained stolen goods.

"Kitty," Mr. Pennyfeather said to her one evening, "I have studied our verminous leaders for thirty years, and I believe I have learned their biggest weakness. They are greedy for everything—money, power, status, you name it—and quarrel incessantly about them all. But nothing arouses their passions more than magical trinkets."

She nodded. "Magic rings and bracelets, you mean?"

"Doesn't have to be jewelry," Anne said. She and Eva were with them in the backroom of the shop, sitting beside stacked rolls of paper. "Might be anything—staves, pots, lamps, pieces of wood. That mouler glass we chucked at you; that counts as one, doesn't it, Chief?"

"It does indeed. Which is why we stole it. Which is why we steal *all* these things, whenever we can."

"I think that glass came from the house in Chelsea, didn't it?" Anne said. "The one where Eva and Stanley shinned up the drainpipe to the upstairs window while the party was going on at the front of the house."

Kitty was open-mouthed. "Isn't that terribly dangerous? Aren't magicians' houses protected by . . . all sorts of things?"

Mr. Pennyfeather nodded. "Yes, though it depends on the power of the magician concerned. That one merely had magical tripwires laced across the room. . . . Naturally, Stanley evaded them easily. . . . We got a good cluster of objects that day."

"And what do you do with them?" Kitty asked. "Apart from throwing them at me, that is."

Mr. Pennyfeather smiled. "Artifacts are a major source of every magician's power. Minor officials, such as the Assistant Secretary for Agriculture—I think he was the owner of the mouler glass—can afford only weak objects, while the greatest men and women aspire to rare pieces of terrible force. They all do so because they are decadent and lazy. It is much easier to use a magical ring to strike down a foe than it is to summon some demon from the pit to do it."

"Safer, too," Eva said.

"Quite. So you see, Kitty, the more items we can get a hold

of, the better. It weakens the magicians considerably."

"And we can use them instead," Kitty added promptly.

Mr. Pennyfeather paused. "Opinion is a little divided on this. Eva here"—he curled his lip back slightly, showing his teeth— "believes it is morally dangerous to follow too closely in the magicians' footsteps. She believes the items should be destroyed. *I* however—and it is *my* company, is it not, so *my* word goes— believe that we must use whatever weapons we can against such enemies. And that includes turning their own magic against them."

Eva shifted in her seat. "It seems to me, Kitty," she said, "that by using such things, we become no better than the magicians themselves. It's far better to remain detached from the tempta- tions of evil things."

"Hah!" The old man gave a disparaging snort. "How else can we undermine our rulers? We need direct attacks to desta- bilize the government. Sooner or later, the people will rise up in support of us."

"Well, *when*?" Eva said. "There's been no—"

"We do not study magic like the magicians," Mr. Pennyfeather interrupted. "We are in no moral danger. But by doing a little research—a little reading in stolen books, for instance—we can learn to operate basic weapons. Your mouler glass, Kitty—that required only a simple Latin command. This is enough for small . . . demonstrations of our displeasure. The more complex artifacts we can stockpile safely, out of magi- cians' hands."

"I think we're going about it the wrong way," Eva said qui- etly. "A few little explosions will never make any difference. They'll always be stronger. We—"

Mr. Pennyfeather slammed his stick hard upon his workbench, making both Eva and Kitty jump. "Would you rather do nothing?" he yelled. "Very well! Go back out among the herds of sheep, put your head down and waste your lives!"

"I didn't mean that. I just don't see—"

"My shop is closing! It is late. You are no doubt expected home, Ms. Jones."

Kitty's mother and father had been greatly relieved by her prompt payment of the court fine. In keeping with their incurious personalities, they did not inquire too closely into where the money came from, gratefully accepting Kitty's stories about a generous benefactor and a fund for miscarriages of justice. In some surprise, they watched Kitty's gradual detachment from her old habits as, throughout the summer holidays, she spent more and more time with her new friends in Southwark. Her father, in particular, did not hide his satisfaction. "You're better off keeping away from that Hyrnek boy," he said. "He'll only get you into trouble again."

Although Kitty continued to visit Jakob, her visits were generally brief and unsatisfactory. Jakob's strength was a long time returning, and his mother kept sharp vigil at his bedside, sending Kitty packing as soon as she detected exhaustion in her son. Kitty could not tell him about Mr. Pennyfeather; and Jakob, for his part, was preoccupied with his streaked and itching face. He grew inward-looking and perhaps, Kitty thought, slightly resentful of her health and energy. Gradually, her trips to the Hyrnek household became less frequent, and after some months, they ceased.

Two things kept Kitty involved with the company. First, gratitude for the payment of her fine. She felt herself to be under a definite obligation to Mr. Pennyfeather. For all that he never mentioned it again, it was possible that the old man sensed her feelings on the matter; if so, he did not attempt to gainsay them.

The second reason was in many ways the more important. Kitty wanted to learn more about the "resilience" that Mr. Pennyfeather had discovered in her and to find out what it could do. Joining the company seemed the only way of achieving this; it also promised her a direction, a sense of purpose, and the glamour of a small and secret society hidden from the world at large. It was not long before she was accompanying the others out on foraging expeditions.

At first she was an onlooker, keeping watch while Fred or Eva scrawled anti-government graffiti on walls, or broke into magicians' cars and houses in search of artifacts. Kitty would stand in the shadows, fingering the silver pendant in her pocket, ready to whistle at any sign of danger. Later, she accompanied Gladys or Stanley as they followed magicians home, tracing the aura of the objects they carried. Kitty noted down the addresses in preparation for later raids.

Occasionally, late in the evening, she would observe Fred or Martin departing the shop on missions of a different kind. They wore dark clothes, their faces smudged with soot; they carried small, heavy bags under their arms. No one referred openly to their objectives, but when the next morning's newspaper carried reports of unexplained attacks on government properties, Kitty drew her own conclusions.

In time, because she was intelligent and decisive, Kitty began to assume a more prominent role. It was Mr. Pennyfeather's practice to send his friends out in small groups, within which each member had a different job; after some months, he let Kitty take charge of one such group, consisting of Fred, Stanley, and Eva. Fred's mulish aggression and Eva's outspoken opinions were notoriously incompatible, but Kitty managed to harness their characters with such effectiveness that they returned from a tour of the magicians' warehouses with several choice prizes—including a couple of large, blue orbs, which Mr. Pennyfeather said were possibly Elemental Spheres, very rare and valuable.

For Kitty, time spent away from the company soon became infinitely tedious; she grew steadily more contemptuous of the small-minded outlook of her parents and the propaganda fed to her at school. By contrast, she reveled in the excitement of the company's nightly operations, but these were fraught with risk. One evening, a magician discovered Kitty and Stanley clambering out of his study window with a magical box in their grasp. He summoned a small creature in the shape of a stoat, which pursued them, belching gouts of fire from its open mouth. Eva, waiting in the street below, threw a mouler glass at the demon, which, distracted by the appearance of the mouler, halted for a moment, allowing them to get away. On another occasion, in a magician's garden, Timothy was assailed by a sentry demon, which crept up and embraced him with its thin blue fingers. It would have gone badly for him had Nick not managed to lop off the creature's head with an antique sword he had stolen moments before. Because of his resilience, Tim survived, but complained thereafter of a faint odor he could never shift.

Aside from demons, the police were a continual problem and eventually led to disaster. As the company's thefts grew more ambitious, greater numbers of Night Police appeared on the streets. One autumn evening in Trafalgar Square, Martin and Stanley noticed a disguised demon carrying an amulet that gave off a vibrant magical pulse. The creature made off on foot, but left a strong resonance in its wake, which Tim was able to follow with ease. It was soon cornered in a quiet alley, where the company weathered the demon's most ferocious assaults. Unfortunately, this magical outburst attracted the attention of the Night Police. Kitty and her colleagues scattered, pursued by things that resembled a pack of dogs. The following day, all but one reported back to Pennyfeather. That one was Tim, who was never seen again.

Timothy's loss hit the company hard, and resulted in a second, almost immediate, casualty. Several of the group, Martin and Stanley in particular, called loudly for a more audacious strategy against the magicians.

"We could lie in wait in Whitehall," Martin said, "when they're driving into Parliament. Or hit Devereaux when he leaves his palace at Richmond. That'll shake 'em up, if the P. M. goes. We need something seismic now to start the uprising."

"Not yet," Mr. Pennyfeather said testily. "I need to do more research. Now get out and leave me in peace."

He was a slight boy, Martin, with dark eyes, a thin, straight nose, and an intensity about him that Kitty had never noticed in anyone else before. He had lost his parents to the magicians, someone said, but Kitty never learned the circumstances. He never looked anyone full in the eyes while speaking; always a little down and to the side. Whenever Mr. Pennyfeather refused his demands for action, he would argue his case passionately at first, then suddenly withdraw into himself, blank-faced, as if unable to express the strength of his feelings.

A few days after Tim's death, Martin did not turn up for the evening's patrol; when Mr. Pennyfeather entered his cellar, he discovered that his secret weapons store had been opened. An

Elemental Sphere had been taken. Hours later, an attack on Parliament took place. An Elemental Sphere was thrown into the midst of the MPs, killing several people. The Prime Minister himself narrowly escaped. Sometime the next day, the body of a youth was washed up on the shingle of the Thames.

Almost overnight, Mr. Pennyfeather became more solitary and irritable, rarely visiting the shop except on Resistance business. Anne reported that he was throwing himself deeper into his researches in the stolen books of magic. "He wants to access better weapons," she said. "We've only scratched the surface before. We need greater knowledge if we're to get revenge for Tim and Martin."

"How can he manage that?" Kitty protested. She had liked Tim particularly, and the loss had affected her deeply. "Those books are written in a hundred languages. He'll never make head or tail of them."

"He's made a contact," Anne said. "Someone who can help us out."

And indeed, it was around this time that a new associate joined the group. Mr. Pennyfeather valued his opinions highly. "Mr. Hopkins is a scholar," he said, on introducing him to the group for the first time. "A man of great wisdom. He has many insights into the cursed ways of the magicians."

"I do my best," Mr. Hopkins said modestly.

"He works as a clerk at the British Library," Mr. Pennyfeather went on, clapping him on the shoulder. "I was nearly caught when trying to, um . . . appropriate a book on magic. Mr. Hopkins shielded me from the guards, allowed me to escape. I was grateful; we began talking. I have never met a commoner with so much knowledge! He has taught himself many things by reading the texts there. Sadly, his brother was killed by a demon years ago and, like us, he seeks revenge. He knows—how many languages, Clem?"

"Fourteen," Mr. Hopkins said. "And seven dialects."

"There! How about that? He does not have resilience as we do, sadly, but he can provide back-up support."

"I'll do what I can," Mr. Hopkins said.

Whenever Kitty tried to bring Mr. Hopkins to mind, she found it was an oddly difficult task. It wasn't that he was unusual in any way—quite the opposite, in fact. He was extremely ordinary. His hair, perhaps, was straight and mousy, his face was smooth, clean-shaven. It was hard to say if he was old or young. He had no standout features, no funny quirks or unusual ways of speaking. All in all, there was something so instantly forgettable about the man that even in his company, as he was actually speaking, she would find herself switching off him, listening to the words, but ignoring the speaker. It was a decidedly curious thing.

Mr. Hopkins was treated with some suspicion by the company at first, primarily because, lacking resilience, he did not go out on forays to bring artifacts home. Instead, his forte was information, and in this he quickly proved his worth to the group at large. His job at the library, together, perhaps, with his oddly unmemorable character, allowed him to eavesdrop on the magicians. As a result, he was often able to predict their movements, allowing raids to be carried out on their properties while they were away; he heard tell of artifacts newly sold by Pinn's, enabling Mr. Pennyfeather to organize appropriate burglaries. Above all, Mr. Hopkins uncovered a wider range of incantations, allowing new weapons to be used in a wider range of Resistance attack. The accuracy of his tips was such that soon everyone came to rely on him implicitly. Mr. Pennyfeather was still the group's leader, but Mr. Hopkins's intelligence was their guiding light.

Time passed. Kitty left school at the standard age of fifteen. She had what few qualifications the school provided, but saw no future in the joyless factory work or the secretarial jobs offered by the authorities. An agreeable alternative presented itself: at Mr. Pennyfeather's suggestion, and to the satisfaction of her parents, she became an assistant working in his art shop. Among a hundred other tasks, she learned to keep the ledger, cut watercolor paper, and sort brushes into a dozen varieties of bristle. Mr. Pennyfeather did not pay well, but Kitty was content enough.

At first, she enjoyed the danger of her activities with the company; she liked the warm and secret thrill she got when passing government workers struggling to paint over some grafittied slogan, or seeing an outraged headline in *The Times* complaining about the latest thefts. After a few months, to escape her parents' scrutiny, she rented a small room in a run-down tenement five minutes from the shop. She kept long hours, working in the shop by day and with the company at night; her complexion grew pale, her eyes hardened by the perpetual threat of exposure and repeated loss. Each year brought further casualties: Eva killed by a demon at a house in Mayfair, her resilience unable to withstand its attack; Gladys lost during a warehouse blaze, when a dropped sphere started a fire.

As the company contracted, there came a sudden sense that the authorities were striving to hunt them down. A new magician, named Mandrake, was active: demons in the guise of children were seen, making inquiries about the Resistance and offering magical goods for sale. Human informers appeared in pubs and cafés, flourishing pound notes in return for information. There was a beleaguered air to the meetings in the backroom of Mr. Pennyfeather's shop. The old man's health was waning; he was irritable and his lieutenants restless. Kitty could see that a crisis was coming.

Then came the fateful meeting, and the biggest challenge of all.

21

"They're here."

Stanley had been keeping watch at a grille in the door, peering out into the main room of the shop. He had been there some time, tense and still; now he sprang into action, pulled back the bolt and opened the door. He stepped aside, pulling his cap from his head.

Kitty heard the familiar slow tapping of the stick approaching. She rose from her seat, arching her back to smooth out the aches and chill. Beside her, the others did likewise, Fred rubbing his neck and swearing under his breath. Of late, Mr. Pennyfeather had grown more insistent on these little courtesies.

The only light in the backroom came from a lantern on the table; it was late, and they did not want to attract the attention of passing spheres. Mr. Hopkins, who came in first, paused in the doorway to let his eyes adjust, then moved aside to guide Mr. Pennyfeather through the door. In the half-light, their leader's shrunken form looked even more diminished than usual; he shuffled in like an animated skeleton. Nick's reassuring bulk brought up the rear. All three entered the room, Nick closing the door softly behind them.

"Evening, Mr. Pennyfeather, sir." Stanley's voice was less chipper than normal; to Kitty's ears it carried a nauseating false humility. There was no reply. Slowly, Mr. Pennyfeather approached Fred's wicker chair; each step seemed to give him pain. He sat. Anne moved across to place the lantern in a niche beside him; his face was wreathed in shadow.

Mr. Pennyfeather rested his stick against his chair. Slowly, one finger at a time, he plucked his gloves from his hands. Mr. Hopkins stood beside him, neat, quiet, instantly forgettable. Anne, Nick, Kitty, Stanley, and Fred remained standing. This was a familiar ritual.

"Well, well, sit, sit." Mr. Pennyfeather placed his gloves on his knee. "My friends," he began, "we have come a long way together. I need not dwell on what we have sacrificed, or."— he broke off, coughed—"for what end. It has lately been my opinion, reinforced by my good Hopkins here, that we lack the resources to carry the fight to the enemy. We do not have enough money, enough weapons, enough knowledge. I believe we can now rectify this."

He paused, made an impatient signal. Anne hurried forward with a glass of water.

Mr. Pennyfeather gulped noisily. "That's better. Now. Hopkins and I have been away, studying certain papers stolen from the British Library. They are old documents, nineteenth century. From them, we have discovered the existence of an important cache of treasures, many of considerable magical power. If we can gain possession of it, we stand to revolutionize our fortunes."

"Which magician has them?" Anne asked.

"At present, they are beyond the magicians' reach."

Stanley stepped forward eagerly. "We'll travel wherever you want, sir," he cried. "To France, or Prague, or . . . or the ends of the earth." Kitty rolled her eyes skyward.

The old man chuckled. "We do not have to go quite as far as that. To be precise, we only have to cross the Thames." He allowed the ripple of bemusement to subside. "These treasures are not in some far temple. They are very close to home, some-

where we have all passed a thousand times. I will tell you—"
He raised his hands to quell the rising hubbub. "Please, I will
tell you. They are at the heart of the city, the heart of the magicians' empire. I am talking about Westminster Abbey."

Kitty heard the others' intakes of breath, and felt a shiver of
excitement run up her spine. The abbey? But no one would
dare—

"You mean a tomb, sir?" Nick asked.

"Indeed, indeed. Mr. Hopkins—if you would explain further?"

The clerk coughed. "Thank you. The abbey is the burial site
of many of the greatest magicians of the past—Gladstone,
Pryce, Churchill, Kitchener, to name but a few. They lie
entombed in secret vaults deep beneath the floors, and with
them lie their treasures, items of power that the faltering fools
of today can only guess at."

As always when Mr. Hopkins spoke, Kitty scarcely acknowledged *him*; she was toying with his words, with the possibilities
they suggested.

"But they laid curses on their tombs," Anne began. "Terrible
punishments await those who open them."

From the depths of his chair, Mr. Pennyfeather let out a
wheezing laugh. "Today's leaders—poor excuses for magicians,
all—certainly avoid the tombs like the plague. They are cowards, every one. They quail at the thought of the revenge their
ancestors might take, were they to disturb their bones."

"The traps can be avoided," Mr. Hopkins said, "with careful
planning. We do not share the magicians' almost superstitious
fear. I have been looking among the records and I have
discovered a crypt that contains marvels you could scarcely
dream of. Listen to this . . ." From his jacket, the clerk produced

a folded piece of paper. In dead silence, he opened it, drew a small pair of spectacles from his pocket and perched them on his nose. He read: "Six bars of gold, four jeweled statuettes, two emerald-headed daggers, a set of onyx globes, a pewter chalice, an—ah, this is the interesting bit—an enchanted pouch of black satin, filled with fifty gold sovereigns—" Mr. Hopkins glanced up at them over his spectacles. "This pouch is unremarkable to look at, but consider this—no matter how much gold is removed from the pouch, it never grows empty. An unending source of revenue for your group, I think."

"We could buy weapons," Stanley muttered. "The Czechs would supply us with stuff, if we could pay."

"Money can get you anything," Mr. Pennyfeather chuckled. "Go on, Clem, go on. That isn't all, by any means."

"Let me see . . ." Mr. Hopkins returned to the paper. "The pouch . . . ah yes, and an orb of crystal, in which—and I quote—'glimpses of the future and the secrets of all buried and hidden things can be descried.'"

"Imagine that!" Mr. Pennyfeather cried. "Imagine the power *that* would give us! We could anticipate the magicians' every move! We could locate lost wonders of the past, forgotten jewels . . ."

"We'd be unstoppable," Anne whispered.

"We'd be rich," Fred said.

"If true," Kitty remarked quietly.

"There is also a small bag," Mr. Hopkins went on, "in which demons may be trapped—that might prove useful, if we can discover its incantation. Also a host of other, lesser items, including, let me see, a cloak, a wooden staff, and sundry other personal effects. The pouch, the crystal ball, and the bag are the pick of the treasures."

Mr. Pennyfeather leaned forward in the chair, grinning like a goblin. "So, my friends," he said. "What do you think? Is this a prize worth having?"

Kitty felt it was time to inject a note of caution. "All very well, sir," she said, "but how come these marvels haven't been taken before? What's the catch?"

Her comment seemed to puncture the mood of elation slightly. Stanley scowled at her. "What's the matter?" he said. "This job not big enough for you? *You're* the one who's been moaning on about needing better strategy."

Kitty felt Mr. Pennyfeather's gaze upon her. She shivered, shrugged.

"Kitty's point is valid," Mr. Hopkins said. "There *is* a catch, or rather a defense around the crypt. According to the records, a Pestilence has been fixed to the keystone of the vault. This is triggered by the opening of the door. Should anyone enter the tomb, the Pestilence balloons from the ceiling and smites all those in the vicinity"—he glanced back at the paper—"'to rend the flesh from their bones.'"

"Lovely," Kitty said. Her fingers toyed with the teardrop pendant in her pocket.

"Er . . . how do you propose we avoid this trap?" Anne asked Mr. Pennyfeather politely.

"There *are* ways," the old man said, "but at present they are beyond us. We do not have the magical knowledge. However, Mr. Hopkins here knows someone who might help."

Everyone looked at the clerk, who adopted an apologetic expression. "He is, or was, a magician," Mr. Hopkins said. "Please"—his words had sparked a chorus of disapproval—"hear me out. He is disaffected with our regime for reasons of his own, and seeks the overthrow of Devereaux and the rest.

He has the necessary skill—and artifacts—to enable us to escape the Pestilence. He also"—Mr. Hopkins waited until there was silence in the room—"has the key to the relevant tomb."

"Who is he?" Nick said.

"All I can tell you is that he's a leading member of society, a scholar, and a connoisseur of the arts. He is an acquaintance of some of the greatest in the land."

"What's his name?" Kitty said. "This is no good."

"I'm afraid he guards his identity very carefully. As should we all, of course. I have not told him anything about you either. But if you accept his assistance, he wishes to meet with one of you, very soon. He will pass on the information we require."

"But how can we trust him?" Nick protested. "He could be about to betray us."

Mr. Hopkins coughed. "I do not think so. He has helped you before, many times. Most of the tip-offs I have given you have been passed on by this man. He has long wished to advance our aims."

"I examined the burial documents from the library," Mr. Pennyfeather added. "They seem genuine. It is too much effort for a forgery. Besides, he has known of us for years, through Clem here. Why does he not betray us if he wishes the Resistance harm? No, I believe what he is saying." He got unsteadily to his feet, his voice turning harsh, congested. "And it is *my* organization, after all. You would do well to trust my word. Now, are there any questions?"

"Just this," Fred said, snapping his flick-knife open. "When do we start?"

"If all goes well, we shall raid the abbey tomorrow night. It just remains—" The old man broke off, doubled over in a sudden fit of coughing. His hunched back cast strange shadows on the wall. Anne stepped across and helped him sit. For a long moment he was too short of breath to speak again.

"I am sorry," he said finally. "But you see how my condition goes. My strength is lessening. In truth, my friends, Westminster Abbey is the best opportunity I have. To lead you all to—to something better. This will be a new beginning."

And an appropriate end for *you*, Kitty thought. This is your last chance to achieve something concrete before you die. I just hope your judgment holds up, that's all.

As if he had read her mind, Mr. Pennyfeather's head twisted suddenly in her direction. "It just remains," he said, "to visit our mysterious benefactor and discuss terms. Kitty, since you are so sprightly today, *you* will go to meet him tomorrow."

Kitty returned his gaze. "Very well," she said.

"Now, then." The old man turned to regard them all, one by one. "I must say I am a little disappointed. None of you has yet asked the identity of the person whose tomb we are about to enter. Are you not curious?" He laughed, wheezing.

"Er, whose is it, sir?" Stanley asked.

"Someone with whom you will all be familiar from your school days. I believe he still figures prominently in most lessons. None other than the Founder of our State, the greatest and most terrible of all our leaders, the hero of Prague himself"—Mr. Pennyfeather's eyes glittered in the shadows—"our beloved William Gladstone."

Part Three

22

Nathaniel's plane was due to leave the Box Hill aerodrome at six-thirty sharp. His official car would arrive at the Ministry an hour earlier, at five-thirty. This meant that he had approximately half a day to prepare himself for the most important assignment of his brief career in government: his trip to Prague.

His first task was to deal with his servant and proposed traveling companion. On his return to Whitehall, he found a free summoning chamber and, with a clap of the hands, summoned Bartimaeus once more. When it materialized, it had rid itself of its panther guise, and was in one of its favored forms: a young dark-skinned boy. Nathaniel noted that the boy was not wearing its usual Egyptian-style skirt; instead, it was lavishly dolled up in an old-fashioned tweed traveling suit, with spats, gaiters and, incongruously, a leather flying helmet, complete with goggles, loose upon its head.

Nathaniel scowled. "And you can lose those for starters. You're not flying."

The boy looked wounded. "Why not?"

"Because I'm traveling incognito, and that means no demons waltzing through customs."

"What, do they put us in quarantine now?"

"Czech magicians will be scanning all incoming flights for magic, and they'll subject a British plane to the finest scrutiny of all. No artifact, book of magic, or idiot demon will get through. I shall have to be a 'commoner' for the duration of my flight; *you* I'll have to summon once I've arrived."

The boy raised its goggles, the better to look skeptical. "I thought the British Empire ruled the roost in Europe," it said. "You broke Prague years ago. How come they're telling you what to do?"

"They're not. We control the balance of power in Europe still, but officially we have a truce with the Czechs now. For the moment, we're guaranteeing no magical incursions into Prague. That's why this trip has to be done subtly."

"Speaking of subtle . . ." The boy gave a broad wink. "I did pretty well earlier, eh?"

Nathaniel pursed his lips. "Meaning what?"

"Well, I was on my best behavior this morning—didn't you notice? I could have given your masters plenty of lip, but I restrained myself to help you out."

"Really? I thought you were your normal irritating self."

"Are you kidding? I was so oily, my feet practically slipped from under me. I can still taste that false humility on my tongue. But that's better than being popped into one of dear Jessica's Mournful Orbs again." The boy shuddered. "*My* sucking up only lasted a few minutes, though. It must be horrible kowtowing to them *perpetually*, as *you* do, and knowing that you could stop that game at any time you wished, and go your own way—except that you haven't got the bottle to do it."

"You can stop right there. I'm not interested in your opinion." Nathaniel was having none of this—demons often threw half-truths at magicians to disorientate them. It was best to close your ears to their wiles. "Besides," he added, "Duvall, for one, is not my master. I despise him."

"And Whitwell's different, is she? I didn't notice any great love between you."

"Enough. I must pack, and I have to visit the Foreign Office before I go." Nathaniel looked at his watch. "I shall require you again in . . . twelve hours' time, at my hotel in Prague. Until I summon you again, I bind you into a nexus here. Remain silent and invisible, in this circle, beyond the knowledge or senses of all sentient things, until I send for you."

The boy shrugged. "If I must."

"You must."

The figure in the pentacle shimmered and faded slowly, like the memory of a dream. When it was entirely gone, Nathaniel worked a couple of backup charms, to prevent anyone unknowingly releasing the djinni if they chose to use the circle, and left hurriedly. He had a busy few hours ahead of him.

Before departing for his home to pack, Nathaniel called in at the Foreign Office, a building not dissimilar to the British Museum in size, bulk, and brooding gray power. Here, much of the day-to-day running of the Empire took place, magicians relaying advice and instructions by means of telephone and messenger to their counterparts in smaller offices across the world. As he climbed the steps to the revolving door, Nathaniel looked up at the roof. Even on the three planes that he was able to observe, the sky above the building was thick with the hurrying of insubstantial forms: fleet couriers carrying orders in magically coded envelopes, larger demons acting as their escorts. As always, the sheer scale of the great Empire, which could be sensed only in sights such as this, left him awestruck and a little preoccupied. In consequence, he had some trouble with the revolving entrance door; in pushing vigorously the wrong way, he unfortunately sent an elderly, gray-haired lady sprawling backward into the foyer on the other side, her armload of papers streaming out across the marbled floor.

After negotiating the door successfully, Nathaniel hurried forward and with a dozen flustered apologies, helped his victim to her feet before beginning the task of scooping up the papers. As he did so, accompanied by a continuous volley of reedy complaints from the old woman, he saw a familiar slim form emerge from a door on the opposite side of the foyer and make her way across. Jane Farrar, Duvall's apprentice, as elegant and glisteningly dark-haired as ever.

Nathaniel's face went scarlet; he speeded up frantically, but there were many papers to gather and the foyer was not large. Long before he had finished, and while the old lady was still spiritedly telling Nathaniel what she thought of him, Ms. Farrar had arrived on the scene. He glimpsed her shoes out of the corner of one eye: she had halted and was watching. He could well imagine her air of detached amusement.

With a deep breath, he stood and thrust the papers into the old woman's hands. "There. Once again, I'm sorry."

"I should think so, too—of all the careless, arrogant, most pestilential little—"

"Yes, let me help you through that door . . ."

With a firm hand he spun her around and, with a guiding shove between her shoulder blades, set her speedily on her way. Brushing himself down, he turned and blinked, as if in vast surprise.

"Ms. Farrar! What a pleasure this is."

She smiled a lazy, secret smile. "Mr. Mandrake. You seem a little out of breath."

"Do I? Well, I *am* rather urgently engaged this afternoon. And then that poor old woman's legs gave way, so I tried to help . . ." Her cool eyes appraised him. "Well . . . I'd better be getting along. . . ."

He moved aside, but Jane Farrar suddenly stepped a little closer. "I *know* you're busy, John," she said, "but I would *love* to pick your brains about something, if I might be so bold." She twizzled a strand of long, black hair idly with a finger. "What luck for me. I'm *so* glad we met by chance. I heard through the grapevine that you managed to summon a fourth-level djinni recently. Is that *really* true?" She looked at him with wide, dark eyes, brimming with admiration.

Nathaniel took a slight step back. He felt perhaps a little hot, certainly a little flattered, but still very unwilling to discuss matters as private as his choice of demon. It was unfortunate that the incident at the British Museum had been so public—speculation would be rife about his servant now. But it was never wise to be unguarded: *safe, secret, secure.* He gave a harried smile. "It *is* true. You were not misinformed. It's nothing too difficult, I assure you. Now, if you don't mind—"

Jane Farrar gave a little sigh and adjusted a strip of hair becomingly behind one ear. "You *are* clever," she said. "You know, I've tried to do exactly that—to raise a demon of the fourth level—but I must be getting muddled somehow, because I just can't do it. I can't *think* what the problem is. Couldn't you come along with me now, and run me through the incantations? I've got a summoning circle all of my own. It's in my apartment, not far from here. It's very private—we wouldn't be disturbed. . . ." She tilted her head slightly to one side and smiled. Her teeth were very white.

Nathaniel was conscious of a bead of sweat trickling in an ungainly fashion down the side of his forehead. He contrived to smooth his hair back and brush the drip away in what he hoped was a casual motion. He felt distinctly odd: languorous, yet fired up and energetic all at once. After all—it would be an easy thing to help Ms. Farrar. Summoning a djinni was pretty straightforward when you'd done it a few times. It was no big deal. He suddenly realized he rather desired her gratitude.

She touched his arm gently with slender fingers. "What do you say, John?"

"Um . . ." He opened and shut his mouth, frowning. Something was holding him back. Something about time, or lack of it. What was it? He'd come to the Ministry to—to do what, exactly? It was so hard to recall.

She gave a little pout. "Are you worried about your master? She'll never find out. And I won't tell mine. I know we're not *supposed* to. . . ."

"It's not that," he said. "It's just—"

"*Well* then."

"No—I've got to do something today . . . something important." He tried to tear his eyes away from hers; he couldn't concentrate, that was the problem, and his heart was beating far too noisily for his memory to make itself heard. She was wearing a delightful fragrance, too, not your normal Rowan Tree Rub-On, but a perfume much more oriental and flowery. It was very nice, but a bit overpowering. The scent of her proximity muddled him.

"What *is* that something?" she asked. "Maybe I can help you with it."

"Um, I'm going somewhere. . . . To Prague . . ."

She pressed a little closer. "Are you? What for?"

"To investigate . . . er . . ." He blinked, shook his head. Something was wrong.

"Tell you what," she said, "we could sit together and have a nice talk. You could tell me everything you're planning."

"I suppose . . ."

"I've got a lovely long couch."

"Have you?"

"We can cozy up together and drink iced sherbet and you can tell me all about this demon you summon, this Bartimaeus. I'd be *so* impressed."

As she spoke the name, a little warning note sounded in his mind, cutting through his luxurious befuddlement. Where had she learned Bartimaeus's name? It could only be from Duvall, her master, who had himself learned it that very morning in the summoning chamber. And Duvall—Duvall was no friend of his. He would want to stymie anything Nathaniel was doing, even his trip to Prague. . . . He stared at Jane Farrar with growing suspicion. Realization came flooding back, and for the first time he noticed his sensor web emitting a dull pulse in his ear, warning him of the presence of a subtle magic on his person. A Charm, or perhaps a Glamour . . . Even as he thought this, the luster of her hair seemed to fade a little, the sparkle in her eyes flickered and dimmed.

"I—I'm sorry, Ms. Farrar," he said huskily. "Your invitation is very kind, but I must decline. Please give my regards to your master."

She regarded him silently, the look of doe-eyed admiration replaced, fleetingly, by one of bottomless contempt. A moment later, the familiar, measured coolness had returned to Jane Farrar's face. She smiled. "He will be pleased to receive them."

Nathaniel gave a short bow and left her. When he glanced back, from the other side of the foyer, she had already gone.

He was still a little disoriented by this encounter five minutes later, when he emerged from a lift on the third floor of the Ministry, crossed a broad, echoing corridor, and arrived at the Second Secretary's door. He adjusted his cuffs, composed himself for a moment, knocked, and entered.

It was a high-ceilinged room of oak-paneled walls; light streamed in from elegantly tapering windows overlooking the busy traffic of Whitehall. The room was dominated by three great wooden tables, their upper surfaces inlaid with stretches of stippled green leather. Upon these were a dozen unfurled maps of varying size: some of pristine paper, others of ancient, cracking vellum, all pinned carefully onto the leather tabletops. A small bald man, the Second Secretary of the Foreign Office, was stooped over one such map, tracing some detail with his finger. He glanced up and nodded affably.

"Mandrake. Good. Jessica said you'd be calling. Come in. I've got the Prague maps ready for you."

Nathaniel crossed over to stand beside the Secretary, whose diminutive frame barely reached the level of his shoulder. The man's skin was yellow-brown, the color of sun-stained parchment, and had a dry and dusty quality. He stabbed a finger down upon the map. "Now, that's Prague: a fairly recent map, as you can see—it shows the trenches left by our troops in the Great War. You're familiar with the city in principle, I take it."

"Yes, sir." Nathaniel's efficient mind smoothly accessed the relevant information. "The castle district is on the West Bank of the Vltava, the Old Town on the East. The old magical quarter used to be near the castle, didn't it, sir?"

"That's right." The finger shifted. "Over here, hugging the hill. Golden Lane was where most of the Emperor's magicians and alchemists were based—until Gladstone's lads marched in, of course. Nowadays, what magicians the Czechs *do* have are barracked out of the town center in the suburbs, so there's little, if anything, going on near the castle. It's all run down there, I believe. The other old magical center"—the finger moved east across the river—"is the ghetto, *here*. That was where Loew created the first golems, back in Rudolf's day. Others in that area continued the practice up until the last century, so I imagine it's there, if anywhere, that the appropriate lore will have been guarded." He glanced up at Nathaniel. "You realize this is a fool's errand, don't you, Mandrake? If they've had the ability to create golems all this time, why haven't they been doing so? Heaven knows, we've defeated them in battle often enough. No, I can't see it, myself."

"I'm only acting on information received, sir," Nathaniel said, respectfully. "Prague seems the appropriate place to begin." His neutral tone and posture concealed the fact that he agreed wholeheartedly with everything the Secretary had said.

"Mm. Well, you know best." The Second Secretary's voice made it clear he thought Nathaniel didn't. "Now . . . see this packet? That contains your fake passport for the trip. You'll be traveling as Derek Smithers, a young apprentice working for Watt's Wine Company of Marylebone. Your pack contains documents confirming that, should Czech customs get fussy."

"Derek . . . Smithers, sir?" Nathaniel did not look too enthused.

"Yes. Only name we could get. Poor lad died of dropsy last month, at about your age; we've since appropriated his identity for government service. Now, you're officially going to Prague with a view to importing some of their excellent beer. I've put a list of brewers in your packet for you to memorize on the flight."

"Yes, sir."

"Right. Above all, you've got to be low-key on this mission, Mandrake. Don't draw attention to yourself in any way. If you have to use magic, do it quietly and do it quickly. I hear you might be using a demon. If so, *keep it under control.*"

"Of course, sir."

"The Czechs are not to know that you're a magician. Part of our current treaty with them is that we promise not to conduct any magical activities in their territories. And vice versa."

Nathaniel frowned. "But sir, I heard that Czech infiltrators have been active in Britain recently. Surely they're breaking the treaty."

The Secretary flashed an irritated side-glance at Nathaniel and tapped his fingers on the map. "That is so. They are quite untrustworthy. Who knows, they may even be behind this 'golem incident' of yours, too."

"In that case—"

"I know what you're about to say, Mandrake. Of course, there's nothing we'd like better than to march our armies into Wenceslas Square tomorrow and show the Czechs what's what, but we can't do that right now."

"Why not, sir?"

"Because of the American rebels. We're unfortunately a trifle stretched just at this moment. Won't last long. We'll mop up the Yankees and then turn our attention back to Europe. But just at this point, we don't want anything causing ructions. Got that?"

"Of course, sir."

"Besides, *we're* breaking the truce in a dozen ways as well. That's diplomacy for you. In truth, the Czechs have been getting above themselves for the last ten years. Mr. Devereaux's campaigns in Italy and central Europe were inconclusive, and the Prague Council has begun to probe our Empire for weaknesses. They're nipping at us the way a flea does a dog. Never mind.

All will come right in time. . . ." The Second Secretary wore an expression in which hardness and complacency were equally mingled. He turned his attention to the map again. "Now then, Mandrake," he said, briskly, "you'll be wanting a contact in Prague, I suppose. Someone to help you get your bearings."

Nathaniel nodded. "Do you have someone there, sir?"

"We do. One of our top agents. . . . His name is Harlequin."

"Harlequin . . ." In his mind's eye, Nathaniel saw a slender, masked figure, stealing with a dancing step among the shadows, carrying an air of carnival and menace in its wake. . . .

"Indeed. That is his agent's title. His real name I cannot tell you; possibly it is unknown even to himself. If you're visualizing a slender, masked gentleman, colorfully costumed, and spry of foot, then think again. Our Harlequin is a plump, elderly man of funereal temperament. Also, he is given to wearing black." The Secretary made a face of refined distaste. "Prague does that to you, if you stay there too long. It is a melancholy city. Several of our agents have been driven to suicide over the years. Harlequin seems sound enough so far, but he is a trifle morbid in his sensibilities."

Nathaniel swept his hair out of his eyes. "I'm sure I can handle that, sir. How will I meet him?"

"At midnight this evening, leave your hotel and make your way to the cemetery in the ghetto—that is here, by the way, Mandrake . . . see? Just along from the Old Town Square. You are to wear a soft cap, with a blood-red feather in it, and stroll among the tombstones. Harlequin will find you. You will recognize him by the distinctive candle that he carries."

"A distinctive candle."

"That's right."

"What—is it particularly long or wonky, or what?"

"He did not furnish me with that information."

Nathaniel made a face. "Pardon me, but it all seems a bit . . . melodramatic, doesn't it, sir? All these cemeteries and candles and blood-red feathers. Couldn't he just give me a ring in my hotel room when I've had a shower, and meet me in a café downstairs?"

The Secretary smiled bleakly. He passed the packet across to Nathaniel and made his way behind the farthest table to a plush leather chair, in which he sat with a small sigh. He swiveled it to face the windows, where watery clouds could be seen hanging low over London. It was raining far off to the west: smudged marks in the sky angled down into unseen folds of the city. The Secretary gazed out for a time without speaking.

"Behold the modern city," he said at last, "built to the finest modern templates. Look at the proud buildings of Whitehall: none of them more than a hundred and fifty years old! Of course there are tatty, unreconstructed areas still—that is inevitable, with so many commoners about—but the heart of London, where we work and live, is entirely forward-looking. A city of the future. A city worthy of a great empire. Your Ms. Whitwell's apartment, Mandrake—a fine building; it exemplifies the modern trend. There should be many more like that. Mr. Devereaux plans to bulldoze much of Covent Garden next year, rebuild all those little timber-framed houses as glorious visions of concrete and glass. . . ."

The chair swiveled back toward the room; he gestured at the maps. "Prague now—that's different, Mandrake. By all accounts it is a peculiarly *gloomy* sort of spot, far too nostalgic for the glories of its vanished past. Bit of a morbid fixation on things that are dead and gone: the magicians, the alchemists, the great Czech Empire. Well, any doctor could tell you that's an unhealthy sort of outlook—if Prague were a human, we'd lock her in a sanatorium. Now, I daresay we could shake Prague out of her daydreams if we chose, Mandrake, but we *don't* choose. No. Far better to have her mind muddled and mysterious, rather than clear-cut and farsighted like London's. And people such as Harlequin, who keep an eye on things there for us, have to think in the same way as the Czechs do. Or they wouldn't be any good to us, would they? Harlequin is a better spy than most, Mandrake. Hence his colorful instructions. I suggest you follow them to the letter."

"Yes sir, I'll certainly do my best."

23

I could tell it was Prague as soon as I materialized. The shabby ostentation of the gold chandelier hanging from the hotel-room ceiling; the ornate and grimy moldings around the uppermost edges of the walls; the dusty folds of the drapery above the small four-poster bed; the melancholy tingle in the air—all pointed only one way. As did the expression of foul distemper upon my master's face. Even as he mumbled out the last syllables of the summoning, he was looking around the room as if he half-expected it to rise up and bite him.

"Pleasant journey?" I inquired.

He completed a few protective bonds and stepped from the circle, signaling me to do the same. "Hardly. There were still some magical traces on me when I went through customs. They collared me and took me to a drafty backroom where I had to talk pretty fast—I said my wine warehouse was right next to a government compound and occasional deviant spells permeated the walls. In the end, they bought it and let me go." He scowled. "I can't understand it! I changed all my clothes before leaving home to prevent any traces sticking to me!"

"Underpants, too?"

He paused. "Oh—I was in a hurry. I forgot them."

"That'll be it, then. You'd be surprised what builds up down there."

"And look at this room," the boy continued. "This is meant to be their top hotel! I swear it hasn't been redecorated this century. Look at the cobwebs on those drapes! Appalling. And can you tell what color that carpet's supposed to be? Because *I* can't." He kicked out at the bed irritably; a cloud of dust ballooned outward. "And what's this stupid four-poster thing, anyway? Why can't they just have a nice clean futon or something, like at home?"

"Cheer up! At least you've got your own facilities." I investigated a forbidding-looking side door: it swung open with a theatrical squeak to reveal a dingily tiled bathroom, lit by a single bulb. A monstrous three-legged bath lurked in one corner; it was the kind brides are bumped off in, or where pet crocodiles grow to vast size, fed on unusual meats.[1] A similarly imposing toilet waited opposite, its chain hanging from the ceiling like a gallows rope.[2] Cobwebs and mold fought keenly for dominion of the far reaches of the ceiling. A complex series of metal pipes wound around each other across the wall, connecting bath and toilet and looking for all the world like the spilled intestines of a—

I shut the door. "On second thought, I wouldn't bother looking in there. Just a bathroom. Nothing special. How's the view?"

He glowered at me. "Check it out."

I parted the heavy scarlet curtains and looked out on a charming vista of a large municipal graveyard. Lines of neat headstones stretched away into the night, shepherded by rows of gloomy ash and larch. At intervals, yellow lanterns hanging from trees gave off mournful light. A few hunched and solitary

---

[1] This is one of Prague's odd qualities: something in its atmosphere, perhaps caused by five centuries of gloomy sorcery, brings out the macabre potential of every object, no matter how mundane.

[2] See what I mean?

individuals could be seen wandering the gravel paths between the stones; the wind carried their sighs up to the window.

I drew the curtains smartly. "Yes. . . . Not exactly uplifting, I admit."

"Uplifting? This is the dreariest place I've ever been!"

"Well, what do you expect? You're British. Of course they'll put you in a lousy room with a view of a graveyard."

The boy was sitting at a heavy desk, inspecting some papers from a small brown packet. He spoke absently. "I should get the best room for exactly that reason."

"Are you kidding? After what Gladstone did to Prague? They don't forget, you know."

He looked up at this. "That was warfare. We won, fair and square. With minimum loss of civilian life."

I was Ptolemy at this point, standing by the curtains, arms folded, glowering at him in my turn. "You reckon?" I sneered. "Tell that to the people of the suburbs. There are still waste-lands out there, where the houses burned."

"Oh, you'd know, would you?"

"Of course I'd know! I was there, wasn't I? Fighting for the Czechs, I might add. Whereas everything *you've* learned was concocted by Gladstone's Ministry of Propaganda after the war. Don't lecture me about it, *boy*."

He looked, for a moment, as if he might erupt into one of his old furies. Then a switch seemed to go off inside him, and he instead became all cold and careless. He turned back to his papers, blank-faced, as if what I had said was of no account and even bored him. I would have preferred the anger, somehow.

"In London," he said, almost to himself, "the cemeteries are outside the city boundaries. Much more hygienic that way. We have special funeral trains to take the bodies out.

That's the modern method. This place is living in the past."

I said nothing. He didn't deserve the benefit of my wisdom.

For perhaps an hour, the boy studied his papers by the light of a low candle, making small notes in the margins. He ignored me; I ignored him, except to subtly send a breeze across the room to make the candle gutter over his work in an irritating manner. At half-past ten, he rang down to reception and, in perfect Czech, ordered a dish of grilled lamb and a carafe of wine to be delivered to his room. Then he put down his pen and turned to me, smoothing his hair back with his hand.

"Got it!" I said, from the depths of the four-poster, where I was taking my ease, "I know who you remind me of now. It's been bugging me since you summoned me last week. Lovelace! You fiddle with your hair just like he did. Can't leave it alone."

"I want to talk about the golems of Prague," he said.

"It's a vanity thing—must be. All that oil."

"You've seen golems in action. What kind of magician uses them?"

"I reckon it shows insecurity as well. A constant need to preen."

"Was it always Czech magicians who created them? Could a British one do it?"

"Gladstone *never* fiddled—with his hair or anything else. He was always very still."

The boy blinked; he showed interest for the first time. "You knew Gladstone?"

"*Knew*'s putting it a trifle strongly. I saw him from afar. He was usually present during battle, leaning on his Staff, watching his troops cause carnage; here in Prague, across Europe. . . . Like I say, he was very still; he observed everything, said little;

then, when it counted, every movement was decisive and considered. Nothing like your prattling mages of today."

"Really?" You could tell the boy was fascinated. No prizes for guessing who he modeled himself on. "So," he said, "you kind of admired him, in your poisonous, demonic sort of way?"

"No. Of course not. He was one of the worst. Church bells rang across occupied Europe when he died. You don't want to be like him, Nathaniel, take it from me. Besides"—I plumped up a dusty pillow—"you haven't got what it takes."

Oh, he bristled at that. "Why?"

"You're not nasty enough by a long way. Here's your supper."

A knock at the door heralded the arrival of a black-coated servant and an elderly maid, bearing assorted domed platters and chilled wine. The boy spoke courteously enough to them, asking a few questions about the layout of the streets nearby and tipping them for their trouble. For the duration of their visit, I was a mouse curled cozily between the pillows; I remained in this guise while my master scoffed his food. At last he clattered his fork down, took a last swig from his glass and stood up.

"Right," he said. "No time for talk. It's a quarter past eleven. We've got to go."

The hotel was on Kremencova, a short street on the edge of Prague Old Town, not far from the great river. We exited and wandered north along the lamp-lit roads, making our way slowly, steadily, in the direction of the ghetto.

Despite the ravages of war, despite the dissolution into which the city fell after its Emperor was killed and its power transferred to London, Prague still maintained something of its old mystique and grandeur. Even I, Bartimaeus, indifferent

BARTIMAEUS

as I normally am to the various human hellholes where I've been imprisoned, recognized its beauty: the pastel-colored houses, with their high, steep terra-cotta roofs, congregating thickly around the spires and bell towers of the endless churches, synagogues, and theaters; the great gray river winding past, spanned by a dozen bridges, each created to a different style by its own workforce of sweating djinn;[3] above it all, the castle of the Emperors, brooding wistfully on its hill.

The boy was silent as we went. Unsurprising, this—he had seldom left London in his life before. I guessed him to be gazing about in dumbstruck admiration.

"What an appalling place," he said. "Devereaux's slum-clearance measures would come in useful here."

I looked at him. "Do I take it the golden city does not meet with your approval?"

"Well . . . it's just so *messy*, isn't it?"

True, as you worm your way deeper into the Old Town, the streets become narrower and more labyrinthine, connected by a capillary system of snickelways and side courts, where the gable overhangs become so extreme that daylight barely hits the cobblestones below. Tourists probably find this warren charming; for me, with my slightly more soiled outlook, it perfectly embodies the hopeless muddle of all human endeavor. And for Nathaniel, the young British magician used to the broad, brutal Whitehall thoroughfares, it was all a bit too messy, a bit too out of control.

"Great magicians lived here," I reminded him.

---

[3] I was involved in constructing the Stone Bridge, the noblest of all, back in 1357. Nine of us performed the task, as required, in a single night, fixing the foundations with the usual sacrifice: the entombment of a djinni. We drew straws for the "honor" as dawn broke. Poor Humphrey is presumably there still, bored rigid, though we gave him a pack of cards with which to pass the time.

269

"That was then," he said, sourly. "This is now."

We passed the Stone Bridge, with its ramshackle old tower on the eastern side; bats were swirling about its protruding rafters, and flickering candlelight shone in the topmost windows. Even at this late hour, plenty of traffic was abroad: one or two old-fashioned cars, with high, narrow bonnets and cumbersome retracting roofs, passing slowly across the bridge; many men and women on horseback, too; others leading oxen, or driving two-wheeled carts full of vegetables or beer kegs. Most of the men wore soft black caps in the French style, fashions evidently having changed since my time here so many years before.

The boy made a disparaging face. "That reminds me. I'd better get this charade over with." He was carrying a small leather rucksack; into this he now delved, pulling out a large floppy cap. Further rummaging revealed a curled and rather crumpled feather. He held this up so it caught the lantern light.

"What color would you call that?" he said.

I considered. "I don't know. Red, I suppose."

"What kind of red? I want a description."

"Erm, brick red? Fiery red? Tomato red? Sunburn red? Could be any or all."

"Not blood-red, then?" He cursed. "I was so short of time—that was all I could get. Well, it'll have to do." He pushed the feather through the fabric of the cap and placed the ensemble on his head.

"What's this in aid of?" I asked. "I hope you're not trying to be dashing, because you look like an idiot."

"This is strictly business, I assure you. It's not my idea. Come on, it's almost midnight."

We turned away from the river now, heading into the heart of the Old Town, where the ghetto guarded Prague's deepest secrets.[4] The houses became smaller and more ramshackle, crowded in upon each other so tightly that some were doubtless held up only by the proximity of their neighbors. Our moods shifted in opposite directions as we went. My essence felt energized by the magic seeping from the old stones, by the memories of my exploits of the past. Nathaniel, conversely, seemed to become ever gloomier, muttering and grumbling under his outsize hat like a cantankerous old man.

"Any chance," I said, "of telling me exactly what we're doing?"

He looked at his watch. "Ten to midnight. I have to be in the old cemetery when the clocks start chiming." He tutted again. "*Another* cemetery! Can you believe it? How many *are* there in this place? Well, a spy will meet me there. He will know me by this cap; I will know him by his—and I quote—'unusual candle.'" He held up a hand. "Don't ask—I haven't got a clue. He may, perhaps, be able to point us in the direction of someone who knows something of golem lore."

"You think some Czech magician is causing the trouble in London?" I said. "That's not necessarily so, you know."

He nodded, or at least his head did something abrupt under his enormous cap. "Quite. An insider must have stolen the clay eye from the Lovelace collection: there's a traitor working somewhere. But the knowledge to use it must have come from Prague. No one in London's ever done it before. Perhaps our

---

[4] In Rudolf's time, when the Holy Roman Empire was at its height and six afrits patrolled the newly fashioned walls of Prague, the Jewish community here supplied the Emperor with most of his money and much of his magic. Forcibly restricted to the crowded alleys of the ghetto, and at once distrusted and relied on by the rest of Prague society, the Jewish magicians grew powerful for a time. Since pogroms and slander against their people were commonplace, their magic was largely defensive in outlook—as exemplified by the great magician Loew, who created the first golem to protect the Jews against attack by human and djinni alike.

spy can help us." He sighed. "I doubt it, though. Anyone who calls himself Harlequin is obviously pretty far gone already."

"No more deluded than the rest of you, with your silly fake names, Mr. *Mandrake*. And what am I to do, while you meet this gentleman?"

"Keep hidden and keep watch. We're in enemy territory, and I'm not going to trust Harlequin or anyone else. All right, this must be the cemetery. You'd better change."

We had arrived at a cobbled yard, surrounded on all sides by buildings with small, black windows. Before us was a flight of steps, leading up to an open metal gate, set in a tumbledown railing. Beyond rose a dark and toothy mass—the uppermost headstones of Prague's old cemetery.

This graveyard was little more than fifty meters square, by far the smallest in the city. Yet it had been used for many centuries, over and over, and this contributed to its distinctive flavor. In fact, the sheer weight of burials in this restricted space had led to bodies being interred one on top of another, time and again, until the surface of the cemetery had risen six feet higher than the surrounding yard. The headstones were packed in likewise, with large ones overhanging small, small half-buried in the ground. With its higgledy-piggledy disregard for clarity and order, the cemetery was exactly the kind of place calculated to unsettle Nathaniel's tidy mind.[5]

"Well, get on with it, then," he said. "I'm waiting."

"Oh, that's what you're doing, is it? I couldn't tell under that hat."

"Turn yourself into a loathsome snake or plague rat, or

---

[5] Actually, it made me shiver a little, too, but for different reasons. Earth was very strong here—its power extended upward into the air, leaching my energies away. Djinn were not welcome; it was a private place, working to a different magic.

whatever foul creature of the night you desire. I'm going in. Get ready to protect me if necessary."

"Nothing will give me greater pleasure."

I chose to be a long-eared bat this time, leather-winged, tufted of head. It's a flexible guise, I find—fast-moving, quiet, and very much in keeping with the tone of midnight graveyards. I flittered off into the clotted wilderness of jumbled stones. As an initial precaution, I made a sweep of the seven planes: they were clear enough, though so steeped in magic that each one vibrated gently with the memories of past deeds. I noticed no traps or sensors, though a few protective hexes on buildings nearby implied that magicians of a sort still dwelled here.[6] There was no one about; at this late hour, the graveyard's tangle of narrow paths was empty, swathed in black shadow. Rusty lamps nailed to the railings emitted half-hearted light. I found an overhanging headstone and hung elegantly from it, tucked inside my wings. I surveyed the main path into the cemetery.

Nathaniel stepped through the gate, his shoes crunching gently on the path. Even as he did so, the dozen clocks of the churches of Prague began to chime, marking the beginning of the secret, midnight hour.[7] The boy gave an audible sigh,

---

[6] They were weak defenses. An armless imp could have pried his way through. As a center of magic, Prague was a century into a steep decline.

[7] For complex reasons possibly connected with astronomy and the angle of Earth's orbit, it is at the twin points of midnight and noon that the seven planes draw closest together, allowing sensitive humans glimpses of activity that would normally be invisible to them. At these times, therefore, there is the most talk of ghosts, specters, black dogs, doppelgängers, and other revenants—which are generally imps or foliots doing errands in one guise or another. Because night particularly stimulates human imagination (such as it is), people pay less attention to apparitions at noon, but they're still present: flickering figures glimpsed in heat haze; passersby who on inspection lack a shadow; pale faces in the midst of crowds, which, when you look directly, are nowhere to be seen.

shook his head disgustedly, and began to stroll tentatively along the path, one hand outstretched, feeling his way between the stones. An owl hooted close by, possibly as a harbinger of violent death, possibly commenting on the ridiculous scale of my master's hat. The blood-red feather waved to and fro behind his head, glimmering faintly in the meager light.

Nathaniel paced. The bat hung motionless. Time passed as slowly as it always does when you're hanging out in cemeteries. Once only was there movement in the street below the railing: a strange four-legged, two-armed creature with a kind of double head came shuffling out of the night. My master caught sight of it and halted in doubt. It passed beneath a lantern, to be revealed as a courting couple, heads resting together, arms entwined. They kissed assiduously, giggled a bit, moved off along the road. My master watched them go with an odd expression on his face. I think he was trying to look contemptuous.

From then on, his pacing, never particularly energetic, became distinctly half-hearted. He scuffed along, kicking unseen pebbles, and wrapping his long black coat about him in a hunched, uncaring sort of way. His mind did not seem to be on the job. Deciding he needed a pep talk, I fluttered over and hovered by a headstone.

"Perk it up," I said, "you're looking a bit lackluster. You'll put this Harlequin bloke off if you're not careful. Imagine you're on a romantic assignation with some pretty, young girl magician."

I couldn't swear to it—it was dark and all—but I think he might have blushed. Interesting. . . . Perhaps this was fertile ground to furrow, in due time.

"This is *hopeless*," he whispered. "It's nearly half-past twelve. If he was going to show, we'd have seen something by now. I think . . . are you listening to me?"

"No." The bat's keen ears had picked up a scrabbling noise from way off across the graveyard. I rose a little higher, peered out into the dark. "This might be him. Feather at the ready, Romeo."

I banked and swooped low among the stones, taking a circular course to avoid direct collision with whatever it was that was coming our way.

For his part, the boy adopted a more upright pose; with his hat at a rakish angle, hands casually behind his back, he dawdled along the path as if in deep, profound thought. He gave no sign that he noticed the increasingly persistent scuffling sounds, or the strange pale light that now approached him from among the gravestones.

24

From the corner of his eye, Nathaniel saw the bat flitter away toward an age-old yew tree, which had somehow managed to survive centuries of burials in one corner of the cemetery. A particularly desiccated branch offered a good view of the path. The bat alighted under it and hung still.

Nathaniel took a deep breath, adjusted his hat, and strolled forward as nonchalantly as he could. All the while, his eyes were fixed on something moving in the depths of the cemetery. Despite the profound skepticism he felt for the whole farrago, the dankness and solitude of this lonely place had infected his spirits. Against his wishes, he found his heart thudding painfully against his chest.

What was it that he saw before him? A pale corpse light drifting nearer, a greenish milky white in color, staining the stones it passed with an unhealthy radiance. Behind it came a moving shadow, hunched and shambling, weaving ever nearer through the stones.

Nathaniel narrowed his eyes: on none of the three observable planes could he see any demonic activity. This thing, presumably, was human.

At last, the crunch of gravel indicated that the shadow had stepped out upon the path. It did not stop, but came smoothly onward, a ragged cloak or cape drifting drearily behind. As it drew close, Nathaniel noticed a pair of unpleasantly white hands protruding from the front of the cape, holding something that let off the feeble witch light. He tried hard to make out a face, too, but this was concealed by a heavy black hood that curved down like an eagle's talon. Nothing else of the figure could be seen. He turned his attention to the object held in the pale hands, the thing that shed the strange, white glow. It was a candle, firmly wedged into . . .

"Euuch!" he said, in Czech. "That's disgusting."

The figure stopped short. A high, thin voice sounded indignantly from under the cowl. "'Ere, what d'you mean?" It coughed hastily; a deeper, slower, altogether more eerie voice emerged at once: "That is to say— What . . . do you mean?"

Nathaniel curled his lip. "That horrible thing you're carrying. It's foul."

"Beware! It is an item of power."

"It's unhygienic, that's what it is. Where did you get it?"

"I cut it down from a gallows myself, by the light of a gibbous moon."

"I bet it isn't even pickled. Yes! Look—there's bits falling off it!"

"No, there aren't. That's drips of candlewax."

"Well, maybe, but it's still wrong to be carrying it around with you. I suggest you toss it behind those gravestones, then wash your hands."

"Do you realize," said the figure, who now had one fist wedged irritably against his hip, "that you are referring to an object that has the power to send my enemies into a stupor and can detect watchful magic at fifty paces? This is a valuable item. I'm not binning it."

Nathaniel shook his head. "You ought to be locked up. That kind of behavior wouldn't be tolerated in London, I can tell you."

The figure gave a sudden start. "London? What's that to me?"

"Well, you're Harlequin, aren't you? The agent."

A long pause. "Might be."

"Of course you are. Who else would be wandering through the graveyard at this time of night? I don't need to see that icky candle thing to know it's you, do I? Besides, you're speaking Czech with a British accent. Enough of this! I need some information fast."

The figure held up its free hand. "One moment! I don't yet know who *you* are."

"I'm John Mandrake, on government service. As you well know."

"That's not good enough. I must have proof."

Nathaniel rolled his eyes. "See that?" He pointed upward. "Blood-red feather."

The figure considered it. "That looks brick-red to me."

"It's *blood*-red. Or it will be in a minute if you don't stop this nonsense and get down to business."

"Well . . . all right, then. But first . . ." The figure adopted an eerie stance. "I must check that no watchers are among us. Stand back!" It held up the object in its hand, spoke a word. Instantly, the pale fire flared outward, becoming a luminous hoop of light that hovered in the air between them. On another command, and with a sudden rushing, the hoop expanded, rippling out in all directions across the graveyard. Nathaniel glimpsed the bat drop like a stone from its perch upon the tree, just before the band of light passed by. What happened to the bat he did not see; the hoop continued out beyond the edge of the graveyard and swiftly faded into nothing.

The figure nodded. "It is safe to talk."

Nathaniel pointed to the candle, which had resumed its previous dimensions. "I know that trick. That's an Illuminated Circlet, triggered by an imp. You don't need a dead man's extremities to pull that off. This gothic stuff is all jiggery-pokery, suitable for gawping commoners. It won't work on me, Harlequin."

"Perhaps . . ." A gaunt hand disappeared inside the cowl and scratched something ruminatively. "Even so, I think you're being overly fastidious, Mandrake. You're ignoring the fundamental basis of our magic. It isn't so clean and pure as you make out. Blood, ritual, sacrifice, death . . . they are at the heart of every incantation we utter. We all rely on 'gothic stuff,' when all's said and done."

"Here in Prague, maybe," Nathaniel said.

"Never forget, London's power was built on Prague's. So then . . ." Harlequin's voice turned suddenly businesslike. "The imp that reached me said you were here on a top secret mission. What is it, and what information do you want from me?"

Nathaniel spoke quickly and with some relief, outlining the main events of the previous few days. The man under the hood heard him out in silence.

"A golem abroad in London?" he said, when Nathaniel drew to a halt. "Wonders *will* never cease. There's your gothic stuff coming home to roost, whether you like it or not. Interesting . . ."

"Interesting *and* intelligible?" Nathaniel asked, hopefully.

"I don't know about that. But I may have some details for you—quick! Duck down!" With the speed of a snake, he threw himself to the ground; without hesitation, Nathaniel did likewise. He lay with his face pressed against the graveyard soil, listening to the sound of jackboots echoing on the cobblestones outside. A faint scent of cigarette smoke drifted on the wind. The sounds faded. After another minute or so, the agent got slowly to his feet. "Patrol," he said. "Fortunately, their sense of smell is deadened by those fags they smoke; we're all right for now."

"You were saying . . ." Nathaniel prompted.

"Yes. First, the issue of the golem's eye. Several of these objects are kept in magical repositories belonging to the Czech government. The Prague Council prevents any access to them. As far as I know, they have not been used for magical purposes, but they are of high symbolic value, since the golems were instrumental in causing great damage to Gladstone's army back in his first European campaign. Several years ago, one of the eyes was stolen, and the culprit never found. I speculate—and it is only speculation, mark you—that this missing eye is the one later found in the collection of your friend Simon Lovelace."

"Pardon me," Nathaniel said, stiffly, "but he was not my friend."

"Well, he's nobody's friend *now*, is he? Because he failed. If he'd won, you'd all have been hanging on his every word and inviting him to dinner." The agent gave a long, melancholy sniff of disparagement from somewhere within the hood. "Hang on to this a minute, I need a drink."

"Euuch! It's all cold and clammy. Hurry up!"

"Coming." Harlequin's hands were rummaging within his cloak in a complex sort of way. A moment later, they emerged, holding a dark green bottle with a cork stopper. He pulled out the cork and tilted the bottle into the depths of his cowl. A gulping noise ensued, followed by the smell of strong liquor.

"*That's* better." Unseen lips smacked, cork returned to bottle, and bottle returned to pocket. "I'll take that back. You didn't damage it, did you? It *is* a bit fragile. Now," Harlequin went on, "perhaps Lovelace intended to use the eye himself; if so, his plan was thwarted by his death. Someone else, maybe an associate of his—who knows?—has now stolen it from our government, and appears to have got the thing to work.... This is where it gets difficult."

"They need the formative spell, too," Nathaniel said. "It is written on a parchment and inserted into the golem's mouth before it comes to life. That's the bit that nobody's known for all these years. No one in London, anyway."

The agent nodded. "The secret *may* have been lost; equally, it may still be known in Prague, but just remain unused. The Council does not want to enrage London at present; the British are too strong. They prefer to send spies and small groups over to London to work quietly, gathering information. This golem of yours . . . it's too dramatic a move for the Czechs—they would expect invasion to follow as a direct result. No, I think you are hunting for a maverick, someone working for their own individual ends."

"So where do I look?" Nathaniel asked. He couldn't help yawning as he spoke; he had been awake since the British Museum incident the previous night. It had been a taxing day.

"I must consider . . ." The agent remained lost in thought for a few moments. "I need time to make inquiries. We will meet again tomorrow night, when I will give you names." He wrapped his cloak about himself with a dramatic sweep. "Meet me—"

Nathaniel interrupted him. "I hope you're not going to say 'in the shadow of the gibbet' or 'at Execution Dock' or anything dreary like that."

The figure drew itself up. "Ridiculous. The very idea."

"Good."

"I was going to suggest the old plague pits on Hybernska Street."

"*No.*"

The agent seemed rather miffed. "All right," he growled.

"Six o'clock at the hot–dog stand in the Old Town Square. That mundane enough for you?"

"That'll do nicely."

"Until then, then . . ." With a billow of the cloak and a creak of hidden knees, the figure turned and swept its way up the cemetery path, its corpse light flickering dimly into the distance. Soon the light was gone, and nothing but a fleeting shadow and a muffled curse when it knocked into a gravestone indicated it had ever been.

Nathaniel sat down on a headstone, waiting for Bartimaeus to show. The meeting had been satisfactory, if a little irritating; now he had plenty of time to rest before the following evening. His weary mind drifted. The memory of Jane Farrar came back to him. How pleasant it had been to have her so close. . . . It had affected him almost like a drug. He frowned— of *course* it was like a drug. She'd worked a Charm on him, hadn't she? And he'd nearly fallen for it, completely ignoring his sensor's warning. What a *fool* he was.

The girl had either wanted to delay him, or learn more about what he knew. Either way, she would be working for her master, Duvall, who evidently did not want Internal Affairs having any sort of success in this matter. When he got back, he would doubtless face more hostility of the same kind. Duvall, Tallow, Farrar . . . Even his master, Ms. Whitwell, was not to be relied on, if he didn't produce the goods for her.

Nathaniel rubbed his eyes. He suddenly felt very tired.

"*Bless*, you look ready to drop." The djinni was sitting on an opposite gravestone, in its familiar boy guise. It was crossing its legs in identical fashion to Nathaniel, and pulling an extravagant yawn. "You should have been tucked up *hours* ago."

"Did you hear everything?"

"Most of it. I missed a bit after he let loose that Circlet. It nearly hit me, and I had to take evasive action. Good job those tree roots had dislodged a few gravestones. I was able to drop into an underground cavity while the probe passed over." The boy paused to shake a bit of gray dust out of its hair. "Not that I generally recommend graves as a place to hide. You never know what you might find. But the occupant of this particular one was quite hospitable. Let me cuddle up to him for a few moments." It gave a knowing wink.

Nathaniel shuddered. "How perfectly foul."

"Speaking of which," the djinni said. "That candle the bloke was carrying. Was it really . . . ?"

"Yes. I'm trying not to think about it. Harlequin is more than half-mad, which is no doubt what comes of living in Prague too long." Nathaniel stood and buttoned up his coat. "But he does have his uses. He's hoping to give us some contact names tomorrow night."

"Good," the boy said, busily buttoning its coat in a similar fashion. "Then perhaps we'll have a bit of action. My recipe for informers is either to roast them over a slow flame or hang them by a leg out of a high window. That usually makes a Czech spill the beans."

"There'll be none of that if we can possibly avoid it." Nathaniel began to walk down the path out of the graveyard. "The authorities mustn't know we're here, so we can't draw attention to ourselves. That means no violence or obvious magic. Got that?"

"Of *course*." The djinni smiled broadly as it fell in step beside him. "You know me."

25

At 9:25 on the morning of the great raid, Kitty was heading down a backstreet in London's West End. She went quickly, almost jogging; the bus had been held up by traffic on Westminster Bridge, and she was running late. A small rucksack bounced on her back; her hair streamed behind her as she went.

At precisely 9:30, disheveled and a little out of breath, Kitty arrived at the Stage Door of the Coliseum Theatre, pushed gently, and found it unlocked. She took a quick look behind her at the rubbish-strewn street, saw nothing, slipped inside.

A drab and dirty corridor was filled with buckets and obscure wooden constructions presumably destined for the stage. A little light filtered through a grubby window; there was a strong smell of paint in the stale air.

Ahead was another door. Obeying her memorized instructions, Kitty soundlessly crossed to it and passed through into a second room, this one filled with quiet racks of costumes. The staleness of the air increased. Someone's bygone lunch—pieces of sandwich and potato chips, and half-filled cups of coffee—lay scattered on a table. Kitty entered a third room and found a sudden change: beneath her feet was a thick carpet and the walls were papered. The air now smelled distantly of smoke and polish. She was near the front of the theater, in the public corridors.

She paused and listened. In all the empty building, not a sound.

Yet somewhere above, someone was waiting.

* * *

She had received her instructions that morning, in an atmosphere of fevered preparation. Mr. Pennyfeather had closed the shop for the day and had retired to the cellar storeroom to begin sorting their equipment for the raid. Everyone else was busy, too, assembling dark clothes, polishing tools and, in Fred's case, practicing knife-throwing in the privacy of the cellar. Mr. Hopkins had given Kitty directions to the Coliseum. The mysterious benefactor, he said, had chosen the disused theater as a suitably neutral venue, a place where magician and commoner might meet on equal terms. There she would be given the assistance they required to break into Gladstone's tomb.

Despite certain misgivings about the whole enterprise, Kitty could not help thrilling to the name. *Gladstone*. Stories of his splendor were legion. Friend to the People, Terror of their Enemies . . . To desecrate his tomb was an act so unthinkable her mind scarcely comprehended it. And yet, if they succeeded, if they returned home with the Founder's treasures, what wonders the Resistance might yet accomplish.

If they should fail, Kitty was under no illusion about the consequences. The company was crumbling. Pennyfeather was old: despite his passion, despite his fury, his strength was dwindling. Without his stern guidance, the group would splinter—they would all return to their humdrum lives beneath the magicians' heels. But if they had the crystal ball and the magic purse, what then? Perhaps their fortunes might be turned around and new blood won to fight their cause. It made her heart pound to think of it.

But first, she had to meet the unknown benefactor and win his aid.

*   *   *

Kitty passed a number of half-open doors along the corridor; through them she could see the shrouded reaches of the theater's auditorium. It was very still, every sound muffled by the heavy carpet and the elegant furred paper on the walls. The carpet was a wine-dark red, the wallpaper striped with pink and terra-cotta. Fading theatrical posters and chipped brass candelabras, which emitted a weak, flickering light, were the only decoration. Kitty walked swiftly until she reached the stairs.

Up a long, curving flight of shallow steps, then—doubling almost back upon herself—up a second flight, along a silent corridor and so to the place where six curtained alcoves waited along the left-hand side. Each was the entrance to one of the boxes used by the magicians, overlooking the stage.

Each alcove had a number inscribed on a brass plaque above the curtain. Without pausing, Kitty made her way to the last alcove in the line. This was number 7; the place where the benefactor would be waiting.

As with all the others, the curtain was fully drawn. Kitty stopped outside, listened, heard nothing. A wisp of hair had fallen down over her face. She smoothed it back and, for luck, touched the silver pendant in her pocket. Then she grasped the curtain firmly and stepped through.

The box was empty except for two heavy golden chairs facing the stage. A curtain had been drawn across from the left, shielding the box from the auditorium below. Kitty frowned in perplexity and frustration. Had she mistaken the number, or come at the wrong time? No. More likely, the benefactor had gotten cold feet and hadn't shown up.

A small piece of paper was pinned to the arm of one of the chairs. Kitty stepped over to pull it loose. As she did so, she became aware of a slight shift in the air, the faintest of noises behind her. Her hand jerked to her coat. A small, sharp pressure was applied to the back of her neck. She froze.

A voice, quiet and reflective. "Please do not attempt to turn around at any time, my dear. The pinprick you feel is the tip of a stiletto, forged in Rome for the Borgias. Sharpness is not its only quality—a finger's width up the blade is a bead of poison; should this touch your wound, death will follow in thirteen seconds. I mention this simply so that we observe the proper niceties. Without turning, please take hold of the chair, and align it facing the wall. . . . Good. Now sit. I shall sit close behind you, then we shall talk."

Kitty dragged the chair to face the wall, moved slowly around, and sat gingerly upon it, feeling all the while the little sharpness on her neck. She heard a rustle of cloth, the squeak of leather shoes, a soft sigh as someone sat and took his ease. She looked at the wall and said nothing.

The voice came again. "Good. Now we are ready and I hope we can do business. You understand that the precautions I take here are merely safeguards? I do not wish you harm."

Kitty remained looking at the wall. "Nor we you," she said levelly. "Nevertheless, we have taken precautions, too."

The voice grunted. "Which are?"

"A colleague of mine waits outside the theater. She carries a small leather bag. Within it are six small demons trapped in an explosive gel. It is, I believe, an effective weapon of war and can level a whole building. We stole it recently from a Ministry of Defense storehouse. I mention this to impress you: we are capable of remarkable acts. But also because, if I do not return within fifteen minutes, my friend will activate the imps and toss them into the theater." Kitty's face was expressionless. This was a complete lie.

A chuckle. "Nicely put, my dear. Well then, we must hurry. As Mr. Hopkins no doubt told you, I am a gentleman of leisure with many contacts among the magicians; I have even dabbled in the art myself upon occasion. However, like you I am sick of their rule!" A note of anger entered the voice. "Owing to a small financial disagreement, the government has robbed me of my wealth and my estates! I am now a pauper, where once I slept on Tashkent silks! It is an intolerable situation. *Nothing* would give me greater pleasure than to see the magicians fall. That is why I will help your cause."

These remarks had been spoken with great emotion; at each emphasis, the stiletto point jabbed the back of Kitty's neck. She moistened her lips. "Mr. Hopkins said you had valuable information for us."

"I do indeed. You must understand, I have no sympathy for the commoners whose cause you serve. But your activities unsettle the great ones of the government, and that pleases me. So, to business. Hopkins has explained the nature of the proposition?" Kitty nodded carefully. "Well now, through my connections, I have had access to Gladstone's papers and have made some small study of them. By deciphering certain codes, I discovered details of the Pestilence he left guarding his remains."

"That seems a meager defense, for one of his power," Kitty said. "If I may say so."

"You are an intelligent, opinionated girl," the voice said approvingly. "When he died, Gladstone was old and weak, a spindly husk, capable of nothing more than that simple spell. Even so, it has done its job. No one has disturbed it, for fear of being raddled by the Pestilence. However, it can be bypassed, if you bring proper precautions. I can give you that information."

"Why should we trust you?" Kitty said. "I don't understand. What's in this for you?"

The voice did not seem to resent the questions. "If I wished to destroy your group," it said peaceably, "you would have been in police custody the moment you poked your head through this curtain. Besides, I have already told you that I wish to see the magicians fall. But you are right, of course. There *is* something else in it for me. When I scoured Gladstone's archive, I discovered the list of his grave goods. It contains objects to interest both you and me."

Kitty shifted a little in the broad gold chair. "It will take me at least two minutes to leave the building," she said. "I assure you, my friend is very punctual."

"I will be brief. Mr. Hopkins will have told you of the wonders the crypt contains—you may have them, magical weapons and all. I do not need them; I am a man of peace. But I *do* collect unusual objects, and I would be grateful to have Gladstone's cloak, which was folded and placed upon his sarcophagus. It has no magical properties, so it is of no use to you. Oh, and if his oaken staff has survived, I would like that, too. It is of negligible magical value—I believe he charged it with a small hex for keeping away insects—but I would be pleased to see it in my humble collection."

"If we get the other treasures," Kitty said, "we will be glad to give those to you."

"Very well, we have an agreement. We will both prosper by it. Here is the equipment you need." With a slight rustling, a small black bag was pushed along the carpet into view. "Do not touch it yet. The bag contains a casket and hammer. These will protect you from the Pestilence. Full instructions are included. Obey them, and you will live. Listen carefully," the voice continued. "Tonight, at eleven-thirty, the curators of the abbey will depart. Go to the cloisters door: I will arrange for it to be left open. A second door bars the way to the abbey itself; ordinarily it is secured by two medieval deadlocks and a drawbar. I will leave this unlocked, too. Find your way to the north transept and locate Gladstone's statue. Behind it, set in a pillar, is the entrance to the tomb. To gain entry, you merely have to turn the key."

Kitty stirred. "The key?"

Something small and glinting fell through the air to land beside the bag. "Guard it well," the voice said, "and *do* remember to cloak yourself in my magic before opening the tomb, or all this tiresome subterfuge will have been for nothing."

"We'll remember," Kitty said.

"Good." She heard the sound of someone rising from the chair. The voice spoke above her, close behind. "Then that is all. I wish you well. Do not turn around."

The sharp sensation in the back of her neck lessened, but so softly, so stealthily, that Kitty at first was hardly able to detect that it had gone. She waited a full minute, motionless, eyes wide and staring in her head.

Finally, she lost patience.

She turned in a single fluid motion, her knife already in her hand.

The box was empty. And when she ducked out into the silent corridor, key and bag safely in her grasp, she saw no trace of anyone in the vicinity.

26

At some time in the distant past, long before the first magicians arrived in London, the great church of Westminster Abbey had exerted considerable power and influence on the surrounding town. Built over centuries by a dynasty of forgotten kings, the abbey and its grounds extended over a wide area, with a population of scholarly monks conducting its services, studying in its library, and working in its fields. The main church rose more than a hundred feet into the air, with snub-nosed towers rising at the west end and at the center of the building, high above the sanctuary. The building was constructed of a strong white stone, which gradually became discolored with the smoke and magical effusions emanating from the growing city.

Years passed; the kings fell from power, to be replaced by a succession of parliaments, which met at Westminster Hall, not far from the abbey. The influence of the church slowly reduced, as did the waistlines of the surviving monks, who now fell on hard times. Many of the abbey outbuildings deteriorated, and only the cloisters—four broad, enclosed walkways around a central open square of grass—remained in good condition. When Parliament was itself taken over by a new authority—a group of powerful magicians, who had little time for the traditions of the Church—it seemed as if the ancient abbey itself might soon fall into ruin.

But one tradition saved the building. The greatest leaders of the country, whether kings or parliamentary ministers, had long been buried in the abbey crypts. Countless tombs and memorials already clustered among the pillars of the nave, while the ground below was honeycombed with crypts and sepulchres. The magicians, who courted eternal renown as much as any king before them, decided to continue this practice; it became a matter of great honor for any individual to be interred within the church.

The remaining monks were cast out, a small clergy installed to conduct occasional services, and the abbey survived into the modern age as little more than a gigantic tomb. Few commoners went there by day, and by night, even its perimeter was shunned. It had an unhealthy reputation.

Security on the building was, therefore, comparatively weak. There was really no likelihood of the company meeting any kind of guard, when, at 11:30 precisely, the first of them arrived at the unlocked door of the cloisters outhouse, and noiselessly slipped inside.

Kitty had wanted to visit the abbey during its opening hours to do a proper reconnaissance and to view the exterior of Gladstone's tomb. But Mr. Pennyfeather had forbidden her. "We must arouse no suspicions," he said.

In fact, Kitty need not have worried. Mr. Hopkins had been his normal useful self during the course of that long and nervous day, rustling up numerous maps of the abbey and its environs. He showed them the layout of the transept, below which most of the tombs were hidden; he showed them the covered cloisters, where once the monks had sat to read or, in bad weather, taken their constitutionals. He showed them the surrounding roads, highlighting guardhouses of the Night Police and known routes of the vigilance spheres. He pointed out the doors that would be unlocked, and suggested, in case of random patrols, that they assemble at the abbey one by one. It was all very well organized by Mr. Hopkins.

"I only wish I had resilience like you," he said sadly. "Then I could take part in the mission myself."

Mr. Pennyfeather was supervising Stanley, who was laboring under a box of weapons taken from the cellar. "Now, now, Clem," he cried. "You have done your part! Leave the rest to us. We are the professionals at theft and stealth."

"Pardon me, sir," Kitty said. "Are you coming, too?"

The old man's face mottled with fury. "Of course! This will be the crowning moment of my life! How dare you suggest otherwise? You think I am too weak?"

"No, no, sir. Of course not." Kitty bent to the abbey maps again.

A great expectancy and unease had stolen across the company that day; all of them, even the normally equable Anne, were tetchy and highly strung. During the morning, the equipment was doled out, and each person prepared their kit in silence. When Kitty returned with the benefactor's gifts, Mr. Pennyfeather and Mr. Hopkins retired to the backroom of the shop to study the instructions. The others prowled among the paints and easels, saying little. Anne prepared sandwiches for lunch.

That afternoon, Kitty, Fred, Stanley, and Nick walked to the cellar to practice their skills. Fred and Stanley took turns throwing discs at a pitted beam, while Nick engaged Kitty in a mock knife fight. When they returned, they found Mr. Hopkins and Mr. Pennyfeather still locked in consultation. At 5:30, in a brittle atmosphere, Anne brought in trays of tea and almond biscuits. An hour later, Mr. Pennyfeather emerged from the backroom. With great deliberation, he poured lukewarm tea into a cup.

"We have deciphered the instructions," he said. "Now we are truly ready." He raised the cup in a solemn toast. "To whatever tonight may bring! We have righteousness on our side. Be confident and keen, my friends. If we are bold and do not falter, our lives will never be the same again!"

He drank, clicked his cup back decisively on its saucer.

The final discussions began.

Kitty was the second of the company to enter the abbey outhouse. Anne had preceded her less than a minute before. She stared into the darkness, hearing Anne's breathing close by. "Shall we risk a light?" she whispered.

"Pencil torch," Anne said. "I've got it."

A thin beam lit the wall opposite, then, briefly, Kitty's face. Kitty blinked and raised a hand. "Keep it low," she said. "We don't know about windows."

Crouching down to the flagstoned floor, Anne swung the torch about her speculatively, casting fleeting light upon piles of paint pots, spades, garden forks, a shiny new lawn mower, and sundry other tools. Kitty shifted her rucksack from her back, plunked it down before her and checked her watch. "Next one's due," she said.

As if in answer, a faint scrabbling sounded somewhere outside, beyond the door. Anne turned off the torch. They crouched in darkness.

The door was opened and closed, accompanied by the sound of heavy breathing. Air drifted briefly through the room, bringing with it a powerful waft of aftershave.

Kitty relaxed. "Hello, Fred," she said.

At five-minute intervals, the remainder of the company arrived. Last to appear was Mr. Pennyfeather himself, already weary and out of breath. He gave a wheezed command: "Frederick Stanley! Lanterns . . . on! There are—there are . . . no windows in this room. We have nothing to be afraid of."

In the light of two powerful lanterns, the six of them stood revealed: all carrying rucksacks, all wearing black. Mr. Pennyfeather had even painted his stick black, and had muffled its tip with a plug of fabric. He leaned on it now, scanning the party one by one with slow deliberation, gathering his resources. "Very well," he said, at last. "Anne—headgear, please."

Dark woolen balaclavas were produced and distributed. Fred eyed his distrustfully. "I don't like these things," he growled. "They scratch."

Mr. Pennyfeather clicked his tongue impatiently. "Blackheads alone will not be sufficient tonight, Frederick. It is too important. Put it on. Right—final check. Then cloisters. So, Nicholas—you have the casket with the Hermetic Mantle?"

"I do."

"And the hammer with which to strike it?"

"That, too."

"Frederick—you have the jimmy? Good. And your useful array of knives? Excellent. Stanley—rope and compass? Kitty—sticking plaster, bandages, and ointment? Good, and I have the key to the tomb. As for weapons—we should all have at least one mouler glass and an Elemental Sphere of some description. Very well."

He took a moment to regain his breath. "A couple of things," he added, "before we go through. The weapons are to be used only as a last resort, if we are disturbed. Otherwise, we must be subtle. Unseen. If the door to the abbey is locked, we retreat. In the tomb itself, we locate the treasures; I will divide them out among you. Fill your bags and return the way we came. We will meet back in this room. If anything should go wrong, at the first opportunity make your way to our cellar. Avoid the shop. If, for any reason, I am a casualty, Mr. Hopkins can advise you further. He will wait at Druid's Coffeehouse tomorrow afternoon. Any questions? No? Nicholas—if you would . . ."

At the end of the outhouse was a second door. Nick passed to it silently and pushed. It swung open; beyond was the ink-blue darkness of the open air.

"We go," Mr. Pennyfeather said.

This was the order they went in: Nick, followed by Kitty, then Fred, Anne, Stanley, and Mr. Pennyfeather bringing up the rear.

With the silence of bats they flitted through the cloisters, flecks of moving graininess against the wall of black. Faint slabs of a lighter shade marked out the arched windows to their right, but the inner court of the cloisters was invisible to them. There was no moon to show the way. Their sneakered feet scuffed the stone slabs with the gentle rustling of dead leaves nudged by the wind. Mr. Pennyfeather's stick, muffled at its padded tip, tapped along behind. Up ahead, Nick's covered lantern swung silently from its long chain, weaving its illumination close to the ground like a will-o'-the-wisp; he carried it low, below the level of the windowsills, for fear of watching eyes.

Kitty counted the arches as she went. After the eighth gray slab, the guide light darted to the right, around the corner of the cloisters. She ducked around, too, and continued on without breaking stride, counting the arches again. One, two . . . The weight of her rucksack pressed against her back; she heard its contents shifting. She devoutly hoped the spheres were properly protected in their wrapping cloth. Four, five . . . Automatically, she ran through the position of her other weapons: a knife in her belt, a throwing disc in her jacket. These gave her a much greater feeling of security than any magical weapon: they weren't tainted with the touch of demons.

Six, seven . . . They were at the end of the northern side of the cloisters. The guide light jerked and slowed. Kitty nearly ran up against Nick's back, but stopped herself in time. Behind, the rustling of feet continued for a moment, then ceased.

She sensed Nick turn his head. His voice carried in a half-whisper: "Nave door. Now we'll see."

He raised the lantern, sweeping it in front of him for an instant. Kitty glimpsed the black surface of an ancient door, heavily pitted and studded with giant nails, their shadows leaping and rotating as the illumination passed. The light was lowered. Darkness, silence, a faint scrabbling. Kitty waited, fingers brushing against the pendant in her pocket. She imagined Nick's fingers running across the dark grain and the imbedded nails, searching for the giant metal latch. She heard a slight scuffle, and the sounds of sustained and suppressed exertion—little gasps and curses from Nick, the rustling of his jacket. He was evidently in difficulties.

"Come *on*." A soft clink; dim light spread across the flagstones. Nick had lowered the lantern to the floor and was wrestling two-handed with the latch. Close behind, almost directly in her ear, Kitty heard Fred let out a muttered imprecation. She realized that in her tension, she was clamping her teeth together so hard that her jaw ached. Was the benefactor wrong? Was the door still locked? If so, they were stymied good and proper. It was their only way in and the door could not be destroyed. They couldn't risk any kind of explosion.

Something brushed past her; from the scent, she knew it to be Fred.

"Let me. Shift over . . ." More rustling as Nick stood aside, a short burst of scrabbling, then a grunt from Fred. A loud crack and thud followed instantly, together with a squeal of rusted hinges. Fred's voice held a note of satisfaction. "I thought there was a problem. That wasn't even stiff."

He returned to his position in the line; without further words, the company passed through the door and closed it behind them. With that, they were in the nave of Westminster Abbey.

Nick adjusted the cover on his lantern, restricting it to the smallest of circular glows. They waited a few moments, allowing their eyes to adjust. The church was not entirely dark: gradually Kitty began to glimpse the ghostly shadows of great arched windows opposite them, running along the north wall of the nave. Their outlines grew stronger, lit from outside by distant lights, including passing cars. Strange figures were depicted on the window glass—but the light was not strong enough to see them clearly. No sound came from the roads beyond; she felt as if she were enclosed in a giant cocoon.

Close beside her, Kitty made out a stone column, its upper regions lost in the arching shadows. Other pillars rose at intervals along the nave, surrounded near their bases by hulking patches of black, oddly proportioned and very numerous. The look of them gave her an aching feeling in her gut: they were all memorials and tombs.

A subdued tapping suggested Mr. Pennyfeather was moving on. His words, though whispered from beneath his balaclava, awoke a host of echoes that drifted sighing back and forth among the stones. "Quickly, then. Follow me."

Across the open body of the nave, under the hidden roof, following the glowing light. Mr. Pennyfeather went first, as fast as he was able, the others crowding at his heels. Stanley dawdled to the left. As they passed a shapeless knot of blackness, he raised his lantern curiously—and let out a yell of fright. He jumped back, the swinging light sending shadows racing around them. Reverberations of his yell danced in their ears.

Mr. Pennyfeather spun around; Kitty's knife leaped to her hand; silver discs appeared in those of Fred and Nick. "What *is* it?" Kitty hissed, above the banging of her heart.

A plaintive voice in the dark. "Right beside us—there . . . a ghost . . ."

"Ghosts don't exist. Raise your lantern."

With obvious reluctance, Stanley obeyed. In his trembling light, a stone plinth was revealed nestling in an alcove. It had an arch in its side, from which a skeleton had been carved emerging, wreathed in shrouds and flourishing a spear.

"Oh . . ." Stanley said, in a small voice. "It's a statue."

"You idiot," Kitty whispered. "It's just someone's tomb. Could you have shouted *any* louder?"

"Come on." Mr. Pennyfeather was already moving off. "We're wasting time."

As they left the nave and rounded a wide pillar to enter the north transept, the number of visible memorials cluttering the aisles increased. Nick and Stanley raised their lanterns to shed light upon the tombs; it was somewhere here that Gladstone's was to be found. Many of the statues were life-size representations of the dead magicians: they sat in carved chairs, studying unrolled parchments; they stood heroically in long carved robes, their pale, sharp faces gazing sightlessly down upon the hurrying company. One carried a cage with a forlorn frog sitting within; this particular woman was depicted laughing. Despite her steely resolve, Kitty was unnerved. The sooner they left this place, the better.

"Here," Mr. Pennyfeather whispered.

A modest statue in white marble—a man standing on a low, circular pedestal. His brow was furrowed, his face a model of stern preoccupation. He wore a flowing gown, and beneath it an old-fashioned suit with a high starched collar. His hands were loosely clasped in front of him. On the pedestal was one word, engraved deeply in the marble:

GLADSTONE

Something of the reputation of the name cast its power upon them. They held back from the statue, crowding close together at a respectful distance. Mr. Pennyfeather spoke softly: "The key to the tomb is in my pocket. The entrance is on the pillar there. A small bronze door. Kitty, Anne—you have the sharpest eyes. Find the door and locate the keyhole. According"—he suppressed a cough—"according to the records, it should be on the left-hand side."

Kitty and Anne rounded the statue and approached the pillar, Anne training her pencil torch on the stonework ahead. With careful steps they walked around the column until the dull glint of metal showed within the light. They stepped close. The metal panel was small, only five feet high, and narrow, too. It was entirely bare of ornament, except for a seam of tiny studs around its margins.

"Found it," Kitty whispered. A minuscule hole halfway up,

on the left-hand edge. Anne held the torch close; the hole was plugged with cobwebs.

Mr. Pennyfeather led the others over: they stood gathered beside the pillar.

"Nicholas," he said. "Get the Mantle ready."

For perhaps two minutes, Kitty stood with them in the darkness, breathing steadily through the woolen fibers of her balaclava, waiting for Nick to prepare. Occasionally a muffled drone indicated the passage of a limousine somewhere out in Parliament Square; otherwise, all was still—except for the sound of Mr. Pennyfeather coughing quietly into his gloves.

Nick cleared his throat. "Ready." At that moment, they heard the scream of sirens, growing louder, then passing drearily over Westminster Bridge into the night. They faded. Finally, Mr. Pennyfeather gave a brief nod. "Now," he said. "Stand close, or the Mantle will not protect you."

Neither Kitty nor the others needed to be told. They crowded close into a rough circle, inward facing, their shoulders touching. In their midst, Nick held a neat ebony casket; with his other hand he flourished a small hammer. Mr. Pennyfeather nodded. "I have the key here. The moment the Mantle covers us, I will turn the key in the lock. When that happens, stand still—no matter what occurs."

Nick raised the hammer and brought it down sharply on the lid of the ebony casket. The lid broke in two; the precise crack it made echoed like a pistol shot. A stream of yellow particles flew upward out of the casket, twirling and twinkling with their own light. They spiraled above the company to a height perhaps of fifteen feet, then arched out and downward like water from a fountain, hitting the stone floor, and disappearing into it. Particles continued to rise from the box, loop up, and rain down, forming a faint glimmering canopy that sealed them in, as if inside a dome.

Mr. Pennyfeather held the tiny golden key. With great speed, he reached out, taking care that his hand did not stray beyond the edge of the glittering dome, and inserted the key into the lock. He turned it, then withdrew his hand as fast as a rattlesnake.

They waited. No one moved a muscle. The sides of Kitty's face were swathed in cold sweat.

Soundlessly, the small bronze door swung inward. Beyond was a black space, and out of this a glowing green bulb of light came slowly floating. As it drew level with the opening, it suddenly accelerated, expanding as it did so, with a peculiarly repellent hiss. An instant later, a bright green cloud had erupted out across the transept, illuminating all the statues and memorials like a livid flame. The company cowered within their protective Mantle as the Pestilence burned the air about them, rising to half the height of the transept walls. They were safe, provided they did not stir outside the dome; even so, a smell of such taint and decay drifted to their nostrils that they struggled not to gag.

"I hope," Mr. Pennyfeather gasped, as the green cloud raged back and forth, "that the Mantle's duration is longer than that of the Pestilence. If not—if not, Stanley, I fear the next skeletons you see will be our own."

It was very hot inside the Mantle. Kitty felt her head beginning to swim. She bit her lip and tried to concentrate: fainting now would certainly prove fatal.

With surprising suddenness, the Pestilence blew itself out. The green cloud seemed to implode, as if—lacking victims—it had been forced to consume its own essence. One moment the whole transept was aglow with its unhealthy light; the next, it was sucked down into nothing and the darkness had returned.

A minute passed. Sweat dripped down Kitty's nose. No one moved a muscle.

Then, abruptly, Mr. Pennyfeather began to laugh. It was a high, almost hysterical sound that set Kitty's teeth on edge. It held a tone of exultation carried slightly beyond the normal bounds. Instinctively, she jerked backward, away from him, and stepped out of the Mantle. She felt a tingle as she passed through the yellow canopy, then nothing. She looked about her for a minute, then took a deep breath.

"Well, the tomb's open," she said.

27

Evening was drawing closer; the proprietors of the smaller coffeehouses in the backstreets around the square were stirring themselves at last, lighting lamps that hung from door beams, and stacking up the wooden chairs that had spilled out across the pavement through the day. A peal of eventide bells was being tolled beneath the dark black spires of old Tyn Church, where my good friend Tycho lies entombed,[1] and the streets murmured with Prague's people walking home.

For much of the day, the boy had sat slumped at a white-clothed table outside a tavern, reading a succession of Czech newspapers and cheap pamphlets. If he looked up, he had a good view of the Old Town Square, into which the street opened a dozen yards away; if he looked down, he had an even better view of a medley of empty coffee cups and dishes strewn with sausage scraps and pretzel crumbs, the relics of his afternoon's consumption.

I was sitting at the same table, wearing a large pair of dark glasses and a swanky coat similar to his. For token effect, I had placed a pretzel on my plate and broken it into a few pieces, to

---

[1] Tycho Brahe (1546–1601), magician, astronomer, and duelist, perhaps the least offensive of my masters. Well, in fact quite possibly the *most* offensive, if you were one of his human contemporaries, since Tycho was a passionate fellow, forever getting into fights and trying to kiss friends' wives. That was how he lost his nose, incidentally—it was cut off by a lucky stroke during a duel over a woman. I fashioned him a fine gold replacement, together with a delicate tufted stick for burnishing the nostrils, and with this won his friendship. Thereafter he summoned me mainly when he fancied a good conversation.

make it look like I was trying. But of course I ate and drank nothing.[2]

The Old Town Square was one of the largest open areas in the east of the city, an uneven space of bright cobblestone, spotted with pedestrians and flower stalls. Flocks of birds drifted lazily down in front of the elegant five-story houses; smoke rose from a thousand chimneys. It was as peaceful a scene as could be wished for, yet I was not at ease.

"Will you stop *fidgeting*?" The boy slapped his pamphlet on the table. "I can't concentrate."

"Can't help it," I said. "We're too exposed here."

"Relax—we're in no danger."

I looked around furtively. "So you say. We should have stayed in the hotel."

The boy shook his head. "I'd have gone mad if I'd stayed in that fleapit a moment longer. I couldn't sleep in that bed for dust. *And* a tribe of bedbugs were feasting on me all night—I heard them popping off me every time I sneezed."

"If you were dusty, you should have had a bath."

He looked embarrassed. "Didn't fancy that tub somehow. It was a bit too . . . hungry-looking. Anyhow, Prague's safe enough; there's hardly *any* magic here any more. You've seen nothing all the time we've been sitting here—no imp, no djinni, no spell—and we're in the center of town! No one's likely to see you for what you are. Relax."

I shrugged. "If you say so. It won't be me running around the walls with soldiers jabbing pikes into my trousers."

---

[2] Mortal food clogs our essences something chronic. If we *do* devour anything—such as a human, say—it generally has to be still alive, so that its living essence galvanizes our own. This outweighs the burden of ingesting the useless bone and flesh. Sorry—not putting you off your tea, am I?

He wasn't listening. He'd picked up his pamphlet again and was frowning his way through it. I returned to my afternoon's occupation: namely checking and double-checking the planes.

Here's the thing: the boy was absolutely right—we'd seen nothing magical all day. This was not to say the authorities weren't represented: a few soldiers in dark-blue uniforms with shiny jackboots and highly burnished caps[3] *had* wandered repeatedly through the square. (Once, they had stopped at my master's table and asked for our identification; my master produced his fake ID, while I performed a Glaze upon them, so they forgot the object of their query and wandered on.) But we'd seen none of the magical sorties that were par for the course in London: search spheres, foliots masquerading as pigeons, etc. . . . It all seemed very innocent.

Yet, having said that, I could feel strong magic somewhere in the vicinity, not far from where we were, operating vigorously on all the planes. Each one tingled with it, particularly the seventh, which is usually where the most trouble comes. It wasn't aimed at us—yet; even so, it made me nervous, particularly because the boy—being human, young, and arrogant—sensed nothing and persisted in acting like a tourist. I didn't like being in the open.

"We should have agreed to meet him in a lonely spot," I persisted. "This is just too public."

---

[3] As a rough rule of thumb, the jazzier the uniform, the less powerful the army. In its golden age, Prague's soldiers wore sober outfits with little decoration; now, to my disgust, they minced about under a heavy weight of pompous finery: a fluffy epaulette here, an extra brass knobble there. You could hear their metal bits jingling like bells on cats' collars from far off down the street. Contrast that with London's Night Police: their outfits were the color of river-sludge, yet *they* were the ones to fear.

The boy snorted. "And give him the opportunity to come dressed as a ghul again? I think not. He can wear a suit and tie like everyone else."

Six o'clock drew near. The boy paid our bill and stuffed pamphlets and newspapers hurriedly into his rucksack. "The hot-dog stand it is, then," he said. "As before, hang back and protect me if anything happens."

"Okay, boss. You're not wearing a red feather this time. How about a rose, or a ribbon in your hair?"

"No. Thank you."

"Just asking."

We parted in the crowd; I peeled off, keeping close to the buildings on one side, while the boy continued on out into the center of the square. Since most of the home-goers for one reason or another kept to the edges, this made him look slightly isolated. I watched him go. A flock of sparrows erupted from the cobblestones near his feet and flapped away toward the rooftops high above. I scanned them anxiously, but there were no hidden watchers among them. All was well, for now.

A gentleman with a small struggling mustache and an enterprising nature had affixed a wheeled brazier to a bicycle and had cycled to a vantage point near the middle of the square. Here, he had set his coals alight, and was busily toasting spiced sausages for the hungry citizens of Prague. A small queue had formed, and to this my master attached himself, glancing casually around for the appearance of Harlequin.

I positioned myself nonchalantly by one of the perimeter walls and surveyed the square. I didn't like it: too many windows ablaze with the light of the dying sun; it was impossible to tell who might be looking down from them.

Six o'clock came and went. Harlequin did not appear.

The sausage queue shortened. Nathaniel was last in line. He shuffled forward, fumbling in his pocket for some change.

I checked out the passersby in all the distant fringes of the square. A small knot stood gossiping below the town hall, but most people were still hurrying homeward, entering and departing down the roads that fed into the square.

If Harlequin was anywhere close, he gave no sign.

My feeling of unease grew. There was no magic visible, but still that tingling sensation on every plane.

Out of habit, I checked each exit road. There were seven. . . . That at least was good: plenty of avenues of escape, should the need arise.

Nathaniel was now second in the queue. A small girl was ahead of him, demanding extra ketchup on her sausage.

A tall man strode out across the square. He wore a suit and hat; he carried a battered satchel. I eyed him up. He seemed about the right height for Harlequin, though it was difficult to be sure.

Nathaniel had not yet noticed him. He was watching the small girl stagger off under the weight of her vast hot dog.

The man made for Nathaniel, walking fast. *Too* fast, perhaps—almost as if he had some unseen purpose . . .

I started forward.

The man passed close behind Nathaniel without giving him a glance. He marched away smartly over the cobbles.

I relaxed again. Perhaps the boy was right. I *was* a little jittery.

Now Nathaniel was purchasing his sausage. He appeared to be haggling with the vendor about the amount of extra sauerkraut.

Where was Harlequin? The clock on the tower of the Old Town Hall showed twelve minutes past six. He was very late.

I heard a distant jingling, somewhere amid the pedestrians on the edges of the square—faint, rhythmic, like the bells on Lapland sleighs, heard far off across the snow. It seemed to come from all sides at once. It was familiar to me, yet somehow different from anything I had heard before. . . . I could not place it.

Then I saw the specks of blue weaving their way through the bystanders at the entrance to every one of the seven streets, and understood. Boots slapped on cobblestones, sunlight glinted on rifles, metal paraphernalia jangled on the chests of half of Prague's armed forces as they shouldered their way into view. The crowd melted backward, voices rising in alarm. The soldiers stopped suddenly; solid lines blocked each street.

I was already running out across the square.

"Mandrake!" I shouted. "Forget Harlequin. We have to go."

The boy turned, holding his hot dog. He noticed the soldiers for the first time. "Ah," he said. "Tiresome."

"Too right it is. And we can't go over the roofs, either. We're badly outnumbered there, too."

Nathaniel looked up, treating himself to a grandstand view of several dozen foliots, which had evidently scrabbled up the roofs on the far side, and were now crouching on the uppermost tiles and chimneys of every house in the square, leering down at us and making offensive gestures with their tails.

The hot-dog seller had seen the army cordons; with a yelp of fright, he leaped onto the saddle of his bicycle and veered furiously away across the cobblestones, leaving a trail of sausages, sauerkraut, and hissing red-hot coals behind him.

"They're only human," Nathaniel said. "This isn't London, is it? Let's break our way through them."

We were running now, toward the nearest street—Karlova.

"I thought you didn't want me to use any violence or obvious magic," I said.

"Those niceties are past. If our Czech friends want to start something, we can—oh."

We still had the cyclist in view when it happened. As if crazed with fear, uncertain what to do, he had made two random sorties back and forth across the square; suddenly, head down, feet pumping, he changed tack, charging straight at one of the army lines. One soldier raised a rifle; a shot rang out. The cyclist gave a twitch, his head slumped to one side, his feet slipped from the pedals and jerked and juddered against the ground. Still carried by its own momentum, the bicycle continued forward at a great pace, brazier crashing and banging behind it, until it plowed straight into the breaking line of soldiers and overturned, spilling body, sausages, hot coals, and cold cabbage over the nearest men.

My master halted, panting hard. "I need a Shield," he said. "Now."

"As you wish."

I raised a finger, willed the Shield around us both: it hung there shimmering, visible on the second plane—an uneven, potato-shaped orb that shifted when we moved. "Now," the boy said savagely, "a Detonation. We'll blast our way through."

I looked at him. "Are you *sure* about that? These men aren't djinn."

"Well, just knock them aside somehow. Bruise them gently. I don't care. As long as we get through unscathed—"

A soldier disentangled himself from the mess of sprawling limbs and took swift aim. A shot: a bullet whistled across the thirty-yard space, straight through the Shield and out again, parting Nathaniel's hair on the crown of his head en route.

The boy glared at me. "And what sort of Shield do you call this?"

I made a face. "They're using silver bullets.[4] The Shield's not safe. Come on—" I turned, reached out for the scruff of his neck, and in the same movement, made a necessary change. The slim, elegant form of Ptolemy grew and roughened; skin turned to stonework, dark hair to green lichen. All across the square, the soldiers had a fine view of a swarthy, bow-legged gargoyle stumping off at speed, dragging an angry adolescent beside him.

"Where are you going?" the boy protested. "We're cut off out here!"

The gargoyle gnashed its horny beak. "Quiet. I'm thinking."

Which was hard enough to do in all that kerfuffle. I sprinted back into the center of the square. From every street, soldiers were advancing slowly, rifles at the ready, boots thudding, regalia rattling. Up on the roofs, the foliots chittered eagerly and began to stalk forward, down the steep inclines, claws on tiles clicking like the sound of a thousand insects. The gargoyle slowed and stopped. More bullets whizzed past us. Dangling as he was, the boy was vulnerable. I swung him up in front of me; stone wings descended about him, blocking off the line of fire. This had the extra advantage of muffling his complaints.

A silver bullet ricocheted off my wing, stinging my essence with its poison touch.

---

[4] Just as silver is deeply poisonous to our essences, so is it capable of cutting through many of our magical defenses like a hot knife through butter. Low in magic though Prague had now become, it seemed they hadn't forgotten all the old tricks. Not that silver bullets were mainly used on djinn in the old days—they were generally employed against a hairier enemy.

We were surrounded on all sides: silver at street level, foliots up high. Which left only one option. The middle way.

I retracted a wing briefly, held the boy up so he had a quick view of the square. "Take a look," I said. "Which house do you think has the thinnest walls?"

For a moment, he was uncomprehending. Then his eyes widened. "You're not—"

"*That* one? With the pink shutters? Yes, maybe you're right. Well, let's see . . ."

And with that, we were off, careering through a shower of bullets—me, beak forward, eyes narrowed; him, gasping, trying to curl up into a ball and shield his head with his arms all at once. On foot, gargoyles can put together a pretty fine turn of speed, provided we pump our wings as we run, and I'm pleased to say we left a thin scorched trail on the stones behind us as we went.

A brief description of my objective: a quaint four-story building, square, broad, with tall arches at its base marking out a shopping arcade. Behind it rose the bleak spires of Tyn Church.[5] The owner of this house loved it. Each window had twin shutters that had recently been repainted a delightful pink. Long, low flower boxes sat on every sill, crammed to bursting with pink-white peonies; frilly net curtains hung chastely across the inside of each window. It was all remarkably

---

[5] I could almost hear old Tycho urging me on. He loved a gamble, Tycho did. He once bet me my freedom that I couldn't jump across the Vltava in a single bound on a given day. If I succeeded he was mine to do with as I wished. Of course, the cunning hound had calculated the date of the spring tides in advance. On the given day, the river burst its banks and flooded a much wider area than normal. I landed hooves first in the drink, much to my master's cruel amusement. He laughed so hard his nose fell off.

twee. The shutters didn't quite have hearts carved in their wood, but it was a close thing.

Soldiers ran forward from two side streets; they converged to cut us off.

Foliots skittered off gutters and descended on looping parachutes of arm skin.

I thought, on balance, the second floor was the one to aim for, midway between our enemies.

I ran, I jumped, my wings creaked and flapped; two tons of gargoyle launched proudly into the air. Two bullets rose to meet us; also, a small foliot, somewhat ahead of his fellows, descended into our path. The bullets shot by on either side; for his part, the foliot was met by a stony fist, which concertinaed him into something round and flat, resembling an aggrieved pie plate.

Two tons of gargoyle hit a window on the second floor.

My Shield was still in force. The boy and I were thus largely protected from the glass and timber, the bricks and plaster exploding all around us. This didn't stop him from crying out in woe, which was more or less what the old lady sitting in her Bath chair did as we flew past her at the topmost point of our arc. I had a brief glimpse of a genteel bedroom, in which ornamental lacework was given undue prominence; then we were out of her life once more, exiting swiftly through the opposite wall.

Down we fell, down into the cool shadows of a backstreet in a storm of bricks, through a tangle of washing that some thoughtless individual had hung on a line outside his window. We landed heavily, the gargoyle absorbing most of the impact in his hoary calves, the boy flung from his grasp and rolling off into the gutter.

I got wearily to my feet; the boy did likewise. The outcry behind us was muffled now, but neither soldiers nor foliots would be long in coming. A narrow street led away into the heart of the Old Town. Without a word, we took it.

Half an hour later, we were slumped in the shady overgrowth of an untended garden, catching our breath. No sounds of pursuit had been heard for many minutes. I had long since returned to Ptolemy's more unobtrusive form.

"So," I said. "That not-drawing-attention-to-ourselves business. How are we doing?"

The boy didn't answer. He was looking at something gripped tightly in his hands.

"I suggest we forget Harlequin," I said. "If he's got any sense, he'll be emigrating to Bermuda after all this fuss. You'll never track him down again."

"I don't need to," my master said. "Besides, it wouldn't do any good. He's dead."

"Eh?" My famed eloquence had been sorely tested by events. It was at this point that I realized the boy was still holding his hot dog. It was looking a trifle forlorn after its adventure, the sauerkraut having been largely replaced by a scrumptious coating of plaster, wood, splinters of broken glass, and flower petals. The boy was staring at it intently.

"Look, I know you're hungry," I said. "But that's going a bit far. Let me find you a burger or something."

The boy shook his head. With dusty fingers he pried apart the bread. "This," he said slowly, "is what Harlequin promised us. Our next contact in Prague."

"A sausage?"

"No, you fool. This . . ." From underneath the hot dog, he

drew out a small piece of card, somewhat bent and ketchup-stained. "Harlequin was the hot-dog seller," he continued. "That was his disguise. And now he's died for his country, so avenging him is part of our mission. But first—this is the magician we must find."

He held out the card. Scrawled on it were just four words:

Kavka,

13 Golden Lane

28

To my great relief, the boy appeared to learn something from our close shave in the Old Town Square. I saw no more of the casual English tourist now; instead, for the rest of that dark, uncomfortable evening, he allowed me to guide him through Prague's maze of crumbling alleys in the appropriate manner—the stealthy, painstaking progress of two spies abroad in an enemy land. We made our way north with infinite patience, dodging the foot patrols that were now radiating out from the square by enmeshing ourselves under Concealments or, on occasion, entering derelict buildings to skulk as the soldiery tramped by. We were aided by darkness and the comparative scarcity of magical pursuit. A few foliots tripped across the rooftops, flashing out questing Pulses, but I diverted these easily without detection. Beyond that, there was nothing: no demi-afrits unleashed, no djinn of any capacity. Prague's leaders were heavily reliant on their unobservant human troops, and of this I took full advantage. Less than an hour after we had begun our flight, we had crossed the Vltava on the back of a vegetable lorry and were making our way on foot through a region of gardens toward the castle.

In the great days of the Empire, the low hill on which the castle stood had been illuminated, each day at dusk, by a thousand lanterns; these changed color, and occasionally position, at the Emperor's whim, casting multifarious light upon the trees and houses clinging to its slopes.[1] Now the lamps were broken and rusted to their posts. Except for a few feeble orange spots that marked out windows, Castle Hill was dark before us, enfolded by night.

We came at length to the base of a steep flight of cobbled steps. Up above was Golden Lane—I glimpsed its lights glinting high against the stars, on the very edge of the cold black slab of hill. Beside the bottom of the steps was a low wall, and behind this was a midden; I left Nathaniel lurking there, while I flew, as a bat, on a quick reconnaissance up the steps.

The eastern steps had changed little, since that distant day when my master's death had released me from his service. Too much to hope that an afrit would leap out to grab my current master now. The only presences I could detect were three fat owls, hidden in the avenues of dark trees on either side of the way. I double-checked; they were owls even on the seventh plane.

Far off across the river, the hunt was still in operation. I could hear soldiers' whistles shrilling with sad futility, a sound that gave a thrill to my essence. Why? Because Bartimaeus was too fast for them, that's why; because the djinni they wanted was far away already, flitting and flapping the 256 steps up Castle Hill. And because somewhere ahead of me in the night silence was the source of the disturbance that I still felt tingling on each plane— the odd, unidentified magical activity. Things were going to get interesting.

The bat passed the tumbled husk of the old Black Tower,

---

[1] Each lantern contained a sealed glass pod in which an irritable imp resided. The Master of Lamps, an hereditary official among the court magicians, stalked along the hillside each afternoon, instructing his captives in the colors and intensity required for the night to come. By subtle phrasing of each charge, the nuances achieved could be subtle or spectacular, but were always in accordance with the mood at court.

once occupied by the Elite Guard, but home now to no one but a dozen sleeping ravens. Beyond it was my objective. A street, narrow and unassuming, walled by a series of humble cottages—all tall stained chimneys, small windows, cracked plaster-fronts, and plain wooden doors leading straight onto the road. The place was always like this, even in the great years. Golden Lane worked under different rules.

The roofs, always sagging, were now beyond repair—a mess of warped frames and loose tiles. I settled on an exposed rib of wood on the endmost cottage and surveyed the street. In the days of Rudolf, greediest of the emperors, Golden Lane was a center of great magical effort, the objective of which was nothing less than the creation of the Philosopher's Stone.[2] Each house was rented to a different alchemist and, for a time, the tiny cottages hummed with activity.[3] Even after the search was abandoned, the street remained home to foreign magicians

---

[2] A fabled pebble accredited with the ability to turn base metals into gold or silver. Its existence is, of course, utter moonshine, as might be discovered by asking any imp. We djinn can alter the *appearance* of things by casting a Glamour or an Illusion; but to permanently shift the true nature of something is quite impossible. But humans never listen to something that doesn't suit them, and countless lives were expended on this futile search.

[3] The magicians came from all over the known world—from Spain, from Britain, from snowbound Russia, from the fringes of the Indian deserts—in the hope of winning incalculable reward. Each was master of a hundred arts, each the tormentor of a dozen djinn. Each drove their slaves for years in the great quest; each, in turn, failed utterly. One by one, their beards turned gray, their hands weakened and palsied, their robes grew faded and discolored from ceaseless summonings and experiments. One by one, they tried to give up their positions, only to find Rudolf was unwilling to let them go. Those who attempted to slip away found soldiers waiting for them on the castle steps; others, attempting a magical departure, discovered a strong nexus around the castle, sealing them in. They did not escape. Many ended in the dungeons; the rest took their own lives. It was, to those of us spirits who watched the process, a deeply moral tale: our captors had been caught in the prison of their own ambitions.

working for the Czechs. The government wanted them close beside the castle, where it could keep an eye on them. And so the situation remained, right through to the bloody night when Gladstone's forces took the city.

No foreign magicians dwelled here now. The buildings were smaller than I remembered, huddled together like seabirds on a headland. I sensed the old magics, still seeped into the stonework, but little that was new. Except . . . the faint tremoring on the planes was stronger now, its source much closer. The bat looked about carefully. What could it see? A dog, ferreting in a hole at the foot of one old wall. A lit window, fringed by thin curtains; inside it, an old man hunched beside a fire. A young woman, in the glare of a streetlight, walking carefully along the cobblestones in high-heeled shoes, perhaps making for the castle. Blank windows, shut casements, roof holes, and broken chimneys. Litter blowing in the wind. An upbeat scene.

And number 13, halfway down the street, a hovel indistinguishable from the rest in its griminess and melancholy, but with a glowing green nexus of force surrounding it on the sixth plane. Someone was in, and that someone did not want to be disturbed.

The bat made a quick sortie up and down the street, carefully avoiding the nexus where it curved up into the air. The rest of Golden Lane was dark and quiet, fully obsessed with its little activities of evening. I swooped quickly back the way I had come, down to the bottom of the hill to rouse my master.

"I've found the place," I said. "Mild defenses, but we should be able to get in. Hurry, while no one's around."

I've said it before, but humans are simply useless when it comes to getting about. The *time* it took for that boy to climb those measly 256 steps, the sheer number of huffs and puffs and gratuitous pauses for breath he needed, the remarkable color he became—I've never seen the like.

"I wish we'd brought a paper bag or something," I told him. "Your face is glowing so much it can probably be seen from the other side of the Vltava. It's not even a very big hill."

"What—What—kind of—defenses are there?" His mind was strictly on the job.

"Flimsy nexus," I said. "No problem. Don't you exercise at all?"

"No. No time. Too busy."

"Of course. You're too important now. I forgot."

After ten minutes or so, we reached the ruined tower and I became Ptolemy again. In this guise, I led the way to a place where a shallow incline dropped down onto the street. Here, while my master gasped and wheezed gently against the wall, we looked out at the hovels of Golden Lane.

"Appalling lack of condition," I commented.

"Yes. They should . . . knock them all down . . . and start again."

"I was talking about *you*."

"Which—which one is it?"

"Number thirteen? That one on the right, three along. White plaster front. When you've finished dying, we'll see what we can do."

A cautious walk along the shadows of the lane took us to within a few meters of the cottage. My master was all for marching up to the front door. I reached out an arm. "Stop right there. The nexus is directly in front of you. A fingertip farther and you'll set it off."

He stopped. "You think you can get inside?"

"I don't *think*, boy. I know. I was doing this kind of stuff when Babylon was a small-time cattle station. Stand aside, watch and learn."

I stepped up to the frail glowing net of filaments that blocked our way, bent my head close. I chose a small hole between the threads and blew gently toward it. My aim was true: the tiny sliver of Obedient Breath[4] passed into the hole and hung there, neither slipping through, nor withdrawing. It was too light to trigger the alarm. The rest was easy. I expanded the sliver slowly, gently; as it grew, it pried apart the filaments. In a few minutes, a large round hole had been created in the net, not far above the ground. I remodeled the Breath into the shape of a hoop and stepped nonchalantly through it. "There," I said. "Your turn."

The boy frowned. "To do what? I still can't see anything."

With some exasperation, I refigured the Breath to make it visible on the second plane. "Happy now?" I said. "Just step carefully through that hoop."

He did so, but still seemed unimpressed. "Huh," he said. "You could be making this up for all I know."

"It's not my fault humans are so blind," I snapped. "Yet again you're taking my expertise for granted. Five thousand years of experience at your command, and not even a thank-you comes my way. Fine. If you don't believe there's a nexus there, I'll happily set it off for you. You'll see the magician Kavka come running."

"No, no." He was hasty now. "I believe you."

"Are you *sure*?" My finger hovered back toward the glowing lines.

---

[4] A type of conjuration formed by an expiration of air from the mouth and a magic sign. Not remotely connected to the Noisome Wind, which is created in a rather different way.

"Yes! Calm down. Now—we'll creep in at a window and catch him unawares."

"Fine. After you."

He stepped grimly forward, straight into the lines of a *second* nexus I hadn't noticed.[5] A loud siren noise, seemingly consisting of a dozen bells and chiming clocks, went off in the house. The noise continued for several seconds. Nathaniel looked at me. I looked at Nathaniel. Before either of us reacted, the noise was discontinued, and a rattling noise sounded behind the cottage door. The door was flung open and a tall wild-eyed man wearing a skullcap rushed out,[6] shouting furiously.

"I *told* you," he cried. "This is too early! It will not be ready until dawn! Will you not leave me in p— Oh." He took heed of us for the first time. "What the devil?"

"Close," I said. "Kind of depends on your point of view." I leaped forward and grappled him to the ground. In an instant, his hands were up behind his back and nicely tied by the cord of his dressing gown.[7] This was to prevent any quick hand gestures that might have summoned something to his aid.[8] His mouth was stuffed with a section of Nathaniel's shirt, in case of uttered commands. This done, I bundled him to his feet and had him back indoors before my master could even open his

---

[5] Very subtle, it was. Seventh plane only, the thinnest of thin threads. Anyone could have missed it.

[6] He didn't *just* have a skullcap on; he wore other clothes as well. Just in case you were getting excited. Look, I'll get to the details later; it's a narrative momentum thing.

[7] See? He had a dressing gown on. And pajamas, for that matter. All perfectly respectable.

[8] Also the rude ones, which might have upset the kid.

mouth to speak an order. *That's* how fast a djinni can act when necessary.

"Look at that!" I said proudly. "Not even any noticeable violence."

My master blinked. "You've *ruined* my shirt," he said. "You've torn it in half."

"Shame," I said. "Now close the door. We can discuss this inside."

With the door closed, we were able to take stock of our surroundings. Mr. Kavka's house could best be described by the term *scholarly squalor.* The entire floor, and every item of furniture on it, was covered with books and loose manuscripts: in places they formed intricate strata many inches thick. These in turn were covered with a thin crust of dust, scatterings of pens and quills, and numerous dark and pungent items, which had the nasty look of being leftovers from the magician's lunches over the preceding month or two. Beneath all this was a large worktable, a chair, a leather sofa and, in the corner, a primitive rectangular sink, with a single tap. A few stray parchments had migrated into the sink, too.

It seemed that the first floor of the cottage was entirely taken up by the one room. A window at the back looked down onto the hillside and the night: lights from the city far below shone dimly through the glass. A wooden ladder extended up through a hole in the ceiling, presumably to a bedchamber. It did not look as if the magician had gone that way for some time: on close inspection, his eyes were gray rimmed, his cheeks yellow with fatigue. He was also extremely thin, standing with crumpled posture, as if all energy had drained out of him.

Not a particularly imposing sight, then—either the magician or his room. Yet this was the source of the trembling on the seven planes: I felt it, stronger than ever. It made my teeth rattle in my gums.

"Sit him down," my master said. "The sofa will do. Push that rubbish out of the way. Right." He sat on the corner of the worktable, one leg on the floor, the other dangling casually. "Now," he continued, addressing his captive smoothly in Czech, "I haven't much time, Mr. Kavka. I hope you will cooperate with me."

The magician gazed at him with his tired eyes. He gave a noticeable shrug.

"I warn you," the boy went on. "I am a magician of great power. I control many terrifying entities. This being you see before you"—here I rolled my shoulders back and puffed my chest up menacingly—"is but the meanest and least impressive of my slaves." (Here I slumped my shoulders and stuck my stomach out.) "If you do not give me the information I desire, it will be the worse for you."

Mr. Kavka made an incoherent noise; he nodded his head and rolled his eyes.

The boy looked at me. "What's that mean, d'you think?"

"How do I know? I suggest taking out the gag and finding out."

"All right. But if he utters one syllable of any kind of spell, destroy him instantly!" To accompany this, the boy attempted an expression of terrible malignity that made him look as if he had an ulcer. I removed the gag. The magician coughed and spluttered for a time. He was no more coherent than before.

Nathaniel rapped his knuckles on an exposed bit of table. "Pay attention, Mr. Kavka! I want you to listen very carefully to all my questions. Silence, I warn you, will get you nowhere. To begin—"

"I know why you have come!" The voice erupted from the magician's mouth with all the force of a river in spate. It was defiant, aggrieved, endlessly weary. "You do not need to tell me. It is the manuscript! Of course! How could it be anything else, when I have applied my all to its mysteries for the last six months? It has eaten up my life during this time; see—it has robbed me of my youth! My skin shrivels with every scratch of the pen. The manuscript! It could be nothing else!"

Nathaniel was taken aback. "A manuscript? Well, possibly. But let me make myself cl—"

"I have been sworn to secrecy," Mr. Kavka continued; "I have been threatened with death—but what do I care now? Once was quite enough. Twice—that is impossible for any single man. See how my energy has withered—" He held up his bound wrists against the light; they were sticklike and shaking, the skin so thin the light shone through between the bones. "*That* is what he has done to me. Before this, I burned with life."

"Yes—but what—"

"I know exactly who you are," the man continued, speaking over my master as if he did not exist. "An agent of the British government. I expected you in time, though not, I admit, someone so young and hopelessly inexperienced. If you had arrived a month ago, you might have saved me. As it is, it means little enough. I care not." He gave a heartfelt sigh. "It is behind you, on the table."

The boy looked back, reached out and picked up a paper. As he did so, he cried out in sudden pain; dropped it instantly. "Aahh! It's charged! A trick—"

"Don't show your youth and inexperience," I said. "You're embarrassing me. Can't you see what that *is*? Anyone with eyes could tell you it's the center of all the magical activity in Prague. It's no wonder it gave you a shock. Use that poncy handkerchief in your pocket and study it more closely. Then tell me what it is."

I knew already, of course. I'd seen such things before. But it did me good to see that trumped-up boy shivering with fright, too startled to disobey my instructions, wrapping his hand in his flouncy handkerchief, and picking the document up again with the utmost care. It was a large-scale manuscript, cut from calfskin, no doubt stretched and dried in accordance with the old methods—a thick, creamy parchment, beautifully smooth and crackling with power. This power came, not from the material, but from the words upon it. They were written in an unusual ink, equal parts red and black,[9] and flowed beautifully from right to left, from the base of the page up toward the top; line upon line of intricate, calligraphic runes. The boy's eyes were wide with wonder. He sensed the artistry, the labor that had gone into this work, even if he could not read the marks. Perhaps he would have articulated this astonishment if he'd been able to get a word in. But the magician, old Kavka, was still singing like a canary, good and true.

"It isn't finished yet," he said. "You can see that. Another half-line needs to be added. A full night's work before me: a night that will be my last in any case, since he will surely kill me, if the ink itself does not drain my blood. You see the space at the top—that small, square box? His employer will write his own name there. That is the only blood *he* needs to expend to

---

[9] I speculate that these symbolize the power of earth (black) and the blood of the magician (red), which gives that earth its life. But this is only speculation: I am not privy to golem magic.

control the creature. It works out very well for *him*, oh yes. Less so for poor Kavka."

"What *is* his name?" I asked. Best to get right to the point, I find.

"The employer?" Kavka laughed—a harsh sound, like an insane old bird. "I do not know. I have never met him."

The boy was still staring at the manuscript in a daze. "This is for another golem" he said slowly. "It'll be put in its mouth to animate it. He's giving the paper his lifeblood, which will feed into the golem. . . ." He looked up at Kavka, with horrified wonder on his face. "*Why* are you doing this?" he asked. "It's killing you."

I made an urgent gesture. "That's not what we need to know," I said. "We've got to find out *who*. Time's running out and dawn's not far off."

But the magician was talking again, a faint dullness in his gaze suggesting he no longer saw us clearly. "Because of Karl, of course," he said. "And Mia. I have been promised their safe return if I create these things. You must understand that I do not *believe* this, but I cannot give up the one small hope I have. Perhaps he will honor it. Perhaps not. Probably they are already dead." He broke into a hideous, wracking cough. "In truth—I fear this must be so."

The boy was blank. "Karl, Mia? I don't understand."

"They are the only family I have," the magician said. "How sad it is they have been lost. It is an unjust world. But when you are offered a chink of light, you climb toward it—even you, a cursed Briton, must understand that. I could not ignore the only chance I had to see their faces again."

"Where are they, your family?" Nathaniel asked.

"Hah!" The magician stirred at this; a brief light flared in his eyes. "How do I know? Some godforsaken prison ship? The Tower of London? Or are their bones already burned and buried? That is *your* province, English boy—you tell *me*. You *are* from the British government, I suppose?"

My master nodded.

"The person you seek wishes your government no good." Kavka coughed again. "But then—you know this. That is why you are here. *My* government would kill me, if it knew what I had done. They do not want a new golem created in case it brings another Gladstone down upon Prague, wielding that terrible Staff."

"I take it," the boy said, "that your relatives are Czech spies? They went to England?"

The magician nodded. "And were captured. I heard nothing of them. Then a gentleman came calling, said his employer would restore them to me, alive, if I revealed the secrets of the golem, if I created the necessary parchment. What could I do? What would any father do?"

Uncharacteristically, my master was silent. Uncharacteristically, I was, too. I looked at Kavka's emaciated face and hands, his dulling eyes, saw in them the endless hours spent stooped over his books and papers, saw him pouring his life into the page on the small off chance that his family might be returned to him.

"The first parchment I completed a month ago," Kavka said. "That was when the messenger altered his demands. *Two* golems were required now. In vain, I argued that it would kill me, that I would not live to see Mia and Karl again. . . . Ah, he is cruel. He would not listen."

"Tell us about this messenger," the boy said suddenly, "and if your children are alive, I will return them to you. I guarantee it."

The dying man made a great effort. His eyes focused on my master; their dimness was replaced by a searching strength. He appraised Nathaniel carefully. "You are very young to be making such promises," he whispered.

"I am a respected member of the government," Nathaniel said. "I have power—"

"Yes, but can you be trusted?" Kavka gave a heavy sigh. "You *are* British, after all. I will ask your demon—" He did not look away from Nathaniel as he spoke. "What do you say? Is he trustworthy?"

I puffed out my cheeks, blew hard. "Tricky one. He's a magician. By definition he'd sell his own grandmother for soap. But he's marginally less corrupt than some of them. Possibly. A bit."

Nathaniel looked at me. "Thanks for that ringing endorsement, Bartimaeus."

"You're welcome."

But rather to my surprise, Kavka was nodding. "Very well. I leave it to your conscience, boy. I will not live to see them in any case. In truth, I am worn away. I care not a fig for you *or* him—you can go on tearing each other's throats out until all Britain lies ravaged. But I will tell you what I know, and let that be an end." He began to cough weakly, his chin low against his chest. "Be assured of one thing. I will not complete this manuscript now. You will not have two golems enlivening the streets of London."

"Now, that *is* a pity," a deep voice said.

29

Quite how he had arrived there, Nathaniel could not have said. Neither external nexus had been triggered, and not one of them—Nathaniel, Kavka, even Bartimaeus—had heard him enter the house itself. Yet there he was, leaning casually against the loft ladder, brawny arms folded across his chest.

Nathaniel's mouth opened. No words came out—nothing but a horrified gasp of recognition.

The bearded mercenary. Simon Lovelace's hired assassin.

After the fighting at Heddleham Hall some two years earlier, the mercenary had evaded capture. Government agents had hunted for him high and low, in Britain and across the Continent, but without success—no trace was ever found. In time, the police moved on; they closed their files and gave up the search. But Nathaniel could not forget. One terrible image was seared on his memory: the mercenary emerging from the shadows of Lovelace's study, carrying the Amulet of Samarkand, his coat stained with the blood of a murdered man. For years, the image had hung like a cloud in Nathaniel's mind.

And now the assassin stood two meters away, cold eyes surveying them each in turn.

As before, he radiated a malign vitality. He was tall and muscular, blue-eyed and heavy of brow. He appeared to have trimmed his beard a little, but wore his black hair longer, halfway down his neck. His clothes were jet-black—a loose shirt, a padded tunic, trousers broad above the knee, high boots that swelled about the calf. His swaggering confidence battered against Nathaniel like a fist. Nathaniel was immediately conscious of his own paltry strength, of the weakness of his limbs.

"Don't bother introducing us, Kavka," the man said. His voice was lazy, deep, and slow. "We three are old acquaintances."

The old man gave a long, sad sigh, which was hard to interpret. "It would be pointless in any case. I know none of your names."

"Names have never been an issue for us."

If the djinni was startled, it gave no sign. "You got your boots back, I see," it said.

The dark brows knotted. "I *said* that you'd pay for that. And so you will. You *and* the boy."

Until this moment, Nathaniel had been sitting on Kavka's desk, transfixed by shock. Now, in a concerted effort to assert some authority, he pushed forward and stood upright, hands on hips.

"You're under arrest," he said, glaring fiercely at the mercenary as he spoke.

The man returned his gaze with such baleful unconcern that Nathaniel felt himself shrinking and cowering where he stood. In fury, he cleared his throat. "Did you hear what I said?"

The man's arm moved—so fast that Nathaniel barely registered it—and a sword rested in his hand. It pointed lazily in Nathaniel's direction. "Where is *your* weapon, child?"

Nathaniel jutted out his chin defiantly and jerked a thumb toward Bartimaeus. "There," he said. "He's an afrit at my sole command. One word from me and he'll tear you apart."

The djinni seemed a little taken aback. "Er, yes," it said doubtfully. "That's right."

A glacial smile spread beneath the beard. "This is the creature you had with you before. It failed to kill me then. What makes you think it'll have more luck this time?"

"Practice makes perfect," the djinni said.

"How true." Another flicker of movement, another blur about his person—and in his other hand he held an S-shaped metal disc. "I have practiced long with this," the mercenary said. "It will cut through your essence and *still* return to my outstretched hand."

"By that point, you wouldn't have a hand left to catch *with*," Nathaniel said. "He's fast, my afrit is. Like a striking cobra. He'd have you before that thing left your grasp." He glanced between djinni and mercenary. Neither looked overly convinced.

"*No* demon is as fast as me," the mercenary said.

"Is that so?" Nathaniel replied. "You just try him."

Bartimaeus raised a hasty finger. "Now look here—"

"Give him your best shot."

"I might just do that."

"See what happens to you."

"Hey, steady on," the djinni said. "This macho posturing is all very well, but leave me out of it, please. Why don't you two have an arm wrestle, or compare biceps or something? Work your tensions out that way."

Nathaniel ignored him. "Bartimaeus," he began, "I order you—"

At that moment something unexpected happened. Kavka stood up.

"Stay where you are!" The mercenary's eyes swiveled, the sword point shifted.

Kavka did not seem to have heard. He swayed slightly where he was, then tottered forward, away from the sofa, across the paper-strewn floor. His bare feet made little crunching noises as he trod upon the parchments. In a couple of steps he had reached the table. A bone-thin arm shot out and seized the golem manuscript from Nathaniel's loose grasp. He stood back, hugging it to his chest.

The mercenary made as if to hurl his disc, but paused. "Put that down, Kavka!" he growled. "Think of your family—think of Mia."

Kavka's eyes were closed; he was swaying again. He raised his face toward the ceiling. "Mia? She is lost to me."

"Complete that paper tonight, and you will see her tomorrow, I swear it!"

The eyes opened. They were dull, but lucid. "What matter? I will be dead by dawn. My life force is already drained away."

A look of intense irritation had appeared on the mercenary's face. He was not the kind of man who enjoyed negotiation. "My employer assures me that they are safe and well," he said. "We can remove them from prison tonight and fly them to Prague by morning. Think hard—do you wish *all* this work to be wasted?"

Nathaniel glanced at the djinni. It was shifting position slowly. The mercenary did not appear to have noticed. Nathaniel cleared his throat, sought to distract him further. "Don't listen to him, Kavka," he said. "He's lying."

The mercenary flashed Nathaniel a look. "It is a matter of intense displeasure to me," he said, "that you were not caught this afternoon in the square. I gave the police the most careful instructions, yet *still* they bungled it. I should have tackled you myself."

"You *knew* we were here?" Nathaniel said.

"Of course. Your timing was most inappropriate. Another day or two and it would have been irrelevant—I'd have been back in London with the completed manuscript. Your investigations would have come to nothing. As it was, I needed to keep you occupied. Hence my tip-off to the police."

Nathaniel's eyes narrowed. "*Who* told you I'd be coming?"

"My employer, of course," the mercenary said. "I told the Czechs and they followed that bumbling British agent around all day, knowing he would eventually lead them to you. Incidentally, they believe you to be in Prague to plant a bomb. But all that is academic now. They let me down."

He had the sword and disc outstretched as he spoke, his eyes flicking between Nathaniel and the magician. Nathaniel's head was awhirl—hardly *anyone* had known he was coming to Prague, yet somehow the mercenary had been informed. Which meant . . . No, he had to concentrate. He saw Bartimaeus still inching sideways, subtle as a snail. A little farther and the djinni would be out of view, in just the right position to attack.

"I see you found another foul traitor to replace Lovelace," he snapped.

"Lovelace?" The man's brows flickered with mild amusement. "He was not my main employer even then. He was nothing but a sideshow, an amateur, much too eager for success. My master encouraged him, as far as it went, but Lovelace was not his only tool. Nor am I his only servant now."

Nathaniel was beside himself with fury. "*Who* is it? Who do you work for?"

"Someone who pays well. Surely that is obvious. You are a strange little magician."

At that moment, the djinni, which had shuffled successfully to the fringes of the mercenary's gaze, raised its hand to strike. But in the same instant, Kavka acted. All this while, he had been standing beside Nathaniel, holding the golem parchment in his hands. Now, without a word, his eyes tight shut, he tensed suddenly, and ripped the manuscript in half.

The effect was unexpected.

An outpouring of magical force surged from the torn parchment and blasted around the cottage like an earthquake. Nathaniel was tossed into the air amid a maelstrom of flying objects: djinni, mercenary, table, sofa, paper, pens, splashing ink. For a split second Nathaniel could see the three visible planes shaking at different rates: everything was multiplied three times. The walls shuddered, the floor tipped. The electric light crackled and went out. Nathaniel crashed heavily against the floor.

The surge poured away, through the floorboards, down into the earth. The manuscript's charge was gone. The planes steadied, the reverberations died. Nathaniel raised his head. He was slumped beneath the upturned sofa, looking toward the window. The lights of the city still shone through it, but seemed oddly higher than before. It took a moment to grasp what had happened. The entire cottage had tipped, and was perched right on the edge of the hill. The floorboards ran down in a gentle gradient toward the window. As he watched, many little objects came sliding past, to rest up against the tilted wall.

The room was quite dark and filled with the rustling noise of gently settling paper. Where was the mercenary? Where was Bartimaeus? Nathaniel lay very still beneath the sofa, eyes wide as a rabbit's in the night.

He could see Kavka well enough. The old magician was lying faceup on his tilted sink with a dozen sheets of paper floating down upon him in a makeshift shroud. Even from a distance, Nathaniel could see that he was dead.

The weight of the sofa pressed heavily upon one of Nathaniel's legs, pinning it to the floor. He dearly wanted to shift it off, but knew it was too risky. He lay quiet, watched and listened.

A footstep; a figure coming slowly into view. The mercenary paused beside the body on the sink, inspected it for a moment, uttered a quiet curse, and moved on to rummage through the scattered furniture near the window. He went slowly, legs tensed against the gradient of the floor. He no longer held his sword, but something silvery shone in his right hand.

Finding nothing among the debris, the mercenary began to climb back across the room, head swinging methodically from side to side, eyes squinting in the darkness. In horror, Nathaniel saw that he was drawing ever closer to the sofa. Nathaniel could not retreat: the sofa that protected him from view also trapped him. He bit his lip, trying to recall the words of an appropriate summoning.

The mercenary appeared to notice the upturned sofa for the first time. For two seconds, he stood very still. Then, silver disc in hand, he bent his knees and crouched down to lift the sofa from Nathaniel's cringing head.

And Bartimaeus appeared behind him.

The Egyptian boy was floating above the tilted floor; its feet hung limp, its hand was outstretched. A silver nimbus played about its form, flashing upon the white cloth around its waist and shining darkly in its hair. The djinni whistled once, a jaunty sound. In a blur of movement the mercenary spun; the disc left his hand; it whistled through the air, cut through the radiance at Bartimaeus's side and looped out across the room.

"Nah-nah, you missed," the djinni said. An Inferno erupted from its fingers and engulfed the mercenary where he stood. A gobbet of flame enveloped his upper body; he cried out, clutching at his face. He stumbled forward, casting a red-yellow radiance on the room, glaring through his fiery clutching fingers.

The whistling disc reached the farthest point of the room; with a change of timbre, it doubled back, shooting toward the mercenary's hand. En route it sliced through the Egyptian boy's side. Nathaniel heard the djinni cry out; saw the boy's form flicker and shake.

The disc returned to the burning hand.

Nathaniel pulled his leg clear of the sofa; he pushed it frantically from him and, stumbling on the uneven floor, clawed himself to his feet.

The Egyptian boy vanished. In its place, lit by the flames, a limping rat scurried into the shadows. The burning man stalked after it, eyes blinking in the heat. His clothes were blackening on his body; the disc glinted redly in his fingers.

Nathaniel tried to command his thoughts. Next to him was the loft ladder, which had toppled to lodge diagonally against the ceiling. He steadied himself against it.

The rat hurried across an aged parchment. The paper cracked loudly under its feet.

The disc sliced the parchment in half; the rat gave a squeak and rolled to the side.

Burning fingers moved; two more discs appeared in them. The rat scampered away frantically, but was not fast enough. A disc embedded itself in the floorboards, snaring the rat's tail beneath a silver barb. The rat thrashed weakly, trying to pull itself free.

The mercenary stalked over. He raised a smoldering boot.

With a furious effort, Nathaniel dislodged the loft ladder, causing it to fall heavily upon the mercenary's back. Caught off-guard, the man lost his balance and fell sideways in a shower of sparks. He landed on the cottage floor, setting light to manuscripts all around.

The rat gave a great heave, pulled its tail free. With a jerking leap, it landed by Nathaniel's side. "Thanks for that," it gasped. "Did you see how I lined him up for you?"

Nathaniel was staring wide-eyed at the lumbering figure, who was hurling the ladder from him in a spasm of rage, seemingly indifferent to the surrounding flames. "How *can* he survive?" he whispered. "The fire's all over him. He's burning up."

"Just his clothes, I fear," the rat said. "His body's quite invulnerable. But we've got him by the window now. Watch out."

It raised a small pink paw. The bearded man turned and saw Nathaniel for the first time. He snarled in rage, lifted a hand; something silver sparkled there. He reached back—

And was met with the full force of a Hurricane head on: it rushed from the rat's paw, lifted him off his feet, and sent him backward through the window, surrounded by a glittering cascade of broken glass and burning scraps of paper that were whipped up with him off the floor. Out into the night he fell, outward and far away down the hill into the night, his descent marked by the flames still licking up from his body. Nathaniel saw him bounce once, distantly, then lie still.

The rat was already racing up the sloping floor toward the cottage door. "Come on," it cried. "Think that'll stop him? We've five minutes, maybe ten."

Nathaniel scrambled after it, over piles of smoldering paper and out into the night, triggering first one nexus, then the other. The drone of the alarms rose up into the sky and roused the inhabitants of Golden Lane from their melancholic dreams, but rat and boy were already beyond the ruined tower and racing down the castle steps as if all the demons ever summoned were clamoring at their heels.

Late the following morning, wearing fresh clothes and a milliner's wig, and flourishing a newly stolen pass, Nathaniel crossed the Czech border into British-controlled Prussia. Hitching into the town of Chemnitz in a baker's van, he went straight to the British consulate and explained his position. Phone calls were made, passwords checked, and his identity verified. By midafternoon he was aboard a plane departing the local aerodrome for London.

The djinni had been dismissed at the border, since the stress of the prolonged summoning was wearing Nathaniel out. He had had little sleep for days. The aircraft was warm, and despite his desire to puzzle through the mercenary's words, his weariness and the hum of the engines had their effect. Almost before the plane left the ground, Nathaniel was asleep.

An attendant woke him at Box Hill. "Sir, we have arrived. A car awaits you. You are requested to make haste."

He emerged onto the exit stairs under a light, cold drizzle. A black limousine was waiting beside the landing strip. Nathaniel descended slowly, still scarcely awake. He half-expected to see his master there, but the backseat was empty. The chauffeur touched his cap as he opened the door.

"Ms. Whitwell's compliments, sir," he said. "You are to come to London immediately. The Resistance have struck in the heart of Westminster, and— Well, you will see the results for yourself. There is no time to lose. We have an unfolding disaster on our hands."

Wordlessly, Nathaniel climbed into the car. The door clicked shut behind him.

30

The flight of stairs kept to the contour of the pillar above, circling down clockwise into the ground. The passageway was tight and the ceiling low. Even Kitty was forced to stoop, and Fred and Nick—who were practically bent double—had to descend sideways, in the manner of two awkward crabs. The air was hot and faintly foul.

Mr. Pennyfeather led the way, his lantern set to its strongest illumination. Everyone else did likewise, their spirits rising with the renewed light. Now that they were safely underground, there was no chance that anyone would see them. The dangerous part was over.

Kitty followed the scuffling Nick, with Stanley treading close behind. Even with his lantern at her back, the shadows seemed intent on closing in; they darted and leaped incessantly at the corners of her vision.

A goodly number of spiders had made their homes in crevices on either side of the stairs. From Mr. Pennyfeather's curses, it was evident that he was having to clear his path through a hundred years of choking cobwebs.

The descent did not take long. Kitty counted thirty-three steps, and then she was stepping through a hinged metal grille and out into an open space, ill defined by lantern light. She stepped aside to allow Stanley to exit from the stairwell, too, then pulled her balaclava off. Mr. Pennyfeather had just done likewise. His face was faintly flushed, his ring of gray-white hair spiky and disheveled.

"Welcome," he whispered, in a high, hoarse voice, "to Gladstone's tomb."

Kitty's first sensation was of the sheer imagined weight of ground above her. The ceiling had been constructed from neatly carved stone blocks; with the passing years, the alignment of these stones had shifted. Now they bulged ominously in the center of the chamber, pressing down against the weak light as if they wished to snuff it out. The air was full of taint, and smoke twirled from the lanterns and wreathed thickly against the ceiling. Kitty found herself clutching instinctively at each breath.

The crypt itself was fairly narrow, perhaps only four meters wide at its broadest point; its length was indeterminate, extending away into the shadow beyond the radiance of their lights. Its floor was flagged and bare, except for a thick carpeting of white mold that, in places, had extended halfway up the walls. The industrious spiders of the stairwell seemed not to have ventured through the grille: there were no cobwebs to be seen.

Cut into the side wall of the chamber, directly opposite the entrance, was a long shelf, bare except for three glass hemispheres. Although the glass was dirty and cracked, Kitty could just make out the remnants of a circlet of dried flowers inside each one: ancient lilies, poppies, and sticks of rosemary, dotted with brackish lichen. The burial flowers of the great magician. Kitty shuddered and turned to the main focus of the company's attention—the marble sarcophagus directly below the shelf.

It was eight feet long and five feet high, plainly carved without ornament or inscription of any kind, except for a bronze plaque that had been affixed to the center of one side. Its lid, also of marble, sat on top, though Kitty thought it looked slightly askew, as if it had been dropped into place hurriedly and left unadjusted.

Mr. Pennyfeather and the others were crowding around the sarcophagus in great excitement.

"It's in the Egyptian style," Anne was saying. "Typical grandiosity, wanting to follow the pharaohs. No hieroglyphs, though."

"What's this say?" Stanley was peering at the plaque. "Can't make it out."

Mr. Pennyfeather was squinting, too. "It's in some devilish tongue. Hopkins might have read it, but it's no good to us. Now—" He straightened and tapped his stick against the sarcophagus lid. "How can we get this thing open?"

Kitty's brow furrowed with distaste and something approaching apprehension. "Do we need to? What makes you think the stuff's in there?"

Mr. Pennyfeather's nervousness revealed itself in his brittle irritation. "Well, it's hardly going to be lying about on the floor—is it, girl? The old ghoul will have wanted it close by him, even in death. The rest of the room's empty."

Kitty held her ground. "Have you *checked*?"

"Ah! A waste of time! Anne—take a lantern and check the far end. Make sure there aren't any alcoves in the far side. Frederick, Nicholas, Stanley—we'll need all our strength to shift this. Can you get purchase on it, your side? We may need the rope."

As the men gathered around, Kitty stood back to watch Anne's progress. It immediately became obvious that Mr. Pennyfeather was correct. After a few steps, Anne's lantern illuminated the far wall of the chamber, a smooth surface of clear stone blocks. She swept the light across it a few times, check-ing for niches or the outline of doors, but there was nothing to be seen. Shrugging at Kitty, she returned to the center of the room.

Stanley had produced his rope and was assessing one end of the lid. "It's going to be hard to loop it," he said, scratching the back of his head. "Can't wind it around anything. And it's too heavy to lift. . . ."

"We might lug it sideways," Fred said. "I'm game."

"Nah, it's too heavy. Solid stone."

"There may not be much friction," Nick pointed out. "The marble's smooth enough."

Mr. Pennyfeather wiped the sweat from his brow. "Well, boys—we'll have to try. The only alternative is igniting a sphere on it, and that might damage the goods. If you, Fred, set your boots against the wall, we'll get extra leverage. Now, Nick—"

While the discussion proceeded, Kitty bent down to inspect the bronze plaque. It was thickly covered in neat little wedge-shaped marks, arranged together to form what were evidently words or symbols. Not for the first time, Kitty regretted her own ignorance. Knowledge of obscure scripts was not some-thing you were taught at school, and Mr. Pennyfeather had refused to allow his company to study the spell books they had stolen. She wondered idly whether Jakob's father would have been able to read this script, and what it would have told him.

"Kitty, shift out of the way, will you? There's a good girl." Stanley had taken hold of one corner of the lid, Nick was on another, and Fred—who had an end all to himself—had braced a foot against the wall, just beneath the shelf. They were readying themselves for the first effort. Biting her lip at Stanley's facetiousness, Kitty got to her feet and moved away, wiping her face against her sleeve. Sweat was beading her skin; the air in the crypt was very close.

"Now, boys! Push!" With snarls of effort, the men set to. Anne and Mr. Pennyfeather held lanterns up around the three to illuminate their progress. Light glistened on contorted faces, grinning teeth, dripping brows. Just for a moment, a faint grinding noise could be heard above their groaning.

"All right—rest!" Nick, Fred, and Stanley collapsed with gasping cries. Mr. Pennyfeather hobbled around, clapping them soundly on the shoulders. "It moved! Definite movement! Well done, my lads! No sign of the interior yet, but we'll get there. Take a breather, then we'll try again."

And so they did. And yet again. Each time, their gasps grew louder, their muscles cracking with the effort; each time, the lid moved sideways a little more, then stubbornly stopped again. Mr. Pennyfeather urged them on, dancing about them like a demon, his limp almost forgotten, his face contorted in the bouncing light. "Push—that's it!—our fortune is inches below your noses, if you just'll put in the effort! Oh—push, damn you, Stanley! A little further! Break your backs for it, boys!"

Picking up a discarded lantern, Kitty idled about the empty crypt, scuffing her sneakers in the thick white mold, marking time. She dawdled to the far end of the chamber, almost to the wall, then turned and dawdled back.

Something occurred to her, a half-perceived oddity waving vaguely at the back of her mind. For a moment, she couldn't pin down what it was, and the cheer that came from the others after a particularly successful heave provided further distraction. She spun on her heels, looking back toward the far wall, and raised her lantern.

A wall—no more, no less.

Then what was it that . . . ?

The mold. The lack of it.

All around her, underfoot, the white mold stretched; scarcely a single flagstone remained free. And on both sides, the walls had been subjected likewise. The mold was gradually extending up toward the ceiling. One day, perhaps, the whole room would be swathed in it.

Yet on the far wall, there was not a single scrap of mold. The blocks were clean, their outlines as sharp as if the builders had departed that very afternoon.

Kitty turned to the others. "Hey—"

"That's it! One more turn'll do it, lads!" Mr. Pennyfeather was practically capering. "I can see a space now in the corner! Another heave and we'll be the first to see old Gladstone since they tucked his bones away!"

No one heard Kitty; no one paid her the slightest bit of attention.

She turned back to the far wall. No mold at all . . . It didn't make sense. Perhaps these clean blocks were made of a different kind of stone?

Kitty stepped across to touch the blocks; as she did so, her shoe caught on the uneven floor and she fell forward. She raised her hands to brace herself against the wall—and fell right through it.

An instant later, she crashed hard against the flagstones of the floor, jarring her wrists and knee. The lantern bounced from her outstretched hand and clattered down beside her.

Kitty screwed up her eyes in pain. Her knee was throbbing badly, and all her fingers tingled with the shock of the fall. But her strongest sensation was one of puzzlement. How had it happened? She was sure she'd fallen against the wall, yet she seemed to have passed through it as if it wasn't there.

Behind her came a fearsome grinding, followed by a terrific crash, several whoops of triumph and also, somewhere amid it all, a cry of pain. She heard Mr. Pennyfeather's voice. "Well *done*, my boys! Well done! Stop sniveling, Stanley—you're not badly hurt. Gather around—let's take a look at him!"

They'd done it. This she had to see. Stiffly, painfully, Kitty raised herself on hands and knees and reached out for the lantern. She got to her feet and, as she did so, the lantern light illuminated a little of the space she was in.

Despite herself, despite the time she had spent out on campaign, despite all the narrow escapes, the traps, the demons, and the deaths of her friends, the shock of what she now saw set her gasping and trembling again like the child she'd been on the iron bridge so many years before. Her pulse thudded in her ears; her head swam. She heard a long, high, piercing wail echoing across the chamber, and jumped, before realizing that it came from her own mouth.

Behind her, the eager celebrations went suddenly silent. Anne's voice. "What was that? Where's Kitty?"

Kitty was still staring straight ahead. "I'm here," she whispered.

"Kitty!"

"Where are you?"

"Drat the girl—has she gone up the stairs? Nicholas, go and look."

"*Kitty!*"

"I'm right here. At the far end. Can't you see?" She could not raise her voice; her throat felt too tight. "I'm here. And I'm not alone. . . ."

The true end of the chamber was not much farther than the illusory one through which she had fallen, perhaps only three meters away from where she stood. The white mold had disregarded the false barrier and marched straight through: it clad the walls and floor and what lay on the floor, and shone with a sickly radiance in the cold light of her lantern. But despite its thick coating, it did not obscure the objects that lay arranged in a neat row between the walls; their nature was all too clear. There were six of them lying packed together, side by side, their heads flung out toward Kitty, their legs pointing away toward the back wall of the chamber, their bony hands resting quietly on their chests. The sealed conditions of the crypt had ensured that their flesh had not entirely rotted through; instead it had shrunk about the skeletons, so that the jaws of the skulls were drawn downward by the tightening skin, giving them permanent expressions of unbridled terror. The skin itself was blackened like fossil wood or tortured leather. The eyes had entirely shriveled away. All six were clothed strangely, in old-fashioned suits; heavy boots rested on their lolling feet. The ribcage of one poked through his shirt. Their hair remained exactly as it had been in life; it flowed from the dreadful heads like river weed. Kitty noticed that one of the men still had a mop of beautiful auburn curls.

Her companions were still calling out her name; their stupidity amazed her.

"I'm *here*!" With a sudden effort, she broke through the inertia of her shock, turning and shouting back along the chamber. Nick and Anne were both close by; at the sound of her voice, their heads darted around, but their eyes remained blank and puzzled, passing over Kitty as if she were not there. Kitty groaned in exasperation and stepped toward them; as she did so, a strange fizzling sensation passed across her body.

Nick cried out. Anne dropped her lantern.

"You'd better come and see this," Kitty said tersely; then, when they did not reply: "What the devil's wrong with you?"

Her anger snapped Nick out of his shock. "L–look at you," he stammered. "You're half in, half out of the wall." Kitty looked down—sure enough, from this side, the illusion held quite fast: her stomach, chest, and front foot protruded from the stones as if they sliced right through her. Her body tingled at the margins where the magic touched.

"Doesn't even glimmer," Anne whispered. "I've never seen an illusion so strong."

"You can walk through," Kitty said dully. "There's things behind it."

"Treasure?" Nick was eagerness itself.

"No."

In moments, the rest of the company had approached the wall and, after some slight hesitation, stepped through the illusion one by one. The stones did not so much as ripple. From the other side, the barrier was quite invisible.

All six stared in shocked silence at the illuminated corpses.

"I vote we get out now," Kitty said.

"Look at the *hair*," Stanley whispered. "And their nails. Look how long they are."

"Laid out like sardines on a plate . . ."

"How d'you think—?"

"Suffocated, maybe . . ."

"See his chest—that hole? That didn't come natural. . . ."

"We don't need to worry. They're very *old*." Mr. Pennyfeather spoke with hearty assurance, designed perhaps to comfort himself as much as the others. "Look at the color of the skin. They're practically mummified."

"Gladstone's time, you think?" Nick asked.

"Undoubtedly. The style of clothes proves it. Late nineteenth century."

"But, six of them. . . . One for each of us. . . ."

"Shut up, Fred."

"But why would they be——?"

"Some kind of sacrifice, perhaps . . . ?"

"Mr. Pennyfeather, listen, we really——"

"No, but why conceal them? It makes no sense."

"Grave robbers, then? Punished by entombment."

"We *really* need to go."

"That's more likely. But again, why hide them?"

"And who did it? And what about the Pestilence? That's what I don't understand. If they triggered it . . ."

"Mr. Pennyfeather!" Kitty stamped her foot and shouted; the noise reverberated across the chamber. The discussion stopped abruptly. She forced the words out through a tightened throat. "There's something here that we don't know about. Some kind of trap. We should forget the treasure and leave now."

"But these bones are *old*," Stanley said, adopting Mr. Pennyfeather's decisive manner. "Calm down, girl."

"Don't patronize *me*, you little twerp."

"I agree with Kitty," Anne said.

"But my *dears*——" Mr. Pennyfeather placed a hand upon Kitty's shoulder and rubbed it with false good humor. "This is very unpleasant, I agree. But we mustn't let it get out of proportion. However these poor fellows died, they were placed here a very long time ago—probably while the tomb was still open. That would be why the illusory wall that hides them has got no mold, see? It's all grown up since then. The walls were clean and new when they met their end." He gesticulated at the corpses with his stick. "Think about it. These boys were lying here *before* the tomb was sealed—otherwise the Pestilence would have been triggered when they broke in. And it wasn't—because we've just seen it and dispersed it."

His words had a muted effect upon the group; there was some nodding and mumbling of agreement. But Kitty shook her head. "We've got six dead men calling out to us," she said. "We'd be fools to ignore them."

"Huh! They're *old*." From the relief in Fred's voice, it seemed the implications of this concept had only just dribbled through to him. "Old bones." He stretched out a boot and nudged the nearest skull derisively; it rolled to the side, away from the neck, and rocked briefly on the flagstones with a gentle sound like rattling crockery.

"You must learn, Kitty dear, to be less emotional," Mr. Pennyfeather said, removing a handkerchief from his pocket and wiping his brow. "We have already opened the old devil's sarcophagus—and the earth's not swallowed us up, has it? Come and *look*, girl: you haven't seen it yet. A silken winding sheet laid out prettily on top—it alone must be worth a fortune. Five minutes, Kitty. Five minutes is all we'll need to lift that sheet and whisk the purse and crystal ball away. We won't disturb Gladstone's sleep for long."

Kitty said nothing; she turned and stalked white-faced through the barrier and back along the chamber. She could not trust herself to speak. Her anger was directed as much at herself—for her own weakness and unreasoning fear—as at her leader. His words seemed facile to her; too glib and easy. But she was not used to directly opposing his will; and she knew the mood of the group was with him.

The *tap-tap-tap*ping of Mr. Pennyfeather's stick came close behind her. He was slightly out of breath. "I hope, Kitty dear, that you—you would do me the honor—of taking the crystal ball itself—in your bag. I trust you, you see—I trust you implicitly. We shall all be strong for five minutes more, then leave this cursed place forever. Gather around, and get your knapsacks ready. Our fortune awaits us!"

The lid of the sarcophagus remained where it had fallen, at an angle between the tomb and the floor. A section of one corner had snapped off on impact, and lay a little apart amid the mold. A lantern sat on the floor burning merrily, but no light was cast up into the gaping black interior of the tomb. Mr. Pennyfeather took up position at one end of the sarcophagus, leaned his stick up against the stone, and grasped the marble for support. He smiled around at the company and flexed his fingers.

"Frederick, Nicholas—hold your lanterns up and over. I'd like to see *exactly* what I'm touching." Stanley giggled nervously.

Kitty glanced back up the chamber. Through the dark, she could just glimpse the impassive outline of the fake wall, its dreadful secret hidden behind. She took a deep breath. Why? It made no sense . . .

She turned back to the sarcophagus. Mr. Pennyfeather leaned in, took tentative hold of something, and pulled.

31

The silken sheet rose from the sarcophagus almost soundlessly, with the faintest of dry whispers and a delicate cloud of brown dust that erupted up like spores from a bursting puffball. The dust wheeled in the crowding lantern light, then sank slowly. Mr. Pennyfeather gathered up the sheet and rested it carefully on the marble rim; then, and only then, did he lean forward and look inside.

"Lower the light," he whispered.

Nick did so; everyone craned their heads over and looked.

"Ahh . . ." Mr. Pennyfeather's sigh was that of a gourmet at his table, whose meal sits before him and who knows that gratification is near. A chorus of gasps and gentle cries echoed him. Even Kitty's misgivings were momentarily forgotten.

Each one of them knew the face as if it were his or her own. It was a centerpiece of life in London, an unavoidable presence in every public place. They had seen its image a thousand times, on statues, memorials, on roadside murals. It was inscribed in profile on school textbooks, on government forms, on posters and placards erected on high billboards in every market. It looked down with austere command from plinths in half the leafy squares; it gazed up at them from the pound notes drawn crumpled from their pockets. Through all their hurrying and scurrying, through all their daily hopes and anxieties, the face of Gladstone was a constant companion, watching over their little lives.

Here, in the tomb, they looked upon the face with a thrill of recognition.

It was fashioned, perhaps, from gold, thinly beaten and finely shaped; a death mask fit for the founder of an empire. While the body still lay cooling, skilled craftsmen had taken the likeness, made the cast, poured in the liquid metal. Upon burial, the mask had been set back on the face, an incorruptible image to gaze forever into the darkness, while the flesh beneath it fell away. It was an old man's face: hook-nosed, thin-lipped, gaunt about the cheeks—where suggestions of the sideburns lingered in the gold—and incised by a thousand wrinkles. The eyes, sunk back deep within the sockets, had been left blank, the gold cut through. Two gaping holes stared blackly at eternity. To the company, gazing open-mouthed, it seemed that they looked upon the face of an emperor from ancient times, wreathed in his awful power.

All about the mask was a pillow of white hair.

He lay neatly, in a pose not dissimilar to the bodies in the secret annex, hands clasped upon his stomach. The fingers were entirely bone. He wore a black suit, still buttoned, taut enough above the ribs, but sagging nastily elsewhere. Here and there, industrious worms or mites in the material had started the process of decay, and small patches of white shone through. The shoes were small, black, and narrow, wearing an additional patina of dust over the dull leather.

The body rested on red satin pillows, on a high shelf that took up half the width of the sarcophagus interior. While Kitty's eyes had lingered on the golden mask, the others' had been drawn to the rather lower shelf alongside.

"Look at the glow . . ." Anne breathed. "It's incredible!"

"It's *all* worth taking," Stanley said, grinning stupidly. "I've never seen an aura like it. *Something* here must be really strong, but it's all got power—even the cloak."

Across the knees, and neatly folded, was a garment of black and purple, topped by a small gold brooch. "The Cloak of State," Mr. Pennyfeather whispered. "Our friend and benefactor wants that. He's welcome to it. Look at the rest. . . ."

And there they were, piled high upon the lower shelf: the marvelous grave goods they had come to find. There was a clustering of golden objects—small statuettes fashioned in the shape of animals, ornate boxes, jeweled swords and daggers, a fringe of black onyx globes, a small triangular skull of some unknown creature, a couple of sealed scrolls. Up by the head sat something small and domed, covered in a black cloth now gray with dust—presumably the prophetic crystal ball. Near the feet, between a flask with a stopper carved like a dog's head and a dull pewter chalice, a satin purse sat inside a glass container. Alongside was a small black bag, fixed with a bronze clasp. Down the whole length of the sarcophagus, close to the body itself, ran a ceremonial sword and, beside it, a staff of blackened wood, plain and unadorned, except for a pentacle carved within a circle at the top.

Even without the others' gifts, Kitty could feel the power emanating from this assembly. It practically vibrated in the air.

Mr. Pennyfeather pulled himself together with a start. "Right, action stations. Bags open and at the ready. We're taking the lot." He glanced at his watch and gave a gasp of surprise. "Almost one o'clock! We've wasted far too much time already. Anne—you first."

He leaned his body against the lip of the sarcophagus, stretching inside and seizing objects in both hands. "Here. Egyptian these, if I'm not mistaken. . . . There's the purse. . . . *Careful* with it, woman! Bag full? Right—Stanley, take her place. . . ."

While the sarcophagus was being despoiled, Kitty stood back, her rucksack open, arms loosely at her sides. The unease that had engulfed her upon the discovery of the bodies drifted in on her once more. She kept glancing over toward the fake wall and back toward the entrance stairs, her skin prickling and crawling with imaginary fears. This anxiety was accompanied by a growing regret at the night's activities. Never had her ideals— her desire to see the magicians vanquished and power returned to the commoners—seemed so divorced from the reality of Mr. Pennyfeather's group. And what a grotesque reality it was. The naked greed of her companions, their excited cries, Mr. Pennyfeather's red, glistening face, the soft clinking of the valuables as they disappeared into the outstretched bags—all of it seemed suddenly repugnant to her. The Resistance was little more than a band of thieves and grave robbers—and she was one of them.

"Kitty! Over here!"

Stanley and Nick had filled their bags and moved aside. It was her turn. Kitty approached. Mr. Pennyfeather was now stretching in farther than ever, his head and shoulders invisible within the sarcophagus. He emerged briefly, handed her a small funerary pot and a jar decorated with a snake head and tipped himself forward again. "Here . . ." His voice echoed oddly in the tomb. "Take the cloak . . . and the staff, too. Both those are for Mr. Hopkins's benefactor, who has—oof!—guided us so well. I can't reach the other bits from this side; Stanley, can you take over, please?"

Kitty took the stick and shoved the cloak deep into her bag, recoiling a little from its cold and faintly greasy touch. She watched Stanley raise himself onto the lip of the sarcophagus and swing his top half down, reaching into the depths while his legs waved momentarily in the air. At the opposite end, Mr. Pennyfeather leaned against the wall, wiping his brow. "Just a few things left," he panted. "Then we—oh, drat the boy! *Why* can't he be more careful?"

Perhaps in an overabundance of enthusiasm, Stanley had fallen headfirst inside the sarcophagus, knocking his lantern backward onto the floor. There was a dull thud.

"You little fool! If you've broken anything . . ." Mr. Pennyfeather leaned forward to look inside, but could see nothing in the well of darkness. Intermittent rustling sounds came from below, together with sounds of uncoordinated movement. "Pick yourself up *carefully*. Don't damage the crystal ball."

Kitty rescued the lantern from where it was rolling on the flagstones, muttering at Stanley's stupidity. He had always been an oaf, but this was priceless, even for him. She clambered over the broken lid to hold the lantern above the sarcophagus, but jumped back in shock as, with great speed and suddenness, Stanley's head popped up above the rim. His cap had fallen down over his face, obscuring it completely.

"Whoops!" he said, in a high, irritating voice. "Clumsy, *clumsy* me."

Kitty's blood boiled. "What d'you think you're doing, startling me like that? This isn't a game!"

"Hurry it up, Stanley," Mr. Pennyfeather said.

"*So* sorry. *So* sorry." But Stanley didn't seem sorry at all. He didn't adjust his cap or emerge any farther from the tomb.

Mr. Pennyfeather's mood turned dangerous. "I'll take my stick to you, boy," he cried, "if you don't get moving."

"Move? Oh, I can do that." With that, Stanley's head began to jerk to and fro inanely, as if to a rhythm only it could hear.

To Kitty's stupefaction, it then ducked down out of sight, paused a moment and sprang up again with a giggle. This action appeared to give Stanley childish pleasure; he repeated the motion, accompanying it with assorted whoops and cries. "Now you see me!" he cried, his voice muffled behind his cap. "And now . . . you don't!"

"The boy's gone mad," Mr. Pennyfeather said.

"Get out of there *now*, Stanley," Kitty said, in an altogether different tone. Suddenly, unaccountably, her heart was beating fast.

"Stanley, am I?" the head said. "Stanley . . . mmm, suits me, that does. Good honest British name. Mr. G. would approve."

Fred was beside Kitty now. "Hey . . ." He was unusually hesitant in manner. "How come his voice has changed?"

The head stopped dead still, then tilted coquettishly to one side. "Well now," it said. "*There's* a question. I wonder if anyone can guess." Kitty took a slow step backward. Fred was right. The voice no longer sounded much like Stanley's, if it ever had.

"Oh, don't try to leave, little girl." The head shook vigorously back and forth. "Then it'll only get messy. Let's take a look at you." Skeletal fingers, extending from a tattered black sleeve, rose from the sarcophagus. The head tipped sideways. With loving care, the fingers removed the cap from the face and placed it on the head at a rakish angle. "*That's* better," the voice said. "Now we can see each other clearly."

Beneath the cap, a face that was not Stanley's flashed with a glint of gold. A spray of white hair showed all around.

Anne gave a sudden wail and ran for the staircase. The head gave a jerk of surprise. "The bloody cheek! We haven't been introduced!" With a sudden flick of a bony wrist, something was scooped from inside the sarcophagus and hurled forward through the air. The crystal ball landed with a crack at the foot of the stairs, rolling directly in Anne's path. She screamed and collapsed back upon the floor.

Everyone in the company had watched the ball's precipitate flight. Everyone saw it land. Now everyone turned slowly back to the sarcophagus, where something was rising to its feet, stiffly and awkwardly, with a clittering of bones. It stood upright at last, shrouded in darkness, brushing dust from its jacket and tut-ting away all the while like a persnickety old woman. "Will you *look* at this mess! Mr. G. would be quite distraught. And the worms have wreaked *havoc* with his underclothes. There're holes down there where the sun don't shine."

It bent suddenly and extended an arm, long bone fingers plucking a fallen lantern from the floor beside the sarcophagus. This it held up like a watchman, and by its light, considered each horrified face in turn. The neck vertebrae rasped as the skull behind the mask moved, and the golden death mask flashed dully inside its halo of long white hair.

"So then." The voice from behind the mask had no consistent tone. With each syllable it shifted, first high like a child's, then deep and husky; first male, then female, then growling like a beast. Either the speaker could not decide, or relished the variety. "So then," it said. "*Here* you are. Five lonely souls, far underground, with nowhere safe to run to. What, pray, are your names?"

Kitty, Fred, and Nick were standing motionless, halfway to the metal grille. Mr. Pennyfeather was farther back, shrinking against the wall below the shelf. Anne was closest to the stairs, but sprawling, sobbing soundlessly. Not one of them could bring themselves to reply.

"Oh, come *on*." The golden mask tipped sideways. "I'm trying to be friendly. Which is exceptionally decent of me, I reckon, given I've just woken to find a leering lout with an out-size cap rifling through my possessions. Worse still—look at this scuff on the funeral suit! He did that with all his thrashing. Kids today, I ask you. Which reminds me. What year is it? You. The girl. The one who isn't mewling. Speak up!"

Kitty's lips were so dry, she barely got the words out. The golden mask nodded. "I *thought* it had been a long time. Why? Because of the boredom, you'll say. Yes, and you'd be right. But also the ache! Ah, the pain of it you wouldn't believe! It got so's I couldn't concentrate, with the agony and the solitude of it, and the noise of the worms gnawing in the dark. It would have driven a lesser fellow mad. But not me. I solved the pain years ago, and the rest I endured. And now, with a bit of light and some company to chat with, I don't mind telling you, I feel *good*." The skeleton clicked a bony finger and jigged from side to side. "Bit stiff—unsurprising, no tendons left—but that'll pass. All bones present and correct? Check. All possessions too? Ah, no . . ." The voice grew wistful. "Some little mice have come and spirited them away. *Naughty* little mice. . . . Catch them by their tails and pull their whiskers out."

Kitty had been slowly inserting a hand into her bag, beneath the cloak and other objects, to locate her Elemental Sphere. She had it now, clasped in a clammy palm. Beside her, she sensed Fred doing likewise, but with less precision; she feared his rustling movements would soon be noticed. She thus spoke more as a distraction than with any real hope.

"Please, Mr. Gladstone, sir," she stammered. "We have all your possessions here, and will happily return them to you exactly as they were."

With an unpleasant grinding, the skull swiveled 180 degrees on its vertebrae to look behind it. Seeing nothing, it cocked sideways in puzzlement and swiveled back. "To whom are you referring, little girl?" it asked. "To *me*?"

"Er—yes. I thought—"

"Me—Mr. Gladstone? Are you mad, or featherheaded as a dabchick?"

"Well—"

"Look at this hand." Five bone fingers were held up to the light and rotated on a knobbly wrist. "Look at this pelvis. Look at this rib cage." In each case, the fingers moved rotting cloth aside to provide a glimpse of yellowed bone. "Look at this face." For an instant, the golden mask was tipped askew, and Kitty caught a glimpse of the skull, with grinning teeth and hollow sockets. "In all honesty, little girl, does Mr. Gladstone look alive to you?"

"Er—not really."

"'*Not really* . . .' The answer's *no!* No, he doesn't. Why? you ask. Because he's dead. A hundred and ten years dead and rotting in his grave. *Not really*. What kind of an answer is that? You really are clots, little girl, you and your friends. Speaking of which . . ." It pointed a bony finger down at the bronze plaque on the side of the sarcophagus. "Can't you read?"

Dumbly, Kitty shook her head. The skeleton clapped its fingers to its forehead in derision. "Can't read Sumerian, and she goes ferreting in Gladstone's grave! So you didn't see the bit about 'leaving the Glorious Leader to rest in peace'?"

"No, we didn't. We're very sorry."

"Or the bits about 'perpetual guardian,' or 'savage vengeance,' or 'no apologies accepted'?"

"No, none of that." Out of the corner of her eye, Kitty saw

Fred lower his bag a little, his right hand still hidden within it. He was ready now.

"Well, what can you expect, then? Ignorance reaps its own reward, which in this case is an unpleasant death. The first lot apologized profusely, too. You should have seen them get down on their knees and bawl for mercy. That's them over there." It jerked a bony thumb in the direction of the false wall. "They were eager beavers, sure enough. Came within weeks. One was Mr. G.'s private secretary, if I recall, a very loyal specimen; he'd managed to make a duplicate key and stave off the Pestilence somehow. I hid them away, just to be tidy, and if you're good I'll do the same with you. Wait right there."

The skeleton hitched one stiff trouser leg over the side of the sarcophagus. Kitty and Fred caught each other's eye. As one, they drew the Elemental Spheres from their knapsacks and hurled them at the skeleton. It raised a resentful hand; something invisible blocked the spheres' flight; they fell heavily to the floor, where, instead of exploding, they seemed to implode with damp, pathetic squeals, leaving nothing but small black stains upon the flagstones.

"I really *can't* have a mess being made here," the skeleton said reprovingly. "In Mr. Gladstone's day, guests were more considerate."

From his own bag, Mr. Pennyfeather drew forth a silver disc; leaning on his stick, he threw it at the skeleton from the side. It sliced into the forearm of the dusty suit and stuck fast. The voice emanating from behind the golden mask let out a shrill yell. "My essence! I *felt* that. Silver is something I really can't abide. See how *you* like being willfully assaulted, old timer." A bright green bolt erupted from the mask and lanced across into Mr. Pennyfeather's chest, driving him back hard against the wall. He crumpled to the floor. The skeleton gave a grunt of satisfaction and turned back to the others. "That'll learn him," it said.

But Fred was moving again, retrieving from secreted spots about his person one silver disc after another and throwing them in the same blink of an eye. The skeleton ducked the first, leaped over the second and had a lock of hair shaved off by the third. It had extricated itself from the sarcophagus now, and seemed to have rediscovered its power of movement; with every bound and step, it grew more sprightly, until its outline almost seemed to blur. "This is fun!" it cried, as it dodged and twirled. "I really am most obliged to you fellows!"

Fred's supply of missiles seemed inexhaustible; he kept up a constant rain, while Nick, Anne, and Kitty steadily retreated toward the stairs. All at once another green bolt stabbed out and struck Fred across the legs, sending him crashing to the ground. In another moment, he was back on his feet, a little unsteady, brows furrowed with pain, but very much alive.

The skeleton paused in surprise. *Well, now,*" it said. "Natural resilience. Deflects magic. Haven't seen that since Prague." It tapped its gold mouth with a bony finger. "What *am* I going to do, I wonder? Let me think. . . . Aha!" With a bound it was back at the sarcophagus and rummaging inside. "Out of the way, Stanley; I need to get . . . yes! I thought so." Its hand reappeared, holding the ceremonial sword. "No magic involved here. Just a length of sturdy Empire steel. Think you can deflect this, Mr. Spotty? We'll see." It flourished the sword above its head and stalked forward.

Fred stood his ground. He drew his flick-knife from his jacket, opened it with a snick.

Kitty was at the metal grille, hovering in doubt at the foot of the stairs. Nick and Anne had already disappeared above; she could hear their frantic ascent. She looked over toward Mr. Pennyfeather, whose own resilience had stood him in good stead. He was shuffling on his hands and knees toward her. Ignoring her instincts, which screamed at her to turn tail and run, she darted back into the vault, grasped Mr. Pennyfeather around his shoulders and, exerting all her strength, dragged him toward the stairs.

Out of sight behind her, she heard Fred give a snarl of fury. There was a whooshing sound, followed by a soft impact.

Kitty pulled Mr. Pennyfeather onward with a strength she didn't know she had.

Through the grille and up the first few steps. She had Mr. Pennyfeather on his feet now; in one hand he still grasped his stick; the other clenched Kitty's jacket. His breathing was rapid, shallow, painful. He could not talk. Neither had a lantern now; they went in utter darkness. Kitty supported herself on the staff from the tomb. It fumbled on each step.

A voice came calling, somewhere behind and below them. "Yoo-hoo! Is anybody up there? Little mice a–scuffling in the wainscot. How many mice? One mice . . . two. Oh dear, and one of them lame."

Kitty's face was swathed in cobwebs. Mr. Pennyfeather's breathing was now a gasping whine.

"*Won't* you come down to me?" the voice implored. "I'm lonely. Neither of your friends want to talk anymore."

She felt Mr. Pennyfeather's face close to her ear. "I—I—have to rest."

"No. Keep going."

"I can't."

"If you won't come down, then . . . I'll have to come up!"

Deep down in the earth, the metal grille creaked.

"Come *on*."

Another step. And another. She couldn't remember how many there were; in any case, she had lost count. Surely they were almost there. But Mr. Pennyfeather was slowing; he held her back like a dead weight.

"Please," she whispered. "One last try."

But he had stopped altogether now; she sensed him crouched upon the stairs beside her, gasping for each breath. Vainly she tugged at his arm, vainly she beseeched him to respond.

"I'm sorry, Kitty . . ."

She gave up, leaned back against the curving stones, drew her knife from her belt, and waited.

A rustle of cloth. A rattling in the dark. Kitty raised her knife.

Silence.

And then, with a sudden rushing and a single brief and gasping cry, Mr. Pennyfeather was pulled into the darkness. One moment he was there, the next moment he was gone, and something heavy was being dragged away from her and down the steps, *bump, bump, bump.*

Kitty was frozen to the spot for perhaps five seconds; then she was careering up the steps, through veils of drifting cob-webs as if they did not exist, knocking repeatedly into the wall, tripping on the uneven stairs; spying at last a rectangle of gray light ahead, falling out into the airy dimness of the nave, where streetlights glittered against the windows and the stat-ues of the magicians gazed down implacably at her hopeless-ness and distress.

She fled away across the transept, narrowly avoiding several pedestals and actually colliding with a row of wooden chairs; the sound of their brattling collapse boomed back and forth across the enormous space. Passing one great pillar, then another, she slowed and, with the entrance to the tomb now a good way behind her, gave herself up to breathless weeping.

Only then did she realize she might have turned the key in the lock.

"Kitty." A small voice in the shadows. Kitty's heart pounded against her chest; with the knife outstretched before her, she backed away.

"Kitty, it's me." A thin beam of light from the pencil torch. Anne's face, pale, gray-eyed. She cowered behind a high, wooden lectern.

"We've got to get out." Kitty's voice was cracking. "Which way's the door?"

"Where's Fred? And Mr. Pennyfeather?"

"*Which way's the door*, Annie? Can you remember?"

"No. That is, I think *that* way, maybe. It's so difficult in the dark. But—"

"Come on, then. Turn off the torch for now."

She went on at a jog, Anne stumbling after her. In the first moments of her panic, Kitty had simply run unthinkingly, with no sense of direction. It had been the foul blackness below ground that had done it—numbing her brain, stopping her from thinking clearly. But now, dark and musty though it still was, the air was at least fresh—it was helping her master her surroundings, orient her position. A line of pale windows shone high above: they were back in the nave again, on the opposite side to the cloisters door. She halted, allowing Anne to catch up with her.

"It's just across here," she hissed. "Tread carefully."

"Where's—?"

"Don't ask." She stole forward a few more steps. "What about Nick?"

"He's gone. I didn't see . . ."

Kitty swore under her breath. "Never mind."

"Kitty—I dropped my bag."

"Well, that doesn't matter now, does it? We've lost everything." Even as she said it, she suddenly became aware that she was still holding the magician's staff in her left hand. It surprised her somewhat; throughout the desperate flight, she had not been at all aware of it. The rucksack, with the cloak and other valuables, had been lost somewhere on the stairs.

"What was that?"

They stopped dead, in the center of the nave's black space.

"I didn't hear—"

"Something scuttling. Did you—?"

"No . . . *No*, I didn't. Keep going."

A few steps more; they sensed a column rising high in front of them. Kitty turned to Anne. "Past the pillar, we'll need the torch to pinpoint the door. I don't know how far we've come."

"All right." At that moment, a skittering rush sounded directly behind them. Both squealed and lurched in opposite directions. Kitty fell half against the pillar, lost her balance and collapsed to the floor. Her knife was jarred out of her grasp. As quickly as she could she got to her feet and turned around.

Darkness; somewhere a faint scraping. The pencil torch was lying on the ground, spilling a miserly beam of light against the column. Anne was nowhere to be seen.

Slowly, slowly, Kitty backed away behind the pillar.

The door to the cloisters was somewhere close, she was sure of it, but exactly where she could not tell. Still holding the staff, she slipped forward, hand outstretched, feeling her way blindly toward the south wall of the nave.

To her surprise and almost unsupportable relief, her fingers touched coarse wood and the cold breath of true fresh air fell upon her face. The door was hanging open, a little; she scrabbled at it desperately to shove it aside, squeeze through.

It was just then that she heard the familiar noise; somewhere behind her in the nave. The *tap-tap-tap*ping of a lame man's stick.

Kitty dared not breathe; she remained frozen where she was, half in and half out of the abbey door.

Tap, tap, tap. The faintest of whisperings. "Kitty . . . help me . . ."

It couldn't be. *It couldn't.* She made to step out into the cloisters; paused.

"Kitty . . . please . . ." The voice was weak, the footsteps faltering.

She closed her eyes tight; took a long, deep breath; slipped back inside.

Someone was shuffling along in the middle of the nave, tapping hesitantly with the stick. It was too dark to make the figure out; it seemed confused, directionless, wandering this way and that, coughing feebly and calling out her name. Kitty watched it from behind a column, jerking back whenever it appeared to turn toward her. From what she could see, it was the right shape, the right size for him; it moved in the right way. The voice sounded familiar, too, but despite all this, her heart misgave her. The thing was trying to trap her, surely. Yet she couldn't just turn and run, and never know for certain that she hadn't left Mr. Pennyfeather there, alone and still alive.

What she needed was the torch.

The meager beam of light was still shining redundantly against the next pillar, Anne's torch lying exactly where it had fallen. Kitty waited until the limping figure had passed a little way along the nave, then she crept forward with feline stealth, knelt, and collected the torch in her hand. She switched it off and retreated into the darkness.

The figure seemed to have sensed the movement. Halfway across the nave, it turned, emitting a quavering sigh. "Is . . . someone there?"

Hidden behind the pillar, Kitty made no sound.

"Please . . . it will find me soon." The taps started up once more. Steadily, they came nearer.

Kitty bit her lip. She would dart out, torch on; take a look, run. But fear held her rigid, her limbs refused to move.

Tap, tap . . . then, with a hollow clattering, she heard the stick fall upon the stones, followed by the muffled impact of a body collapsing to the floor.

Kitty came to a decision. Holding the torch between her teeth, she drew something small from her trouser pocket: Grandmama Hyrnek's silver pendant, cold and heavy in her hand. She grasped the torch once more and stepped out from behind the column. She switched the torch on.

Right beside her, the skeleton leaned nonchalantly against the pillar, hand on hip, gold mask glinting. "Surprise," it said. And leaped at her.

With a scream, Kitty fell back, dropping the torch, thrusting her silver pendant out toward the onrushing blackness. A swirl of air, a creak of bones, a hoarse cry. "Now, *that's* not fair." The form pulled up short. For the first time, she glimpsed its eyes: two red glowing dots flaring with annoyance.

Kitty backed away, still holding the silver pendant before

her. The two eyes crept with her, keeping pace, but wheeling and swerving in the darkness, as she waved the pendant from side to side.

"Put that *down*, little girl," the skeleton said in a tone of great vexation. "It burns me. Must be good quality to do that, as it's so small."

"Back off," Kitty snarled. Somewhere behind her was the cloister door.

"Now, *am* I likely to do that? I'm on a charge, you know. In fact, I'm on two. Protect Gladstone's possessions, first of all. Check Well done, Honorius. No problem there. Destroy all invaders of the tomb, second. Marks so far? Ten out of twelve. Not bad, but room for improvement. And *you*, little girl, *are number eleven*." It made a sudden lunge; Kitty sensed the bony fingers swiping in the dark; with a cry, she ducked, held up the pendant. There was a brief flurry of green sparks and an animal howl.

"Ow! Curse you! Put it down!"

"Now, *am* I likely to do that?" Kitty felt a cold breeze behind her, took two more retreating steps and nearly collided with the open door. She edged around it, down the step and into the cloister.

The skeleton was a shadowy form hunched in the archway. It shook a fist. "I should have brought my sword for you, Kitty," it said. "I've half a mind to go back and fetch ..." Then it stiffened and cocked its head. Something had caught its attention.

Kitty backed steadily away along the corridor.

"The stars ... I'd quite forgotten." The figure in the arch gave a sudden hop and stood on a ledge, looking up toward the sky. "So many of them ... so bright and pearly blue."

Even from the far end of the cloister, several yards away and retreating fast, Kitty could hear it sniffing the air and muttering to itself, and letting out little cries of fascination and delight. It appeared to have entirely forgotten her existence.

"No stone. No worms. What a change that would make! No mold, no deathly dustly silence. No none of it. So many stars . . . and so much space . . ."

Kitty rounded the corner and made a dash for the cloister door.

Part Four

32

Nathaniel's limousine sped through the outer suburbs of South London, a region of heavy industry, of brickworks and alchemists' factories, where a faint red smog hung permanently around the houses and glowed evilly in the waning sun. For greater speed and convenience, the magicians' highway from the aerodrome had been raised on embankments and viaducts above the maze of polluted slums. The road was little used, and nothing but rooftops stretched around; at times the car appeared to be drifting alone across a sea of dirt-red waves. Nathaniel gazed out across this great expanse, deep in thought.

The chauffeur was of the usual taciturn type, and despite Nathaniel's best efforts, had revealed little of the previous night's disaster. "I don't know much myself, sir," he said. "But there was crowds gathered in the street outside my flat this morning. A lot of panic among the commoners, sir. Very frightened, they were. A disturbance."

Nathaniel leaned forward. "What sort of disturbance?"

"I believe a monster is involved, sir."

"A monster? Can you be specific? Not a big stone man, shrouded in darkness?"

"I don't know, sir. We'll be at the abbey shortly. The ministers are meeting there."

Westminster Abbey? With great dissatisfaction, Nathaniel had settled back in the seat and composed himself to wait. All would be made clear in time. Quite possibly, the golem had struck again, in which case his account of events in Prague would be anxiously awaited. He sorted through everything he knew, trying to make sense of it, setting successes against setbacks in an effort to see whether he came out with credit. On balance, it was a close thing.

On the credit side, he had landed a definite blow against the enemy: with the help of Harlequin, he had discovered the source of the golem parchments and had destroyed it. He had learned of the involvement of the terrible bearded mercenary and, behind him, some other shadowy figure who had, if the mercenary was to be believed, also been involved in the Lovelace conspiracy two years before. The existence of such a traitor was important news. Set against this, however, Nathaniel had not discovered who the traitor was. Of course, it was hard to see how he could have done so, since even the wretched Kavka hadn't known the name.

Here, Nathaniel shifted uncomfortably in his seat, remembering his rash promise to the old magician. The Czech spies, Kavka's children, were—apparently—still alive in a British prison. If so, it would be extremely difficult for Nathaniel to secure their release. But what did it matter? Kavka was dead! It didn't matter to *him* now one way or the other. The promise could quietly be forgotten. Despite this clear-cut logic, Nathaniel found it hard to dismiss the matter from his mind. He shook his head angrily and returned to more important matters.

The traitor's identity was a mystery, but the mercenary had given Nathaniel one important clue. His employer *knew* Nathaniel was coming to Prague and had instructed the mercenary to take action. But Nathaniel's mission had been almost spontaneous, and kept very quiet. Hardly anyone was aware of it.

Who, in fact, *had* known? Nathaniel counted them out on the fingers of one hand. Himself; Whitwell, of course—she'd

sent him there in the first place; Julius Tallow—he'd been present at the meeting. Then there was the Second Secretary of the
Foreign Office, who'd briefed Nathaniel before the flight—
Whitwell had asked him to prepare the maps and documents.
And that was it. Unless . . . hold on . . . a faint uncertainty
nagged at Nathaniel. That encounter with Jane Farrar in the
foyer, when she'd used the Charm . . . Had he let anything slip
there? It was so hard to remember; her spell had fogged his
mind a little. . . . No good. He couldn't recall.

Even so, the range of suspects was remarkably small.
Nathaniel chewed the edge of a fingernail. He had to be very
careful from now on. The mercenary had said something else,
too: his employer had many servants. If the traitor was as close
as Nathaniel now guessed, he had to watch his step. Someone
among the powerful was operating the golem in secret, directing it through the watch-eye. They would not wish Nathaniel
to investigate further. Attempts might well be made on his life.
He would need Bartimaeus to stick close to him.

Despite these concerns, Nathaniel was feeling fairly pleased
with himself by the time the viaducts lowered and the car
neared central London. When all was said and done, he had
prevented a second golem's being unleashed on the capital, and
for that, he would surely receive full praise. Inquiries could be
carried out and the traitor discovered. The first thing he would
do would be to report to Whitwell and Devereaux. No doubt,
they would drop everything and respond.

This happy certainty had begun to ebb a little even before the
car drew into Westminster Green. Nearing the Thames,
Nathaniel began to notice certain unusual things: pockets of
commoners standing in the street, deep in conference; here and

there, what looked like debris in the road—smashed chimneys, chunks of masonry and broken glass. Westminster Bridge itself had a Night Police cordon across it, guards checking the driver's pass before allowing him through. As they crossed the river, Nathaniel saw thick smoke rising from an office downstream: a clock-face on the side of the building had been smashed, the hands ripped off and embedded in the walls. Other groups of bystanders loitered on the embankment, in blatant disregard of vagrancy laws.

The car swept past the Houses of Parliament and up to the great gray mass of Westminster Abbey, where the final remnants of Nathaniel's complacency shriveled down to nothing. The grass before the west end was covered with official vehicles— ambulances, Night Police vans, a host of gleaming limousines. Among them was one with Devereaux's gold standard fluttering from the bonnet. The Prime Minister himself was here.

Nathaniel alighted and, flashing his identity card to the guards on the door, entered the church. Inside, the activity was intense. Internal Affairs magicians swarmed about the nave with imps in attendance, measuring, recording, combing the stonework for information. Dozens of Security officials and gray-coated Night Police accompanied them; the air hummed with muttered conversations.

A woman from Internal Affairs noticed him, gestured with her thumb. "They're up in the north transept, Mandrake, by the tomb. Whitwell's waiting."

Nathaniel looked at her. "What tomb?"

Her eyes were alive with contempt. "Oh, you'll see. You'll see."

Nathaniel walked up the nave, his black coat dragging limply behind. A great trepidation was upon him. One or two

Night Police were standing guard beside a broken walking stick lying on the flagstones; they laughed openly as he passed.

He emerged into the north transept, where statues of the Empire's great magicians clustered in a thicket of marble and alabaster. Nathaniel had been here many times before, to look with contemplation upon the faces of the wise; it was with some shock then that he saw that half the statues were now defaced: heads had been ripped off and replaced back to front, limbs had been removed; one sorcerer wearing a particularly broad hat had even been turned upside down. It was an appalling act of vandalism.

Dark-suited magicians thronged everywhere, carrying out tests and scribbling notes. Nathaniel wandered among them in a daze, until he arrived at an open space, where, sitting in a ring of chairs, Mr. Devereaux and his senior ministers were assembled. They were all present: the burly, brooding Duvall; the diminutive Malbindi; the bland-featured Mortensen; the corpulent Fry. Jessica Whitwell was there, too, scowling into space, arms folded. On a chair a little removed from the others sat Mr. Devereaux's friend and confidante, the playwright Quentin Makepeace, his cheery face solemn and anxious. All were silent, gazing at a large luminous orb hovering several feet off the floor tiles. It was the viewing globe for a vigilance sphere, Nathaniel could see this at once; currently it depicted what appeared to be an aerial view of part of London. In the distance, and rather out of focus, a small figure was leaping from roof to roof. Small green explosions erupted where it landed. Nathaniel frowned, stepped closer to get a better look—

"So, you're back from chasing shadows, are you?" Yellowed fingers caught his sleeve; Julius Tallow stood beside him, sharp nose jutting, features arranged in an expression of distaste.

"About time. All hell's broken loose here."

Nathaniel pulled himself free. "What's going on?"

"Did you discover the mysterious mastermind behind the golem?" Tallow's voice dripped sarcasm.

"Well, no, but—"

"How surprising. It might interest you to know, Mandrake, that while you were gallivanting abroad, the Resistance have struck again. Not some mystery golem, not a mystery traitor wielding forgotten powers, but the same human Resistance that you've been failing to deal with all this time. Not content with destroying half the British Museum the other night, they've now broken into Gladstone's tomb and unleashed one of his afrits. Which, as you can see, is now happily at large across the city."

Nathaniel blinked, tried to take it all in. "The Resistance did this? How do you know?"

"Because we've found the bodies. No giant clay golem was involved, Mandrake. You can give that idea up right now. And we'll soon be out of our jobs. Duvall—"

He drew back. Nathaniel's master, Jessica Whitwell, had left her seat and was making her thin and stately way toward him. He cleared his throat.

"Ma'am, I need to speak to you urgently. In Prague—"

"I blame *you* for this, Mandrake." She bore down on him, eyes flashing furiously. "Thanks to your distracting me with your demon's lies, we look more incompetent than ever! I have been made to look a fool and have lost the Prime Minister's favor. Duvall was given control of my Security department this morning. He has also taken charge of anti-Resistance operations."

"Ma'am, I'm sorry, but listen, please—"

"Sorry? Too late now, Mandrake. The British Museum debacle was bad enough, but *this* was the last straw. Duvall has gotten just what he wanted. His wolves are everywhere now and he—"

"Ma'am!" Nathaniel could no longer restrain himself. "I located the Czech magician who created the golem's parchment. He was making a second one—for a traitor in our government!" He ignored Tallow's expressions of incredulity.

Ms. Whitwell regarded him. "Who is the traitor?"

"I don't yet know."

"Have you proof of your story? The parchment, for instance?"

"No. It was all destroyed, but I think—"

"Then," Ms. Whitwell said, with crushing finality, "it is no good to me, and neither are *you*. London is in an uproar, Mandrake, and a scapegoat needs to be found. I intend to distance myself from you—and if Mr. Tallow has any sense, he will do the same."

She turned on her heel and marched back to her chair. Tallow followed, grinning at Nathaniel over his shoulder. After a moment's hesitation, Nathaniel shrugged and drifted closer to the swirling surveillance orb. The demi-afrit relaying the image was attempting to get closer to the bounding figure on the rooftops. The image zoomed in; Nathaniel caught sight of a black suit, white hair, a gold face. . . . Then, quick as thought, a green light shot from the figure: with an emerald flash, the sphere went dead.

Mr. Devereaux sighed. "A third sphere gone. We'll be running out soon. Right—any comments or reports?"

Mr. Mortensen, the Home Office Minister, stood up and swept a lock of greasy hair over his scalp. "Sir, we must take action against this demon at once. If we don't act, the name of Gladstone will be dragged through the mud! Is he not our greatest leader? The one to whom we owe our prosperity, our dominance, our self-belief? And now what is he? Nothing but a murderous bag of bones dancing across our capital, causing bedlam in its wake! The commoners will not be slow to notice this, you know; nor will our enemies abroad. I say—"

Marmaduke Fry, the Foreign Minister, spoke. "We have had several instances of mass panic, which no amount of strong-arm stuff from Duvall's police has been able to prevent." He cast a sly side glance at the Chief of Police, who grunted angrily.

"The creature is evidently deranged," added the Information Minister, Ms. Malbindi, "and as Mortensen says, that adds to the embarrassment of the situation. We have our Founder's remains capering on rooftops, dangling from flagpoles, dancing down the middle of Whitehall and, if our sources are to be believed, cartwheeling repeatedly through Camberwell Fish Market. Also the thing persists in killing people, apparently at random. Young men and girls, it goes for; mostly commoners, but also people of consequence. It claims it is looking for the 'last two,' whatever that means."

"The last two survivors of the raid," Mr. Fry said. "That's obvious enough. And one of 'em's got the Staff. But our immediate problem is that the commoners know whose corpse they're seeing."

From the edges of the group came Jessica Whitwell's icy voice. "Let me get this clear," she said. "Those really *are* Gladstone's bones? It isn't just some guise?"

Ms. Malbindi raised two fastidious eyebrows. "They're his bones all right. We've entered the tomb, and the sarcophagus is empty. There are plenty of bodies down there, believe you me, but our Founder is very much gone."

"Strange, isn't it?" Mr. Makepeace spoke for the first time. "The guardian afrit has encased its own essence within the bones. Why? Who knows?"

"*Why* is not important." Mr. Devereaux spoke with heavy formality, driving a fist into his cupped palm. "Our first priority must be to get rid of it. Until it is destroyed, the dignity of our State is hopelessly compromised. I want the creature dead and the bones back in the ground. Every senior minister must put a demon on the case from this afternoon. That means all of *you*. Lesser ministers have conspicuously failed so far. The thing *is* Gladstone's, after all; it has some power. Meanwhile, there is the issue of the Staff to consider."

"Yes," Mr. Fry said. "In the long run this is much more important. With the American wars coming up—"

"It mustn't be allowed to get into enemy hands. If the Czechs got hold of it—"

"Quite." There was a brief silence.

"Excuse me." Nathaniel had been listening to everything with silent respect, but his frustration now got the better of him. "This is Gladstone's Staff of Office we're talking about? The one he used to destroy Prague?"

Mr. Devereaux looked at him coldly. "I am glad you have finally deigned to join us, Mandrake. Yes, it is the same Staff."

"So if its Command Words can be mastered, we might harness its energies for new campaigns?"

"We—or our enemies. Presently its whereabouts are unknown."

"Are we sure?" Helen Malbindi asked. "The . . . skeleton, or afrit, or whatever it is—*it* doesn't still have the Staff?"

"No. It carries a bag on its back—which we suspect holds

most of Gladstone's treasures. But the Staff itself has vanished. One of the grave robbers must have it."

"I've sealed the ports and aerodromes," Mr. Mortensen said. "Spheres are on watch along the coast."

"Pardon me," Nathaniel asked. "But if this Staff has *always* been in the abbey, why have we not utilized it before?"

Several of the magicians shifted in their seats. Mr. Duvall's eyes flashed. "This is supposed to be a senior meeting of the Council, not a crèche. I suggest, Rupert, that this changeling be removed."

"A moment, Henry." Mr. Devereaux seemed as annoyed as his ministers, but he still spoke civilly. "The boy has a point. The reason, Mandrake," he said, "is for fear of a disaster such as this. On his deathbed, Gladstone swore vengeance on any who disturbed his tomb, and we all know that his power was not easily transgressed. Exactly what hexes he wrought or demons he employed were not known, but—"

"I have done a little research into the business," Quentin Makepeace said, interrupting with an easy smile. "Gladstone has always interested me. At the funeral, the tomb was sealed with a Pestilence inside—a potent little number, but nothing that could not easily be bypassed. But Gladstone had made preparations for his sarcophagus himself; contemporary sources say the aura of magic emanating from his body killed several imps officiating with the candles. If that was not warning enough, not long after his death several magicians in his government ignored his prohibitions and set out to collect the Staff. They froze the Pestilence, descended into the tomb: and were never seen again. Accomplices waiting outside heard something locking the door from within. No one since has been foolish enough to test the grand old man's defenses. Until last night."

"You believe the Resistance accomplished this?" Nathaniel asked. "If there are bodies remaining, they must furnish some clues. I would like—"

"Pardon me, Mandrake," Duvall said. "That is no longer your job. The police are in charge now. Suffice it to say that my Graybacks will be carrying out enquiries." The Police Chief turned to the Prime Minister. "I think this is the moment, Rupert, for some harsh words to be said. This boy, Mandrake, was meant to be pursuing the Resistance. Now Westminster Abbey, resting place of the great, has been broached and Gladstone's tomb defiled. The Staff has been stolen. And the boy has been doing nothing."

Mr. Devereaux looked at Nathaniel. "Do you have anything to say?"

For a moment, Nathaniel considered recounting the events in Prague, but he knew it would be hopeless. He had no proof. Besides, it was more than probable that the traitor was sitting right there, watching him. He would bide his time. "No, sir."

"I am disappointed, Mandrake, deeply disappointed." The Prime Minister turned away. "Ladies, gentlemen," he said. "We must track down the remnants of the Resistance and recover the Staff. Anyone who succeeds will be well rewarded. First, we must destroy the skeleton. Assemble your best magicians in"—he glanced at his watch—"two hours' time. I want everything resolved. Is that clear?" There was a subdued murmur of assent. "Then this Council is adjourned."

The gaggle of ministers departed the abbey, Ms. Whitwell and Tallow anxiously taking up the rear. Nathaniel made no move to follow them. Very well, he thought, I shall distance myself from you, too. I'll carry out investigations on my own.

A junior magician was sitting on a pew in the nave, consulting her notebook. Nathaniel squared his shoulders and approached with as much of a swagger as he could muster. "Hello, Fennel," he said, gruffly. "Bad business, this."

The woman looked startled. "Oh, Mr. Mandrake. I didn't know you were still on the case. Yes, a bad business."

He nodded back toward the tomb. "Found out anything about them?"

She shrugged. "For what it's worth. Papers on the old man identify him as one Terence Pennyfeather. Owned an artists' supply shop in Southwark. The others are much younger. They may have worked with him in the shop. Don't yet know their names. I was just going down to Southwark to consult his records."

Nathaniel glanced at his watch. Two hours till the summoning. He had time. "I'll come with you. One thing, though . . .". He hesitated, his heart beating a little faster. "Back in the crypt . . . Was there a girl among them—slim, with dark, straight hair?"

Fennel frowned. "Not the bodies I saw."

"Right. Right. Well then, shall we go?"

Burly Night Police were stationed outside Pennyfeather's Art Supplies, and magicians from several departments were busily combing the interior. Nathaniel and Fennel showed their passes and entered. They ignored the hunt for stolen artifacts going on about them, and instead began sifting through a pile of battered account books found behind the counter. Within minutes, Fennel had uncovered a list of names.

"It's a list of payments to employees," she said. "A couple of months back. They might all be Resistance. None of them are here today."

"Let's have a look." Nathaniel scanned it quickly. *Anne Stephens, Kathleen Jones, Nicholas Drew* . . . These names meant nothing to him. Wait—*Stanley Hake* and *Frederick Weaver*. Fred and Stanley, clear as day. He was on the right track, but there was no sign of a Kitty here. He flipped the page to the next month's payments. Same again. He handed the ledger back to Fennel, tapping his fingers on the glass counter.

"Here's another, sir."

"Don't bother. I've already seen—*hold on.*"

Nathaniel almost snatched the paper from Fennel's hands, peered at it closely, blinked, peered again. There it was, the same list, but with a single difference: *Anne Stephens, Kitty Jones, Nicholas Drew* . . . No doubt about it: Kitty Jones, Kathleen Jones, one and the same.

During his many months of hunting, Nathaniel had scoured official records for evidence of Kitty, and found nothing. Now it was clear he had been looking for the wrong name all this time.

"Are you all right, Mr. Mandrake?" Fennel was staring at him anxiously.

Everything snapped back into focus. "Yes, yes, I'm fine. It's just . . ." He smiled at her, adjusted a cuff. "I think I may have had a good idea."

33

It was the biggest joint summoning that I'd been involved in since the great days of Prague. Forty djinn materializing more or less at once, in a vast chamber built for that purpose in the bowels of Whitehall. As with all such things, it was a messy business, despite the best efforts of the magicians. *They* were all lined up in tidy rows of identical pentacles, wearing the same dark suits and speaking their incantations quietly, while the officiating clerks scribbled their names down at tables to the sides. We djinn, of course, were less concerned with regimental decorum: we arrived in forty very different guises, trumpeting our individuality with horns, tails, iridescent flanges, spikes, and tentacles; with colors ranging from obsidian-black to delicate dandelion-yellow; with a menagerie full of hollerings and chitter; with a magnificent range of sulfurous guffs and stenches. Out of sheer boredom, I had reverted to one of my old favorites, a winged serpent with silver feathers arching from behind my head.[1] To my right was a kind of bird thing on stilt legs, to my left an eerie miasma of blue-green smoke. Beyond him was a slavering griffin, and beyond *him*—more disconcerting than menacing, this one—was a stumpy and immobile footstool. We all faced our masters, waiting for our charges.

---

[1] That used to bring the house down in the Yucatán, where you'd see the priests tumbling down the pyramid steps or diving into alligator-infested lakes to escape my mesmerizing sway. Didn't have quite the same effect on the boy here. In response to my undulating menace, he yawned, picked his teeth with a finger and began scribbling in a notepad. Is it me, or have kids today simply seen too much?

The boy hardly paid any attention to me; he was too busy writing down some notes.

"Ahem." The serpent of silver plumes gave a polite cough. "A-*hem*." Still no response. How impolite was this? You call someone up, then take them for granted. I coughed a little louder. "A-*thaniel*."

That got a response. His head jerked up, then swiveled from side to side. "Shut *up*," he hissed. "Anyone could have heard that."

"What *is* all this?" I said. "I thought we had a private thing going. Now every man and his imp are joining in."

"It's top priority. We've got an insane demon on the loose. We need it destroyed."

"It won't be the only mad thing about if you let this lot go." I flicked my tongue in a lefterly direction. "Check out that one at the end. He's taken the form of a footstool. Weird . . . but somehow I like his style."

"That *is* a footstool. No one's using that pentacle. Now, listen. Things are moving fast. The Resistance have broken into Gladstone's tomb and freed the guardian of his treasures. It's at large in London, causing merry hell. You'll recognize it by its mildewed bones and general smell of decay. The Prime Minister wants it gone; that's why this group is being assembled."

"*All* of us? It must be potent. Is it an afrit?"[2]

"We think so, yes. Powerful—and embarrassing. It was last seen gyrating Gladstone's pelvis on Horseguards' Parade. But

---

[2] I'd had a few close encounters with Gladstone's afrits during his war of conquest and it was fair to say I wasn't anxious for another. They were a prickly lot, in general, made restless and aggressive by unpleasant treatment. Of course, even if this afrit had started out with the loving personality of a gentle babe (unlikely), it would not have been improved by a century's inhumation in a tomb.

listen, I want you to do something more. If you find the de—, the afrit, see if you can get any information concerning the Resistance: particularly about a girl called Kitty. I think she may have escaped with a precious Staff. The creature may be able to give a description."

"Kitty . . ." The serpent's tongue flicked back and forth musingly. A Resistance girl of that name had crossed our paths before. If I remembered correctly, she was a feisty specimen with big trousers. . . . Well, several years on, her feistiness evidently hadn't failed her.[3] I recalled something else. "Wasn't she the one who nicked your scrying-glass?"

He made his patented bulldog-who's-sat-on-a-thistle face. "Possibly."

"And now she's pinched Gladstone's Staff . . . Talk about going up in the world."

"There was nothing wrong with that scrying glass."

"No, but you'll admit it'd never laid Europe to waste. That Staff's a formidable piece of work. And you say it's been lying in Gladstone's tomb all this time?"

"Apparently." The boy glanced carefully around him, but all the neighboring magicians were busily delivering their charges to their slaves, shouting over the general caterwauling. He leaned forward in a conspiratorial manner. "It's ridiculous!" he whispered. "Everyone's always been too scared to open the tomb. And now some bunch of commoners has made a fool of the whole government. But I intend to find the girl and rectify that."

I shrugged my hood. "You could always just wish her well and leave her alone."

"And let her sell the Staff to the highest bidder? Don't make

---

[3] I had no information on the trousers so far.

me laugh!" My master bent closer. "I think I can track her down. And when I do . . . well, I've read a lot about that Staff. It's powerful, all right, but its Words of Command were fairly straightforward. It needs a strong magician to control it, but in the right hands—who knows what it could achieve?" He straightened impatiently. "What's the delay here? They should be giving the general order to move off. I've got more important things to do."

"They're waiting for Buttercup there in the corner to finish his incantation."

"Who? *Tallow?* What's that idiot playing at? Why doesn't he just summon his green monkey thing?"

"Judging by the amount of incense he's employed, and the size of that book he's holding, he's going for something big."

The boy grunted. "Trying to impress everyone with a higher-level demon, I suppose. Typical. He'd do *anything* to keep Whitwell's favor."

The winged serpent swayed back violently. "Whoa, there!"

"What's the matter now?"

"It was your face! Just for a moment there, you had a really unpleasant sneer on it. Horrible, it was."

"Don't be ridiculous. You're the one who's a giant snake. Tallow's been on my back too long, that's all." He cursed. "Him and all the rest. I can't trust anyone around here. Which reminds me . . ." He bent closer once more; the serpent dipped its majestic head to hear him. "I'm going to need your protection more than ever. You heard what that mercenary said. Someone in the British government tipped him off that we were coming to Prague."

The plumed serpent nodded. "Glad you caught up. I figured that out long ago. By the way, have you freed those Czech spies yet?"

His brow darkened. "Give me a chance! I've got more urgent things to consider. Someone near the top's controlling the golem's eye, stirring up trouble here. They might try to silence me."

"Who knew you were coming to Prague? Whitwell? Tallow?"

"Yes, and a minister in the Foreign Office. Oh, and possibly Duvall."

"That hairy Police Chief? But he left the meeting before—"

"I know he did, but his apprentice, Jane Farrar, might have wormed the information out of me." Was it the light, or had the boy flushed a little?

"*Wormed* it? How's that, exactly?"

He scowled. "She used a Charm and—"

Rather to my disappointment, this interesting story was suddenly disrupted by an abrupt and, to the assembled magicians, disconcerting occurrence. The stocky, yellow magician, Tallow, who was standing in a pentacle at the end of the next row, had finally finished his long and complex invocation, and with a flex of his pinstriped arms, lowered the book from which he had read. A few seconds passed; the magician waited, breathing hard, for his summons to be heard. All at once, a billowing column of black smoke began to issue from the center of the second pentacle, small yellow forks of lightning crackling in its heart. It was a bit hackneyed, but quite well done in its way.[4]

The magician went gog-eyed with foreboding; rightly so as

---

[4] Several of us hovering nearby had been half-watching with the detached interest of the connoisseur. It's always interesting to study one another's styles when you get the chance, since you never know when you might pick up a new tip on presentation. In my youth, I was always one for the dramatic entrance. Now, in keeping with my character, I gravitate more toward the subtle and refined. Okay, with the occasional feathered serpent thrown in.

it turned out. The smoke coalesced into a muscular black form some seven feet high, complete with four waving arms.[5] It shuffled slowly around the perimeter of the pentacle, testing for weaknesses.

And to its evident surprise, found one.[6]

The four arms froze for a moment, as if in doubt. Then a dribble of smoke emerged from the base of the figure and prodded the edge of the pentacle with experimental care. Two such prods was all it took. The weak spot was pinpointed: a little hole in the incantatory barrier. Instantly, the pseudopodium extended forward and began to stream through the breach, narrowing almost to a point as it passed through, expanding again on the other side. Faster and faster streamed the smoke; it swelled and grew and became a bulging tentacle that darted eagerly across the space to the other pentacle, where the magician stood transfixed in horror. The trails of rosemary and rowan that he had placed around its edges were scattered to the winds. The smoke ballooned up about his shoes, rapidly encasing his legs in a thick black column. The magician made a few incoherent noises at this point, but he didn't have time for much; the figure in the first pentacle had now dwindled to nothing; all its essence had passed through the gap and was enveloping its prey. In less than five seconds, the whole magician, pinstriped suit and all, had been swallowed by the smoke.

---

[5] This guise suggested the djinni's career had included a spell in the Hindu Kush. Amazing how these influences stay with you.

[6] The words of a summons act as crucial reinforcements of the runes and lines drawn upon the floor. They create invisible bands of power that circle the pentacle, knotting and reknotting, and looping in upon themselves, until an impassable boundary is formed. However, just one word a smidgen out of place can leave a fatal weakness in the whole defense. As Tallow was about to discover.

Several triumphalist lightning bolts were emitted near the head of the column, then it sank away into the floor like a solid thing, taking the magician with it.

An instant later, both pentacles were empty, except for a telltale scorch where the magician had once stood, and a charred book lying beside it.

Throughout the summoning chamber, there was stunned silence. The magicians stood dumbfounded, their clerks limp and sagging in their seats.

Then the whole place erupted into noise; those magicians who had already suitably bound their slaves, my master among them, stepped from their pentacles and gathered around the scorch mark, stewy-faced and jabbering. We higher beings began a cheery and approving chatter. I exchanged a few remarks with the green miasma and the stilt-legged bird.

"*Nice* one."

"Stylishly done."

"That *lucky* beggar. You could tell she could hardly believe it."

"Well, how often does a chance like that come along?"

"All too rarely. I remember one time, back in Alexandria. There was this young apprentice—"

"The fool must have mispronounced one of the locking injunctions."

"Either that or a printer's error. You saw he was reading straight out of a book? Well, he said *exciteris* before *stringaris*; I heard him."

"No! Really? A beginner's mistake."

"Exactly. It was the same with this young apprentice I mentioned; he waited till his master was away, then—now, you're not going to *believe* this—"

"Bartimaeus—attend to me!" The boy strode back to his pentacle, coat billowing behind him. The other magicians were doing likewise, all across the hall. There was a sudden sense of businesslike intensity about them. My fellow slaves and I reluctantly faced our masters. "Bartimaeus," the boy said again, and his voice was shaking, "as I bade you, so you must do: go out into the world and hunt down the renegade afrit. I bid you return to me only when it is destroyed."

"All right, steady on." The plumed serpent eyed him with something like amusement. He was getting all uptight and official with me suddenly, lots of "bids" and "bades"—this suggested he was quite upset. "What's the matter with you?" I said. "You're coming over all shocked. I thought you didn't even like the bloke."

His face colored. "Shut up! Not another word! I am your master, as you so regularly forget. You will do as I command!"

No more conspiratorial confidences for us. The boy was back to his old foot-stamping ways again. Strange what a small jolt of reality will do.

There was no point talking to him when he was in a mood like this. The plumed serpent turned its back, coiled in upon itself and, in company with its fellow slaves, vanished from the room.

34

There was plenty of activity above the roofs of London that evening. As well as the forty or so heavy-duty djinn, such as me, who, after leaving the Whitehall chamber, had more or less spontaneously scattered in all directions of the compass, the air was rife with imps and foliots of varying levels of ineptitude. Barely a tower or office block existed that didn't have one or two of them skulking on lookout from its top. Down below, battalions of Night Police were marching, combing the streets with some reluctance for signs of the rogue afrit. In short, the capital was awash with government servants of every type. It was a wonder the afrit wasn't tracked down in the first few seconds.

I spent a little time meandering vaguely around central London in gargoyle form, without any definite plan in mind. As always, my inclination to stay out of harm's way vied with my desire to complete the job and hasten my release as swiftly as possible. Trouble was, afrits are tricky blighters: very difficult to kill.

After a while, lacking anything better to do, I flew across to an unappetizing modern high-rise—a magician's fancy, constructed of concrete and glass—to speak to the sentries on duty there.

The gargoyle alighted with balletic grace. "Here, you two. Has that skeleton passed by here? Speak up." This was relatively polite, given that they were small blue imps—always a trying sort.

The first imp spoke up promptly. "Yes."

I waited. It saluted and went back to polishing its tail. The gargoyle gave a tired sigh and coughed heavily. "Well, *when* did you see it? Which way did it go?"

The second imp paused in a detailed examination of its toes. "It came by about two hours ago. Don't know where it went. We were too busy hiding. It's mad, you know."

"In what way?"

The imp considered. "Well, all you higher spirits are pretty nasty, of course, but most of you are predictable. This one . . . it says strange things. And one minute it's happy, the next— *well*, look what it did to Hibbet."

"He seems happy enough."

"That's Tibbet. It didn't catch Tibbet. Or me. It said it'd get us next time."

"Next time?"

"Yeah, it's been past five times so far. Each time it gives us a really boring lecture, then eats one of us. Five down, two to go. I tell you, the combination of fear and tedium takes some beating. Do you think this toenail's ingrowing?"

"I have no opinion on the subject. When is the skeleton due back?"

"In about ten minutes, if it keeps to his current schedule."

"*Thank* you. At last—some definite information. I shall await it here."

The gargoyle shrank and dwindled, and became a blue imp only moderately less hideous than the other two. I took myself upwind of them and sat cross-legged on a ledge overlooking the London skyline. Chances were, another djinni would have caught up with the afrit before he returned here, but if not, I'd have to have a go. Quite why he was going around and around the city was anyone's guess; possibly his long vigil in the tomb had sapped his wits. Anyhow, there was plenty of backup in the vicinity: I could see several other djinn drifting about within a couple of streets.

As I waited, a few idle thoughts ran through my mind. No question about it, a lot of funny things were happening in London, all at the same time. First: the golem was causing trouble, instigator unknown. Second, the Resistance had broken into a high-security tomb and made off with a valuable item. Third, and as a direct result of the second, we had an unbalanced afrit loose, too, causing additional mayhem. All this was having a result: I'd tasted the fear and confusion among the magicians during the general summoning. Could it be coincidence? I thought it unlikely.

It didn't seem plausible to me that a bunch of commoners could have gained access to Gladstone's tomb all on their lonesome. I guessed instead that someone must have put them up to it, given them a few tips so they got past the first safeguards and down into the vault. Now, either that very helpful person didn't know about the guardian of the tomb, or maybe he (or she) *did*; either way, I doubted very much that the girl Kitty and her friends had much idea what they were going up against.

Still, she at least had survived. And now, while the magicians tied themselves in knots trying to catch up with Gladstone's roving skeleton, the dreaded Staff was at large in the world.[1]

---

[1] In the 1860s, when Gladstone's own remarkable health and vigor were fading, the old codger had endowed his Staff with considerable power, the better for him to access easily. It ended up containing several entities, whose natural aggression was exaggerated by being cooped up together in a single thimble-sized node within the wood. The resulting weapon was perhaps the most formidable since the glory days of Egypt. I'd glimpsed it from afar during Gladstone's wars of conquest, carving the night with sickle-shaped bursts of light. I'd seen the old man's silhouette, static, high-shouldered, holding the Staff, he and it the single fixed points within the parabolas of fire. Everything within its range—forts, palaces, well-built walls—it pounded into dust; even the afrits cringed before its power. And now this Kitty had pinched it. I wondered if she knew precisely what she'd got herself into.

Someone was going to take advantage of this, and I didn't think it would be the girl.

I recalled the unknown intelligence that I'd sensed watching me through the golem's eye, as the creature tried to kill me at the museum. It was possible, if you looked at the whole affair dispassionately, to imagine a similar shadowy presence behind the abbey job, too. The same one? I thought it more than likely.

As I waited, engaged in lots of clever speculation such as this,[2] I scanned the planes automatically, keeping watch for trouble. And so it chanced that, by and by, upon the seventh plane, I saw an amorphous glow approaching through the evening light. It flitted here and there among the chimney pots, sometimes flaring clearly as it passed into the shadows, sometimes getting lost in the red gleam of the sunlit tiles. On planes two to six the glow was identical; it had no obvious form. It was something's aura, all right—the trail of something's essence—but its material shape was impossible to make out. I tried the first plane, and there, drained of all color by the descending sun, I caught my first glimpse of a leaping man-shaped form.

It sprang from gable to weathervane with the precision of a mountain goat, teetering on the smallest crest, spinning around like a top, then bounding on. As it drew nearer, I began to hear thin cries, like those of an excited child, erupting from its throat.

My fellow imps were possessed by sudden eleventh-hour anxiety. They left off picking their toenails and polishing their

---

[2] There were plenty more incredibly intelligent thoughts, which I won't bother troubling your pretty little heads with. Take it from me it was all good, damn good.

tails and began to skitter to and fro about the roof, attempting to hide behind each other and sucking in their bellies in an attempt to look less obvious. "Uh-oh," they said. "Uh-oh."

I spied one or two of my fellow djinn following the leaping figure at a cautious distance. Quite why they hadn't yet attacked, I couldn't fathom. Perhaps I would soon find out. It was coming my way.

I got up, tucked my tail over my shoulder for neatness' sake, and waited. The other imps darted around me, squeaking incessantly. Eventually, I stuck out a foot and tripped one up. The other cannoned into him and ended up on top. *"Quiet,"* I snarled. "Try showing a bit of dignity." They looked at me in silence. "That's better."

"Tell you what . . ." The first imp nudged the other and pointed at me. "*He* could be next."

"Yeah. It might take *him* this time. We could be saved!"

"Get behind him. Quick."

"Me first! After me!"

There followed such an undignified display of scuffling and scurrying, as they fought with each other to hide behind my back, that my attention for the next few moments was entirely taken up with administering some well-deserved slaps, the noise of which echoed around the town. In the midst of this performance, I looked up; and there, standing astride a parapet at the edge of the tower-block roof, not two meters away, was the renegade afrit.

I admit his appearance startled me.

I don't mean the golden mask, shaped with the deathly features of the great magician. I don't mean the wispy hair drifting out behind it on the breeze. I don't mean the skeletal hands resting easily on the hips, or the vertebrae peeping out above the necktie, or the dusty burial suit hanging so limply off his frame. None of that was particularly exciting; I've taken on the guise of a skeleton dozens of times—haven't we all? No, what surprised me was the realization that this was *not a guise*, but real bones, real clothes, and a real golden mask up top. The afrit's own essence was quite invisible, hidden somewhere within the magician's remains. He did not have a form of his own—on this, or any of the other planes. I'd never seen this done before.[3]

Whatever the skeleton had been getting up to during the course of the day, it had evidently been quite energetic, since the clothes were looking the worse for wear: there was a trendy slit across the knee,[4] a burn mark on one shoulder, and a ragged cuff that looked as if it had been sliced by claws. My master would probably have paid good money for that ensemble if he'd seen it in some Milanese boutique, but for an honest afrit it was a pretty shoddy affair. The bones below the cloth seemed complete enough, however, the joints hinging smoothly as if they had been oiled.

The skeleton regarded the heap of imps with its head cocked to one side. We stood stock still, our mouths agape, frozen in the middle of our scuffle. At last it spoke.

---

[3] It is a simple fact that, upon materializing in the human world, we have to take on *some* form or other, even if it is just a drift of smoke or a dribble of liquid. Although some of us have the power to be invisible on the lower planes, on the higher, we must reveal a semblance: that is part of the cruel binding wrought by the magicians. Since we have no such definite forms in the Other Place, the strain of doing this is considerable and gives us pain; the longer we remain here, the worse that pain gets, although changing form can alleviate these symptoms temporarily. What we *don't* do is "possess" material objects: the less we have to do with earthen things the better, and anyway, this procedure is strictly forbidden by the terms of our summoning.

[4] Less trendy was the bony patella poking out.

"Are you breeding?"

"No," I said. "Just a bit of rough-and-tumble."

"I mean your numbers. There were two of you last time."

"Reinforcements," I said. "They called me over to hear you speak. And to get eaten, of course."

The skeleton pirouetted on the edge of the parapet. "How charming!" it cried gaily. "What a compliment to my eloquence and clarity! You imps are more intelligent than you look."

I glanced at Tibbet and his friend, who were both standing stock still, mouths wide and dribbling. Rabbits in headlights would have looked on them with scorn. "I wouldn't count on it," I said.

In response to my searing wit, the skeleton gave a trilling laugh and an impromptu tap dance with arms aloft. About fifty yards beyond, loitering behind a chimney stack like two shifty teenagers, I could see the other djinn, waiting and watching.[5] So I reckoned we pretty much had Gladstone's bones surrounded.

"You seem in a very upbeat mood," I observed.

"And why shouldn't I be?" The skeleton came to a halt, clicking its fingerbones like castanets in time to its shoes' final climactic tap. "I'm free!" it said. "Free as can be! That rhymes, you know."

"Yes . . . well done." The imp scratched its head with the tip of its tail. "But you're still in the world," I said slowly. "Or at least you are from where I'm sitting. So you're not really *free*, are you? Freedom comes only when you break your bond and return home."

---

[5] One was my friend from the mass summoning—the bird with stilt legs. The other was shaped like a pot-bellied orangutan. Good honest traditional forms, in other words; no messing about with moldy bones for them.

"That's what I *used* to think," the skeleton said, "while I was in that smelly tomb. But not anymore. Look at me! I can go wherever I want, do whatever I like! If I want to gaze at the stars—I can gaze to my heart's content. If I want to stroll amid the flowers and the trees—I can do that, too. If I want to grab an old man and throw him head over heels into the river—no problem either! The world calls me: Step right on up, Honorius, and do whatsoever you please. Now, imp; I'd call that freedom, wouldn't you?"

It made a menacing sort of scurry toward me as it said this, its fingers making little clutching spasms and a murderous red light suddenly flaring in the blank sockets behind the eyes of the golden mask. I hopped back hurriedly out of range. A moment later, the red light faded a little and the skeleton's advance became a merry dawdle. "Look at that sunset!" it sighed, as if to itself. "Like blood and melted cheese."

"A delightful image," I agreed. No question about it, those imps were right. The afrit was quite insane. But insane or not, a few things still puzzled me. "Excuse me, Sir Skeleton," I said, "as a humble imp of limited understanding, I wonder if you would enlighten me. Are you still acting under a charge?"

A long curved fingernail pointed to the golden mask. "See him?" the skeleton said, and its voice was now saturated with melancholy. "It's all his fault. He bound me into these bones with his last breath. Charged me to protect them forever, and guard his possessions too. Got most of them here—" It swung around to reveal a modern rucksack hanging incongruously on its back. "And also," it added, "to destroy all invaders of his tomb. Listen, ten out of twelve's not *too* bad, is it? I did my best, but the ones that got away keep nagging at me."

The imp was soothing. "It's very good. No one could have

done better. And I suppose the other two were tough nuts to crack, eh?"

The red light flared again; I heard teeth grinding behind the mask. "One was a man, I think. I didn't see. He was a coward; he ran while his comrades fought. But the other . . . Ah, she was a spry little whippet. I'd have loved to get her white neck between my fingers. But—would you credit such guile in one so young? She had purest *silver* on her person; gave Honorius such a jarring in his poor old bones when he reached out to stroke her."

"Disgraceful." The imp shook its head sadly. "And I bet she never even told you her name."

"*She* didn't, but I overheard it—oh, and I so *nearly* caught her, too." The skeleton gave a little dance of rage. "Kitty she is and, when I find her, Kitty she'll die. But I'm in no hurry. There's time enough for me. My master's dead, and I'm still obeying my orders, guarding his old bones. I'm just taking them along with me, that's all. I can go where I want, eat whatever imp I please. Especially"—the red eyes flared—"the talkative, opinionated ones."

"Mmm." The imp nodded, mouth tight shut.

"And do you want to know the best of it?" The skeleton spun right around (away on the next roof over, I saw the two djinn duck back behind the chimney stack) and bent down close to me. "There is no pain!"

"Mm-*mmm*?" I was still being quiet, but I tried to express sufficient interest.

"That's right. *None at all.* Which is exactly what I'm telling any spirit whom I meet. This pair—" It pointed at the other imps, who had by now summoned enough gumption to creep off to the opposite end of the roof. "This pair have heard it all several times over. You, no less hideous than they, are privileged to hear it now as well. I wish to share my joy. These bones protect my essence: I have no need to create my own, vulnerable form. I nestle snugly within, like a chick inside my nest. My master and I are thus united to our mutual advantage. I am obeying his command, but can still do whatever I wish, happily and without pain. I can't *think* why no one's thought of this before."

The imp broke its vow of silence. "Here's a thought. Possibly because it involves the magician's being dead?" I suggested. "Most magicians aren't going to want to make that sacrifice. *They* don't mind that our essences shrivel while we serve them; in fact, they probably prefer it, since it concentrates our minds. And they certainly don't want us wandering about doing any old thing we wish, do they?"

The gold mask considered me. "You are a most impertinent imp," it said at last. "I shall consume you next, since my essence requires some stoking.[6] But you speak sense, nevertheless. Truly I am unique. Unlucky as I once was, trapped for long dark years in Gladstone's tomb, I am now the most fortunate of afrits. Henceforward I shall roam the world, taking my leisurely revenge on human and spirit alike. Perhaps one day, when my vengeance is sated, I shall return to the Other Place—*but not just yet*." It gave a sudden lunge in my direction; I somersaulted backward, just out of reach, landing with my rear end teetering over the edge of the parapet.

"So it doesn't bother you then that you've lost the Staff?" I

---

[6] You could tell Honorius was far gone by the fact that he evidently hadn't bothered checking through the planes. If he had, he'd have seen that I was an imp only on the first three planes. On the rest, I was Bartimaeus, in all my lustrous glory.

said quickly, making frantic signals with my tail to the djinn on the opposite roof. It was time we put an end to Honorius and his megalomania.[7] Out of the corner of my eye I saw the orangutan scratch his armpit. Either this was a subtle signal promising swift aid, or else he hadn't seen me.

"The Staff . . ." The skeleton's eyes flashed. "Yes, my conscience pricks me a little. Still, what matter? The girl Kitty will have it. She is in London; and sooner or later I will find her." It brightened. "Yes . . . And with the Staff in my hand, who knows *what* I could do. Now stand still, so that I can devour you."

It reached out a leisurely hand, evidently not expecting further resistance. I suppose the other imps must have sat quietly, accepting their fate, not being a very decisive bunch. But Bartimaeus was made of sterner stuff, as Honorius was about to learn. I gave a little skip between the outstretched arms, jumped up, and bounded over the horrid white head, ripping the death mask off as I did so.[8]

It came away without difficulty, having been held on by only a few tightened strands of the skeleton's dirty white hair. Honorius gave a yelp of surprise and wheeled around, his leering skull fully exposed. "Hand that back!"

For answer, the imp danced away around the rooftop. "You don't want this," I called over my shoulder. "It belonged to your

---

[7] I have to say that his ramblings were not without interest, in an odd sort of way. Since time out of mind, every one of us, from the toughest marid to the smallest imp, has been cursed by the twin problems of obedience and pain. We have to obey the magicians, and it hurts us to do it. Through Gladstone's injunction, Honorius seemed to have found a way out of this cruel vise. But he had lost his sanity in the process. Who would rather stay on Earth than return home?

[8] My six imp's fingers came in handy here; each one had a small sucker on the end.

master and he's dead. Euuch, and he didn't have very good teeth, did he? Look at that one hanging by a thread."

"Give me back my face!"

"Your 'face'? That's not healthy talk for an afrit. Ooops, there it goes. Clumsy me." With all my strength, I spun it away like a small gold Frisbee, off the edge of the building and down into the void.

The skeleton roared with rage and sent three Detonations off in rapid succession, singeing the air around me. The imp flipped and sprang, over, under, over, and down below the parapet, where I promptly used my suckers to cling to the nearest window.

From this vantage point, I waved again at the two djinn lurking over by the chimney, and whistled as shrilly as I could. Evidently, Honorius's proficiency with his Detonations had been the reason for their previous caution, but I was relieved now to see the stilt-legged bird shift itself, followed reluctantly by the orangutan.

I could hear the skeleton standing on the verge above, craning its neck out in search of me. Its teeth snapped and ground in anger. I pressed myself as flat as I could to the window. As Honorius now discovered, one definite drawback to his residency in the bones was that he could not change his form. Any honest afrit would by now have grown wings and shot down to find me, but without a nearby ledge or roof to hop to, the skeleton was stymied. Doubtless he was considering his next move.

In the meantime, I, Bartimaeus, made mine. With great stealth, I shimmied sideways along the window, across the wall and around the corner of the building. There, I promptly clambered upward and peered over the top of the parapet. The skeleton was still leaning out in a precarious manner. From behind it looked rather less threatening than from the

front: its trousers were ripped and torn, and sagged so cata-
strophically that I was treated to an unwanted view of its coccyx.

If it would just hold that position a moment more . . .

The imp hopped up onto the roof and changed back into
the gargoyle, which tiptoed across, palms outstretched.

It was just then that my plan was shattered by the sudden
appearance of the bird and the orangutan (now complete with
orange wings), who descended in front of the skeleton from
the sky. Each fired off a burst of magic—a Detonation and an
Inferno, to be precise; the twin bolts slammed into the skeleton, knocking it backward away from the precipice. With the
swift thinking that is my hallmark, I abandoned my idea and
joined in likewise, choosing a Convulsion for variety's sake.
Flickering inky bands swarmed over the skeleton, seeking to
shake it to pieces, but to no avail. The skeleton uttered a word,
stamped its foot, and the remnants of all three attacks spun away
from it, shriveling and fading.

Bird, orangutan, and gargoyle fell back a little on all sides.
We anticipated trouble.

Gladstone's skull rotated creakily to address me. "Why do
you think my master chose *me* for the honor of inhabiting his
bones? I am Honorius, a ninth-level afrit, invulnerable to the
magic of mere djinn. Now—leave me be!" Arcs of green
force crackled out from the skeleton's fingers; the gargoyle
leaped from the roof to avoid them, while the bird and
orangutan tumbled unceremoniously out of the sky.

With a bound, the skeleton dropped to a lower roof and
made off on its sprightly way. The three djinn held a hurried
midair consultation.

"I don't like this game much," the orangutan said.

"Nor me," said the bird. "You heard him. He's invulnerable.

I remember one time, back in old Siam. There was this royal afrit, see—"

"He's not invulnerable to silver," the gargoyle interrupted. "He told me so."

"Yep, but nor are we," protested the orangutan. "It'll make my fur fall off."

"*We* don't have to touch it, do we? Come on."

A swift descent to the thoroughfare below resulted in a minor accident, when the driver of a lorry saw us in passing, and jackknifed off the road. Nasty, but it could have been worse.[9]

My colleague paused in indignation. "What's the matter with him? Hasn't he ever seen an orangutan before?"

"Not one with wings, possibly. I suggest we become pigeons on the first plane. Now, break me off three of those railings. They're not iron, are they? Good. I'm going to find a jeweler's."

A quick examination of the retail district revealed something even better: a veritable silversmith's, boasting a complex window display of jugs, tankards, golfing trophies, and memorial plates that had evidently been assembled with loving care. Bird and orangutan, who had managed to secure three long rails, held back fearfully from the shop, since the freezing aura of the silver raddled our essences even halfway across the street. But the gargoyle had no time for delay. I seized one of the railings, gritted my teeth, and, hopping over to the window, staved the

---

[9] The lorry, which was delivering a cargo of melons somewhere, careered into the glass front of a fishmonger's, sending an avalanche of ice and halibut cascading out onto the pavement. The trap at the back of the lorry opened, and the melons bounced out into the street, where, following a natural incline, they gathered pace along the road. Several bicycles were upended, or forced sideways into the gutter, before the melons' descent was halted by a glassware store at the foot of the hill. The few pedestrians who managed to avoid the rolling missiles were subsequently knocked flying by the horde of alley cats converging on the fish shop.

glass in.[10] With a quick stab of the rail, I lifted a large silver tankard by its handle and backed away from the shop, ignoring plaintive cries from within.

"See this?" I dangled the tankard at the end of the rail before my bemused companions. "One spear. Now we need two more."

It took twenty minutes of low-level flying to locate the skeleton once again. This was easy really; we just followed the sound of the screams. It seemed that Honorius had rediscovered the delights of frightening people, and was sauntering along the embankment, swinging from streetlights and popping up behind the river wall to scare witless any passerby. It was a harmless enough hobby, but we had our collective charge, and that meant we had to act.

Each one of us had a homemade spear, complete with its silver object. The bird had a darts cup swinging on the end of his rail, while the orangutan, who had spent a couple of fruitless minutes trying to balance a large plate on the tip of his, had settled at last for a toastrack. I had hurriedly schooled them both in tactics, and we approached the skeleton in the manner of three sheepdogs tackling an obstinate ram. The bird flew up along the Embankment from the south, the orangutan flew down from the north, and I came at him from the landward side. We cornered him in the region of Cleopatra's Needle.[11]

---

[10] Imagine the discomfort of closely approaching a raging fire: this was the effect so much silver had on me—except that it was *cold*.

[11] *Cleopatra's Needle*: a sixty-foot Egyptian obelisk, weighing 180-odd tons, that has nothing to do with Cleopatra at all. I should know, since I was one of the workers who erected it for Tuthmosis III in 1475 B.C. As we'd plunked it in the sand at Heliopolis, I was rather surprised when I saw it in London 3,500 years later. I suppose someone pinched it. You can't take your eyes off anything these days.

Honorius saw the bird first. Another swinging jet of power shot out, cut between his bandy legs, and vaporized a public convenience. In the meantime, the orangutan darted close and thrust the toastrack between Gladstone's shoulder blades. A burst of greenish sparks, a smell of burning cloth; the skeleton leaped high into the air. It fell to earth with a keening cry, bounded away toward the road, only to narrowly avoid a swipe from my oncoming tankard.

"Ahh! You traitors!" Honorius's next attack shot past the gargoyle's ear; yet while he struggled to keep my fleeing frame in view, the bird stole close and tickled his bony leg with the darts trophy. As he spun around to tackle this new danger, the toastrack went to work again. And so it went. However much the skeleton turned and twisted, one silver weapon or another was always in action behind its back. Before long, its missiles became erratic, lacking force; it was more interested in retreat than engagement. Howling and cursing, it fled across the Embankment's width, nearer and nearer the river wall.

The three of us closed in with great caution. For a moment I couldn't work out why this felt so unusual. Then I realized: it was a chase, and for once *I* was doing the chasing. Usually it's the other way around.

In minutes, we had the skeleton pressed up against the foot of the obelisk. The skull rotated frantically left and right, the red dots flaring, seeking avenues of escape.

"Honorius," I said, "this is your last chance. We understand the stresses you've been under. If you can't dematerialize voluntarily from those bones, doubtless one of today's magicians can free you from your binding instead. Surrender now, and I will ask my master to research the necessary spell."

The skeleton gave a screeching cry of contempt. "*Ask* your

master? Will it really be so easy? Are you on such equal terms? I doubt it very much. *All* of you are subject to the whims of human masters, and I alone am free!"

"You're trapped in a festering bag of bones," I said. "Look at you! Not even able to turn into a bird or fish to get away."

"I'm in a better state than *you*," the skeleton snarled. "How many years have you been working for them? Change shape all you like, the fact remains you're a slave, with threats and manacles binding you to your task. Ooh, look—now I'm an imp, now I'm a devil! Who cares? Big deal!"

"Gargoyle, actually," I muttered. But only quietly; his point had hit home.

"If you had half a chance, you'd be here with me, roaming London at will, teaching those magicians a thing or two. Hypocrite! I defy you!" The vertebrae cracked, the torso turned, white bones reached up and grasped the granite column. With a heave and a gasp, Gladstone's skeleton was climbing up the obelisk, using the ancient carved hieroglyphs for footholds.

My companions and I watched it climb.

"Where's he think he's going?" the bird asked.

The gargoyle shrugged. "There's nowhere for him *to* go," I said. "He's just postponing the inevitable." I spoke angrily, since Honorius's words had contained more than a grain of truth, and that knowledge hurt me. "Let's finish him off."

But as we rose, spears lifted, silver ornaments glinting darkly in the dusk, the skeleton reached the uppermost point of the ancient stone. There, it clambered awkwardly to its feet and raised its ragged arms toward the west and the setting sun. The light shone through the long white hair and danced on the hollow innards of the skull. Then, without another sound, it bent its legs and launched itself up and out over the river in a graceful swan dive.

The orangutan hurled its spear after it, but really there was no need.

The Thames that evening was at high tide and in full spate; the skeleton hit the surface far out and was submerged instantly. Once only did it reappear, way downstream, with water gushing from the eye sockets, jaw champing, arm bones flailing. But still it made no sound. Then it was gone.

Whether the skeleton was carried straight out to sea, or drawn down into the mud at the bottom of the Thames, the watchers on the bank could not say. But Honorius the afrit, together with Gladstone's bones that housed him, was seen no more.

35

Kitty did not cry.

If her years in the Resistance had achieved nothing else, they had succeeded in hardening her emotions. Weeping was no good to her now. The magnitude of the disaster was so great that normal responses were inadequate. Neither during the crisis in the abbey, nor immediately afterward—when she first halted her desperate flight in a silent square a mile away—did she allow herself to slump into self-pity.

Fear drove her on, for she could not believe that she had escaped the demon. At every corner, using old Resistance techniques, she waited thirty seconds, then peeped back the way she had come. On every occasion, the road behind was empty of pursuit: she saw only slumbering houses, flickering lanterns, silent avenues of trees. The city seemed indifferent to her existence; the skies were filled with impassive stars and the blank-faced moon. There was no one out in the depths of the night and there were no vigilance spheres abroad.

Her feet made the faintest tripping sounds as she jogged along the pavement, keeping to areas of shadow.

She heard little: once a car humming past on a nearby road; once a distant siren; once a baby squalling thinly in an upper room.

She still carried the staff in her left hand.

In her first hurried shelter, a ruined basement of a tenement block within sight of the abbey's towers, she had almost abandoned the staff under a pile of rubble. But useless though it was—good for nothing but killing insects, the benefactor had said—it was the only thing to have come out of the horror with her. She could not let it go.

She rested a few minutes in the cellar, but did not allow herself to sleep. By dawn, central London would be swarming with police. It would be fatal to remain there. Besides, if she shut her eyes, she dreaded what she might see.

Throughout the deepest hours of night, Kitty worked her way east along the bank of the Thames, before reaching Southwark Bridge. This was the most exposed and dangerous part of the whole journey, particularly with the staff in tow. She had heard from Stanley how magical objects radiated their nature to those with eyes to see, and she guessed that demons might perceive her burden from far across the water. So she waited in bushes beside the bridge for many minutes, plucking up her courage, before making a dash to the other side.

As the first lights of dawn began to glow above the city, Kitty pattered under a little arch and into the mews courtyard where the weapons cellar was concealed. It was the only place she could think of to gain immediate shelter, and the need for this was pressing. Her feet were stumbling with weariness; worse, she was beginning to see things—flashes of movement in the corner of her eye—that made her heart pound. She could not go to the art shop—that was clear enough, with Mr. Pennyfeather now (how vividly she imagined it) lying neatly stacked away for the authorities to find. Visiting her rented room was unwise, too (Kitty savagely returned to the practical business in hand), since magicians investigating the shop would learn of it and soon come calling.

Blindly, she located the cellar key; blindly, she turned it in the lock. Without pausing to switch on the electric light, she felt her way down a number of twisting corridors, until she reached the inner room, where the ceiling pipe still dripped into its overflowing bucket. Here, she tossed the staff down, stretched out beside it on the concrete floor, and slept.

She awoke in darkness and lay there, stiff and cold, for a long time. Then she rose, felt for the wall and switched on the single bulb. The cellar was just as it had been the afternoon before—when the others had been there, too. Nick practicing his combat moves, Fred and Stanley throwing discs. She could still see the holes in the joist where Fred's disc had struck. Much good it had all done them.

Kitty sat beside the pile of logs and stared at the opposite wall, hands lying loosely in her lap. Her head was clearer now, though rather light from lack of food. She took a deep breath and tried to focus on what she should do. This was hard, for her life had been turned upside down.

For more than three years, her energies and emotions had helped to build the Resistance; now, in a single night, as if by a raging torrent, it had all been swept away. True, it had been a rickety enough construction at the best of times: none of them had agreed much on their strategies, and the divisions between them had grown bigger in recent months. But now there was nothing left at all. Her companions had gone, and with them the ideals they shared.

But what *were* these ideals, exactly? The events in the abbey had not only changed her future, they had transformed her sense of the past, too. The futility of the whole affair now seemed transparent. The futility—and the foolishness, too. When she tried to bring Mr. Pennyfeather to mind now, she saw not the principled leader she had followed for so long, but little more than a grinning thief, red-faced and sweating in the lantern light, rummaging through loathsome places in search of wicked things.

What had they ever expected to achieve? What would the artifacts have truly accomplished? The magicians would not have been toppled, even with a crystal ball. No, they'd been kidding themselves all along. The Resistance was nothing but a flea biting the ears of a mastiff: one swipe of a paw and that was that.

She drew the silver pendant from her pocket and stared dully at it. Grandmama Hyrnek's gift had saved her: nothing more, nothing less. It was the purest luck she had survived at all.

In her heart, Kitty had long known that the group was dying, but the revelation that it could so easily be snuffed out still came as an overwhelming shock. A single demon had attacked—and their resilience had come to nothing. All the group's brave words—all Mr. Hopkins's clever counsel, all Fred's boasting, all Nick's earnest rhetoric—were proved worthless. Kitty could hardly recall their arguments now: her memories had been wiped clean by events in the tomb.

Nick. The demon had said (Kitty had no difficulty bringing *its* words to mind) that it had killed ten out of twelve intruders. Taking the historical victims into account, that meant Nick had survived, too. Her mouth curled into a faint sneer; he'd gotten out so fast that she hadn't even seen him go. No thought from *him* of helping Fred, or Anne, or Mr. Pennyfeather.

Then there was the clever Mr. Hopkins. . . . As she thought of the bland-faced scholar, a thrill of anger ran through Kitty. Where had *he* been all this time? Far away, safe and sound. Neither he nor the mystery benefactor, the gentleman whose information about Gladstone's defenses had proved so sadly lacking, had dared be present at the tomb. If it hadn't been for their influence over Mr. Pennyfeather in the last few months, the rest of the group would still be alive that morning. And what had they gotten for their sacrifice? Nothing but a knobbly length of wood.

The staff lay beside her amid the debris on the floor. In a sudden flurry of rage, Kitty got to her feet, seized it in both hands and brought it down hard over her knee. To her surprise, she achieved nothing but a jarring of both wrists: the wood was much stronger than it looked. With a cry, she hurled it against the nearest wall.

Almost as soon as it began, Kitty's anger was replaced by a great emptiness. It was conceivable, perhaps, that she could contact Mr. Hopkins in due course. Discuss a possible plan of action. But not today. For now, she needed something different, something to counteract the feeling of being utterly alone. She needed to see her parents again.

It was already late afternoon when Kitty emerged from the cellar into the mews courtyard and listened. Faint sirens and one or two bangs sounded, drifting distantly on the wind from central London, where something was evidently afoot. She shrugged. So much the better. She would not be disturbed. She locked the door, hid the key, and set off.

Despite traveling light—she had left the staff lying in the cellar—Kitty took most of the evening to walk to Balham, and the skies were darkening by the time she reached the familiar knot of roads close to her old home. By now she was tired, footsore, and hungry. Apart from a couple of apples stolen from a grocer's store, she had eaten nothing. Imagined tastings of her mother's cooking began to roll tantalizingly over her tongue, accompanied by thoughts of her old room, with its comfy little bed and the wardrobe with the door that didn't close. How long had it been since she'd slept there? Years, now. If just for one night, she would gladly curl up there again.

Dusk was falling when she walked up the old street and, slowing her pace unconsciously, drew near to her parents' house. A light was on in the living room: this drew forth a wrenching sob of relief, but also a spur of anxiety. Unobservant though her mother was, she must *not* guess something was wrong, not until Kitty had had a chance to work out what to do. She inspected herself in the blank reflection of a neighbor's window, smoothed back her tousled hair, and brushed down her clothes as best she could. She could do nothing about the dirt on her hands, or the bags beneath her eyes. She sighed. Not great, but it would have to do. With that, she stepped up to the door and knocked. Her keys had been left back in her rooms.

After a slight delay, during which Kitty was driven to knock again, a familiar slim shadow appeared in the hall. It hovered halfway down it, as if uncertain whether to open the door. Kitty tapped on the glass. "Mum! It's me."

Diffidently, the shadow came near; her mother opened the door a little and looked out. "Oh," she said, "Kathleen."

"Hello, Mum," Kitty said, smiling as best she could. "Sorry this is unexpected."

"Oh. Yes." Her mother did not open the door any farther. She was looking at Kitty with a startled, slightly wary expression.

"Is anything wrong, Mum?" Kitty asked, too weary to care.

"No, no. Not at all."

"So can I come in, then?"

"Yes . . . of course." Her mother stood aside to allow Kitty to enter, presented a cold cheek to be pecked, and shut the door carefully behind them.

"Where's Dad? In the kitchen? I know it's late, but I'm starving."

"I think perhaps the living room would be best, dear."

"Okay." Kitty stepped down the hall and into the small lounge. Everything was much as she remembered: the frayed carpet, denuded of color; the little mirror over the mantelpiece; the elderly sofa and chair that her father had inherited from *his* father, complete with lacy antimacassars on the headrests. On the little coffee table was a steaming teapot and three cups. On the sofa sat her father. In the chair opposite sat a young man.

Kitty stopped dead. Her mother quietly closed the door.

The young man looked up at her and smiled, and Kitty was immediately reminded of Mr. Pennyfeather's expression when he had looked upon the treasures of the tomb. It was a gleeful, acquisitive smile, struggling hard to be contained.

"Hello, Kitty," the young man said.

Kitty said nothing. She knew what he was quite well.

"Kathleen." Her father's voice was barely perceptible. "This is Mr. Mandrake. From the, the Department of Internal Affairs, I believe?"

"That's right," Mr. Mandrake said, smiling.

"He wants—" Her father hesitated. "He wants to ask you some questions."

A sudden wail came from her mother's mouth. "Oh *Kathleen*," she cried. "What have you been *doing*?"

Still Kitty did not reply. She had a single throwing disc in her jacket, but was otherwise defenseless. Her eyes flicked across to the drawn curtains over the window. It was a sash opener; she could climb out that way—if her father had oiled the latch. Or smash it in a pinch—the coffee table would go through it. Or there was the hall, with a choice of exits, but her mother was standing in front of the door . . .

The young man gestured at the sofa. "Would you like to sit down, Ms. Jones?" he said politely. "We can discuss things in an agreeable manner if you wish." The edges of his mouth twitched. "Or are you going to leap from the window at a single bound?"

By articulating the very thought that was running through her mind, the magician—intentionally or not—caught Kitty off guard. Now was not the time. She flushed, pursed her lips, and sat on the sofa, where she regarded the magician as calmly as she could.

So *this* was the Mandrake whose servants had pursued the Resistance for so many months. She would have known his profession a mile off; his clothes were the giveaway—a long black coat, a ridiculously tight black suit, shiny patent leather shoes. An outsize red handkerchief rose up from his breast pocket like a leaf of coral. His hair grew long about his face, which was thin and pale. Kitty realized for the first time how very young he truly was: still in his teens, certainly no older than she, perhaps considerably younger. As if to offset this, he had steepled his hands in an assertive manner, legs crossed, one foot twitching with the motion of a lapcat's tail, and adopted a smile that would perhaps have been urbane, had his eagerness not kept showing through.

His youth gave Kitty a little confidence. "What do you want, Mr. Mandrake?" she asked in a level voice.

The magician reached out, picked up the nearest cup and saucer and took a sip of tea. With ostentatious care, he placed the ensemble down upon the armrest of his chair and arranged it carefully. Kitty and her parents watched him in silence. "Very nice, Mrs. Jones," he said at last. "A very tolerable beverage. Thank you for your worthy hospitality." This pleasantry elicited only a small sob from Kitty's mother.

Kitty did not look at her. Her gaze was fixed on the magician. "What do you want?" she said.

This time, he replied. "First to tell you that you are, as of this moment, under arrest."

"On what charge?" Kitty knew her voice was shaking.

"Well, let me see . . ." The steepled fingers tapped together, beating out the list. "Terrorism; belonging to an outlaw group; treachery against Mr. Devereaux, his government and the Empire; wanton damage of property; conspiracy to murder; malicious theft; desecration of a sacred resting place . . . I could go on, but it would only distress your mother. It is a melancholy situation that two such honest, loyal parents should have been cursed with a daughter like you."

"I don't understand," Kitty said levelly. "These are serious charges. What is your evidence?"

"You have been witnessed in the company of known criminals, members of the so-called Resistance."

"Witnessed? What does that mean? Who says so?"

"Kathleen, you stupid girl, tell him the truth," her father said.

"Shut up, Dad."

"These known criminals," the magician went on, "were found this morning, lying dead in a vault in Westminster Abbey, which they had previously ransacked. One of them was a Mr. Pennyfeather, whom I believe you work for."

"I always knew he was a bad lot," Kitty's mother whispered.

Kitty took a deep breath. "I regret to hear this, but I can

hardly be expected to know everything my employer got up to in his own private time. You'll have to do better than that, Mr. Mandrake."

"Then you deny associating out of hours with this Pennyfeather?"

"Certainly I do."

"What about his fellow traitors? Two youths: Fred and Stanley by name?"

"Many people worked for Mr. Pennyfeather part-time. I knew them, but not well. Is that it, Mr. Mandrake? I don't believe you have *any* proof at all."

"Well, if it comes to that . . ." The magician sat back in his chair and grinned. "One might ask why your clothes are so covered in white stains. It almost looks like grave-mold, when seen in a certain light. One might ask why you were not at your employer's shop this morning, when it was your duty to open the doors. One might possibly draw attention to documents that I have just been reading in the Public Records Office. They relate to a certain trial: *Kathleen Jones versus Julius Tallow*—a most interesting case. You have a previous criminal record, Ms. Jones. Fined a considerable sum for an attack on a magician. And then, not least, there's the witness who saw you fencing stolen goods in the company of the sadly deceased Fred and Stanley; a witness whom you attacked and left for dead."

"And who *is* this precious witness?" Kitty snarled. "Whoever he is, he's lying."

"Oh, I think he's *very* reliable." The magician gave a little chuckle and pushed the hair back from the sides of his face. "Remember now?"

Kitty looked at him blankly. "Remember what?"

The magician's forehead runkled. "Well— *Me*, of course."

"You? Have we met before?"

"You don't recall? Well, it was several years ago; I admit I was different then."

"Less foppish, perhaps?" Kitty heard her mother give a faint moan of distress; the sound had as little effect on her as if it had been uttered by a stranger.

"Don't cheek me, girl." The magician recrossed his legs—with some difficulty, owing to the tightness of his trousers, and smiled thinly. "Mind you—why not? Fire off all the cheap comments you like. It won't make any difference to your fate."

Now that the end had come, Kitty found she had no fear; only an overwhelming sense of irritation at the jumped-up youth sitting opposite. She folded her arms and looked him fully in the face. "So go on, then," she said. "Enlighten me."

The boy cleared his throat. "Perhaps *this* will refresh your memory. Three years ago in North London . . . One cold December night . . . No?" He sighed. "An incident in a back alley?"

Kitty shrugged wearily. "I've had a lot of incidents in alleys. You must have a forgettable face."

"Ah, but I never forgot *yours.*" His anger leaped to the surface now; he leaned forward in his seat, knocking the cup with an elbow, and spilling tea upon the chair. His eyes flashed guiltily at Kitty's parents. "Oh—sorry."

Kitty's mother launched herself at the spot, dabbing with a napkin. "Don't worry, Mr. Mandrake! *Please* don't worry."

"You see, Ms. Jones," the magician went on, lifting the cup off the chair arm so that Kitty's mother could dab around it more effectively, "I never forgot *you,* though I saw you only for a moment. Nor did I forget your colleagues, Fred and Stanley, since it was they who robbed me, they who tried to kill me."

"Robbed you?" Kitty frowned. "What did they take?"

"A valuable scrying glass."

"Oh . . ." A dim memory swam into Kitty's mind. "You were that kid in the alley? The little spy. I remember you now—*and* your glass. That was a shoddy piece of work."

"I made that!"

"We couldn't even get it to start."

Mr. Mandrake gathered himself with difficulty and spoke in a dangerously controlled voice. "I notice that you have stopped denying the charges."

"Oh, yes," Kitty said, and as she did so felt more consciously alive than she had done for many months. "They're true, all right. All of what you said, and more. I'm only sorry it's all over now. No wait—I deny one thing. You said I left you for dead in that alley. That isn't so. Fred would have cut your throat, but I spared you. Heaven knows why, you miserable little sneak. I should have done the world a favor."

"She doesn't mean this!" Her father had jumped to his feet and was standing between them, as if his body would shield the magician from his daughter's words.

"Oh, but she does, she does." The boy was smiling, but his eyes danced with rage. "Go ahead, let her talk."

Kitty had barely paused for breath. "I despise you *and* all the other magicians! You care nothing for people like us! We're just here to . . . to provide your food and clean your houses and make your clothes! We slave away in your factories and work-shops, while you and your demons live in luxury! If we cross your paths we suffer! Like Jakob did! You're all callous and wicked and heartless and vain!"

"Vain?" The boy adjusted the tilt of his handkerchief.

"How wonderfully hysterical. I'm just well turned out. Presentation's important, you know."

"*Nothing's* important to you—get *off* me, Mum." In her fury, Kitty had risen; her mother, half-maddened by distress, was clutching at her from the side. Kitty pushed her away. "Oh" she snarled, "and if you want a tip on presentation, those trousers are far too tight."

"Is that so?" The boy rose too, his coat billowing about him. "I've heard enough. You'll be able to refine your sartorial opinions at leisure in the Tower of London."

"No!" Kitty's mother sank to the floor. "Please, Mr. Mandrake . . ."

Kitty's father was standing as if his bones pained him. "Is there nothing we can do?"

The magician shook his head. "I'm afraid your daughter has long since chosen her path. I regret it for your sakes, since you are loyal to the State."

"She has always been a headstrong girl," Kitty's father said quietly, "but I never realized she was wicked, too. That incident with Jakob Hyrnek should have taught us something, but we always hoped for the best, Iris and me. And now, with our armies going off to war in America, and threats as never before on every side, to find our girl's a traitor, neck-deep in crime . . . Well, it's broken me, it really has, Mr. Mandrake. I always tried to bring her up right."

"I'm sure you did," the magician said hastily. "Nevertheless—"

"I used to take her to watch the march-pasts, see the soldiers during the festivals. I had her on my shoulders on Imperial Day, when the crowds in Trafalgar cheered the Prime Minister for an hour. You might not remember that, Mr. Mandrake, you're so young yourself, but it was a grand occasion. And now that little daughter of mine's gone, and in her place is this surly vixen, who's got no respect for her parents, her betters . . . or her country." There was a catch in his voice as he finished.

"You really are an idiot, Dad," Kitty said.

Her mother was still half-kneeling on the floor, beseeching the magician. "Not the Tower for her, Mr. Mandrake, *please*."

"I'm sorry, Mrs. Jones—"

"It's all right, Mum—" Kitty did not hide her contempt. "You can get off your knees. He won't be taking me to the Tower. I don't see how he can."

"Oh yes?" The boy looked amused. "You doubt that, do you?"

Kitty peered into the far corners of the room. "You seem to be alone."

A faint smile. "Only in a manner of speaking. Now, then. An official car waits in the next street. Are you going to come with me quietly?"

"No, Mr. Mandrake, I am not." Kitty launched herself forward; swung a fist. It caught the boy on his cheekbone with a dull crack; he capsized, sprawling into the chair. Kitty stepped over her prone mother and made for the door, but a firm grasp on her shoulder jerked her back. Her father: white-faced, eyes blank and staring.

"Dad—leave off!" She wrenched at his sleeve, but his grip was iron-strong.

"What have you done?" He looked at her as if she were something monstrous, an abomination. "What have you *done*?"

"Dad . . . Just let me go. Please, just let me go."

Kitty struggled, but her father only gripped the harder. From her position on the floor, her mother reached out to clutch Kitty's leg halfheartedly, as if uncertain whether she intended supplication or restraint. Over in the chair, the magician, who had been shaking his head like a fuddled dog, turned his gaze toward them. His eyes, when they focused, were venomous. He spoke a few harsh syllables in a strange tongue and clapped his hands. Kitty and her parents stopped their struggle; a brackish vapor seeped from nowhere into the air. At its heart, a dark form: blue-black, with slender horns and leathery wings, appraising them with a wicked leer.

The magician rubbed the side of his jaw and flexed it. "The girl," he said. "Secure her and don't let go. You may grasp her hair as painfully as you wish."

The creature chirruped harshly in answer, beat its wings, and flew out of its vapor nest. Kitty's father gave a low moan; his grasp on Kitty's shoulder loosened. Her mother flung herself back against the corner of the dresser and hid her face.

"Is that the best you can do?" Kitty said. "A mouler? *Please*." She stretched out a hand, and before the startled creature could even reach her, seized it by its neck, swung it around her head a few times, and threw it back into the magician's face, where it burst with a flatulent sound. An eruption of purple, bitter-smelling droplets peppered his suit and coat and the surrounding furnishings. He cried out in shock; reaching for his handkerchief with one hand, he made a mystic sign with the other. Instantly, a small red-faced imp appeared at his shoulder, bounded onto the dresser and opened its mouth. A bolt of orange flame shot out at Kitty, catching her on her chest and knocking her back against the door. Her mother screamed; her father cried out. The imp capered with triumph—and stopped, mid-caper. Kitty was straightening up, dusting off her smoldering jacket and staring at the magician with a grim smile. With a quick movement, she drew her throwing disc from her jacket and flourished it; the magician, who had lurched toward her in his fury, stepped hurriedly back. "You can wear the tightest trousers you please, Mr. Mandrake," she said, "but the fact remains, you're a conceited small-timer. If you follow me, I'll kill you. Good-bye. Oh, and don't worry, Mum, Dad"—she turned to look at each one calmly—"I won't ruin your reputation any further. You won't see me again."

With that, and leaving parents, magician, and imp staring at her back, she turned, opened the door, and passed through. Then she walked slowly and deliberately up the hall and out of the front door into the warm evening. In the street, she chose a direction arbitrarily and walked off, never looking behind her. Only when she had rounded the nearest corner and had begun to run did her tears finally begin to flow.

36

Nathaniel's fury at the failure of his swoop knew no bounds. He returned to Whitehall in a vicious temper, urging his chauffeur to ever greater speeds and beating the leather seat with his fist at any mild delay. He dismissed the car outside Internal Affairs, and, despite the lateness of the hour, stomped across the courtyard to his office. Here he snapped on the lights, threw himself into his chair, and began to think.

He had badly miscalculated, and the fact that he had been so close to success made his failure all the more galling. He had been absolutely right to check the Public Records in search of Kathleen Jones's name: he'd uncovered the typescript of her trial—together with her home address—in less than an hour. He'd been right to visit the parents, too. They were malleable fools, both of them, and his original plan—to get them to detain their daughter should she return home, while secretly informing him—would have worked out perfectly, had the girl not arrived back earlier than expected.

Yet even *that* would have been fine, had she not unexpectedly displayed some kind of personal defense against the minor demons. Perplexing . . . The parallels with the mercenary were obvious, of course; the real question was whether their powers were their own, or the product of some spell. His sensors had not detected anything.

If Bartimaeus had been with him, it might have shed some light on the source of the girl's power and perhaps prevented her escape. It was a great pity the djinni was on the other mission.

Nathaniel regarded his jacket sleeve, now permanently marked with remnants of the mouler. He muttered a curse. *Conceited small-timer* . . . It was hard not to admire the girl's strength of character. Nevertheless, Kitty Jones would pay dearly for that insult.

Alongside his anger, he was uneasy, too. He could, with great simplicity, have requested police backup, or asked Whitwell to provide vigilance sphere surveillance of the parents' house. But he had not done so. He had wanted the success for himself and himself alone. Retrieving the Staff would have enhanced his status immeasurably—the Prime Minister would have lauded him to the skies. Perhaps he would have been promoted, allowed to explore the powers of the Staff . . . Duvall and Whitwell would have been left looking uncomfortably over their shoulders.

But the girl had gotten away—and should anyone learn about his failure, he would be held to account. The death of Tallow had left his colleagues prickly, agitated and even more paranoid than normal. It was not a good time to be found out. He had to locate the girl, and quickly.

At that moment, a ringing in his ear warned him of an approaching magic. He stood alert and, an instant later, saw Bartimaeus materializing in the midst of a blue cloud. It wore its gargoyle form. Nathaniel rubbed his eyes and composed himself.

"Well? You have something to report?"

"Lovely to see you, too." The gargoyle reached down, plumped the cloud into the shape of a cushion, and sat with a sigh. "Yep. *Veni, vidi, vici* and all that. The afrit is no more. I'm knackered. Though not, possibly, as much as you. You look dreadful."

"You disposed of the demon?" Nathaniel perked up. This was good news. It would count for much with Devereaux.

"Sure did. Drowned him in the Thames. Word is already spreading. And by the way, you were right—it *was* that Kitty who nicked the Staff. Have you caught her yet? No? Well, better stop making faces and get busy tracking her down. Hey . . ." The gargoyle peered closer. "You've got a bruise on your cheek. Someone's been fighting!"

"No I haven't. It's not important."

"Scrapping like a street kid! Was it over a girl? A matter of honor? Come on, you can tell me!"

"Just forget about it. Listen—I am pleased at your success. Now we must locate the girl." Nathaniel prodded the bruise gingerly with a finger. It smarted.

The gargoyle sighed. "Easier said than done. Where, pray, do I start?"

"I don't know. I need to think. For the moment, you are dismissed. I'll summon you again in the morning."

"Very well." Gargoyle and cloud drifted backward into the wall and vanished.

When all was still once more, Nathaniel stood beside his desk deep in thought. Night pressed up against the office window; there was no sound from the street outside. He was very weary; his body cried out for its bed. But the Staff was too important to be lost so easily. Somehow, he must trace it. Perhaps a reference book might—

Nathaniel was brought up short by a sudden knocking on the courtyard door.

He listened, heart hammering in his chest. Another three knocks: gentle, but assertive.

Who would be calling at this hour? Visions of the terrible mercenary sprang into his mind; he shrugged them away, squared his shoulders, and approached the door.

Moistening his lips, he turned the handle and swung the door aside—

A short, roundish gentleman stood upon the step, blinking in the light that spilled out from the office. He was dressed in a flamboyant green velvet suit, white spats, and a mauve traveling coat that fastened at his neck. On his head was a small suede hat. He beamed at Nathaniel's discomfiture.

"Hello, Mandrake, my boy. May I come in? It's parky out."

"Mr. Makepeace! Um, yes. Please come in, sir."

"Thank you, my boy, thank you." With a hop and a skip, Mr. Quentin Makepeace was inside. He took off his hat and tossed it across the room, to land with great precision upon a bust of Gladstone. He winked at Nathaniel. "We've had enough of *him*, one way and another, I think." Chuckling at his little joke, Mr. Makepeace wedged himself into a chair.

"This is an unexpected honor, sir." Nathaniel hovered uncertainly. "Can I get you anything?"

"No, no, Mandrake. Sit down, sit down. I've just popped in for a little chat." He smiled broadly at Nathaniel. "I hope I have not disturbed you in your work?"

"Certainly not, sir. I was just thinking of heading home."

"Very good, too. 'Sleep is so vital, and yet so hard to come by,' as the Sultan says in the bathhouse scene—that's Act II, Scene 3 of *My Love's an Eastern Maid*, of course. Did you see it?"

"I'm afraid not, sir. I was too young. My previous master, Mr. Underwood, did not attend the theatre as a rule."

"Ah, a crying shame." Mr. Makepeace shook his head sadly.

"With an education as defective as that, it's a wonder you've turned out such a promising lad."

"I've seen *Swans of Araby*, of course, sir," Nathaniel said hastily. "A wonderful work. Very moving."

"Mmm. It *has* been called my masterpiece by several critics, but I trust I shall outdo it with my next little effort. I have been inspired by the American troubles and turned my attention to the West. A dark continent we know so *little* about, Mandrake. My working title is *Petticoats and Rifles*; it involves a young backwoods lass . . ." As he was speaking, Mr. Makepeace made several intricate signs with his hands; from between his palms rose a scattering of orange sparks that floated up and outward to take up position at points about the room. No sooner were they stationary than the playwright stopped talking in mid-sentence and winked at Nathaniel. "See what I've done, boy?"

"A sensor web, sir. To detect watching ears or eyes."

"Exactly so. And all, for the moment, is quiet. Now then, I didn't come to talk to you about my oeuvre, fascinating though it is. I wanted to sound you out—you being a promising lad—about a certain proposition."

"I would be honored to hear it, sir."

"It goes without saying of course," Mr. Makepeace said, "that the contents of this little talk will be for us alone. It could do us both great harm if a word of it were breathed beyond these four walls. You have a reputation for being just as intelligent as you are young and spry, Mandrake; I'm sure that you understand."

"Of course, sir." Nathaniel composed his features into a mask of polite attention. Beneath this, he was perplexed, if flattered. Why the playwright had now accosted him in such secrecy, Nathaniel could not imagine. Mr. Makepeace's close friendship with the Prime Minister was widely spoken of, but Nathaniel had never thought that the author was much of a magician himself. In fact, on the basis of viewing a couple of the plays he had considered it unlikely: privately, Nathaniel considered them appalling potboilers.

"First, congratulations are in order," Mr. Makepeace said. "The renegade afrit is gone—and I believe your djinni played a part in its removal. Well done! You may be sure the P. M. has taken notice. It is in fact on account of this that I have come to you this evening. Someone of your efficiency may be able to help me in a tricky problem."

He paused, but Nathanel said nothing. It was best to be cautious when confiding in a stranger. Makepeace's objectives were not yet clear.

"You were at the abbey this morning," Mr. Makepeace went on, "and you listened to the debate among the Council. It would not have escaped your notice that our friend the Police Chief, Mr. Duvall, has attained great influence."

"Yes, sir."

"As commander of the Graybacks, he has long been in a position of considerable power, and he makes no secret of his desire to gain more. He has already used the current disturbances to gain authority at the expense of your master, Ms. Whitwell."

"I've noticed some such rivalry," Nathaniel said. He did not think it prudent to say more.

"Very carefully put, Mandrake. Now, as a personal friend of Rupert Devereaux, I don't mind telling you that I've been viewing Duvall's behavior with a good deal of concern. Ambitious men are dangerous, Mandrake. They destabilize things. Boorish, uncivilized individuals such as Duvall—it will shock you to learn he has never attended one of my premieres in his life—are the worst of all, since they have no respect for their colleagues. Duvall has been building up his power base for years, keeping in with the P.M., while undermining other senior figures at the same time. His vaunting ambition has long been obvious. Recent events, such as the unfortunate demise of our friend Tallow, have greatly unsettled our senior ministers, and this perhaps gives Duvall further opportunity to take advantage. In fact—and I don't mind telling *you* this, Mandrake, since you're so uncommonly clever and loyal—with the amount of power Duvall now has, I fear rebellion."

Perhaps because of his background in theater, Mr. Makepeace had a peculiarly lively way of talking: his voice fluted high and tremulous, then dived to become low and resonating. Despite his caution, Nathaniel was fascinated; he leaned in closer.

"Yes, my boy, you heard correctly: *rebellion* is what I fear, and as Mr. Devereaux's most loyal friend, I am anxious to prevent it. I am looking for allies in this regard. Jessica Whitwell is powerful, of course, but we do not get on. She is no great lover of the theater. But you, Mandrake, you are rather more my type. I've followed your career for quite some time, ever since that unfortunate Lovelace affair, in fact, and I think we might do admirably well together."

"That is very kind of you, sir," Nathaniel said slowly. His mind was afire: *this* was what he'd been waiting for—a direct line to the Prime Minister. Ms. Whitwell was no true ally; she'd already made it clear that she planned to sacrifice his career. Well, if he played this carefully, he might gain rapid advancement. Perhaps he didn't need her protection, after all.

But this was dangerous territory. He had to be on his guard. "Mr. Duvall is a formidable opponent," he said blandly. "It is a dangerous thing to act against him."

Mr. Makepeace smiled. "How very true. But haven't you already been doing something along those lines? I believe you paid a visit to the Public Records Office this afternoon—and then set off at speed to an obscure address in Balham."

The words were casual, but they made Nathaniel stiffen with shock. "Forgive me," he stammered, "how did you know—?"

"Word reaches me about many things, my boy. As a friend of Mr. Devereaux, I have long kept my eyes and ears open. Do not look so worried! I have no idea what you were up to, merely that it seemed a *personal* initiative." His smile broadened. "Duvall is in charge of counterrevolutionary tactics now, but I don't think you informed him of your activities?"

Nathaniel certainly had not. His head reeled; he needed to gain time. "Er, you mentioned us collaborating in some way, sir," he said. "What do you have in mind?"

Quentin Makepeace settled back into his chair. "Gladstone's Staff," he said. "That's it, pure and simple. The afrit has been dealt with, and much of the Resistance is dead too, it seems. All well and good. But the Staff is a potent talisman; it confers great power on its bearer. I can tell you that, as we speak, Mr. Duvall is applying all his efforts to find the person who took it. Should he do so"—the magician fixed Nathaniel directly with his bright blue eyes—"he might decide to use it *himself*, rather than restore it to the government. I believe the situation is as serious as that. Much of London might be threatened."

"Yes, sir." Nathaniel said. "I have read about the Staff and I believe its energies can be easily accessed by a few simple incantations. Duvall might well use it."

"Indeed. And I think we should preempt him. If you find the Staff and return it to Mr. Devereaux yourself, your standing will be greatly enhanced, and Mr. Duvall will have suffered a setback. I will be content, too, since the Prime Minister will continue to help finance my works worldwide. What do you think of this proposal?"

Nathaniel's head was awhirl. "An . . . interesting plan, sir."

"Good, good. So, we are agreed. We must act swiftly." Mr. Makepeace leaned forward and clapped Nathaniel on the shoulder.

Nathaniel blinked. In his comradely enthusiasm, Makepeace was taking his acceptance entirely for granted. The proposal *was* beguiling, of course, but he felt uncertain, outmaneuvered; he needed a moment to work out what to do. Yet he *had* no time. The magician's knowledge of his activities had caught him horribly off guard, and he was no longer in control. Nathaniel made a reluctant decision: if Makepeace knew of his visit to Balham, there was no point concealing it anyway. "I have already conducted some investigations," he said stiffly, "and I believe the Staff might be in the hands of a girl, one Kitty Jones."

The magician nodded approvingly. "I can see my high opinion of you was correct, Mandrake. Any idea where she might be?"

"I—I nearly caught her at her parents' house this evening, sir. I . . . missed her by minutes. I don't believe she had the Staff on her at the time."

"Hmm," Mr. Makepeace scratched his chin; he made no attempt to cross-examine Nathaniel on the details. "And now she will have fled. She will be hard to trace . . . unless we can encourage her out of hiding. Did you arrest the parents? A few well-publicized tortures might draw the girl out."

"No, sir. I did consider it, but they were not close to her. I do not believe that she would give herself up for them."

"Even so, it is an option. But I have another possible idea, Mandrake. I have a contact who has one foot in London's murky underworld. He is acquainted with more beggars, thieves, and cutpurses than you could cram into a theater. I shall talk to him tonight; see if he can give us word on this Kitty Jones. With a bit of luck, we shall be able to act tomorrow. In the meantime, I suggest you go home to get some sleep. And remember, we are playing for high stakes, my boy, and Mr. Duvall is a dangerous rival. Not a word of our little agreement to anyone."

37

Midday, and the shadows were at their smallest. The sky above was eggshell blue, flecked with amiable clouds. The sun shone pleasantly upon the rooftops of the suburb. It was an upbeat hour, all told, a time for honest enterprises and decent work. As if in proof, a few industrious tradesmen passed along the street, wheeling their barrows from house to house. They doffed their caps to old ladies, patted the heads of little children, smiled politely as they introduced their wares. Bargains were struck, goods and money exchanged; the tradesmen strolled away, whistling temperance hymns.

Hard to believe that anything wicked was about to happen.

Perched in the depths of a tangled elderberry bush set back from the road, a hunched black form surveyed the scene. It was a mess of bedraggled feathers, with beak and legs pro-truding as if at random. A medium-sized crow: a bird of ill and unkempt omen. The bird kept its bloodshot eyes trained firmly on the upstairs windows of a large and rambling house at the other end of an overgrown garden.

Once again, I was loitering with intent.

The thing to remember about this summoning business is that nothing is ever strictly speaking your own fault. If a magi-cian binds you to a task, you do it—and quickly—or suffer the Shriveling Fire. With that kind of injunction hanging over your head, you soon learn to discard any scruples. This means that during the five thousand years I'd been back and forth across the earth, I'd been unwillingly involved in a good many shabby enterprises.[1] Not that I *have* a conscience, of course, but even we hardened djinn sometimes feel a little soiled by the things we're called upon to do.

This, on a small scale, was one such occasion.

The crow squatted drably in his tree, keeping other fowl at bay by the simple expedient of letting off a Stench. I didn't want any company just then.

I shook my beak in mild despondency. *Nathaniel.* What was there to say? Despite our occasional[2] differences, I'd once hoped that he might turn out slightly different from the normal run of magicians. He'd shown a lot of initiative in the past, for instance, and more than a crumb of altruism. It had been barely possible that he might follow his *own* path through life, and not just go down the old power/wealth/notoriety road that every one of his fellows chose.

But had he? Nope.

The signs now were worse than ever. Perhaps still unsettled by witnessing the demise of his colleague Tallow, my master had been curt to the point of rudeness when he summoned me that morning. He was at his palest and most taciturn. No friendly conversation for me, no tactful pleasantries. I received no further praise for my dispatch of the renegade afrit the night before, and despite changing into a few beguiling female

---

[1] There was the sad overthrow of Akhenaton, for instance. Nefertiti never forgave me for that, but what could I do? Blame the High Priests of Ra, not me. Then there was that uncomfortable business of Solomon's magic ring, which one of his rivals charged me to pinch and chuck into the sea. I needed some fast talking on that occasion, I can tell you. Then there were all the other countless assassinations, abductions, thefts, slanders, intrigues, and deceits . . . come to think of it, actual bona fide *non*shabby assignments are rather few and far between.

[2] Well, all right: perpetual.

shapes, didn't get a single rise out of him. What I *did* get was a prompt new task—of the sort that fits squarely into the "nasty and regrettable" category. It was a departure for Nathaniel, the first time he'd sunk to these depths, and I must admit it surprised me.

But a charge is a charge. So here I was, an hour or two later, loitering in a bush in Balham.

Part of my instructions was to keep the whole thing as quiet as possible, which was why I didn't just bust my way through the ceiling.[3] I knew my prey was home and probably upstairs; so I waited, with my little beady eyes fixed upon the windows.

No magician's house, this. Peeling paint, rotting window frames, weeds growing through holes in the tiled porch. A sizable property, yes, but unkempt and a little sad. There were even a few rusting children's toys buried in the foot-high grass.

After an hour or more of immobility, the crow was getting twitchy. Although my master had wanted discretion, he had also wanted speed. Before long I would have to stop dallying and get the business over with. But ideally I wanted to wait until the house had emptied, and my victim was alone.

As if in answer to this need, the front door suddenly opened and a large and formidable woman sallied forth, clutching a canvas shopping bag. She passed directly beneath me and headed off down the street. I didn't bother trying to hide. To her, I was just a bird. There were no nexuses, no magical defenses, no signs that anyone here could see beyond the first plane. It was hardly a proper test of my powers, in other words. The whole mission was sordid from beginning to end.

Then—a movement in one window. A patch of dusty gray

---

[3] I rejected this procedure on aesthetic grounds also. I dislike leaving a mess.

net curtains was shoved aside and a skinny arm reached through to unlatch the clasp and shove the casement up. This was my cue. The crow took off and fluttered up the garden, like a pair of black underpants blown upon the wind. It landed on the sill of the window in question, and with a shuffle of its scaly legs, inched along the dirty net curtains until it located a small vertical tear. The crow shoved its head through and took a look inside.

The room's primary purpose was evident from the bed shoved up against the far wall: a rumpled duvet indicated that it had recently been occupied. But the bed was now half-obscured by a colossal number of small wooden trays, each one subdivided into compartments. Some held semiprecious stones: agate, topaz, opal, garnet, jade, and amber, all shaped, polished, and graded by size. Others held strips of thin metal, or wisps of carved ivory, or triangular pieces of colored fabric. All along one side of the room a rough worktop had been erected, and this was covered by more trays, together with racks of slender tools and pots of foul-smelling glue. In one corner, carefully stacked and labeled, sat a pile of books with new plain leather bindings of a dozen colors. Pencil marks on the bindings indicated where ornamentation was to be added, and in the center of the desk, bathed in a pool of light from two standing lamps, one such operation was in progress. A fat volume in brown crocodile-skin was having a star-pattern of tiny red garnets added to its front cover. As the crow on the windowsill watched, the final gem had a blob of glue applied to its underside and was set in place by a pair of tweezers.

Deeply engaged in this work, and thus oblivious to my presence, was the youth I had come to find. He wore a rather worn-looking dressing gown and a pair of faded blue pajamas.

His feet, which were crossed under his stool, were encased in a huge pair of stripy bed-socks. His black hair was shoulder length, and on a split hairs–general grease rating put even Nathaniel's noxious mane in the shade. The atmosphere of the room was heavy with leather, glue, and odor of boy.

Well, this was it. No time like the present, etc. Time to do the deed.

The crow gave a sigh, took hold of the net curtain in its beak, and with one quick motion of the head, ripped the fabric in two.

I stepped through onto the inner sill and hopped onto the nearest stack of books, just as the boy looked up from his work.

He was very out of shape; the flesh hung heavily on him, and his eyes were tired. He caught sight of the crow, and ran one hand through his hair in a distracted sort of way. A fleeting look of panic passed across his face, then dulled into resignation. He set down his tweezers on the desk.

"What manner of demon are you?" he said.

The crow was taken aback. "You wearing lenses or something?"

The boy shrugged wearily. "My grandmama always said demons came as crows. And normal birds don't slice their way through curtains, do they?"

This last bit was admittedly true. "Well, if you must know," I said, "I am a djinni of great antiquity and power. I have spoken with Solomon and Ptolemy, and hunted down the Sea Peoples in the company of kings. Currently, however, I am a crow. But enough about me." I adopted a more efficient, businesslike tone. "You are the commoner Jakob Hyrnek?" A nod. "Good. Then prepare—"

"I know who sent you."

442

"Er . . . You do?"

"I've guessed this was coming for a long time."

The crow blinked in surprise. "Blimey. *I* found out only this morning."

"It makes sense. He's decided to finish the job." The boy shoved his hands deep into his dressing gown pockets and sighed feelingly.

I was confused. "He has? What job was this? Listen—stop sighing like a girl and explain yourself."

"Killing me, of course," Hyrnek said. "I assume you're a more efficient demon than the last one. Although I have to admit he *looked* a lot more scary. You're a bit drab and weedy. And small."

"Just hold hard a moment." The crow rubbed its eyes with a wing tip. "There's some mistake here. My master never heard of your existence until yesterday. He told me so."

It was the boy's turn to do the perplexed bit. "Why would Tallow say that? Is he mad?"

"Tallow?" The crow was practically cross-eyed with befuddlement. "Slow down! What's *he* got to do with it?"

"He sent the green monkey after me, of course. So I naturally assumed—"

I held up a wing. "Let's start again. I have been sent to find Jakob Hyrnek at this address. Jakob Hyrnek is you. Correct? Right. So far so good. Now, I know nothing about any green monkey—and let me tell you, incidentally, that looks aren't everything. I may not seem much at present, but I'm a good deal more vicious than I appear."

The boy nodded sadly. "I thought you might be."

"Too right, buster. I'm nastier than any monkey you're likely to come across, that's for sure. Now, where was I? I've lost my thread . . . Oh, yes—I know nothing about the monkey and I certainly haven't been summoned by Tallow. Which would be impossible in any case."

"Why?"

"Because he was swallowed by an afrit last night. But that's by the by—"

Not to the boy, it wasn't. At this news, his face lit up: his eyes widened, his mouth curved up and outward in a long, slow smile. His whole body, which had been slumped over his stool like a sack of cement, suddenly began to straighten and gain new life. His fingers gripped the edge of the desk so hard the knuckles cracked.

"He's *dead*? You're sure?"

"Saw it with these eyes. Well—not *these* ones, exactly. I was a serpent at the time."

"How did it happen?" He seemed uncommonly interested.

"A summoning went wrong. The fool misread the words, or something."

Hyrnek's grin broadened. "He was reading from a book?"

"A book, yes—that's generally where incantations are to be found. Now, can we *please* get back to the business at hand? I haven't got all day."

"All right, but I'm very grateful to you for the information." The boy did his best to compose himself, but kept grinning inanely and breaking into little chuckles. It really put me off my stride.

"Look, I'm trying to be serious here. I warn you to take heed—oh hell!" The crow had taken a menacing step forward and stuck its foot into a glue pot. After a couple of tries, I managed to shake it off across the room, and began to scrape my toes clean against the corner of a wooden tray. "Now, listen," I snarled as I scraped, "I've come here—not to kill you, as you surmised—but to take you away, and I advise you not to resist."

That knocked some sense into him. "Take me away? Where?"

"You'll see. Do you want to get dressed? I can spare you a little time."

"No. No, I can't!" All of a sudden he was upset, rubbing at his face and scratching at his hands.

I tried to be reassuring. "I won't try to harm you—"

"But I *never* go out. Never!"

"You have no choice, sonny. Now, how about a pair of trousers? Those pajama bottoms look loose, and I fly at speed."

"Please." He was desperate, pleading. "I *never* go out. I haven't done so for three years. Look at me. *Look* at me. See?"

I looked at him blankly. "What? So you're a bit podgy. There's worse than you out there walking the streets, and you'd solve the problem fast enough if you did some exercise instead of sitting on your backside here. Embossing spell books in your bedroom is no life for a growing boy. It'll play hell with your eyesight, too."

"No—my skin! And my hands! Look at them! I'm hideous!" He was yelling now, thrusting his hands toward my beak, and flicking his hair back from his face.

"I'm sorry, I don't—"

"The coloring, of course! Look at it! All over me." And sure enough, now that he came to mention it, I did see a series of vertical gray-black bands running up and down his face and across the backs of his hands.

"Oh *that*," I said. "What of it? I thought you'd done that intentionally."

Hyrnek gave a sort of silly, sobbing laugh at this, the kind that implies far too much time spent maundering in solitude. I didn't allow him time to speak. "That's a Black Tumbler, isn't it?" I went on. "Well, the Banja people of Great Zimbabwe used to use that—among other spells—to make themselves look more attractive. It was considered very becoming for a young bridegroom to have a full body-coat of stripes before the wedding, and the women went in for it, too, on a more localized basis. Only the wealthy could afford it, of course, as the sorcerers charged the earth. Anyway, from their point of view you look extremely eligible." I paused. "Except for your hair, which *is* pretty bad. But so's my master's, and it doesn't stop him from flouncing about in broad daylight. Now, then"—amid all of that, I thought I'd heard a door slam some-where in the house—"it's time to go. No time for trousers, I fear; you'll have to chance your luck with the updrafts."

I gave a hop along the desk. The boy slipped off his seat in sudden panic and began to back away. "No! Leave me alone!"

"Sorry, can't be done." He was making too much noise; I could sense movement in a room below. "Don't blame me—I haven't got any choice."

The crow jumped onto the floor and began to change, swelling to ominous size. The boy screamed, turned, and flung himself at the door. An answering shout came from beyond it; it sounded maternal. I heard heavy feet hurrying up the stairs.

Jakob Hyrnek wrestled with the handle, but never com-pleted a single twist. A giant gold beak descended on the collar of his dressing gown; steel claws rotated in the carpet, slicing up the boards beneath. He was swung up and around, like a helpless cub dangling in its mother's jaws. Mighty wings flapped once, overturning trays and sending gemstones pattering against the walls. A rush of wind; the boy was launched toward the window. A wing of scarlet feathers rose up to enclose him; glass shattered all around, cold air buffeted his body. He cried out, flailed wildly—and was gone.

Anyone arriving at the gaping wall behind us would have seen nothing, heard nothing, except perhaps the shadow of a great bird flitting across the grass and some distant screams ascending into the sky.

38

That afternoon, Kitty walked past the Druids' Coffeehouse three times. On the first two occasions, she saw nothing and no one of interest, but on the third, her luck changed. Behind a gaggle of excitable European tourists, who took up several outlying tables, she discerned the calm figure of Mr. Hopkins, sitting quietly on his own, and stirring his espresso with a spoon. He seemed engrossed in his occupation, absently adding sugar cube after sugar cube to the dark black mix. But he never touched a drop.

For a long time, Kitty watched him from the shadows of the statue in the center of the square. As always, Mr. Hopkins's face was bland and quite expressionless: Kitty found it impossible to read what he was thinking.

Her betrayal by her parents had left Kitty more exposed than ever, friendless and alone, and a second hungry night in the cellar had convinced her of the need to speak with the one ally she had any hope of finding. Nick, she firmly believed, would have gone deep into hiding; but Mr. Hopkins, always at one remove from the rest of the Resistance, might still be approachable.

And here, sure enough, he was, waiting in the appointed place; yet Kitty still hung back, wracked with uncertainty.

Perhaps it was not strictly Mr. Hopkins's fault that the raid had gone so badly wrong. Perhaps none of the old documents he had studied had mentioned Gladstone's servant. Nevertheless, Kitty could not help but associate his careful advice with the terrible outcome in the tomb. Mr. Hopkins had introduced them to the unknown benefactor; he had helped orchestrate the whole scheme. At the very least, his strategy had been woefully lacking; at worst—he had recklessly endangered them all.

But with the others gone, and the magicians on her heels, Kitty had few options remaining. At last, she stepped out from behind the statue and crossed the cobblestones to Mr. Hopkins's table.

Without a greeting, she pulled out a chair and sat down. Mr. Hopkins looked up; his pale gray eyes appraised her. His spoon made little scratching noises against the edges of the cup as he stirred. Kitty stared at him impassively. A bustling waiter approached; Kitty made a cursory order and allowed him to depart. She did not say anything.

Mr. Hopkins withdrew the spoon, tapped it on the cup's rim and laid it carefully on the table. "I heard the news," he said, abruptly. "I've been looking for you the last day and more."

Kitty uttered a mirthless laugh. "You're not the only one."

"Let me say at once—" Mr. Hopkins broke off as the waiter reappeared, set a milkshake and an iced bun before Kitty with a flourish, and departed. "Let me say at once how . . . dreadfully sorry I am. It is an appalling tragedy." He paused; Kitty looked at him. "If it is any consolation, my . . . informant was profoundly upset."

"Thank you," Kitty said. "It isn't."

"The information we had—and which we shared openly and completely with Mr. Pennyfeather—made no mention of a guardian," Mr. Hopkins continued imperturbably. "The Pestilence—yes, but nothing else. Had we known, we would never of course have countenanced such a scheme."

Kitty studied her milkshake; she didn't trust herself to

speak. All of a sudden, she felt quite sick.

Mr. Hopkins watched her for a moment. "Are all the others—" he began, then stopped. "Are you the only one—?"

"I would have thought," Kitty said bitterly, "that with an information network as sophisticated as yours, you would *know* by now." She sighed. "Nick survived, too."

"Ah? Really? Good, good. And where is Nick?"

"I have no idea. And I don't care. He ran, while the others fought."

"Ah. I see." Mr. Hopkins toyed with his spoon again. Kitty stared at her lap. She realized now that she did not know what to ask of him, that he was as nonplussed as she was. It was no good: she was quite alone.

"It is of course inconsequential now," Mr. Hopkins began, and something in his tone made Kitty look up at him sharply. "Given the nature of the tragedy that has taken place, it is inconsequential and irrelevant, of course, but I suppose—what with the unexpected dangers you encountered, and the misfortune of losing so many of your admirable companions—that you did not manage to bring anything of value out of the tomb?"

This statement was so rambling and circuitous that it immediately had the opposite effect of what its cautious speaker intended. Kitty's eyes widened in disbelief; her brows slowly lowered into a frown.

"You're right," she said crisply. "It is irrelevant." She ate the iced bun in two mouthfuls and took a sip of her milkshake.

Mr. Hopkins began stirring his coffee again. "But then, nothing *was* taken?" he prompted. "You were unable . . ." His voice trailed off.

When Kitty had sat down at the table, she had had the vague intention of mentioning the staff to Mr. Hopkins; it was, after all, of no use to her, and it was possible that the benefactor, who had wanted it for his collection, might be prepared to give her some payment in return—money for survival was now upper-most on her mind. She had assumed, under the circumstances, that Mr. Hopkins would draw a decent line under the whole business; she had not expected to hear him pressing her so openly for booty from the haul. She thought of Anne, death hard on their trail in the darkened nave, agonizing about drop-ping her bag of treasures. Kitty's lips became a hard line.

"We loaded up with the contents of the tomb," she said. "But we couldn't escape. Perhaps Nick managed to get some-thing out; I don't know."

Mr. Hopkins's pale eyes studied her. "But you yourself—you took nothing?"

"I dropped my bag."

"Ah. Of course. I see."

"I had the cloak in it, among other things. You'll have to apologize most profusely to your informant; that was one of the objects he wanted, wasn't it?"

The man made a noncommittal gesture. "I don't recall. I don't suppose you happen to know what became of Gladstone's Staff, do you? I believe he *did* have his eyes on that."

"I imagine that was left behind."

"Yes. . . . Only there was no mention of its being located in the abbey, nor any sign of it in the skeleton's possession as it traveled about London."

"Nick took it then. . . . I don't know. What does it matter? It's not valuable, is it? According to you." Kitty spoke casually, but she was watching the other's face as she did so. He shook his head.

"No. Quite so. My informant will be disappointed, that is

all. He *did* so have his heart set on it, and he would have paid lavishly to have it in his hands."

"We're *all* of us disappointed," Kitty said. "And most of us are dead. He can live with it."

"Yes." Mr. Hopkins tapped his fingers against the tablecloth; he appeared to be thinking. "Well," he said, brightly, "what of you, Kitty? What are your plans now? Where are you staying?"

"I don't know. I'll think of something."

"Do you require help? Somewhere to stay?"

"No, thank you. It would be better if we stayed out of each other's way. The magicians have traced my family; I don't want to put you—or your informant—at any risk." Nor did Kitty wish to associate herself any longer with Mr. Hopkins. His evident unconcern at her colleagues' deaths had startled her; now she wished to be as far removed from him as possible. "In fact" —she pushed her chair back—"I should probably leave now."

"Your concern does you credit. I obviously wish you contin-ued fortune. Before you go, however"—Mr. Hopkins scratched his nose, as if wondering how to phrase something a little dif-ficult—"I think perhaps you should hear something I've learned from one of my sources. It affects you quite closely."

Kitty paused in the act of rising. "Me?"

"I'm afraid so. I heard this little more than an hour ago. It is very secret; most of the government doesn't know about it themselves. One of the magicians hunting for you—his name is John Mandrake, I believe—has been researching your past. He has learned that some years back a Kathleen Jones appeared at the Judicial Courts, charged with assault."

"So?" Kitty kept her face still, but her heart was suddenly beating fast. "That was a long time ago."

"Indeed. Going through the record of the trial, he discovered that you had launched an unprovoked attack on a senior magician, for which you were fined. He regards this as one of the first attacks by the Resistance."

"Ridiculous!" Kitty exploded with fury. "It was an accident! We had no idea—"

"Furthermore," Mr. Hopkins went on, "he knows that you did not launch this attack alone."

Kitty sat very still. "What? He doesn't think—"

"Mr. Mandrake believes—whether rightly or wrongly is perhaps beside the point—that your friend . . . What was his name, now? Jakob something . . ."

"Hyrnek. Jakob Hyrnek."

"That's it. He believes Master Hyrnek is associated with the Resistance, too."

"That's ridiculous—!"

"Even so, at some point this morning, he sent his demon to take your friend away for questioning. Oh dear; I *thought* it might upset you."

It took Kitty a few seconds to gather herself. When she spoke, it was haltingly. "But I haven't even *seen* Jakob for years. He knows nothing."

"Mr. Mandrake will doubtless discover as much. Eventually."

Kitty's head spun. She tried to gather her thoughts. "Where have they taken him? Is it . . . the Tower?"

"I hope, my dear, that you aren't thinking of doing anything rash," Mr. Hopkins murmured. "Mr. Mandrake is considered one of the strongest of the young magicians. A talented boy; one of the Prime Minister's favorites. It would not be advisable—"

Kitty forced herself not to scream. Every moment that they delayed, Jakob might be being tortured; demons worse than the skeleton might be surrounding him, goading him with their claws . . . And he was wholly innocent; he had nothing to do with her at all. What a fool she was! Her reckless actions over the last few years had endangered someone for whom she would once have given her life.

"I would try to forget young Hyrnek," Mr. Hopkins was saying. "You can do nothing—"

"*Please,*" she said. "Is it the Tower of London?"

"As a matter of fact, it is not. That would be the ordinary way of things. But I think Mandrake is trying to do things quietly by himself; to get one up on rivals in the government. He has abducted your friend in secret, and taken him to a safe house for questioning. It is unlikely to be heavily guarded. But there will be demons—"

"I have met Mandrake." Kitty interrupted him fiercely. She was leaning forward urgently now, knocking against the milkshake glass, which jerked sideways, slopping liquid onto the cloth. "I have met him, defied him, and walked away without a backward glance. If this boy hurts Jakob," she said; "if he hurts him in any way at all, believe me, Mr. Hopkins, I will kill him with my own hands. Him and any demon who stands in my path."

Mr. Hopkins raised his palms off the table and lowered them. It was a gesture that might have meant anything.

"Once again," Kitty said. "Do you know where this safe house is?"

The pale gray eyes regarded her for a time, then blinked. "Yes," he said blandly. "I *do* know the address. I can give it to you."

39

Kitty had never been inside Mr. Pennyfeather's secret storeroom, but she knew how to operate the mechanism of the door. She trod down the metal lever hidden among the debris of the cellar floor, and pushed simultaneously against the bricks above the log pile. The brickwork shifted with a slow, weighted inward swing; there was a sudden chemical smell and a crack opening in the wall.

Kitty squeezed through and allowed the door to close behind her.

Utter blackness. Kitty stood frozen. Then she stretched out her hands and felt hesitantly on either side, searching for some kind of switch. First, to her utter horror, she came upon something cold and furred; even as she jerked that hand back, the other closed over a hanging thread.

She pulled it: a click, a hum, and a soft yellow light came on.

The furry object, Kitty was immediately relieved to see, was the hood of an old coat, hung up on a peg. Beside it were three dangling satchels. Kitty selected the largest one, placed the strap over her head, and considered the rest of the room.

It was a small chamber, ringed from floor to ceiling with rough wooden shelves. Here were the remnants of Mr. Pennyfeather's collection: the magical artifacts that Kitty and the rest of his company had managed to steal over the preceding years. Many objects had already been removed for the abbey raid, but there were plenty of items remaining. Neat rows of explosive globes and mouler glasses ran side by side with one or two Elemental Spheres, Inferno sticks, silver throwing stars, and other easily manageable weapons. They gleamed brightly in the light: Mr. Pennyfeather appeared to have kept them well polished. Kitty imagined him descending to the cellar and gloating over his collection alone. For some reason, the thought unnerved her. She set to work, packing as many items as she could in her satchel.

Next she came to a rack of daggers, stilettos, and other knives. Some, perhaps, had magic within them; others were simply very sharp. She selected two, tucking a silver one into a secret casing on the inside of her right shoe, placing the other in her belt. When she stood, her jacket hung down over it, concealing it from view.

Another shelf held several dusty glass bottles, of varying size, mostly filled with colorless liquid. They had been taken from magicians' houses, but their purposes remained unknown. Kitty gave them a glance, then moved on.

A remaining rack of shelves was filled high and low with objects that Mr. Pennyfeather had found no use for: jewelry, ornaments, robes and vestures, a couple of paintings from middle Europe, Asian bric-a-brac, brightly colored shells, and stones with odd whorls and patterns. Stanley or Gladys had observed some kind of magical aura on each one, but the Resistance had been unable to activate them. In such cases, Mr. Pennyfeather had simply stored them away.

Kitty had intended to ignore these shelves, but as she returned to the secret door, she saw, half-hidden at the back, a small, dull disc, heavily covered with cobwebs.

Mandrake's scrying glass.

Without knowing quite why she did so, Kitty picked up the disc and dropped it, cobwebs and all, into the inside pocket of her jacket. Then she turned to the door, which on this side was worked with a conventional handle. She tugged it open and stepped out into the cellar.

The staff was still lying where she had thrown it on the floor that morning. On sudden impulse, Kitty picked it up and carried it back into the secret room. Useless as it was, her friends had died collecting it; the least she could do was stow it away securely. She dropped it in a corner, took a last look around the Resistance's storeroom and clicked the light off. The door creaked mournfully shut behind her as she strode across the cellar toward the stairs.

The safe house where Jakob was being held was in a desolate part of east London, half a mile north of the Thames. Kitty knew the area fairly well: it was a region of warehouses and wastelands, many remaining from the aerial bombardments of the Great War. The Resistance had found it a useful area for operating: they had raided several of the warehouses, and utilized some of the derelict buildings as temporary hideouts. The magicians' presence here was comparatively light, especially after dark. Only a few vigilance spheres tended to pass this way, and those that did could generally be avoided. No doubt this obscurity was exactly why the magician Mandrake had chosen it, too: he wished to conduct his interrogation undisturbed.

Kitty's plan, such as it was, was twofold. If possible, she would extricate Jakob from the house, using her weapons and her natural resilience to hold Mandrake and any demons at bay. She would then attempt to spirit him to the docks, and there take passage to the Continent. Remaining in London was impractical for a time. If rescue and escape proved impossible, her alternative was less pleasant: she intended to give herself up, providing Jakob was set free. The implications of this were clear, but Kitty did not hesitate. She had lived too long as an enemy of the magicians to have qualms about the consequences now.

Keeping to the back roads, she made her way slowly across east London. At nine o'clock, a familiar wailing drone sounded out from the towers of the city: in response to the abbey raid two nights previously, a curfew was in operation. People passed her on both sides of the street, heads down, hurrying home. Kitty paid them little heed; she had broken more curfews than she could remember. Even so, she sat on a bench in a small deserted park for half an hour or more, waiting for the kerfuffle to die away. It was best there were no witnesses when she drew near to her objective.

Mr. Hopkins had not asked her what she planned, and she had not volunteered the information. Other than the address, she wanted nothing more to do with him. His callous indifference at the café had appalled her. From now on, she would rely on nobody but herself.

Ten o'clock came and went; the moon was out now, high and full above the city. Moving cautiously on plimsolled feet, satchel heavy against her side, Kitty flitted through the deserted streets. In twenty minutes she had arrived at her destination: a short, dead-end road, a cul-de-sac, with small factory workshops on either side. Pressed into the shadows at the corner, she took stock of the land ahead.

The street itself was narrow, lit by only two lamps, one a few yards farther on from Kitty's corner, the other away near the end of the road. These, and the white moonlight shining down from above, gave the buildings marginal illumination.

The workshops were generally low, of one or two stories.

Some of them were boarded up; others had their doors and windows caved in, gaping black and open. Kitty stood and watched them for a long time, breathing in the night's stillness. It was a general rule with her that she never passed open, unknown spaces in the dark. But she could see and hear nothing untoward. All was very quiet.

At the end of the road, beyond the second streetlight, was a three-story building, somewhat higher than the rest. Its ground floor had perhaps once been a garage of some kind: there was a wide opening for vehicles to pass through, now poorly covered with netting. Above this, broad blank windows marked out old offices or private housing. All these windows were black and empty—except for one, where a dim light shone.

Kitty did not know which of the buildings was Mandrake's safe house, but this—the only lit window on the entire street—immediately attracted her attention. She kept her eyes fixed on it for a while, but could make out nothing, except possibly some kind of curtain or sheet drawn across. She was too far away to observe it clearly.

The night was cold; Kitty sniffed and wiped her nose on her sleeve. Her heart was beating painfully against her chest, but she ignored its protests. It was time to act.

She crossed to the pavement opposite the first streetlamp and stole forward; one hand on the wall, the other resting easily on her satchel. Her eyes were never still: she scanned the road, the silent buildings, the blackened windows up above, the curtained window far ahead. Every few steps, she stopped and listened, but the city was silent, closed in upon itself; she moved on.

Kitty now drew opposite one of the gaping doorways; she

kept her eyes firmly on it as she passed, her spine-skin prickling. But nothing stirred.

She was close enough now to see that the lit window up ahead was covered with a length of dirty sheet. Evidently, this was not very thick, because she now made out a shadow passing slowly behind it. Her brain struggled unsuccessfully to make sense of the image; it was human, that much she could tell, but more than that was impossible to say.

She crept a little farther down the street. On her immediate left was a broken doorway, the interior a gulf of solid black. Once again, Kitty's hackles rose as she tiptoed by; once again, she kept her eyes fixed firmly on it; once again, she saw nothing to alarm her. Her nose did twitch at a faint scent, an animal smell drifting from the deserted house. Cats, perhaps; or one of the pariah dogs that plagued the derelict zones of the great city. Kitty moved on.

She drew abreast of the second streetlight, and by its light studied the building at the end of the road. Just inside the lip of the wide garage opening, before the rash of netting, she now saw a narrow door set into the side wall. From this distance, it even looked slightly ajar.

Too good to be true? Perhaps. Over the years, Kitty had learned to treat anything this easy with extreme caution. She would reconnoiter the whole area before finally committing to that extremely inviting door.

She set off once more and, in the next five seconds, saw two things.

The first was up at the lit window. For the briefest of moments, the shadow passed again behind the sheet, and this time its profile was clear. Her heart gave a jolt; she knew it for certain then. Jakob was there.

The second was at ground level, a little way ahead, on the opposite side of the road. Here, the streetlight threw its light in a rough circle, spilling out across the street and onto the wall of the building behind. This wall was punctured by a narrow window and, farther on, by an open doorway, and Kitty now noticed, as she edged a little closer, that light entering the window could be seen through the doorway, stretching in a flat diagonal across the internal floor. She also noticed—and this made her halt, mid-stride—that outlined neatly along one edge of this splinter of light was the silhouette of a man.

He was evidently standing pressed flat against the inner wall of the building, just along from the window, because only the very edges of his brow and nose could be discerned in the silhouette. They were rather prominent features—perhaps they protruded farther than their owner had allowed for, just out into the light. Aside from this, he was doing an extremely good job of lying in wait.

Scarcely breathing, Kitty backed up against the wall. With a crashing weight, the realization came: she had passed two doorways already—both had been broken open—and there were at least two more before the street's end. Chances were, each had its hidden occupant. Once she had reached the house at the end, the trap would be sprung.

But whose trap? Was it Mandrake's? Or—a new and dreadful thought, this—Mr. Hopkins's?

Kitty ground her teeth in fury. If she went on, she would be surrounded; if she retreated, she would be leaving Jakob to whatever fate the magicians planned. The first option was possibly suicidal, but the second could not be countenanced at any price.

She adjusted the satchel strap so that it hung more easily

across her shoulder, and flipped the bag open. She took hold of the nearest weapon—an Inferno stick—and edged forward, keeping her eyes fixed on the silhouette in the doorway.

It did not move. Kitty kept close to the wall.

From a concealed place just ahead of her stepped a man.

His dark gray uniform blended perfectly with the night: even in full view, his tall and bulky form seemed only half there, a spirit conjured from the shadows. But his voice, harsh and deep, was real enough.

"This is the Night Police. You are under arrest. Place your bag on the ground and face the wall."

Kitty made no answer. She slowly backed away, angling out into the center of the road, away from the open doorways behind her. The Inferno stick lay lightly in her fingers.

The policeman made no attempt to follow her. "This is your last chance. Stop where you are and lay your weapons down. If you do not, you will be destroyed."

Kitty retreated farther. Then: a movement to her right— the silhouette in the doorway. From the corner of her eye, she saw it shift position. It bent forward and as it did so, the features changed. The protuberant nose began to jut forward alarmingly; the chin swung up to follow it; the bulging brow receded; pointed ears rose from the top of the skull, flexing and shifting. For an instant Kitty glimpsed the actual tip of a jet-black muzzle in the illuminated window, then it dropped to the floor out of view.

The silhouette had vanished from the doorway. From the room came a snuffling, and the sounds of ripping cloth.

Kitty bared her teeth, flicked her eyes back to the policeman in the road. He, too, was altering; his shoulders lurching down and forward, his clothes peeling away from the long, gray bristles erupting along his spine. His eyes shone yellow in the darkness; his teeth snapped angrily as the head descended into shadows.

This was enough for Kitty; she turned and fled.

Something with four feet was pacing at the end of the street, in the dark beyond the lamplight. She saw its burning eyes and, in a gulping mouthful, caught its stink.

She paused, momentarily uncertain. From a doorway to her right stole another low, dark form. It saw her, snapped its teeth and gave a dart in her direction.

Kitty tossed the stick.

It landed on the pavement between the creature's front paws, cracking open and emitting a tall gout of flame. A whimper, a very human squeal; the wolf reared up, front legs pawing like a boxer at the fiery air, and fell back, twisting in retreat.

Kitty already had a sphere—she couldn't tell what type— ready in her hand. She ran toward the nearest closed ground-floor window, threw the sphere against it. An explosion of air almost blew her off her feet; glass shattered, bricks fell down into the road. Kitty vaulted through the newly opened space, snagging her hand on a piece of jagged glass. She landed on her feet in the inner room.

Outside came a snarling and the scrape of claws on cobble-stones.

Ahead of Kitty, in an otherwise naked room, a narrow flight of stairs rose in the darkness. She ran for them, pressing her wounded hand against her jacket to dull the fresh pain of the cut.

On the first step, she turned, faced the window.

A wolf leaped through the opening, jaws agape. The sphere hit it mid-muzzle.

Water exploded through the room, knocking Kitty off her

feet against the bottom steps, momentarily blinding her. When she could open her eyes, a floodtide was draining away around her feet, filling the air with little gushing, sucking noises. The wolf was gone.

Kitty pelted up the stairs.

The upper room had several open windows: silver moonlight lay unrolled across the floor. Something in the street below howled. Kitty immediately scanned for exits, found none, cursed wildly. Worse, she could not secure her back: the steps had opened directly onto the upper floor—there was no trapdoor or other means of shutting off the route. From downstairs came the sound of something heavy splashing into shallow water.

Backing away from the opening, Kitty approached the nearest window. It was old and rotten, the wood around the pane hung slewed in its frame. Kitty kicked at it with a shoe. Wood and glass fell away into space. Almost before it shattered on the road, she was in the gap, silver light spilling across her face, craning her neck upward, looking for a handhold.

Down in the road below, a dark form wheeled and snapped, heavy feet crunching on glass fragments. She sensed it gazing up at her, willing her to fall.

Something bounded up the stairs with such prodigious strength that it almost careered into the opposite wall. Kitty caught sight of a roughened lintel a foot above the window. She tossed a sphere across the room, reached out and swung herself upward, shoes scrabbling on the window rim, muscles cracking, all the time feeling the stinging pain from the cut in her palm.

An explosion below her. Yellow-green plumes of fire jetted out the window beneath her flailing shoes, and for an instant the road was lit as if by a sickly sun.

The magical light died. Kitty hung on to the wall, searching for another handhold. She spied one, tested it, found it secure. She began to climb. A little way above was a parapet; beyond that, perhaps, a flat roof: this was her objective.

Lack of food and sleep had sapped her energy; her arms and legs seemed filled with water. After a couple of minutes, she paused for breath.

A scratching and scrabbling below her; a slavering, curiously near. Cautiously, fingers digging into the soft bricks, Kitty looked over her shoulder, down along the length of her body toward the distant moonlit road. Halfway between her and the pavement was a rapidly ascending form. For the purposes of its climb, it had reverted a little from its full wolf guise: paws had molded into long clawed fingers; animal forelegs had reacquired human elbows, clambering muscles had snapped back into position around the bones. But the face was unchanged: mouth agape, teeth shining in the silver light, tongue lolling and frothing to the side. Its yellow eyes were on her.

This sight almost caused Kitty to lose her grip and tumble away into the void. Instead, she pressed herself close to the bricks, supported her weight with one hand and eased the other into her satchel. She took hold of the first thing she found—a sphere of some kind—and, taking rapid aim, dropped it toward her pursuer.

Glinting as it spun, the sphere missed the brindled back by inches; a moment later, it hit the pavement, sending out brief jets of flame.

The wolf made a gurgling noise deep in its throat. It came on.

Biting her lip, Kitty flung herself back into her climb.

Ignoring the protests of her body, she clambered frantically upward, fearing at any moment the clasp of claws around her leg. She could hear the beast's scratching at her heels.

The parapet . . . With a cry, she pulled herself up onto it, stumbled and fell. The satchel was twisted under her; she could not get access to her missiles.

She twisted around onto her back. Even as she did so, the wolf's head slowly rose above the edge of the parapet, snuffling avidly at a trace of blood smeared from her hand. Its yellow eyes flicked up, looked straight into hers.

Kitty's fingers fumbled in the lining of her shoe; she drew out the knife.

She struggled to her feet.

With a sudden fluid leap, the wolf plunged over the edge of the parapet and onto the roof, crouching a moment on all fours, head lowered, muscles tensed. It stared up at Kitty out of the corners of its eyes, assessing her strength, debating whether to spring. Kitty waved the dagger back and forth warningly.

"See this?" she panted. "It's silver, you know."

The wolf looked at her sidelong. Slowly, its forelegs rose, its humped back elongated and straightened. Now it was standing on its hind legs like a man, towering over her, swaying back and forth, ready for the attack.

Kitty's other hand groped in her satchel for another missile. She knew she didn't have much time before—

The wolf leaped, slashing with its clawed hands, lunging with its red mouth. Kitty ducked, twisted herself around and thrust upward with the knife. The wolf emitted a curiously high-pitched noise, swung an arm out and caught Kitty painfully across the shoulder. Claws snagged through the satchel strap; it fell away. Kitty stabbed again. The wolf bounded back out of reach. Kitty likewise stepped away. Her shoulder was throbbing painfully from the cut. The wolf was clasping a small wound in its side. It shook its head sadly at her. It seemed only mildly inconvenienced. They circled each other for a few seconds, lit by the silver moon. Kitty now had barely enough strength to lift the knife.

The wolf stretched out a clawed foot and drew the satchel toward it across the roof, well out of Kitty's reach. It gave a low, rumbling chuckle.

A small noise behind her. Kitty risked a quick turn of the head. On the other side of the flat roof, tiles rose diagonally to a low gabled crest. Two wolves stood astride it; as she watched, they began a rapid, skittering descent.

Kitty drew the second knife from her belt, but her left hand was weak from the shoulder wound; her fingers could barely grasp the handle. She wondered vaguely if she should throw herself off the edge of the roof—a swift death might be preferable to the wolves' claws.

But that was a coward's way out. She would do a little damage before the end.

Three wolves advanced on her, two on four legs, one walking like a man. Kitty pushed her hair back out of her eyes and raised her knives for the last time.

40

"What a boring evening," the djinni said. "Nothing's going to happen."

Nathaniel paused in his circuit of the room. "Of course it will. Be silent. If I want your opinion, I'll ask for it." He was aware his voice carried no conviction. He glanced at his watch to reassure himself. "The night's still young."

"Sure, sure. I can see you're wildly confident. You've already worn a small furrow in the floorboards. And I bet you're powerful hungry, too, since you forgot to bring provisions."

"I won't need them. She'll turn up soon. Now shut up about it."

From its station at the top of an old wardrobe, the djinni, which was back in the form of a young Egyptian boy, stretched its arms above its head and yawned extravagantly. "All great master plans have their drawbacks," it said. "They all have their little flaws, which make them tumble into ruin. That's human nature: you're born imperfect. The girl won't come; you'll wait; you haven't brought any food; therefore, you and your captive will starve."

Nathaniel scowled. "Don't worry about him. *He's* all right."

"Actually, I *am* quite hungry." Jakob Hyrnek was sitting on a decrepit chair in one corner of the room. Beneath an old army greatcoat, which the djinni had located in one of the safe house attics, he wore nothing but pajamas and a pair of king-size bed socks. "I didn't have any breakfast," he added, rocking back and forth mechanically on his wonky chair. "I could do with a bite."

"There you are, you see," the djinni said. "He's peckish."

"He's not, and if he knows what's good for him, he'll stay *quiet*, too." Nathaniel resumed his pacing, eyeing the captive as he did so. Hyrnek seemed to have gotten over his fear of the flight by now, and since he'd been immediately shut up in the empty house, with no one else to see him, his paranoia about his face had quieted down a bit, too. The actual captivity didn't appear to bother him much, which slightly perplexed Nathaniel; then again, Hyrnek *had* been in a self-imposed prison for years.

The magician's gaze strayed toward the window, hidden behind its swathe of sheeting. He quelled a desire to step across and peer out into the night. Patience. The girl would come; all it took was time.

"How about a game?" The boy on the wardrobe grinned down at him. "I could find us a ball and wall-hoop and teach you two the Aztec ball game. It's great fun. You have to use your knees and elbows to get the ball through the hoop. That's the only rule. Oh, and the losers get sacrificed. I'm very good at it, as you'll discover."

Nathaniel waved his hand wearily. "No."

"I Spy, then?"

Nathaniel blew out hard through his nose. It was difficult enough to remain calm without the djinni's jabbering. He was playing for high stakes here, and the consequences of failure did not bear thinking about.

Mr. Makepeace had visited him early that morning in secret, bringing news. His underworld contact believed he could gain access to the fugitive Kitty Jones and that it would be possible to tempt her out of hiding, if a suitable goad could be discovered. Nathaniel's swift and inventive mind had immediately turned to her childhood friend Jakob Hyrnek, who had been mentioned in the records of her trial and to whom Kitty had a proven loyalty. From what Nathaniel had seen of her—here he gingerly fingered the purpling bruise on his cheek—the girl would not be afraid to come to Hyrnek's aid if danger threatened.

The rest was easy. Hyrnek's capture had been rapidly effected, and Makepeace had conveyed word of it to his contact. All Nathaniel had to do now was wait.

"Psst." He looked up. The djinni was beckoning him over, all the while nodding and winking with furious confidentiality.

"What?"

"Come over here a minute. Out of earshot." It nodded toward Hyrnek, who was rocking back and forth in his chair a little way across the room.

With a sigh, Nathaniel stepped close. "Well?"

The djinni bent its head over the edge of the wardrobe. "I've been thinking," it whispered. "What's going to happen to you when your precious Ms. Whitwell finds out about this? Because she doesn't know you've snatched the boy, does she? I don't understand what game you're playing here. You're usually such a well-behaved little underling, a petted lapdog eager to please."

The barb hit home. Nathaniel bared his teeth. "That time is past," he said. "She won't find out until I have the girl and the Staff under lock and key. Then she'll have to clap with the rest of them. I'll be too close to Devereaux for *any* of them to do anything other than cheer."

The boy arranged itself to sit neatly cross-legged, in a manner reminiscent of an Egyptian scribe. "You're not doing this on your own," it said. "Someone's helped you set it all up.

Someone who knows how to find the girl and tell her we're here. *You* don't know where she is, or you'd have caught her yourself by now."

"I've got contacts."

"Contacts who know a great deal about the Resistance, it would seem. You'd better be careful, Nat. Things like that can work both ways. That hairy Police Chief would give his carnassials to link you somehow with those traitors. If he knew you were doing deals with them . . ."

"I'm not doing deals!"

"Ooh. That was a shout. You're agitated."

"I'm not. I'm just saying. I'm capturing her, aren't I? I just want to do it my own way."

"Fine, but who's your contact? How does he or she know so much about the girl? That's what you should be asking."

"It's not important. And I don't want to talk any more about it." Nathaniel turned his back. The djinni was right, of course: the ease with which Makepeace delved into the underworld was startling. But the theater *was* a disreputable profession; Makepeace was bound to know all kinds of odd commoners—actors, dancers, writers—who were only one notch above the criminal type. Uneasy as he was with his sudden new alliance, Nathaniel was quite happy to reap the benefits of it, provided all went well. But he would be in a parlous position should Duvall or Whitwell discover that he had been acting behind their backs. That was the main risk he was running. Both of them had asked for updates that morning about his activities; to both of them, he had lied. It gave him a prickly sensation at the back of his neck.

Jakob Hyrnek held up a plaintive hand. "Excuse me, sir?"

"What?"

"Please, Mr. Mandrake, I'm getting a little bit chilly."

"Well, get up and walk about, then. But keep those stupid socks out of my sight."

Wrapping the coat tightly about him, Hrynek began to shuffle about the room, his candy-colored striped bed socks peeping out incongruously from under his pajamas.

"Hard to believe *anyone* would risk her life for this specimen," the djinni observed. "If I were his mother, I'd look the other way."

"You haven't met this Kitty," Nathaniel said. "She'll come for him."

"She won't." Hyrnek was standing near the window now; he'd overheard this last exchange. "We used to be close, but not anymore. I haven't seen her for years."

"Even so," Nathaniel said. "She'll come."

"Not since . . . my face was ruined," the boy went on. His voice throbbed with self-pity.

"Oh, give me a break!" Nathaniel's tension exploded into annoyance. "Your face is fine! You can talk, can't you? You can see? Hear? Well, then. Stop complaining. I've seen far worse."

"That's what *I* told him." The djinni negligently stood and hopped down from the wardrobe without a sound. "He's far too het up about it. Look at *your* face—that's permanent, too, and you're not afraid to parade it before the world. Nope, for both of you its your hair that's the real downer. I've seen better styles on the back end of a badger. Just give me five minutes with a pair of shears—"

Nathaniel rolled his eyes and sought to reassert some authority. He grabbed Hyrnek's collar and spun him around. "Back to your chair," he snarled. "Sit down. As for *you*"—he addressed the djinni—"my contact's man will have given the girl this address some hours ago. She will be on her way now, almost certainly with the Staff, since that is her most powerful weapon. When she enters the stair below, a sensory sphere will be triggered and sound the alert up here. You are to disarm her as she comes through the door, hand me the Staff, and prevent her escape. Got that?"

"Clear as daylight, boss. As it was the fourth and fifth times you told me."

"Just don't forget. Get the Staff. That's the important bit."

"Don't I know it? I was at the fall of Prague, remember?"

Nathaniel grunted and resumed his pacing. Even as he did so, there was a sound from the street outside. He turned to the djinni, wide-eyed. "What was that?"

"A voice. Man's."

"Did you hear— There it is again!"

The djinni indicated the window. "Do you want me to look?"

"Don't let yourself be seen."

The Egyptian boy sidled to the window; vanished. A scarab beetle crawled behind the sheet. A bright light flared somewhere beyond the glass. Nathaniel hopped from one foot to the other. "Well?"

"I think your girl's arrived." The djinni's voice sounded small and distant. "Why don't you take a peek?"

Nathaniel ripped the sheet aside and looked out, in time to see a small column of flame flare up from the ground halfway down the road. It died back. On the previously deserted street were many running forms—some on two legs, some on four, and some that were evidently undecided about the matter, but were still gamely lolloping along under the bright moon. There was a snapping and a howling. Nathaniel felt the color drain from his face.

"Oh, hell," he said. "The Night Police."

Another small blast; the room shook mildly. A slight and agile two-legged form sprinted across the road and leaped through a newly blown hole in the wall of a building. A wolf pursued her, only to be engulfed by another explosion.

The scarab beetle whistled approvingly. "Nice use of an Elemental Sphere. Your girl's good. Even so, she'll hardly evade the whole battalion."

"How many are there?"

"A dozen, perhaps more. Look, they're coming over the rooftops."

"You think they'll catch—"

"Oh yes—and eat her. They're angry now. Their blood's up."

"All right—" Nathaniel stood away from the window. He had come to a decision. "Bartimaeus," he said, "go out and get her. We can't risk her being killed."

The scarab beetle chittered in disgust. "Another lovely job. Wonderful. Are you *sure*, now? You'll be going directly against that Police Chief's authority."

"With luck, he won't know it's me. Take her to . . ." Nathaniel's mind raced; he snapped his fingers. "That old library—you know, the one we sheltered in, when Lovelace's demons were after us. I'll take the prisoner and meet you later. We all need to get away from here."

"I'm with you on that one. Very well. Stand clear." The beetle skittered backward on the sill away from the window, rose onto its hind legs and waved its antennae at the glass. A bright light, a spurt of heat; a lopsided hole melted in the middle of the pane. The beetle opened its wing cases and hummed out into the night.

Nathaniel turned back into the room, just in time to meet

a chair swinging into the side of his face.

He fell to the floor awkwardly, half-stunned. One spinning eye caught a skewed glimpse of Jakob Hyrnek hurling the chair aside and hurrying for the door. Nathaniel gabbled a command in Aramaic; a small imp materialized at his shoulder and loosed a lightning bolt at the seat of Hynek's pajamas. There was a sound of rapid scorching and a shrill yelp. Its work done, the imp vanished. Hyrnek halted momentarily, clutching his rump, then continued his stumbling progress toward the door.

By now, Nathaniel had gotten to his feet; he flung himself forward and down in a clumsy tackle; his outstretched hand caught hold of a bed-socked foot and pulled it sideways. Hyrnek fell; Nathaniel clawed himself on top of him and began slapping him frantically about the head. Hyrnek replied in kind. They rolled around for a while at random.

"What an unedifying spectacle."

Nathaniel froze in the act of pulling Hyrnek's hair. He looked up from his prone position.

Jane Farrar stood in the open doorway, flanked by two hulking officers of the Night Police. She wore the crisp uniform and peaked cap of the Graybacks and her eyes were openly scornful. One of the officers at her side made a guttural noise deep in his throat.

Nathaniel cast through his mind for an explanation that might suffice, but found none. Jane Farrar shook her head sadly. "How the mighty have fallen, Mr. Mandrake," she said. "Extricate yourself, if you can, from this half-dressed commoner. You are under arrest for treason."

41

Werewolves in the street, Nathaniel back indoors. Which would *you* choose? Truth to tell, I was glad to get out and about for a bit.

His behavior was disconcerting me more and more. In the years since our first encounter, doubtless under Whitwell's careful tutelage, he'd become an officious little beast, carefully obeying his orders with one eye always on promotion. Now he was deliberately going out on a limb, doing underhanded things, and risking much by so doing. This was no homegrown idea. Someone was putting him up to it; someone was pulling his strings. He'd been many things to me, Nathaniel had, most of them indescribable, but he'd never looked so much of a puppet as he did now.

And already it had all gone wrong.

The scene below was one of chaos. Wounded creatures lay here and there across the street amid piles of broken brick and glass. They writhed and growled and clutched their flanks, their contours altering with each spasm. Man, wolf, man, wolf . . . That's the problem with lycanthropy: it's so hard to control. Pain and strong emotion make the body shift.[1]

---

[1] This chronic unreliability is one of the reasons werewolves get such bad press. As is the fact that they're ravenous, savage, bloodthirsty and very poorly house-trained. Lycaon of Arcadia assembled the first wolf corps as his personal bodyguard, way back about 2000 B.C., and despite the fact that they promptly ate several of his houseguests, the notion of their fulfilling a useful enforcing role stuck fast. Many tyrannical rulers who had recourse to magic have used them ever since: casting complex transformation spells over suitably brawny humans, keeping them in isolation, and sometimes carrying out breeding programs to improve the strain. As with so much else, it was Gladstone who inaugurated the British Night Police; he knew their worth as instruments of fear.

The girl had downed about five, I thought, not including the one blown to pieces by the Elemental Sphere. But several more were pacing redundantly in the road, and others, displaying a little more intelligence, were busily scaling drainpipes or searching for fire escapes to climb.

Nine or ten were left alive. Too many for any human to handle.

But she was still fighting: I saw her now, a little whirling figure on the rooftop. Something bright flashed in each hand—she was waving them high and low in little desperate feints and thrusts to keep three wolves at bay. But with every turn she made, the black forms inched a little closer.

A scarab beetle, for all its many qualities, is not much cop in a fight. Besides, it would have taken about an hour to fly across to join the action. So I made my change, flapped my great red wings twice, and was upon them in a flash. My wings blocked out the moon, casting the four combatants on the roof into the blackest of shadows. For good measure, I uttered the fearsome cry of the roc as it swoops down upon the elephants to snatch away their young.[2]

All this had the appropriate effect. One of the wolves leaped meter backward, its brindled fur fluffed in fright, and disappeared with a howl over the edge of the parapet. Another reared up on its hind legs and received a blow in the midriff from the roc's clenched talons: it shot into the air like a fluffy

---

[2] Indian elephants, usually. The rocs lived on remote isles in the Indian Ocean, appearing inland infrequently in search of prey. Their nests were an acre across, their eggs vast white domes visible far out across the sea. The adults were formidable opponents, and sank most ships sent out to pillage the nesting sites by dropping rocks from great heights. The caliphs paid huge sums for rocs' feathers, cut by stealth from the breasts of sleeping birds.

football and vanished with a clatter behind a chimney.

The third, which was standing upright in parody of a man, was more nimble, quicker thinking. The roc's arrival had caught the girl by surprise, too: gawping up in wonder at the splendor of my plumage, she lowered her knives. Without a sound, the wolf leaped at her throat.

Its teeth clashed together, sending bitter sparks flying into the night.

The girl was already several feet up and rising, suspended from my claws. Her hair streamed in front of her face, her legs dangled above the rapidly diminishing rooftop, the street and all its scurrying inhabitants. The noises of fury and disappointment receded and we were suddenly alone, suspended high above the infinite lights of the city, drawn upward by my protective wings into a place of calm tranquility.

"Ow! That's my leg! Ow! Ah! Curse you, that's silver! Stop it!"

The girl was stabbing a knife repeatedly into the scaly flesh just above my talons. Can you credit it? This same leg, remember, was preventing her from falling to a sooty destruction amid the smokestacks of east London. I ask you. I pointed this out to her with my usual elegance.

"There's no need to swear, demon," she said, desisting for a moment. Her voice was high and faint upon the wind. "And anyway, I don't care. I want to die."

"Believe me, if I could only help you out . . . Stop that!" Another prick of pain, another woozy sensation in my head. Silver does that to you; much more of it and we'd both be falling. I shook her vigorously, until her teeth rattled and her knives plummeted from her hand. But even that wasn't the end of it: now she began twisting and wrenching back and forth in a fevered effort to loose my grip. The roc tightened its hold. "Will you *stop* wriggling, girl? I'm not going to drop you, but I *will* hold you headfirst over a tanner's chimney."

"I don't care!"

"Or dunk you in the Thames."

"I don't care!"

"Or take you to Rotherhithe Sewage Works and—"

"I don't care, I don't care, I don't care!" She seemed apoplectic with rage and grief, and even with my roc's strength it was all I could do to prevent her from prying herself free.

"Kitty Jones," I said, keeping my eyes fixed on the lights of north London—we were nearing our destination now—"do you not want to see Jakob Hyrnek again?"

She went quiet then, all limp and thoughtful, and we flew on for a while in a state of blessed silence. I used the respite to circle for a time, keeping a weather eye out for pursuing spheres. But all was still. We flew on.

A voice sounded from somewhere below my wishbone. It was more measured than before, but the fire had not gone out of it. "Demon," it said, "why didn't you let the wolves devour me? I know that you and your masters plan to kill me in any case."

"I can't comment on that," the roc said. "But feel free to thank me, if you wish."

"Are you taking me to see Jakob now?"

"Yes. If all goes as planned."

"And then?"

I was silent. I had a fairly good idea.

"Well? Speak up! And speak truthfully—if you *can*."

In an attempt to change the subject, the roc affected disdain. "I'd be careful, love. It's unwise to make catty remarks when suspended at high altitude."[3]

"Huh, you're not going to drop me. You just said."

"Oh. Yes. So I did." The roc sighed. "The truth is I do not know what is planned for you. Now, shut your trap a minute. I'm coming in to land."

We sank through the darkness, across the ocean of orange lights, down to the street where the boy and I had sheltered on the night of the Underwood fire. The ruined library was still there: I could see its bulk sandwiched among the lights of the smaller shops nearby. The building had deteriorated somewhat in the intervening years, and a considerable hole now yawned in one place, where a large glass skylight had fallen away. The roc diminished in scale as it approached, judged the angle carefully, and popped the girl feet first through the hole as if posting a letter. We descended into the cavernous space, lit here and there by shafts of moonlight. Only when we were a safe distance from the rubble of the floor did I let my burden go.[4] She dropped with a squeak and rolled briefly.

I alighted a little way off and appraised her properly for the first time. It was the same one, all right—the girl in the alley who had tried to pinch the Amulet. She looked older now, thinner, and more jaded, her face gray and drawn and her eyes wary. The last few years had been hard for her, I reckoned; the last few minutes positively cruel. One arm hung limp, its shoulder slashed and caked with blood. Even

---

[3] As exemplified by Icarus, an early pioneer of flight. According to Faquarl, who admittedly wasn't the most reliable of sources, the Greek magician Daedalus constructed a pair of magical wings, each one housing a short-tempered foliot. These wings were tested by Icarus, a fey and facetious youth, who made cheap remarks at the foliots' expense while at several thousand feet above the Aegean. In protest, they loosed their feathers one by one, sending Icarus and his witticisms plummeting to a watery grave.

[4] We were about six feet up. Hey, she was young and bouncy.

so, the defiance in her was palpable: she got carefully to her feet and, with chin studiedly aloft, stared at me from across a column of silver light.

"I don't think much of *this*," she snapped. "Can't you interrogate me somewhere cleaner? I was expecting the Tower at least."

"This is preferable, believe me." The roc was sharpening a claw against the wall. I wasn't in much of a mood for conversation.

"Well, get on with it, then. Where's Jakob? Where are the magicians?"

"They'll be along in a bit."

"*In a bit?* What kind of outfit is this?" She put her hands on her hips. "I thought you lot were meant to be terrifyingly efficient. This is all cockeyed."

I raised my great plumed head. "Now, *listen*," I said. "Don't forget that I've just saved you from the jaws of the Night Police. A little gratitude wouldn't go amiss here, young lady." The roc rapped its talons meaningfully on the floor and fixed her with the kind of look that sends Persian sailors diving overboard.

She fixed me with the kind of look that curdles milk. "Get lost, demon! I defy you and your wickedness. You don't frighten me!"

"No?"

"No. You're just a useless imp. Your feathers are mangy and covered in mold."

"What?" The roc made a hurried inspection. "Rubbish! That's the moonlight giving them that sheen!"

"It's a wonder they haven't fallen out. I've seen pigeons with better plumage."

"Now, listen—"

"I've destroyed demons with *real* power!" she cried. "Think I'll be impressed by an overgrown chicken?"

The cheek of the girl! "This noble roc," I said with bitter dignity, "is not my only form. It is but one of a hundred thousand guises I can assume. For instance . . ." The roc reared up: I became, in quick succession, a ferocious red-eyed minotaur, frothing at the mouth; a granite gargoyle, champing its jaws; a thrashing serpent, spitting venom; a moaning ghost; a walking cadaver; a floating Aztec skull, gleaming in the dark. It was a motley assortment of nastiness,[5] if I say so myself. "Well?" the skull inquired, meaningfully. "Care to comment?"

She swallowed audibly. "Not bad," she said, "but all those guises are big and showy. I bet you can't do subtle."

"Of course I can!"

"I bet you can't go extra *small*—say small enough to . . . to get into that bottle over there." She pointed at the end of a beer bottle poking out from under a pile of litter, while all the time watching me out of the corner of her eye.

That old one! If it's been tried on me once, it's been tried a hundred times. The skull shook itself slowly from side to side and grinned.[6] "Nice effort, but that didn't work on me even in the old days.[7] Now," I went on. "Why don't you sit down and rest? You look dog-tired."

---

[5] If not particularly inventive. I was tired and out of sorts.

[6] Actually, it was grinning already, grinning being one of the few things skulls do really well.

[7] You know the trick. The clever mortal convinces the stupid djinni to squeeze inside a bottle (or some other confined space), then stoppers him up and refuses to let him out unless he grants three wishes, etc., etc. Ho hum. Unlikely as it may seem, however, if the djinni enters the bottle of his own free will this entrapment actually has a fair degree of power. But even the smallest, doziest imp is unlikely to fall for this chestnut today.

The girl sniffed, pouted, and folded her arms painfully. I could see her looking around, weighing up the exits.

"And don't try anything," I advised. "Or I'll brain you with a rafter."

"Hold it in your teeth, will you?" Ooh, she was disdainful.

In answer, the skull faded and became Ptolemy. I altered without thinking—it's always my preferred form[8]—but as soon as I did so, I saw her give a start and step back a pace. "You! The demon in the alley!"

"Don't get so excited. You can't blame me for that occasion. *You* jumped *me*."

She grunted. "True. The Night Police nearly caught me then, too."

"You ought to be more careful. What did you want the Amulet of Samarkand for anyway?"

The girl looked blank. "The what? Oh, the jewel. Well, it was magical, wasn't it? We stole magical artifacts in those days. It was the whole point of our group. Robbing the magicians, trying to use their stuff ourselves. Stupid. Really stupid." She kicked out at a brick. "Ow."

"Do I take it you no longer espouse this policy?"

"Hardly. Since it got us all killed."

"Except you."

Her eyes flashed in the dark. "You truly expect me to survive tonight?"

She had a point there. "You never know," I said, heartily. "My master may attempt to spare you. He has already saved you from the wolves."

She snorted. "Your master. Does he have a name?"

---

[8] Take it as a mark of respect for what he did for me.

"John Mandrake is the one he uses." I was banned by my vow from saying more.

"*Him?* That pretentious little fool!?"

"Oh, you've met him, then?"

"Twice. And the last time I did I punched his lights out."

"*Did* you? No wonder he kept quiet about it." I was liking this girl more and more with every moment. In truth, she was a breath of fresh air. In all the long centuries of my toil, I've spent remarkably little time in the company of commoners— by instinct, magicians try to keep us shadowy and removed from ordinary men and women. I can count the number of commoners I've properly conversed with on the claws of one hand. Of course, by and large it isn't a rewarding process—the equivalent of a dolphin chatting up a sea slug—but you do get the occasional exception. And this Kitty Jones was one. I liked her style.

I snapped my fingers and caused a small Illumination to fly up and lodge among the rafters. From a nearby heap of rubble, I pulled some planks and breeze blocks and arranged them as a chair. "Sit yourself down," I said. "Make yourself comfortable. That's right. So . . . you punched John Mandrake, did you?"

She spoke with a certain grim satisfaction. "Yes. You seem amused."

I stopped guffawing. "Oh, can you tell?"

"Odd, given that you and he are aligned in wickedness, given that you carry out his every whim."

"Aligned in wickedness? Hey, there *is* a certain master-servant thing going on here, you know. I'm a slave! I've no choice in the matter."

Her lip curled. "Just obeying orders, eh? Sure. That's a *great* excuse."

"It is when to disobey means certain destruction. You try the Shriveling Fire on *your* bones—see if you like it."

She frowned. "It sounds a pretty ropy excuse to me. You're saying all your evil is performed unwillingly?"

"I wouldn't put it *quite* like that, but—yup. From imp to afrit, we're all bound to the magicians' will. We can't do anything about it. They have us over a barrel. At the moment, for instance, I have to help and protect Mandrake, whether I like it or not."

"Pathetic." She spoke decisively. "Absolutely pathetic." And indeed, as I heard myself say all this, it did seem so to me, too. We slaves have dwelled so long in these chains of ours that we rarely speak of them;[9] to hear the resignation in my own voice sickened my essence to its core. I tried to batten down my shame with a spot of righteous indignation.

"Oh, we fight back," I said. "We catch them out if they're careless, and misinterpret when we can. We encourage them to vie with one another, and set them at one another's throats. We load them with luxuries until their bodies grow fat and their minds too dull to notice their own downfalls. We do our best. Which is more than you *humans* manage to do most of the time."

At this, the girl uttered a strange, ragged laugh. "What do you think I've been *trying* to do all these years? Sabotaging government, stealing artifacts, disrupting the city—it's been hopeless, the whole thing. I might as well have been a secretary, like my mother wanted. My friends have been killed or corrupted and demons like *you* have done it all. And don't tell

---

[9] Only a few, such as old Faquarl, openly (and hopelessly) plot revolt. But they've been wittering on about it for so long without results that no one pays any attention.

me you don't enjoy it. That thing in the crypt loved every second of . . ." Her body gave a violent shudder; she broke off, rubbed her eyes.

"Well, there *are* exceptions," I began—then desisted.

As if a thin barrier had been broached, the girl's shoulders shook and she suddenly began to cry with great spasms of pent-up grief. She did so silently, stifling the noise with her fist, as if to save me embarrassment. I didn't know what to say. It was all very awkward. She went on a long time. I sat myself cross-legged a little way off, turned respectfully away from her and gazed off into the shadows.

Where *was* the boy? Come on, come on. He was taking his time.

Pathetic. Absolutely pathetic. Try as I might to ignore them, her words gnawed away at me in the still of the night.

42

Kitty gathered herself at last. The last ructions of despair subsided. She sighed heavily. The ruined building was dark, save for the small area near the roof where the magical light glowed faintly. Its radiance had dimmed. The demon sat close by, still wearing the form of a dark-skinned youth clad in a wrapped skirt. Its face was turned aside, the light casting angular shadows on its thin neck and hunched bare shoulders. It looked oddly frail.

"If it's any consolation," the demon said, "I destroyed that afrit from the crypt." It did not turn around.

Kitty coughed and straightened her back, smoothing her hair out of her eyes. She did not reply at once. The despairing hopelessness that had overcome her when the demon plucked her into the sky had subsided now, washed away by the sudden out-welling of grief for her lost friends. She was left feeling hollow and light-headed. Even so, she tried to gather her thoughts.

Escape. She *could* try to escape. . . . No, there was Jakob to consider, she should wait for him. *If* he was actually coming. . . . She scowled: she had only the demon's word for that. Perhaps it *was* better to flee. . . . She craned her head from side to side, seeking inspiration. "You killed it . . . ?" she said absently. "How?" There was a stairwell close by; they were on the first floor, then. Most of the windows were boarded up.

"Dropped him in the Thames. He was quite mad, you know, after so long. He'd bound his essence into Gladstone's bones. Wouldn't—or couldn't—get himself free. A sad business, but there you go. He was a menace to everything—djinni or human—and is best trapped under hundreds of meters of water."

"Yes, quite . . ." There looked to be a broken window not far off; perhaps she could leap from it. The demon might attack with some magic as she ran, but her resilience would see her through. Then she could drop to the street, seek cover—

"I hope you're not thinking of doing anything rash," the boy said suddenly.

She started guiltily. "No."

"You're thinking of doing *something*; I can hear it in your voice. Well, don't. I won't bother using a magical attack. I've been around, you know. I'm well aware of your defenses. I've seen it all before. I'll just lob a brick at you."

Kitty chewed her lip. Reluctantly, and only for the moment, she dismissed escape from her mind. "What do you mean, seen it before?" she said. "You're talking about the alley?"

The boy flashed a look at her over his shoulder. "Well, there was that, of course—your chums withstood a fairly high-intensity Inferno from me head on. But I mean further back, long before London's precious little magicians started getting above themselves. Time and again, I've seen it. It always happens sooner or later. You know, considering what's at stake you'd think that wretched Mandrake would make a bit of an effort to get here, wouldn't you? We've been here an hour already."

Kitty's brow furrowed. "You mean you've seen people like me before?"

"Of course! A dozen times over. Huh, I suppose the magicians don't let you read the history books—it's no wonder you're so powerful ignorant." The demon shuffled around on his bottom to face her. "How do you think Carthage fell? Or Persia? Or Rome? Sure, there were enemy states ready to take advantage of the empires' weaknesses, but it was the divisions *within* that really did for them. Romulus Augustulus, for instance, spent half his reign trying to control his own people, and all the while Ostrogoths with big mustaches were tramping down through Italy. His djinn couldn't control the plebs any longer, you see. Why? Because so many of them had become like you—resilient to our magic. Detonations, Fluxes, Infernos—scarcely singed their beards. And of course the people *knew* that, so they wanted their rights, they wanted the magicians overthrown at last. There was so much confusion that hardly anyone noticed the barbarian horde before it ransacked Rome." The boy scratched its nose. "In a way, I think it came as a relief. Fresh start and all that. No more magicians in the Eternal City for a long, long time."

Kitty blinked. Her knowledge of history was scanty, and the strange names and places meant little to her, but the implications were startlingly clear. "Are you saying that most of the Romans were resilient to magic?"

"Oh, no. About thirty percent, maybe. In varying degrees, of course. You don't need more than that for a good uprising."

"But we never managed more than eleven! And London's huge!"

"Eleven percent? That's not too bad."

"No. Eleven. That was it."

The boy raised his eyebrows. "Blimey, your recruitment policy can't have been too snappy. But then again, it's early days. How long is it since Gladstone set up shop? Hundred and fifty years or so? Well, that's your answer. Resilience to magic takes a long time to build up in the general population. Magicians had ruled in Rome for five hundred years before the revolutions came. That's an awful lot of magic seeping through the city. Gradually more and more children are born with talents of one sort or another. What else can *you* do, for instance? See us?"

"No." Kitty made a face. "Anne and Fred could do that. I'm just . . . good at surviving."

The boy grinned. "That's no mean talent. Don't knock it."

"Stanley could see magic *in stuff* as well—that's how we knew you had that necklace."

"What? Oh, the Amulet. Yep, that kind of sight's another one. Well, there are probably all sorts of abilities bubbling up in London's population right now. Must be hundreds of people with the power. But you've got to remember, most people won't be aware they've got an ability at all. It takes time for the knowledge to spread. How did you find out?"

It was all Kitty could do to remember that this slight, polite, and very informative boy was actually a demon, something to be loathed and shunned. She opened her mouth to speak and hesitated. The boy rolled its eyes in annoyance and raised its hands. "Look, don't think I'm going to tell anyone this, least of all my master. I don't owe him anything. Still, far be it from me to force it out of you. I'm not a magician." It sounded rather huffy.

"A demon hit me with a Black Tumbler." Her small confidence took Kitty rather by surprise; she found herself saying it without thinking.

"Oh, yes. Tallow's monkey. I forgot." The boy stretched lazily. "Well, you'll be pleased to know Tallow's dead now. An afrit got him. Quite stylishly, too. No—I won't give you the details. Not unless you tell me more about you. What happened after the Tumbler?" And Kitty, despite herself, was soon recounting her story.

At the finish, the demon shrugged ruefully. "You see, the problem with this Pennyfeather was that he was too much like the magicians, wasn't he? Greedy, close, and clasping. Wanted to keep everything nice and secret, all for himself. Small wonder you had only eleven members. If you want to get a revolution going, my tip is to get the people on your side. All those explosions and thefts were never going to get you anywhere."

Kitty scowled. The demon's blithe assurance on the matter rankled. "I suppose not."

" 'Course they weren't. Education's the thing. Knowledge of the past. That's why the magicians give you such ropy schooling. I bet you had endless triumphal stuff about why Britain's so great." He chuckled. "The funny thing is, the people's growing resilience always comes as a surprise to the magicians, too. Each empire thinks it's different, thinks it won't happen to them. They forget the lessons of the past, even recent lessons. Gladstone only got to Prague so fast because half the Czech army was on strike at the time. It seriously weakened the Empire. But my master and his friends have already forgotten this fact. He hadn't a clue why you escaped his mouler the other day. Incidentally, he really *is* taking ages to bring Hyrnek across. I'm beginning to think something might have happened to him. Nothing fatal, unfortunately, or I wouldn't still be here."

Jakob. Kitty had been so caught up in the demon's words that the thought of her friend had half escaped her mind. She flushed. This was the *enemy* she was talking with—a killer, an abductor, an inhuman fiend. How could she have forgotten?

"You know," the demon said in a companionable sort of

way, "I was wondering about something. Why did you come looking for this Hyrnek? You must have known it was a trap. He said you hadn't seen him for years."

"I hadn't. But it's my fault he's in this mess, isn't it?" Kitty gritted the words out.

"Ye-e-s . . ." The demon made a face. "I just think it's odd, that's all."

"What can *you* know about it, demon?!" Kitty was white with rage. "You're a monster! How dare you even *imagine* what I'm feeling!" She was so furious, she almost lashed out.

The boy tutted. "Let me give you a friendly tip," he said. "Now, you wouldn't want to be called 'female mudspawn,' would you? Well, in a similar way, when addressing a spirit such as me, the word *demon* is in all honesty a little demeaning to us both. The correct term is *djinni*, though you may add adjectives such as *noble* and *resplendent* if you choose. Just a question of manners. It keeps things friendly between us."

Kitty laughed harshly. "*No one*'s friendly with a demon!"

"Not normally, no. The cognitive differentials are just too great. But it *has* happened. . . ." It broke off thoughtfully.

"Yeah?"

"Take it from me."

"Such as when?"

"Oh, long ago . . . It doesn't matter." The Egyptian boy shrugged.

"You're making it up."

Kitty waited, but the boy was studying its fingernails intently. It did not continue.

After a long pause, she broke the silence. "So why *did* Mandrake save me from the wolves? It doesn't make sense."

The boy grunted. "He wants the Staff. Obviously."

"The staff? Why?"

"What do you think? Power. He's trying to get it before the others." The boy's voice was terse. It appeared to be in a bad mood.

A dawning realization stole over Kitty. "You mean that staff's important?"

"Of course. It's Gladstone's. You *knew* that, otherwise why break into his tomb?"

In her mind's eye, Kitty saw the theater box again, and the gold key being tossed into view. She heard the voice of their benefactor, mentioning the Staff as if it were an afterthought. She saw Hopkins's pale gray eyes gazing at hers, heard his voice, low amid the bustle of the Druids' Coffeehouse, inquiring after the Staff. She felt the sickness of betrayal.

"Oh. You *didn't* know." The bright eyes of the djinni were watching her. "You were set up. Who by? That Hopkins?"

Kitty's voice was faint. "Yes. And someone else—I never saw his face."

"Pity. It was almost certainly one of the leading magicians. As to which, you can take your pick. They're all as bad as one another. And they'll always have someone else do their dirty work for them, djinni or human." It blinked, as if a thought had struck it. "You don't know anything about the golem, I suppose?" This word meant nothing to Kitty; she shook her head. "Didn't think so. It's a big, nasty magical creature—been causing chaos around London recently. *Someone's* controlling it, and I'd dearly like to know who. Nearly killed me, for starters."

The boy looked so put out as it said this that Kitty almost smirked. "I thought you were a noble djinni of awesome power?" she said. "How come this golem beat you?"

"It's resistant to magic, that's why. Saps my energy if I get close. *You'd* have a better chance of stopping it than me." It made it sound as if this was the most ridiculous thing in the world.

Kitty bridled. "Thanks a lot."

"I'm serious. A golem's controlled by a manuscript hidden in its mouth. If you got close, and whipped the paper out, the golem would return to its master and disintegrate back into clay. I saw it happen once, in Prague."

Kitty nodded absently. "That doesn't sound too difficult."

"Obviously, you'd have to penetrate the choking black mist that hangs about it. . . ."

"Oh . . . right."

"And avoid its swinging fists that can hammer through concrete . . ."

"Ah."

"Other than that, you'd be laughing."

"Well, if it's so *easy*," Kitty demanded hotly, "how come the magicians haven't stopped it?"

The djinni gave a cold smile. "Because it would require personal bravery. They never do *anything* themselves. They rely on us the whole time. Mandrake gives me an order, I obey. He sits at home, I go out and suffer. That's the way it works."

The boy's voice had grown old and tired. Kitty nodded. "Sounds tough."

A shrug. "That's the way it works. No choice. That's why I'm interested in you coming out to rescue Hyrnek. Let's face it, it was a stupid decision, and you didn't have to make it. No one's forcing you to do anything. You got it wrong, but for admirable reasons. Believe me, it makes a change to see that after hanging around with magicians for so long."

"I didn't get it wrong," Kitty said. "How long *has* it been?"

"Five thousand years or more. Off and on. You get the odd break down the centuries, but just as one empire falls, there's always another rising up. Britain's only the latest."

Kitty looked out into the shadows. "And Britain'll fall too, in time."

"Oh, yes. The cracks are already showing. You should read more, you'll see the patterns. Aha . . . someone's below. At last . . ."

The boy stood up. Kitty did likewise. To her ears now came scuffling sounds, a couple of whispered curses drifting up the staircase. Her heart began to beat fast. Once more, she wondered if she should run; once more, she quelled the instinct down.

The djinni looked across at her, grinned. Its teeth flashed very white. "You know, I've quite enjoyed our conversation," it said. "I hope they don't order me to kill you."

Girl and demon stood together, waiting in the darkness. Steps ascended the stairs.

43

Nathaniel was escorted to Whitehall in an armored limousine, accompanied by Jane Farrar and three silent officers of the Night Police. Jakob Hyrnek sat to his left, a policeman to his right. Nathaniel noticed that the officer had great rips and tears in the trousers of his uniform, and that the nails on his great callused hands were torn. The air was thick with the smell of musk. He looked across at Jane Farrar, sitting impassively in the front seat, and found himself wondering whether she was a werewolf, too. Altogether, he doubted it: she seemed too controlled, too slight of build. But then again, you could never tell.

At Westminster Hall, Nathaniel and Jakob were taken straight to the great Reception Chamber, where the ceiling glowed with vigilance spheres and the Prime Minister and his lords sat around the polished table. Unusually, no edible delicacies were on display, indicating the perceived seriousness of the situation. Each minister had only a humble bottle of carbonated water and a glass. The Police Chief now sat in the chair of honor next to the Prime Minister, his face heavy with satisfaction. Ms. Whitwell was relegated to a seat on the margins. Nathaniel did not look at her. His eyes were fixed on the Prime Minister, looking for readable signs; but Mr. Devereaux was gazing at the table.

No one but the chief ministers were there. Mr. Makepeace was not present.

The escorting officers saluted at Police Chief Duvall and, at his signal, shuffled from the room. Jane Farrar stepped forward. She coughed delicately.

Mr. Devereaux looked up. He sighed the sigh of a man about to carry out a regretful task. "Yes, Ms. Farrar? You have something to report?"

"I do, sir. Has Mr. Duvall given you any details?"

"He has mentioned something of the matter. Please be brief."

"Yes, sir. For some days, we have been observing the activities of John Mandrake. Several small discrepancies about his recent affairs made us attentive: he has displayed a certain vagueness and inconsistency in his actions."

"I protest!" Nathaniel interrupted as suavely as he could. "My demon destroyed the renegade afrit—I can hardly be accused of vagueness there."

Mr. Devereaux held up a hand. "Yes, yes, Mandrake. You will have your chance to speak. In the meantime, please be silent."

Jane Farrar cleared her throat. "If I might expand, sir: in the last few days Mandrake has several times embarked on solitary trips across London, at a time of crisis when all magicians were required to remain at Westminster to receive orders. This afternoon, when he once more departed mysteriously, we sent vigilance spheres out to follow him. We traced him to a house in east London, where he met his demon and this unprepossessing youth. They took up station there, evidently waiting for someone. We decided to station officers from the Night Police nearby. Late this very evening, a girl approached the house; challenged by our officers, she proceeded to resist arrest. She was highly armed: two men were killed and four injured in the scuffle. However, our officers were about to effect capture when Mr. Mandrake's demon appeared and helped the suspect escape. At this point, I felt it my duty to arrest Mr. Mandrake."

The Prime Minister took a small sip of water. "This girl? Who is she?"

"We believe her to be a member of the Resistance, sir, a survivor of the abbey raid. It seems clear that Mandrake has been in contact with her for some time. Certainly, he helped her evade justice. I thought it proper that the matter be brought to your attention."

"Indeed." Mr. Devereaux's black eyes scanned Nathaniel for a time. "When your forces encountered her, was the girl carrying Gladstone's Staff?"

Jane Farrar pursed her lips. "No, sir, she was not."

"Please sir, if I may—"

"You may *not*, Mandrake. Henry, you wish to comment?"

The Police Chief had been shuffling restlessly in his seat; now he leaned forward, placing his great thick hands palms-down on the table. He turned his head slowly from side to side, scanning the other ministers one by one. "I have had my doubts about this boy for some time now, Rupert," he began. "When I first saw him I said to myself: 'This Mandrake, he's talented, all right, and outwardly industrious—but deep too, there's something unfathomable about him.' Well now, we all know his ambition, how he's wormed his way into poor Jessica's affections, how she gave him power in Internal Affairs at a remarkably young age. So what was his brief in that office? To tackle the Resistance, destroy it if possible, and make the streets a safer place for us all. What has happened in recent months? The Resistance has gone from strength to strength, and their terror campaign has culminated in the ransacking of our Founder's tomb. There is no end to the outrages they have committed: the British Museum, the emporiums of Piccadilly, the National Gallery—all have been attacked, and no one has been held accountable."

Nathaniel stepped forward angrily. "As I've said many times, those had nothing to do with—"

An olive-green band of gelatinous substance materialized in midair before him and wound tightly around his head, gagging him painfully. Mr. Mortensen lowered his hand. "Go on, Duvall," he said.

"Thank you." The Police Chief made an expansive gesture. "Well, now. At first, Ms. Farrar and I assumed all this singular lack of success was down to simple incompetence on Mandrake's part. Then we began to wonder: Could there be something more to it? Could this talented and ambitious youth be part of something more sinister? We began to keep an eye on him. After the museum's destruction, he made a surreptitious journey to Prague, where—although his movements are a little uncertain—we believe he met with foreign magicians. Yes, you may well gasp, Ms. Malbindi! Who knows what damage this boy may have done, what secrets he may have exposed. At the very least, one of our best spies in Prague—a man who had served us well for many years—was killed during Mandrake's visit."

At this, many of the ministers set up a low muttering. Mr. Duvall drummed the table with his slablike fingers. "Mandrake has been touting an unlikely story about the London attacks, claiming that a golem—yes, you did hear correctly, Ms. Malbindi, a *golem*—might be behind them. Ridiculous as this is, he appears to have gulled poor Jessica easily enough, and the golem story served as his excuse to visit Prague. He came back without proof of his wild assertions, and—as we have just heard—has since been caught communing with the Resistance and defying our police. It's clear enough that he wants Gladstone's Staff; it may even be that he directed the traitors to the tomb in the first place. I suggest that we escort Mr. Mandrake forthwith to the Tower of London for proper interrogation. Indeed, I propose to take care of the matter personally."

There was a murmur of assent. Mr. Devereaux shrugged. Of the ministers, Ms. Whitwell remained silent, stony-faced. The portly Foreign Minister, Fry, spoke: "Good. I never liked the boy. His hair is far too long and he has an insolent face. Do you have any methods in mind, Duvall?"

"Perhaps the Well of Remorse? I suggest suspending him up to his nose in it overnight. That usually makes traitors talk, if the eels have left them their tongues."

Fry nodded. "Eels. That reminds me. What about a second supper?"

Mr. Mortensen leaned forward. "What about the Winch, Duvall? That often proves effective."

"A Mournful Orb is the most tried-and-tested method, I find."

"Perhaps a few hours in each?"

"Perhaps. Shall I remove the wretch, Rupert?"

The Prime Minster blew out his cheeks, sat back in his chair. He spoke hesitantly. "I suppose so, Henry. I suppose so."

Mr. Duvall clicked his fingers; from the shadows stepped four Night Police, each one more muscular than the last. They marched in step across the room toward the prisoner, their leader producing a thin silver manacle from his belt. At this development, Nathaniel, who had been wriggling and gesticulating with vigor for some time, set up such an agitated protest that a small muffled yelp escaped his gag. The Prime Minster seemed to recall something; he held up a hand.

"One moment, Henry. We must allow the boy his defense."

The Police Chief frowned with impatience. "*Must* we, Rupert? Beware. He is a plausible little devil."

"*I* shall decide that for myself, I think." Mr. Devereaux glanced at Mortensen, who made a reluctant gesture. The gelatinous gag around Nathaniel's mouth dissolved, leaving a bitter tang. He took his handkerchief from his pocket and wiped the perspiration from his face.

"Get on with it then," Duvall said. "And mind, no lies."

Nathaniel drew himself upright and passed his tongue across his lips. He saw nothing but hostility in the eyes of the senior magicians, except—and this was his only hope now—perhaps those of Mr. Devereaux himself. There he discerned something that might have been uncertainty, mixed with extreme irritation. Nathaniel cleared his throat. He had long prided himself on his bond with the Prime Minister. Now was the time to put it to the test.

"Thank you for the opportunity to speak, sir," he began. He tried to give his voice an easy, calm assertion, but fear constricted it into a squeak. Simply the thought of the House of Persuasion, an area of the Tower of London given over to interrogation of prisoners, made him tremble. Bartimaeus had been right: by his actions, he had become vulnerable to his enemies. Now he had to out-talk them. "Mr. Duvall's insinuations are groundless," he said, "and Ms. Farrar is, to say the least, overeager. I hope that there is still time to make good the damage that they have done."

He heard Jane Farrar snort discreetly somewhere beside him. Mr. Duvall emitted a snarl of protest that was cut off by a single look from the Prime Minister. Somewhat emboldened, Nathaniel pressed on. "My trip to Prague and the issue of the girl are two entirely separate things, sir. It is true that I believe many of the attacks in London to be the work of a golem; my investigations into that are not yet finished. Meanwhile I have been using this youth"—he nodded toward Hyrnek—"to lure the traitor Kitty Jones out of hiding. He is her old associate and I guessed she might attempt to save him. Once in my power, she would soon tell me the location of the Staff, which I could then deliver into your hands. The arrival of Ms. Farrar's wolves completely ruined my ambush. I trust she will be firmly reprimanded."

Jane Farrar gave a cry of anger. "*My* men had the girl trapped! Your demon spirited her away."

"Of course." Nathaniel was urbanity itself. "Because *your* men would have torn her to pieces. They were filled with bloodlust. How would we have secured the Staff then?"

"They were Imperial Police, directly accountable to Mr. Duvall here—"

"Quite so, and a more crude and haphazard organization would be hard to find." Nathaniel went on the attack. "I acknowledge that I have been secretive, sir," he said sweetly, addressing Mr. Devereaux full on, "but I knew this was a delicate operation. The girl is stubborn and willful. To locate the Staff I had to tread carefully: I had to offer her this boy's safety for its return. I feared lest Mr. Duvall's customary heavy-handedness would jeopardize everything. As, unfortunately, has been the case."

The fury in the Police Chief's eyes was remarkable to behold. His swarthy face went beetroot red, the veins in his neck and hands bulged like mooring ropes, and his fingernails—which seemed slightly longer than a moment previously—jabbed deep into the tabletop. He could barely speak for choking. "Guards! Take this vicious youth away. I shall attend upon him presently."

"You forget yourself, Henry." Mr. Devereaux spoke quietly, but the menace in his voice was clear. "*I* am judge and jury in this government; it is I who shall decide Mandrake's fate. I am by no means satisfied that he is the traitor you claim. John," he continued, "your demon has the girl, this Kitty Jones, in custody?"

"Yes, sir." Nathaniel's face was taut with tension. He was not free yet; the dark shadow of the Well of Remorse still hovered before him. He had to go carefully. "I sent her to a quiet location, where I might carry out my plan. I hope this long delay has not ruined everything."

"And you planned to restore the Staff to me?" Devereaux regarded him out of the corner of one eye.

"Of course, sir! I hoped I would see it one day sitting next to the Amulet of Samarkand in the government vaults, sir." He chewed his lip, waited. That was his trump card, of course—by retrieving the Amulet he had saved Devereaux's life, and he did not want the Prime Minister to forget it now. "I can still do it, sir," he added. "If I take this Hyrnek to the girl, and promise their mutual safety, I believe she will give me the Staff within the hour."

"And the girl? She will go free?"

Nathaniel smirked. "Oh, no sir. Once I have the Staff, she and Hyrnek can be interrogated at leisure." His smile promptly vanished as Jakob Hyrnek kicked out and made contact with his shin.

"The boy is a consummate liar." Mr. Duvall had regained a little of his composure. "Please, Rupert, you are surely not going to be taken in . . ."

"I have made my decision." The Prime Minister leaned forward, steepling his fingers into an arch. "Mandrake has proved himself valuable and loyal in the past; we must give him the benefit of the doubt. We shall take him at his word. Let him get the Staff. If he does, his secretiveness in the matter is forgiven. If he does not, I shall accept Henry's version of events and consign him to the Tower. A happy compromise? Is everyone satisfied?" Smiling, he looked from Mr. Duvall's louring disappointment to Nathaniel's sickly green anxiety and back again. "Good. Mandrake can depart. Now, did someone mention food? A little Byzantine wine to begin!"

A warm breeze spun around the room. Invisible slaves stepped forward, bearing crystal glasses and decanters filled with apricot-colored wines. Jane Farrar ducked as a plate of venison sausages swept past her head. "But sir, surely we aren't going to let Mandrake do this alone!"

"Yes—we must send a battalion of troops!" Duvall impatiently swatted a proffered glass aside. "It would be foolish to trust him."

Nathaniel was already halfway to the door. He hurried back. "Sir, this is a situation of great delicacy. A bunch of wolfheads will ruin everything."

Mr. Devereaux was sampling a glass. "Delightful. The essence of Marmara . . . Well, we shall compromise again. Mandrake will be assigned several vigilance spheres, so we can check up on his movements. Now, can someone pass me that delicious-looking couscous?"

Nathaniel bound Jakob Hyrnek in an invisible bond and, leading him by the arm, departed the hall. He felt no elation. He had stymied Duvall for the moment, but if he did not secure the Staff, and soon, the outlook was bleak. He knew that he had used up all the goodwill the Prime Minister felt for him, and the dislike of all the other ministers was palpable. His career, and his life, hung by a thread.

As they crossed the lobby of the hall, Ms. Whitwell stepped out to intercept them. Nathaniel gazed at her implacably, but did not speak. Her hawk eyes bored into his.

"You may or may not have convinced our dear Prime Minister," she said in a harsh whisper, "and you may or may not acquire the Staff, but *I* know that you have been acting behind my back, seeking advancement at my expense, and I will not forgive you for it. Our association is at an end, and I wish you no success. You are welcome to rot in Duvall's Tower for all I care."

She hurried away, her clothes rustling like dead leaves. Nathaniel stared after her for a time; then, noticing Hyrnek watching him with grim amusement in his eyes, he gathered himself and signaled across the lobby to the knot of waiting chauffeurs.

As the car drove north, four red vigilance spheres materialized above the entrance to the hall and drifted silently in pursuit.

44

I saw the way it was the moment they came up the stairs. I could read it in the forced smile of the boy Hyrnek and the reluctance with which he climbed each step. I could see it in the cold, steely look in my master's eyes, and the menacing closeness with which he trod in his prisoner's wake. Oh yes, Nathaniel was trying to make it appear all nice and relaxed, trying to lull the girl into carelessness. Call me intuitive, but I didn't reckon things were quite as rosy as he wanted her to think. Of course, the invisible foliot perched on Hyrnek's shoulders, clutching his throat tightly in its long clawed feet, was a bit of a giveaway, too. Hyrnek's hands were pinned to his side by a thin, scaly loop of tail, so he was unable to speak, cry out, or make any kind of gesture. Thin talons jabbed into his cheeks, encouraging him to maintain his smile. The foliot was busy whispering something in his ear too, and it is unlikely to have been sweet nothings.[1]

But the girl was oblivious to this. She uttered a small cry when she saw Hyrnek appear up the staircase and made an involuntary step forward. My master gave a warning call: "Please stand away, Ms. Jones!"

She stayed where she was, but didn't take her eyes off her friend. "Hello Jakob," she said.

---

[1] Lesser spirits such as this are often small-minded and vengeful, and take any opportunity to discomfort a human in their power with talk of bloodcurdling tortures. Others have an endless roster of smutty jokes. It's a toss-up which is worse.

The foliot loosened its claws a little, allowing the prisoner to croak. "Hi, Kitty."

"Are you hurt?"

A pause. The foliot tickled Hyrnek's cheek warningly. "No."

She gave a weak smile. "I—I came to rescue you."

A stiff nod was all she got that time. The foliot's claws had reasserted their hold. Hyrnek's fake smile was back, but I could see the desperate warning in his eyes.

"Don't worry, Jakob," the girl said firmly. "I'll get us out of this."

Well, this was all very touching, all very poignant, and I could see the girl's affection for the boy[2] was exactly what my master desired. He was watching their greeting with eager calculation.

"I come in good faith, Ms. Jones," he said, lying blandly. Hanging invisibly around Hyrnek's neck, the foliot rolled its eyes and mouthed a silent chuckle.

Even if I *had* wanted to tip off the girl about the foliot, it was impossible to speak to her with my master standing right there in front of me.[3] Besides, he wasn't the only problem. I now noted a couple of red spheres hovering high up in the rafters. Magicians were observing us from afar. There was no point asking for trouble. As usual, I stood pathetically by and waited for my orders.

"I come in good faith," my master said again. His hands

---

[2] Unaccountable as this was. He seemed a bit wet to me.

[3] Not that I would have, of course. Humans and their sad little affairs are nothing to do with me. If I'd had the option of helping the girl out or dematerializing straight off, I'd probably have vanished with a ringing laugh and a gout of brimstone in her eye. Charming as she was, it never pays a djinni to get close to people. Never. Take it from one who knows.

were outstretched in a sign of peace, palms upward and empty.[4]
"No one else knows you are here. We are alone."

Well, that was another fib. The watching spheres nudged
coquettishly behind a beam, as if embarrassed. The foliot
made a face of mock outrage. Hyrnek's eyes pleaded with the
girl, but she noticed nothing. "And the wolves?" she said
curtly.

"Are far away—still searching for you, for all I know." His
mouth smiled. "You can scarcely want any further proof of my
intentions," he said. "Were it not for me, you would be nothing but bones in a back alley by now."

"Last time I saw you, you were scarcely so considerate."

"True." Nathaniel made what he evidently thought was a
courteous flourish; with all his hair and cuffs flapping it looked
as though he'd tripped. "I apologize for my haste on that occasion."

"You still propose to arrest me? I take it that is why you
abducted Jakob."

"I did think it would winkle you out, yes. But arrest you? In
all honesty, that is up to you. Perhaps we can come to an
arrangement."

"Go on."

"But first—do you require refreshment or first-aid? I see
you carry an injury, and you must be weary. I can send my
slave"—here he clicked his fingers at me—"to get whatever
you desire: food, hot wines, restoratives . . . Ask, and it shall
be done!"

She shook her head. "I want none of your magical filth."

"Surely you have need of something? Bandages? Sweet

---

[4] What you could see of them under his outsize lacy cuffs, that is.

herbs? Whisky? Bartimaeus can produce it all in the blink of an eye." [5]

"No." She was hard-faced, unmoved by his blandishments. "What is your proposal? I assume you want the Staff."

Nathaniel's complexion changed a little at the word; perhaps he was disconcerted by her bluntness, magicians being rarely that honest and direct. He nodded slowly. "You have it?" His body was stiff with tension; he did not breathe.

"I do."

"Can it be swiftly secured?"

"It can."

He exhaled then. "Good. Good. Then here is my proposal. I have a car waiting below. Take me to the location of the Staff and entrust it into my care. Once I have it safely, you and Hyrnek will be given safe conduct anywhere you choose. This amnesty will last for a day. I assume you will wish to leave the country, and that will give you time to do so. Think carefully on my words! This is a handsome offer to an unregenerate traitor such as yourself. Others in the government, as you have seen, would not be so kind."

The girl was unconvinced. "What surety do I have that you will keep your word?"

He smiled, plucked a speck of dust from a sleeve. "None. You will have to trust me."

"Hardly likely."

---

[5] Again, a bit of an overstatement here, unless you had a particularly gummy, rheumatic eye that took a while to unstick. Given a precise command and a partial retraction of my current charge, I can certainly dematerialize, materialize elsewhere, locate the necessary objects, and return, but this is bound to take a good few seconds—or more if the objects are hard to track down. I cannot just spirit things out of thin air. That would be silly.

"What choice do you have, Ms. Jones? You are already in something of a corner. A savage demon stands guard over you—"

She looked from side to side in puzzlement. I coughed. "That's me," I said.

"—and you have *me* to contend with too," my master went on. "I will not underestimate you again. In fact," he added, almost as an afterthought, "I'm curious to know the source of your magical defenses. Very curious, in fact. Where did you get them from? Who gave them to you?" The girl said nothing. "If you share this information with me," Nathaniel said, "if you talk candidly about your time in the Resistance, I will do more than set you free." He stepped forward then, put out a hand to touch her arm. She flinched, but did not pull away. "I can give you wealth, too," he said. "Yes, and status beyond your wildest dreams. Commoners such as yourself—with brains, bravery, and aptitude to spare—can win roles at the heart of government, positions of real power. That's no secret. You will work daily with the great ones of our society, and learn such things that will make your head spin. I can take you away from the drabness of your life, give you glimpses into the marvelous past, the days when the magician-emperors bestrode the world. Then you can become part of our own great story. When the current wars are won, for instance, we shall establish a renewed Colonial Office in America, and will need intelligent men and women to enforce our will. They say there are vast estates to be won out there, Ms. Jones, tracts of land with nothing on them but beasts and a few savages. Imagine— you as a great lady of the Empire . . ."

She moved aside then; his hand dropped from her arm. "Thank you, but I do not think that will suit me."

He scowled. "A pity. What of my first proposal? Do you accept?"

"I wish to talk with Jakob."

"There he stands." Casually, the magician walked away a short distance. I stepped back, too. The girl drew close to Hyrnek.

"Are you truly all right?" she whispered. "You are so silent."

The foliot relaxed its hold on his throat, but flexed its talons before his face as a gentle reminder. He nodded weakly. "I'm fine. Fine."

"I am going to accept Mr. Mandrake's offer. Do you have anything to say?"

The weakest of smiles. "No, no, Kathleen. You can trust him."

She hesitated, nodded, turned away. "Very well, then. Mr. Mandrake, I assume you wish to delay no longer. Where is your car? I will take you to the Staff."

During the journey, Nathaniel was a ripe old mix of emotions. Excitement, agitation, and downright fear mingled unappetizingly in his countenance; he could not sit still, fidgeting on his seat, turning repeatedly to look out of the back window at the passing lights of the city. He treated the girl with a confusing combination of officious politeness and barely concealed scorn, asking eager questions one minute and uttering veiled threats the next. By contrast, the rest of us in the car were grave and silent. Hyrnek and Kitty stared rigidly to the front (Hyrnek with the foliot still entwined about his face), while the chauffeur beyond the glass made stolidity an art form.[6] I—though

---

[6] A block of wood wearing a peaked cap would have had more verve and individuality.

forced through lack of space to assume the form of a stoic guinea pig crouched between the girl's shoe and the glove compartment—was my usual dignified self.

We drove steadily through the London night. There was nothing on the roads. The stars began winking out above the rooftops: dawn was fast approaching. The car engine hummed drearily. Out of sight of Nathaniel, four red lights bobbed and weaved directly above the roof of the limousine.

In contrast to my master, the girl seemed very self-possessed. It occurred to me that she knew he would betray her—let's face it, it didn't need a djinni's brain to guess that much—but was going to her doom calmly nonetheless. The guinea pig nodded regretfully to itself. More than ever, I admired her resolve—and the grace with which she exerted it. But that's free will for you. I did not have that luxury in this world.

Under the girl's direction, we drove south through the center of the city, across the river, and into a downmarket region of light industry and commerce, where ramshackle tenement housing rose three stories tall. A few hunched pedestrians were already in evidence, stumbling to early shifts. A couple of bored demi-afrits drifted past, and once a portly messenger imp also, laboring under a giant package. At length, we turned into a narrow cobbled lane that ran under a low arch and into a deserted mews.

"Here." The girl rapped on the partition glass. The block of wood pulled over and sat motionless, awaiting orders. The rest of us disembarked, stiff and cold in the first light of the dawn. The guinea pig stretched out its essence and returned to Ptolemy's form. I glanced about, and saw the watching spheres loitering at a distance.

On either side of us were rows of narrow, white-painted mews houses, residential and a little unkempt. Without a word, the girl approached a set of steps leading down to a basement door. Nudging Hyrnek in front of him, Nathaniel followed. I brought up the rear.

My master glanced at me over his shoulder. "If she tries any tricks, kill her."

"You'll have to be more specific," I said. "What kind of tricks? Card, coin, Indian rope—what?"

He gave me a look. "Anything that breaks my agreement with her, with the intention of causing me harm or assisting her escape. That clear enough?"

"Crystal."

The girl had been scrabbling around in the dimness by the door; from some crevice or other she withdrew a key. A moment later, the door scraped open. Without a word, she stepped through; the three of us shambled after.

We twisted and turned through a series of labyrinthine basements, Kitty, Hyrnek, Nathaniel, and I, one close after the other as if doing a slow and dreary conga. She seemed to know her way well enough, flicking light switches on at intervals, ducking under low arches that caused the rest of us to bang our foreheads, never looking back. It was a circuitous route; I began to wonder if my minotaur guise wouldn't have been more appropriate.

Looking back, I saw the glow of at least one sphere trailing in our wake. We were still being observed from afar.

When the girl halted at last, it was in a small side room off the main basement. She switched on a meager bulb. The room was empty, except for a pile of logs in the far corner. Water dripped from the ceiling and trickled in rivulets across the floor. Nathaniel wrinkled his nose. "Well?" he snapped. "I don't see anything."

The girl stepped over to the logs and extended a foot

somewhere into the pile. A squeaking; a section of brickwork swung open beyond her. Shadows yawned.

"Stop right there! You're not going in." Leaving Hyrnek for the first time, my master hurried forward to stand between Kitty and the secret door. "Bartimaeus—go inside and report what you find. If the Staff is there, bring it out to me."

Rather more diffidently than is my wont, I approached the door, erecting a Shield about me in case of booby traps. As I drew close, I felt a warning throb on all seven planes, the indication of powerful magic up ahead. I stuck a tentative head through the hole and looked around.

It was little more than a glorified cupboard, a seedy hole half filled with the cheap gimmicks that the girl and her friends had pinched from the magicians. There were the usual glass orbs and metal containers: shoddy stuff all, none of it any good.[7]

The exception to this was the item propped casually in the far corner, incongruously fighting for space with a few explosive lances.

When I'd seen the Staff from afar across the burning roofs of Prague, it had been crackling with a storm's power. Lightning bolts had converged on it from a rent and wounded sky, its shadow extended across the clouds. A whole city was subjugated before its anger. Now it was quiet and dusty and a spider was innocently spinning a web between its carved head and a recess in the wall.

---

[7] Rather in the same way that tinned vegetables are never as nice and nutritious as the real thing, Elemental Spheres, or Inferno sticks, or any other weapon formed by trapping an imp or other spirit inside a globe or box, are never as effective or long-lasting as spells worked spontaneously by the spirits themselves. All magicians use them as often as possible, however—it's so much easier than going through the laborious business of summoning.

Even so, its energy was still latent within it. Its aura pulsed strongly, filling the room (on the higher planes) with light. Such an object is not to be trifled with, and it was with hooked fingertip and thumb, in the reluctant manner of someone extracting a maggot from an apple, that I carried Gladstone's Staff out of the secret storeroom and presented it to my master.

Oh, he was happy then. The relief just poured off him. He took it from me and gazed at it, and the aura of the thing lit the contours of his face with a dull radiance.

"Mr. Mandrake." That was the girl talking. She was standing next to Hyrnek now, one arm around him protectively. The invisible foliot had swung to Hrynek's opposite shoulder and was eyeing her with profound mistrust. Perhaps it sensed her innate resilience. "Mr. Mandrake," she said, "I have completed my half of the bargain. Now you must set us free."

"Yes, yes." My master scarcely looked up from his appreciation of the Staff. "Of course. I will make the appropriate arrangements. An escort will be found for you. But first, let us get out of this gloomy place."

By the time we emerged, the light of early morning had begun to spill into the corners of the cobbled mews and shone faintly on the chrome of the limousine on the opposite side of the lane. The chauffeur sat stock-still in his seat, gazing out in front; he did not appear to have moved in all the time we'd been gone. Now the girl tried again. She was very tired; her voice did not carry great hope. "You do not have to escort us from here, Mr. Mandrake," she said. "We can make our own way."

My master had just clambered up the steps holding the Staff. He did not appear to hear her at first; his mind was far away, dwelling on other things. He blinked, stopped dead in his tracks, and fixed his eyes upon her as if seeing her for the first time.

"You made a promise," the girl said.

"A promise . . ." He frowned vaguely.

"To let us go." I noticed her subtly shifting her weight onto the front of her feet as she spoke, readying herself for sudden movement. I wondered with some interest what she planned to do.

"Ah yes." There might have been a time, a year or two back, when Nathaniel would have honored any agreement he had made. He'd have considered it beneath his dignity to break a vow, despite his enmity with the girl. It may be that, even now, part of him still disliked doing so. Certainly, he hesitated for a moment, as if in actual doubt. Then I saw him glance up at the red spheres, which had emerged from the cellar and were once more hovering above. His eyes went dark. His masters' gazes were on him, and that decided matters.

He tugged at a cuff as he spoke, but his resemblance to the other magicians was now deeper than such outward mimicry. "Promises made to terrorists are scarcely obligatory, Ms. Jones," he said. "Our agreement is void. You will be interrogated and tried for treason forthwith, and I shall make it my business to escort you to the Tower myself. Do not try anything!" His voice rose in warning—the girl had slipped a hand into her jacket. "Your friend's life hangs by a thread. Sophocles, reveal yourself!" The grinning foliot on Hyrnek's shoulders shrugged off its invisibility on the first plane, gave the girl an insolent wink and snapped its teeth beside its prisoner's ear.

The girl's shoulders sagged a little; she looked crestfallen. "Very well," she said.

"Your weapon—whatever it is in your coat. Bring it out. Slowly."

She hesitated. "It's not a weapon."

Nathaniel's voice grew dangerous. "I don't have time for this! Show it, or your friend will lose his ear."

"It's not a weapon. It's a present." So saying, she drew forth her hand. In her fingers was something small, circular, glinting in the light. A bronze disc.

Nathaniel's eyes widened. "That's mine! My scrying glass!"[8]

The girl nodded. "Have it back." She flicked her wrist. The disc flew spinning high into the air. Instinctively, we watched it go: Nathaniel, the foliot, and I. As we watched, the girl acted. Her hands reached out and snared the foliot around its scrawny neck, jerking it backward off Hyrnek's shoulders. It was taken by surprise, its grip was loosened, its talons snicking in midair, but its slender tail looped around Hyrnek's face, fast as a whip, and began to squeeze. Hyrnek cried out, clawing at the tail.

Nathaniel was stepping backward, following the spinning disc. He still held the Staff, but his free hand was stretched out, hoping to catch it.

The girl's fingers bore down upon the foliot's neck; its eyes bulged, its face grew purple.

The tail tightened on Hyrnek's head.

I watched all this with great interest. Kitty was relying on her resilience here, on her power to counteract the foliot's magic. It all depended how strong that resilience was. It was quite possible that the foliot would soon reassert itself, crush Hyrnek's skull, and move on to deal with her. But the girl was strong, and she was angry. The foliot's face swelled; it uttered a reproachful sound. A crisis point was reached. With the sound of a balloon popping, the foliot burst into vapor, tail and all; it dissipated on

---

[8] Recognizable from the dreadful workmanship of the exterior. The cheeky, work-shy imp on the interior is even worse.

the air. Both Kitty and Hyrnek lost their balance, tumbled to the ground.

The scrying glass landed safely in Nathaniel's hand. He looked up, and for the first time took in the situation. His prisoners were unsteadily getting to their feet.

He uttered a cry of annoyance. "Bartimaeus!"

I was sitting myself quietly on a post. I looked over. "Yes?"

"Why didn't you act to halt this? I gave you strict instructions."

"You did, you did." I scratched the back of my head.

"I told you to kill her if she tried anything!"

"The car! Come on!" Already the girl was moving, dragging Hyrnek along with her. They scampered across the cobblestones toward the limousine. This was better watching than the Aztec ball game. If only I'd had some popcorn.

"Well?" He was incandescent with rage.

"You told me to kill her if she broke the terms of your agreement."

"Yes! By escaping—as she's doing now! So get to it! The Shriveling Fire—"

I grinned cheerily. "But that agreement is null and void. You broke it yourself, not two minutes ago—in a particularly noxious manner, if I may say so. So she can hardly be breaking it herself, can she? Listen, if you put that Staff down, you can tear your hair out more easily."

"Ahh! I rescind all previous orders and issue a new one, which you cannot misinterpret! Stop them from departing in that car!"

"Oh, very well." I had to obey. I slouched down from the post and set off in reluctant and leisurely pursuit.

All the while we'd been gabbing, Nathaniel and I had been watching our friends' frantic progress across the lane.

The girl was in the lead; now she reached the limo and swung open the driver's door, presumably with the intention of forcing him to drive them away. The chauffeur, who at no point in the proceedings had evinced even the slightest interest in our scuffling, remained staring forward. Kitty was shouting at him now, frantically issuing orders. She tugged at his shoulder. He gave a sort of limp wobble and slipped sideways out of his seat, knocking into the startled girl, before collapsing face down on the cobblestones. One arm lolled discouragingly.

For a couple of seconds, we all halted what we were doing. The girl remained transfixed, perhaps wondering at her own strength. I contemplated the remarkable work ethic of the traditional British workman. Even my master stopped frothing at the mouth for a moment in perplexity. We all edged nearer.

"Surprise!" Up from behind the body of the car popped a smiling face. Well, it was grinning, really—skulls, as we know, don't really smile. Nevertheless, it exuded a certain irrepressible gaiety, which contrasted sharply with the lank white hair flecked with river slime, with the sodden black rags clogged upon its bones, with the fetid graveyard stench now floating on the breeze.

"Uh-oh." Blindingly articulate, that's me.

With a clacking of bones and a gleeful cry, Honorius the afrit leaped upon the bonnet of the car, femurs akimbo, hands on hip bones, skull cocked at a jaunty angle. From there, framed by the light of the new sun, he appraised us one by one.

45

For the first seconds, Kitty was no longer in the cobbled lane, no longer breathing morning air; she was once more underground, trapped in a black crypt, with the taste of death in her mouth and her friends cut down before her eyes. The terror was the same, and the helplessness; she felt her strength and resolution shrivel into nothing, like scraps of paper consumed by fire. She could scarcely breathe.

Her first thought was anger at the demon Bartimaeus. His claim to have destroyed the skeleton was now revealed as just another falsehood. Her second thought was for Jakob, who stood quivering beside her: because of her actions, he would die—she knew this with utter certainty, and hated herself for it.

Most of the skeleton's clothing had fallen away; what little remained hung shapelessly upon the yellowed bones. The golden mask was missing; tiny red flames burned in the skull's dark sockets. Below, sunlight filtered between the ribs and out through the remnants of the jacket. The trousers and shoes were entirely gone. But the creature's energy was unchanged. It hopped from foot to foot with an appalling jerky swiftness.

"Well, jolly nice, I call it." The merry voice rang clear as a bell from between the dangling teeth. "I couldn't have asked for more. Here I am, happy as a lamb, if a little damp about the cartilage, hard at work. What do I want? Simply to follow the scent of my lost possession, collect it and be off on my way. What do I find? My Staff—yes! Good as new—but more than that . . . Two *other* little lambs to play with—two lambs whom I've

520

been thinking about long and hard, as I swilled around the estuary in the cold, cold water, and my beautiful clothes grew rotten on my bones. Oh, don't look so innocent, my dear"— the high voice dropped to a snarl, the skull jutted down toward Kitty—"you're one of them. The little mouse who disturbed my master's rest, who took his Staff and thinks it ladylike to carry vicious silver in her purse. *You*, I'll deal with last."

The skeleton straightened with a bound, tapped its metatarsals on the limousine bonnet, and jerked out a finger toward Bartimaeus, who still wore the semblance of a dark-skinned boy. "Then there's *you*," it said, "the one who stole my face. The one who drowned me in the Thames. Oh, I'm most terrible mad at you."

If it was anxious, the demon was doing a good job of hiding it. "I can understand that," it said coolly. "In fact, I'm a little disappointed myself. Mind telling me how you got here?"

The skull gnashed its jaw in fury. "Merest chance saved me from oblivion," it whispered. "As I drifted, helpless in the current and the cold, cold dark, the crook of my elbow snagged in a rusted chain rising from an anchor in the riverbed. In an instant I had seized the chain in my fingers and my jaw; I fought against the pull of the ocean, clambered upward to the light. Where did I come out? An old barge, tethered for the night. As the cruel water dropped from my bones, my strength returned. What did I want? Vengeance! But first, the Staff, to give me back my power. I crept along the shore by night and day, snuffling for its aura like a dog. . . . And today"—the voice erupted in sudden riotous delight—"I found it, traced it to this yard, waited here in coziness with that fellow on the floor." It indicated the chauffeur's body with a dismissive toe. "I fear he did *not* have good conversation."

Bartimaeus nodded. "Humans aren't known for their wit. Very dull."

"Aren't they, though?"

"Deathly."

"Mmm. Hey!" The skeleton collected itself indignantly. "You're trying to change the subject."

"Not at all. You were saying you were terribly mad at me."

"Quite. Where was I . . . ? Terribly mad . . . Two little lambs, a girl and a djinni . . ." It appeared to have quite lost its train of thought.

Kitty jerked a thumb at the magician Mandrake. "What about him?"

Mandrake gave a start. "I've never seen this excellent afrit in all my life! He can have no grudge against me."

The flames in the skull's eye sockets flared. "Except that you carry my Staff. *That* is no small matter. And what is more . . . you plan to *use* it! Yes! No denials—you are a magician!"

Its outrage was worth building on. Kitty cleared her throat. "*He* made me steal it," she said. "It's all his fault. Everything. He made Bartimaeus attack you, too."

"Is that so?" The skeleton considered John Mandrake. "How very interesting." It bent toward Bartimaeus again. "She's not correct, is she? Is that fop with the Staff *really* your master?"

The young Egyptian boy looked genuinely embarrassed. "I'm afraid so."

"Tsk. Dear me. Well, don't worry. I'll kill him—after I kill you."

Even as it spoke, the skeleton raised a finger. Green flame erupted where the demon had stood, but the boy was already gone, somersaulting across the cobblestone to land neatly on a dustbin beside the nearest house. As if propelled by a single thought, Kitty, Jakob, and John Mandrake turned and ran, making for the arch that led out of the mews courtyard to the road beyond. Kitty was the swiftest, and it was she who first noticed the sudden darkening of the atmosphere, a rapid leaching away of the dawn light about them, as if some power was thrusting it bodily away from the ground. She slowed and stopped. Thin tendrils of blackness were waving and probing through the archway ahead, and behind them came a dark cloud. The view beyond was utterly blocked out, the courtyard cut off from the world outside.

What *now*? Kitty exchanged a helpless glance with Jakob and looked back over her shoulder. The Egyptian boy had sprouted wings and was swooping to and fro across the courtyard, just out of reach of the bounding skeleton.

"Keep away from that cloud." It was John Mandrake's voice, quiet and faltering. He was near them, eyes wide, slowly retreating. "I think it's dangerous."

Kitty sneered at him. "Like you care." Even so, she too backed away.

The cloud extended toward them. A terrible silence hung about it, and an overpowering smell of wet earth.

Jakob touched her arm. "Can you hear . . . ?"

"Yes." Heavy footfalls in the depths of the shadows, something coming closer.

"We've got to get out of this," she said. "Make for the cellar."

They turned and ran toward the steps that led to Mr. Pennyfeather's cellar store. From across the courtyard, the skeleton, which had been vainly firing bolts of magic at the energetic demon, perceived them and clapped its hands. A tremor—the cobblestones rattled. The lintel above the basement door split in two, and a ton of brickwork descended with a rush upon the stairs. The dust subsided; the door was gone.

With a hop and a skip, the skeleton was upon them. "That darned demon is a bit too spry," it said. "I've changed my mind. You two are first."

"Why me?" Jakob gasped. "I've done nothing."

"I know, dear child." The eye sockets glittered. "But you're full of life. And after my time underwater, I frankly need the energy." It reached out a hand—as it did so, it noticed, for the first time, the dark cloud stealing across the courtyard, sucking the light from the air. The skeleton gazed into the blackness, jaw lolling uncertainly.

"Well, well," it said softly. "What's this?"

Kitty and Jakob scuffled back against the wall. The skeleton paid no heed. It swiveled its pelvis and straightened to face the cloud, calling out something in a strange tongue. Beside her, Kitty felt Jakob give a start. "That was Czech," he whispered. "Something like: 'I defy you!'"

The skull rotated 180 degrees and stared at them. "Excuse me a minute, children. I have unfinished business to take care of. I will attend to you in half a jiff. Wait there."

Bones clicking, it moved away, circling out into the center of the courtyard, its eye sockets fixed upon the swelling cloud. Kitty tried to gather her wits. She looked about her. The road was engulfed by shadows, the sun a veiled disc faintly shimmering in the sky. The exit from the mews was blocked by the menacing darkness; on all other sides, blank walls and barred windows stared down. Kitty cursed. If she had a single sphere, she could blast their way out; as it was, they were helpless. Rats in a trap.

A flurry of air beside her, a lightly descending figure. The demon Bartimaeus folded its gauzy wings behind its back and nodded to her politely. Kitty flinched.

"Oh, don't worry," the boy said. "My orders were to prevent your leaving in that car. Go anywhere near it and I'll have to stop you. Otherwise, do whatever you like."

Kitty frowned. "What's happening? What's this darkness?"

The boy sighed ruefully. "Remember that golem I mentioned? It's turned up. *Somebody* has decided to intervene. No prizes for guessing why. That wretched Staff is the root of all our trouble." It peered out through the smog. "Which reminds me . . . What's he— Oh, he's *not*. Tell me he's not . . . He *is* as well. The little idiot."

"What?"

"My dear master. He's trying to activate the Staff."

Roughly opposite them, not far from the limousine, the magician John Mandrake had retreated to stand against a wall. Ignoring the activities of the skeleton—it was now prancing back and forth across the cobblestone, declaiming insults against the ever-advancing cloud—he leaned upon the Staff, head bowed, eyes seemingly closed, as if asleep. Kitty thought she could see his lips moving, mouthing words.

"This is *not* going to end well," the demon said. "If he's trying some simple activation, without Reinforcement or Muting spells, he's asking for trouble. He hasn't a clue how much energy it contains. Two marids' worth at least. Overambition, that's always been his problem." It shook its head sadly.

Kitty understood little of this and cared even less. "Please . . . Bartimaeus—is that your name? How can we get out? Can you help us? You could break through a wall."

The boy's dark eyes appraised her. "Why should I do that?"

"Erm . . . You . . . you don't mean us harm. You've just been following orders . . ." She did not sound very confident.

The boy scowled. "I'm a wicked demon. You said so. Anyway, even if I *wished* to help you, we don't want to draw attention to ourselves right now. Our friend the afrit has forgotten us for the moment. He's remembered the Siege of Prague, when golems like this one caused havoc among Gladstone's troops."

"It's doing something," Jakob whispered. "The skeleton . . ."

"Yes. Heads down." For some moments, the cloud of darkness had paused in its advance, as if considering the antics of the capering skeleton before it. As they watched, it seemed to make a decision. Tendrils flowed forward, in the vague direction of Mandrake and the Staff. At this, the skeleton raised an arm: a brilliant stream of pale light shot out and slammed into the cloud. There was a muffled thump, as of an explosion behind strong doors; fragments of black cloud dispersed in all directions, twisting and melting away in the suddenly renewed warmth of the morning sun.

Bartimaeus made an appreciative sound. "Not bad, not bad. Won't help him, though."

Jakob and Kitty caught their breath. Standing in the center of the courtyard they saw revealed a giant figure, man-shaped but much greater, stocky and crude of limb, a colossal slablike head perched upon its shoulders. It seemed put out by the destruction of its cloud; it swung its arms uselessly, as if trying to scoop the darkness back around itself. Failing in this endeavor, and studiously ignoring the whoops of triumph uttered by the skeleton, it set off with lumbering steps across the courtyard.

"Mmm, Mandrake had better hurry with his conjuration . . ." Bartimaeus said. "Whoops, there goes Honorius again."

"Keep back!" The skeleton's cry echoed across the courtyard. "The Staff is my property! I defy you! I have not guarded it for a hundred years to see some coward rob me. I see you staring through that eye! I shall pluck it out and crush it in my fist!" With this, it fired several blasts of magic at the golem, which absorbed them without any ill effect.

The stone figure strode on. Kitty could see the details of the head more clearly now: two nominal eyes and above them a larger, far more defined third eye, planted in the center of the forehead. This swiveled left and right; it shone like a white flame. The mouth below was little more than a corrugated hole, token and useless. The demon's words came back to her—somewhere in that terrible mouth was the magical paper that gave the monster its power.

A scream of defiance. Honorius the afrit, apoplectic at the failure of its magic, had flung itself forward into the path of the advancing golem. Dwarfed by the great figure, the skeleton bent its knees and sprang; as it did so, magical energies erupted from its mouth and hands. It landed directly on the golem's chest, bony arms circling the neck, legs twining around the torso. Blue flames erupted where it touched. The golem stopped dead, raised a massive clublike hand, and seized the skeleton by a shoulder blade.

For a long moment, the two adversaries remained locked, motionless, in utter silence. The flames licked higher. There was a smell of burning, a radiation of the utmost cold.

Then, all at once—a rush of sound, a pulse of blue light . . .

The skeleton shattered.

Fragments of bone shot out across the cobblestones like a squall of hail.

"Strange . . ." Bartimaeus was seated cross-legged on the ground. He had the look of a fascinated spectator. "That was really very strange. Honorius didn't need to do that, you know.

It was totally foolhardy, a suicidal act—though brave, of course. Despite being mad, he *must* have known it would destroy him, don't you think? Golems negate our magic, pulverize our essences, even when encased in bone. Very odd. Perhaps he was tired of this world after all. Do *you* understand it, Kitty Jones?"

"Kitty . . ." This was Jakob, plucking urgently at her sleeve. "The exit's clear. We can slip away."

"Yes . . ." She snatched another look across at Mandrake. Eyes closed, he was still reciting the words of some spell.

"Come *on* . . ."

The golem had been stationary since the destruction of the skeleton. Now it moved again. Its watch-eye glittered, swiveled, fixed upon Mandrake and the Staff.

"Looks like Mandrake's for it." Bartimaeus's voice was neutral, matter-of-fact.

Kitty shrugged and began to inch after Jakob, along the edge of the wall.

Just then, Mandrake looked up. At first he seemed oblivious of the coming danger; then his gaze fell upon the advancing golem. His face broadened into a smile. He held the Staff out before him and spoke a single word. A nebulous light of pinks and purples drifted around the body of the Staff, rising toward its top. Kitty paused in her inching. A soft reverberation, a humming—as of a thousand bees trapped underground—a tremble in the air; the ground shook slightly.

"He *can't* have," Bartimaeus said. "He *can't* have mastered it. Not the first time."

The boy's smile widened. He pointed Gladstone's Staff toward the golem, which paused uncertainly. Colored lights played about the carvings on the Staff; the boy's face was alive with their radiance and a terrible joy. In a deep, commanding voice, he uttered a complex charm. The Flux about the Staff flared. Kitty screwed up her eyes, half looked away; the golem rocked back on its heels. The Flux wobbled, sputtered, shot back down the Staff and along the magician's arm. His head jerked back; he was lifted bodily off his feet and straight into the wall behind him with a melancholy thud.

The boy sprawled on the ground, tongue lolling. The Staff clattered from his hand.

"Ah." Bartimaeus nodded sagely. "He *hadn't* mastered it. Thought as much."

"Kitty!" Jakob was already some way off along the wall. He was gesticulating furiously. "While there's still time."

The giant clay figure had resumed its stately progress toward the prone figure of the magician. Kitty made to follow Jakob, then turned back to Bartimaeus.

"What's going to happen?"

"Now? After my master's little error? Simple enough. You'll run off. The golem will kill Mandrake, grab the Staff, and take it to whichever magician's watching through that eye."

"And you? You won't help him?"

"I'm powerless against the golem. I've tried once already. Besides, when you were escaping just now, my master overruled all his previous charges—which included my duty to protect him. If Mandrake dies, *I* go free. It's hardly in my interest to help the idiot out."

The golem was drawing abreast of the limousine now, nearing the body of the chauffeur. Kitty looked again at Mandrake, lying unconscious by the wall. She bit her lip and turned away.

"*I* don't have free will most of the time, you see," the demon said behind her loudly. "So when I do, I'm hardly likely to act in a way that injures myself, if I can help it. That's what makes me superior to muddled humans like you. It's called common sense. Anyway, off you go," it added. "Your resilience might well not work against the golem. It's refreshing to see you doing exactly what I would do and getting out while the going's good."

Kitty blew her cheeks out and took a few steps more. She looked back over her shoulder again. "Mandrake wouldn't have helped *me*," she said.

"*Exactly*. You're a smart girl. Off you go and leave him to die."

She looked at the golem. "It's too big. I could never tackle it."

"Especially once it's past that limousine."

"Oh, *hell*." Then Kitty was running, not toward the stricken Jakob, but out across the cobblestones, toward the lumbering giant. She ignored the pain and numbness in her shoulder, ignored her friend's despairing shouts; most of all, she ignored the voices in her head ridiculing her, screaming out the danger, the futility of her action. She put her head down, increased her speed. She was no demon, no magician—she was better than they were. Greed and self-interest were *not* her only concerns. She scampered around the back of the golem, close enough to see the rough smears on the surface of the stone, to smell the terrible wet earthen taint that drifted in its wake. She leaped onto the bonnet of the limousine, ran along it, level with the torso of the monster.

The sightless eyes stared forward, like those of a dead fish; above them, the third eye sparkled with malign intelligence. Its gaze was fixed firmly upon Mandrake's body; it did not perceive Kitty, at its side, jumping with all her strength to land upon the golem's back.

The extreme cold of the surface made her gasp with pain: even with her resilience, it was like plunging into an icy stream—her breath left her, every nerve stung. Her head swam with the earthen stench, bile rose in her throat. She flung her good arm around the golem's shoulder, clung desperately. Each footstep threatened to shake her free.

She had expected the golem to reach up and tear her off, but it did not do so. The eye did not see her; its controller could not feel her weight on the creature's body.

Kitty reached forward with her wounded arm; her shoulder throbbed, making her cry out. She bent her elbow, reached around the front of the face, feeling for the great gaping mouth. That was what the demon had said: a manuscript, a paper, lodged inside. Her fingers touched the ice-cold stone of the face; her eyes rolled, she almost blacked out.

It was no good. She couldn't reach the mouth—

The golem stopped. With surprising suddenness, its back began to bend. Kitty was flung forward, almost headfirst over its shoulders. She had a brief glimpse of the lumpen hand below reaching out and down toward the unconscious boy: it would seize him by the neck, snap it like a twig.

Still the back bent. Kitty began to topple; her grip failed. Her fingers slapped frantically against the great flat face and, all at once, lit upon the cavity of the mouth; they thrust inside. Rough cold stone . . . jagged snags that might almost have been teeth . . . something else, of a soft coarseness. She grasped at it, and in the same moment, lost all purchase on the creature's back. She tumbled forward over its shoulder, landing heavily on the prone figure of the boy.

She lay on her back, opened her eyes, and screamed.

The golem's face was right above her: the gaping mouth, the

sightless eyes, the third eye fixed upon her, alive with fury. As she watched, the fury dimmed. The intelligence went out. The eye in the forehead was nothing but a clay oval, intricately carved, but dull and lifeless.

Kitty raised her head stiffly, looked at her left hand.

A scroll of yellow parchment was clutched between her finger and thumb.

Painfully, Kitty propped herself up on her elbows. The golem was completely frozen, one fist inches from John Mandrake's face. The stonework was cracked and pitted; it might have been a statue. It no longer radiated extreme cold.

"Mad. Quite mad." The Egyptian boy was standing beside her, hands on hips, shaking its head gently. "You're as mad as that afrit was. Still"—it indicated the magician's body—"at least you got a soft landing."

Behind the demon, she saw Jakob approaching diffidently, wide-eyed. Kitty groaned. Her shoulder wound was bleeding again, and every muscle in her body seemed to ache. With laborious care she righted herself and stood, hauling herself up by pulling on the golem's outstretched hand.

Jakob was gazing down at John Mandrake. Gladstone's Staff lay across his breast. "Is he dead?" He sounded hopeful.

"He's still breathing, more's the pity." The demon sighed; looked sidelong at Kitty. "By your foolhardy actions you've condemned me to further toil." It glanced into the sky. "I would take issue with you, but there were some search spheres here earlier. I think the golem's cloud caused them to retreat, but they'll be back—and soon. It would be best if you depart with haste."

"Yes." Kitty took a few steps, then remembered the parchment in her hand. With sudden disgust she loosened her fingers; it drifted to the cobblestones.

"What about the Staff?" Bartimaeus said. "You *could* take it, you know. No one's here to stop you."

Kitty frowned, glanced back at it. It was a formidable object, she knew that much. Mr. Pennyfeather would have taken it. So would Hopkins, the benefactor, Honorius the afrit, Mandrake himself . . . Many others had died for it. "I don't think so," she said. "It's no good to me."

She turned away, began hobbling after Jakob toward the arch. She half expected the demon to call to her again, but it did not do so. In less than a minute, Kitty was at the arch. As she rounded it, she looked back and saw the dark-skinned boy still staring after her across the courtyard. A moment later he was out of view.

46

A sudden ice-cold shock; Nathaniel gasped, sputtered, opened his eyes. The Egyptian boy stood over him, lowering a dripping pail. Freezing water ran into Nathaniel's ears, nostrils, and open mouth; he tried to speak, coughed, retched, coughed again, and rolled onto his side, conscious of a wrenching pain in his stomach and a dull tingling in every muscle. He groaned.

"Rise and shine." That was the djinni's voice. It sounded extremely cheerful.

Nathaniel raised a shaking hand to the side of his head. "What happened? I feel . . . terrible."

"You *look* it too, believe me. You were hit by a considerable magical backlash through the Staff. Your brains and body will be even more addled than usual for a while, but you're lucky to be alive."

Nathaniel tried to lever himself into a sitting position. "The Staff . . ."

"The magical energies have been gradually ebbing through your system," the djinni went on. "Your skin's been steaming gently and the end of each hair's been glowing at the tip. A remarkable sight. Your aura's gone haywire, too. Well, it's a delicate process, ridding yourself of a charge like that. I wanted to wake you straightaway, but I knew I had to wait several hours to ensure you were safely recovered."

"What! How long has it been?"

"Five minutes. I got bored."

Recent memories flooded back into Nathaniel's mind.

"The golem! I was trying to—"

"Overcome a golem? An almost impossible task for any djinni or magician, and doubly so when operating an artifact as subtle and powerful as that Staff. You did well to activate it at all. Be thankful it wasn't charged enough to kill you."

"But the golem! The Staff! . . . Oh no—" With sudden horror, Nathaniel realized the implications. With both of them gone, he'd have failed utterly, he would be helpless before his enemies. With great weariness, he put his head in his hands, scarcely troubling to stifle the beginnings of a sob.

A hard, firm toe jabbed him sharply on his leg. "If you had the wit to look around you," the djinni said, "you might see something to your advantage."

Nathaniel opened his eyes, peeled his fingers away. He looked; what he saw practically jolted him clear of the cobblestones. Not two feet from where he sat, the golem towered against the sky; it was bent toward him, its clawing hand so close he might touch it, the head lowered menacingly; but the spark of life had vanished from it. It had no more motion than a statue or a lamppost.

And propped up against one of its legs, so casually it might almost have been a gentleman's cane: the Staff of Gladstone.

Nathaniel frowned and looked, and frowned some more, but the solution to this puzzle quite eluded him.

"I'd close your mouth," the djinni advised him. "Some passing bird might use it as a nest."

With difficulty, as his muscles seemed like water, Nathaniel got to his feet. "But how . . . ?"

"*Isn't* it a poser?" The boy grinned. "How *do* you think it happened?"

"I must have done it, just before I lost control." Nathaniel nodded slowly; yes, that was the only possible solution. "I was trying to immobilize the golem, and I must have succeeded, just as the backlash happened." He began to feel rather better about himself.

The djinni snorted long and loud. "Guess again, sonny. What about the girl?"

"Kitty Jones?" Nathaniel scanned the courtyard. He had quite forgotten her. "She—she must have fled."

"Wrong again. I'll tell you, shall I?" The djinni fixed him with its black-eyed stare. "You knocked yourself out, like the idiot you are. The golem was approaching, doubtless planning to take the Staff and crush your head like a melon. It was foiled—"

"By your prompt action?" Nathaniel said. "If so, I'm grateful, Bartimaeus."

"*Me? Save you?* Please—someone I know might be listening. No. My magic is canceled out by the golem's, remember? I sat back to watch the show. In fact . . . it was the girl and her friend. *They* saved you. Wait—don't mock! I do not lie. The boy distracted it while the girl climbed on the golem's back, tore the manuscript from its mouth, and threw it to the ground. Even as she did so, the golem seized her and the boy—incinerated them in seconds. Then its life force ebbed and it finally froze, inches from your sorry neck."

Nathaniel's eyes narrowed in doubt. "Ridiculous! It makes no sense!"

"I know, I know. Why should she save you? The mind boggles, Nat, but save you she did. And if you don't think it's true, well—seeing's believing." The djinni brought a hand out from behind its back, held something out. "This is what she plucked from the mouth." Nathaniel recognized the paper instantly; it was identical to the one he'd seen in Prague, but this time furled and sealed with a daub of thick black wax. He took it slowly, gazed across at the golem's gaping mouth and back again.

"The girl . . ." He couldn't accommodate the thought. "But I was taking her to the Tower; I'd hunted her out. No— she'd kill me, not save my life. I don't believe you, djinni. You're lying. She's alive. She's fled the place."

Bartimaeus shrugged. "Whatever you say. That's why she left the Staff with you when you were helpless."

"Oh . . ." This was a point. Nathaniel frowned. The Staff was the Resistance's great prize. The girl would never willingly give it up. Perhaps she *was* dead. He looked down at the manuscript again. A sudden thought occurred to him.

"According to Kavka, the name of our enemy will be written on the parchment," he said. "Let's look! We can find out who's behind the golem."

"I doubt you'll have time," the djinni said. "Watch out— there it goes!"

With a melancholy hiss, a yellow flame erupted from the surface of the scroll. Nathaniel cried out and dropped the parchment hastily to the cobblestones, where it juddered and burned.

"Once out of the golem's mouth, the spell's so strong it soon consumes itself," Bartimaeus went on. "Never mind. You know what happens now?"

"The golem is destroyed?"

"Yes—but more than that. It returns to its master first." Nathaniel stared at his slave with sudden understanding. Bartimaeus raised an amused eyebrow. "Might be interesting, you think?"

"Very much so." Nathaniel felt a surge of grim elation. "You're sure of this?"

"I saw it happen, long ago in Prague."

"Well, then . . ." He stepped past the smoldering fragments of the parchment and hobbled over to the golem, wincing at the pain in his side. "Ahh, my stomach *really* hurts. It's almost like someone fell on it."

"Eerie."

"No matter." Nathaniel reached the Staff, picked it up. "Now," he said, stepping clear of the golem's bulk once more, "let's see."

The flames died away; the manuscript was nothing but ash drifting in the breeze. An odd dark scent hung in the air.

"Kavka's lifeblood," Bartimaeus said. "All gone now." Nathaniel made a face.

As the last wisp of paper vanished, a shudder ran through the golem's transfixed body; the arms wobbled, the head jerked spasmodically, the chest rose, then fell. A faint sighing, as of a dying breath, was heard. A moment's silence; the stone giant was quite still. Then, with the wrenched creaking of an old tree in a storm, the great back rose, the outstretched arm fell against its side, the golem stood straight once more. Its head tilted, as if deep in thought. Deep in the forehead, the golem's eye was blank and dead: the commanding intelligence rested there no longer. But still the body moved.

Nathaniel and the djinni stood aside as the creature turned and with weary steps began to trudge off across the courtyard. It paid no heed to them. It went at the same remorseless pace that it had always used; from a distance, it carried the same energy as before. But already a transformation was taking place: small cracks extended out across the surface of the body. They began in the center of the torso, where previously the stone had been smooth and strong, and radiated toward the limbs. Little pieces of clay broke from the surface and drifted to the cobblestones in the giant's wake.

Behind the golem, Nathaniel and the djinni fell into step. Nathaniel's body ached; he used Gladstone's Staff as a crutch as he went along.

The golem passed under the arch and departed the mews. It turned left into the street beyond, where, ignoring the regulations of the highway, it proceeded to march directly down the center of the road. The first person to encounter it, a large, bald trader with tattooed arms and a trolley of root vegetables, uttered a piteous squeal on its appearance and scampered pell-mell into a side alley. The golem ignored him, Nathaniel and Bartimaeus likewise. The small procession marched on.

"Assuming that the golem's master is a senior magician," Bartimaeus remarked, "just *assuming*, mark you—we may be heading for Westminster right now. That's the center of town. This is going to cause something of a stir, you know."

"*Good*," Nathaniel said. "That's exactly what I want." With every passing minute, his mood was lightening; he could feel the anxiety and fear of the past few weeks beginning to drain away. The exact details of his escape from the golem that morning were still unclear in his mind, but this mattered little to him now; after the low point of the night before, when the massed ranks of the great magicians were set against him and the threat of the Tower hung above his head, he knew he was clear, he was safe once more. He had the Staff—Devereaux would fall at his feet for that—and better, he had the golem. None of them had believed his story; now they would be groveling with apologies—Duvall, Mortensen, and the rest. He would be welcomed into their circle at last, and whether Ms. Whitwell chose to forgive him or not would, in truth, matter very little. Nathaniel allowed himself a broad smile as he stumped along through Southwark, following the golem.

The fate of Kitty Jones was perplexing, but even here things had worked out well. Despite the prompting of practicality and logic, Nathaniel had felt uneasy with his breaking of his promise to the girl. It could not have been helped, of course—the vigilance spheres were observing them, so he could scarcely have allowed her to go free—but the business *had* weighed a little on his conscience. Now, he did not have to worry. Whether in helping him (he still found this difficult to credit) or in attempting to escape (more likely), the girl was dead and gone, and he did not need to waste time thinking about her. It was a shame in a way. . . . From what he had seen of her, she appeared to have had remarkable energy, talent, and willpower, far more than any of the great magicians, with their endless bickering and foolish vices. In some odd way, she had reminded Nathaniel a little of himself, and it was almost a pity she was gone.

The djinni walked in silence beside him, as if deep in thought. It did not seem much disposed to speak. Nathaniel shrugged. Who could guess what strange and wicked daydreams a djinni had? Better not to try.

As they went, they crushed small pieces of damp clay underfoot. The golem was shedding its material with increasing speed; clusters of holes were visible across its surface, and the outline of its limbs was a little uneven. It moved at its normal pace, but with a slightly bent back, as if growing old and frail.

Bartimaeus's prediction, that the golem would cause something of a stir, was proved increasingly correct with every passing moment. They were now firmly on Southwark High Street, with its market stalls and cloth merchants and general air of shabby industry. As they went, the commoners fanned out screaming up ahead, driven like cattle to gross and excessive panic before the striding giant. People threw themselves into shops and houses, breaking down doors and smashing windows in their efforts to escape; one or two climbed lampposts; several of the thinnest jumped down manholes into drains. Nathaniel chuckled under his breath. The chaos was not altogether regrettable. It would do the commoners good to be stirred up a bit, have their complacency shaken out of them. They should *see* the kinds of dangers the government was protecting them against, understand the wicked magic that threatened them on all sides. It would make them less likely to listen to zealots like the Resistance in the future.

A large number of red spheres appeared over the rooftops and hovered silently above the road, regarding them. Nathaniel composed his face into an expression of sobriety, and glanced with what he hoped was patrician sympathy at the broken stalls and frightened faces all around.

"Your friends are watching us," the djinni said. "Think they're happy?"

"Envious, more like."

As they passed the Lambeth rail terminal and headed west, the golem's outline became noticeably more irregular, its shambling more exaggerated. A large piece of clay, perhaps a finger, detached itself and fell wetly to the ground.

Westminster Bridge was up ahead. There seemed little doubt now that Whitehall was their destination. Nathaniel's mind turned to the confrontation to come. It would be a fairly senior magician, of that he had no doubt, one who had discovered his trip to Prague and so sent the mercenary after him. Beyond that, it was impossible to say. Time would quickly tell.

Gladstone's Staff was comfortable in his hand; he leaned heavily upon it, for his side still hurt him. As he went, he looked at it almost lovingly. This was one in the eye for Duvall and the others. Makepeace would be very pleased with the way things had turned out.

He frowned suddenly. So where would the Staff go now? Presumably, it would be placed into one of the government vaults, until someone needed to use it. But who among them had the ability to do so—other than he? Using nothing but improvised conjurations, he'd almost succeeded in using it the first time of asking! He could master it easily, given the opportunity. And then . . .

He sighed. It was a great pity he could not keep it for himself. Still, once he was back in Devereaux's favor, all things were possible. Patience was the key. He had to bide his time.

They turned at last up a short rise between two glass and concrete watchtowers, onto Westminster Bridge itself. Beyond lay the Houses of Parliament. The Thames sparkled in the morning; little boats meandered with the tide. Several tourists vaulted the balustrade at the sight of the decaying golem and plopped into the water.

The golem strode on, its shoulders slumped, its arms and legs truncated stumps that shed clay in rapid gobbets. Its stride was visibly more disjointed; the legs wobbled unsteadily with each step. As if recognizing its time was short, it had increased its speed, and Nathaniel and the djinni were forced into a half-trot behind it.

Since they reached the bridge, there had been little traffic on the road, and now Nathaniel saw the reason why. Halfway across, a small, nervous unit of Night Police had erected a cordon. It consisted of concrete posts, barbed wire, and a number of savage second-plane imps, all spines and shark teeth, circling in midair. When they perceived the approaching golem, the imps retracted both spines and teeth and retreated with shrill wails. A police lieutenant stepped slowly forward, leaving the rest of his men loitering uncertainly in the shadows of the posts.

"Halt now!" he growled. "You are entering a government-controlled area. Rogue magical effusions are strictly forbidden on pain of swift and awful puni—"With a yelp like a puppy, he sprang sideways out of the golem's path. The creature raised an arm, swatted a post into the Thames and tore through the cordon, leaving small pieces of clay hanging on the ravaged wire. Nathaniel and Bartimaeus sauntered along behind, winking cheerily at the cowering guards.

Over the bridge, past the towers of Westminster, onto the green itself. A crowd of minor magicians—pale-faced bureaucrats from the Ministries along Whitehall—had been alerted to the kerfuffle and had emerged blinking into the light of day. They fringed the pavements in awe, as the shambling giant, now considerably reduced, paused for a moment at the corner of Whitehall, before turning away, left, toward Westminster Hall. Several people called out to Nathaniel as he passed them. He waved a regal hand. "This is what's been terrorizing the city," he called. "I am returning it to its master."

His answer awoke great interest; in ones and twos, and then in a rushing mass, the crowd fell in behind him, keeping always at a safe distance.

The great entrance door of Westminster Hall was ajar, the gatekeepers having fled at the sight of the oncoming creature and the crowd behind. The golem shouldered its way inside, ducking a little under the arch. By now, its head had lost most of its shape; it had melted like a candle by morning. The mouth had merged with the torso; the carved oval eye was skewed, hanging drunkenly midway down the face.

Nathaniel and the djinni entered the lobby. Two afrits, yellow-skinned, with lilac crests, materialized menacingly from pentacles in the floor. They considered the golem and swallowed audibly.

"Yep, I wouldn't bother," the djinni advised them as it passed. "You'll only hurt yourselves. Watch your backs, though—half the city's on our heels."

The moment was coming. Nathaniel's heart was beating fast. He could see where they were going now: the golem was passing along the corridor toward the Reception Chamber, where only elite magicians were allowed. His head spun at the implications.

From a side corridor a figure stepped out—slight, gray-uniformed, with bright green, anxious eyes. "Mandrake! You fool! What are you doing?"

He smiled politely. "Good morning, Ms. Farrar. You seem unduly agitated."

She bit her lip. "The Council have scarcely been to their beds all night; now they have gathered once more and are watching through their spheres. What do they see? Chaos across London! There's pandemonium in Southwark—riots, demonstrations, mass destruction of property!"

"It's nothing that your estimable officers can't control, I'm sure. Besides, I am merely doing what I was . . . requested to do last night. I have the Staff"—he flourished it—"and in addition, I am returning some property to its rightful owner, whoever that may be. Whoops, that was valuable, wasn't it?" Up ahead, the golem, entering a more constricted section of corridor, had sent a vase of Chinese porcelain smashing to the floor.

"You'll be arrested . . . Mr. Devereaux—"

"Will be delighted to learn the identity of the traitor. As would these people behind me. . . ." He did not need to glance over his shoulder. The hubbub of the pursuing crowd was deafening. "Now, if you would care to accompany us. . . ."

A set of double doors ahead. The golem, now little more than a shapeless mass, stumbling and careering from side to side, broke its way through. Nathaniel, Bartimaeus, and Jane Farrar, with the first of the onlookers close behind, stepped after it.

As one, the ministers of the British government rose from their places. A sumptuous breakfast lay before them on the table, but it had been brushed aside to accommodate the swirling nexuses of several vigilance spheres. In one, Nathaniel recognized an aerial view of Southwark High Street, with crowds milling restlessly amid the debris of the market; in another, he saw the people thronging Westminster Green; in a third, a view of the very chamber they were in.

The golem halted in the center of the room. Breaking through the doors had taken its toll and it appeared to have very little energy remaining. The ruined figure swayed where it stood. Its arms had vanished now, its legs conjoined into a single fluid mass. For a few moments, it teetered as if it would fall.

Nathaniel was scanning the faces of the ministers around the table: Devereaux, whey-faced with weariness and shock; Duvall, scarlet with fury; Whitwell, her features hard and set; Mortensen, lank hair disordered and unoiled; Fry, still peaceably crunching the remnants of a wren; Malbindi, her eyes like saucers. To his surprise, he saw, among a knot of lesser ministers hovering to the side, both Quentin Makepeace and Sholto Pinn. Evidently the events of the early morning had drawn everyone of influence to the room.

He looked from face to face, saw nothing but anger and distress. For a moment, he feared he had been wrong, that the golem would collapse now, with nothing proven.

The Prime Minister cleared his throat. "Mandrake!" he began. "I demand an explanation of this—"

He halted. The golem had given a lurch. Like a drunken man, it wobbled to the left, toward Helen Malbindi, the Information Minister. All eyes followed it.

"It may still be dangerous!" Police Chief Duvall appeared less frozen than the rest. He tapped Devereaux on the arm. "Sir, we must vacate the room immediately."

"Rubbish!" Jessica Whitwell spoke harshly. "We are all aware what is happening. The golem is returning to its master! We must stand still and wait."

In dead silence they watched the column of clay shuffle toward Helen Malbindi, who retreated with shaking steps; all at once, its balance shifted, it tipped sideways and to the right, toward the places of Jessica Whitwell and Marmaduke Fry. Whitwell did not move an inch, but Fry gave a mewl of fright, lurched back and choked on a wren bone. He collapsed gasping into his chair, pop-eyed and scarlet-cheeked.

The golem veered toward Ms. Whitwell; it hovered above her, great slabs of clay sloughing off onto the parquet floor.

Mr. Duvall cried out. "We have our answer and must delay no longer! Jessica Whitwell is the creature's master. Ms. Farrar—summon your men and escort her to the Tower!"

The clay mound gave a strange shudder. It tipped suddenly— away from Ms. Whitwell, and toward the center of the table, where Devereaux, Duvall, and Mortensen were standing. All three started back a pace. The golem was scarcely taller than a man now, a crumbling pillar of decay. It lurched up against the table edge and here it paused again, separated from the magicians by a meter of varnished wood.

The clay fell forward onto the tabletop. Then, with a horrible intentness, it moved, shuffling side to side in weak and painful spasms, like a limbless torso wriggling. It moved among the debris of the breakfast, knocking plates and bones aside; it nudged against the nearest vigilance sphere nexus, which instantly flickered and went out; it clawed its way directly toward the motionless form of the Police Chief, Henry Duvall.

The room was very silent now, save for the quiet choking of Marmaduke Fry.

Mr. Duvall, his face ashen, retreated from the table. He pressed back against his chair, which knocked against the wall.

The clay had left almost half its remaining substance amid the scattered plates and cutlery. It reached the opposite side of the table, reared up, swayed like an earthworm, flowed down upon the floor. With sudden speed it darted forward.

Mr. Duvall jerked back, lost his balance, subsided into his chair. His mouth opened and shut, but made no sound.

The sinuous mass of clay reached his jackboots. Summoning the last of its energy, it rose up in a blunt and swaying tower, to teeter for an instant over the Police Chief's head. Then it crashed down upon him, shedding the last vestiges of Kavka's magic as it did so. The clay split, fragmenting into a shower of tiny particles that spattered down upon Duvall and the wall behind him and sent a small oval piece of material tumbling gently down his chest.

Silence in the room. Henry Duvall gazed down, blinking through a clinging veil of clay. From its lodging place on his lap, the golem's eye stared blankly back.

47

The uproar that attended my master's unmasking of Henry Duvall was as tumultuous as it is tedious to relate. For a long while bedlam reigned; word spread in ripples out from the magicians' chamber, across the heart of Whitehall and into the extremities of the city, where even the lowliest commoners wondered at it. The downfall of one of the great is always attended by much excitement, and this was no exception. One or two impromptu street parties were held that very evening and, on the rare occasions when they dared show their faces in the ensuing weeks, members of the Night Police were treated with overt derision.

In the immediate term, confusion was the order of the day. It took an age to place Duvall under arrest—this was through no fault on his part, since he seemed stunned by the direction events had taken, and made no effort to resist or escape. But the wretched magicians lost no time in clamoring to take his place, and for some while squabbled like vultures over who had the right to take charge of the police. My master did not take part in the fray; his actions had done the talking.

In the end, the Prime Minister's lackeys summoned a fat afrit, who had been lurking sheepishly in the lobby out of the way of the golem, and with its help achieved order. The ministers were dismissed, Duvall and Jane Farrar taken into custody, and the excited onlookers shepherded out of the building.[1] Jessica Whitwell loitered till the last, shrilly proclaiming her part in Nathaniel's success, but finally she, too, reluctantly departed.

The Prime Minister and my master were left alone.

Exactly what passed between them, I don't know, as I was sent along with the afrit to restore order in the streets outside. When I returned, some hours later, my master was sitting in a side room alone, eating breakfast. He no longer had the Staff.

I took the semblance of the minotaur again, sat myself in the chair opposite, and tapped my hooves idly on the floor. My master eyed me, but said nothing.

"So," I began. "All well?" A grunt. "Are we restored to favor?" A brief nod. "What's your status now?"

"Head of Internal Affairs. Youngest minister ever."

The minotaur whistled. "*Aren't* we clever."

"It's a start, I suppose. I'm independent from Whitwell now, thank goodness."

"And the Staff? Did you get to keep it?"

A sour expression. He speared his black pudding. "No. It's gone into the vaults. For 'safe-keeping,' allegedly. No one's allowed to use it." His face brightened. "It might be brought out in time of war, though. I was thinking, maybe later in the American campaigns . . ." He took a sip of coffee. "They've not started too well, apparently. We'll see. Anyway, I need time to refine my approach."

"Yeah, like see if you can make it work."

He scowled. "Of course I can. I just left out a couple of restrictive clauses and a directional incantation, that's all."

"In plain language, you fluffed it, mate. What's happened to Duvall?"

---

[1] The vast majority went quickly and without trouble. A few laggards were helped on their way by the application of Infernos to their backsides. A number of pressmen from *The Times*, who were discovered making detailed notes of the magicians' panic, were escorted to a quiet place, where their reports were channeled more favorably.

My master chewed meditatively. "He's been taken to the Tower. Ms. Whitwell is head of Security again. She will be supervising his interrogation. Pass the salt."

The minotaur passed it.

If my master was pleased, I had reason to be satisfied, too. Nathaniel had vowed to release me once the matter of the mystery attacker was solved, and solved it undoubtedly had been, although I felt there were still one or two issues that defied ready explanation. However, this was no business of mine. I awaited my dismissal with easy confidence.

And waited.

Several days passed during which the boy was too busy to listen to my demands. He took control of his department; he attended high-level meetings to discuss the Duvall affair; he moved out of his old master's apartment and, using his new salary and a gift from the grateful Prime Minister, purchased a swanky townhouse in a leafy square not far from Westminster. This last required me to carry out a number of dubious chores, which I haven't time to go into here.[2] He attended parties at the Prime Minister's residence at Richmond, held functions for his new employees, and spent his evenings at the theater, watching abysmal plays for which he had acquired an inexplicable taste. It was a hectic lifestyle.

Whenever possible, I reminded him of his obligations.

"Yes, yes," he would say, on his way out in the mornings. "I'll deal with you presently. Now, for my reception-room curtains, I require an ell of oyster-gray silk; make the purchase from Fieldings, and get a couple of extra cushions while you're at it."

---

[2] They involved whitewash, wallpaper, and copious cleaning fluids. I say no more.

I could do with some Tashkent enameling in the bathroom, too."[3]

"Your six weeks," I said pointedly, "are almost up."

"Yes, yes. Now, I really must go."

One evening he returned home early. I was belowstairs, supervising the tiling of his kitchen,[4] but somehow tore myself away to press my case once more. I found him in his dining room, an ostentatious space currently without furniture. He was staring at the empty fireplace and the cold blank walls.

"You need a *proper* pattern in here," I said. "Wallpaper to suit your age. What about a car motif, or steam trains?"

He wandered to the window, his feet tapping on the hollow boards. "Duvall confessed today," he said at last.

"That's good," I said. "Isn't it?"

He was looking out at the trees of the square. "I suppose . . ."

"Because with my magical powers I detect that you don't seem wildly satisfied."

"Oh . . . Yes." He turned to me, forced a smile. "It clears up a lot of things, but most of them we knew already. We'd found

---

[3] He was no different here from 90 percent of other magicians. When not attempting to stab one another in the back, they spend their time surrounding themselves with the finer things in life. Luxurious pads feature heavily on their wish lists, and it's always the poor djinni who has to do the legwork. Persian magicians were the most extravagant: we had to shift palaces from one country to another overnight, build them on clouds, even underwater. There was one magician who wanted his castle made of solid glass. Aside from the obvious privacy angle, it was a hopeless mistake. We built it for him one evening and he joyfully took possession. Next morning, the sun came up: the walls acted like giant lenses and its rays were refracted through with vigor. By noon the magician and his entire household had been burned to charcoal crisps.

[4] To help carry out the job, he'd presented me with two foliots, which wore the semblance of orphan waifs. They were round-eyed and pitiable enough to melt the hardest of hearts. However, they were also inclined to laziness. I roasted them over a slow flame, and so won their prompt obedience.

the workshop in the cellar of Duvall's house—the pit where the golem was made, the crystal through which he controlled the eye. He worked the creature, no question."

"Well, then."

"Today he acknowledged all that. He said he'd long wanted to expand his role, diminish Ms. Whitwell and the others. The golem was his method: it created chaos, undermined the other ministers. After a few attacks, with no solution found and everyone in disarray, Devereaux was only too happy to give him more authority. The police were given more powers; Duvall got the Security post. From there, he'd have been better placed to overthrow Devereaux in time."

"Sounds fairly clear," I agreed.

"I don't know . . ." The boy screwed down the corners of his mouth. "Everyone's satisfied: Whitwell's back in her old job; Devereaux and the other ministers are heading back to their silly feasts; Pinn's reconstructing his shop already. Even Jane Farrar's been set free, as there's no evidence she knew about her master's treachery. They're all happy to put it out of their minds. But I'm not sure. Several things don't add up."

"Such as?"

"Duvall claimed that he wasn't alone in this. He says someone put him up to it, a scholar named Hopkins. He says this Hopkins brought him the golem's eye, taught him how to use it. He says this Hopkins put him in touch with the bearded mercenary, and encouraged Duvall to send him out to Prague to track down the magician Kavka. When I started investigating, Duvall contacted the mercenary in Prague and told him to stop me. But Hopkins was the brains of the whole thing. This rings true to me—Duvall wasn't bright enough to have worked it all out alone. He was the leader of a bunch of werewolves, not a great magician. But can we find this Hopkins? No. No one knows who he is, or where he lives. He's nowhere to be seen. It's as if he doesn't exist."

"Perhaps he doesn't."

"That's what the others think. They reckon Duvall was trying to shift the blame. And everyone assumes he was involved in the Lovelace conspiracy, too. The mercenary proves it, they say. But I don't know. . . ."

"Hardly likely," I said. "Duvall was trapped with the others in the great pentacle at Heddleham Hall, wasn't he? He wasn't part of that conspiracy. Sounds like Hopkins might have been, though. He's the connection, if you can find him."

He sighed. "That's a big if."

"Perhaps Duvall knows more than he's telling. He might spill more beans."

"Not now." The boy's face sagged insensibly; he suddenly looked tired and old. "On being returned to his cell after this afternoon's interrogation, he transformed into a wolf, overcame his guard, and broke through a barred window."

"And escaped?"

"Not exactly. It was five floors up."

"Ah."

"Quite." The boy was by the great bare mantelpiece now, fingering the marble. "The other question is the Westminster Abbey break-in and the matter of the Staff. Duvall agreed he'd sent the golem to steal it from me the other day—it was too good an opportunity to miss, he said. But he swore he had nothing to do with the Resistance, and nothing to do with breaking into Gladstone's tomb." He tapped his hands on the stone. "I suppose I'll have to be satisfied, like the others. If *only* the girl hadn't died. She could have told us more. . . ."

I made an affirmative sort of noise, but said nothing. The fact that Kitty was alive was a mere detail—it wasn't worth mentioning. Nor was the fact that she'd told me a good deal about the abbey break-in, and that a gentleman named Hopkins was somehow involved with it. It wasn't my business to tell Nathaniel this. I was nothing but a humble servant. I just did what I was told. Besides, he didn't deserve it.

"You spent time with her," he said abruptly. "Did she talk much to you?" He eyed me quickly, turned away.

"No."

"Too frightened, I suppose."

"*Au contraire*. Too disdainful."

He grunted. "Shame she was so willful. She had some . . . admirable qualities."

"Oh, you noticed those, did you? I thought you were too busy reneging on your promise to give much thought to her."

His cheeks flushed red. "I had little choice, Bartimaeus—"

"Don't give me anything about choice," I snapped. "*She* could have chosen to let you die."

He stamped his foot. "I'm *not* going to have you criticizing my actions—"

"Actions nothing. It's your morals I object to."

"Still less my morals! *You're* the demon, remember? Why should it matter to you?"

"It doesn't matter!" I was standing, arms folded now. "It doesn't matter at all. The fact that a humble commoner was more honorable than you'll ever be is hardly my affair. You do what you like."

"I will!"

"Fine!"

"Fine!"

For a few moments there, we'd both been winding ourselves

up into full-blown fury, ready to go at it hammer and tongs, but somehow our hearts weren't in it.

After an interlude of his staring at a corner of the fireplace and my gazing at a crack in the ceiling, the boy broke the silence. "If it's of any interest to you," he growled, "I've spoken to Devereaux and have gotten Kavka's children released from prison. They're back in Prague now. Cost me a few favors to get that done, but I did it."

"How noble of you." I was in no mood to pat his back.

He scowled. "They were low-level spies anyway. Not worth keeping."

"Of course." Another silence. "Well," I said finally. "All's well that ends well. You've got everything you wanted." I gestured across the empty room. "Look at the size of this place! You can fill it with all the silk and silver you desire. Not only that, you're more powerful than ever; the Prime Minister is once more in your debt; and you're out from under Whitwell's thumb."

He looked a little happier at this. "That's true."

"Of course, you're also completely friendless and alone," I went on, "and all your colleagues fear you and will want to do you harm. And if you get too powerful, the Prime Minister will get paranoid and find an excuse to bump you off. But hey, we've all got troubles."

He eyed me balefully. "What a charming insight."

"I'm full of them. And if you don't want any more, I advise you to dismiss me on the instant. Your six weeks are up, and that marks the end of my current bond. My essence aches and I'm tired of white emulsion."

He gave a sudden curt nod. "Very well," he said. "I will honor our agreement."

"Eh? Oh. Right." I was a little taken aback. In all honesty, I'd expected the usual bartering before he agreed to let me go. It's like making a purchase in an Eastern bazaar: haggling is inevitably the order of the day. But perhaps his betrayal of the girl had lodged in my master's mind.

Whatever the reason, he silently led me up to his workroom on the second floor of the house. It was decked out with the basic pentacles and paraphernalia.

We completed the initial procedure in stony silence.

"For your information," he said cattily, as I stood within the pentacle, "you do not leave me entirely alone. I am off to the theater this evening. My good friend Quentin Makepeace has invited me to a gala premiere of his latest play."

"How desperately thrilling."

"It is." He did a dismal job of trying to look pleased. "Well, are you ready?"

"Yep." I performed a formal salute. "I bid the magician John Mandrake farewell. May he live long and never summon me again. . . . By the way, notice something there?"

The magician paused with his arms raised and his incantation at the ready. "What?"

"I didn't say 'Nathaniel.' That's because I see you more as Mandrake now. The boy who was Nathaniel's fading, almost gone."

"Good," he said crisply. "I'm glad you see sense at last." He cleared his throat. "So. Farewell, Bartimaeus."

"Farewell." He spoke. I went. I didn't have time to tell him he'd kind of missed the point.

48

Mrs. Hyrnek had said her good-byes up beyond the customs house, and Kitty and Jakob walked alone together down to the quay. The ferry was nearing departure; smoke rose from the funnels and a brisk breeze was furling the sails. The last of the travelers were ascending a gaily canopied gangway near the stern, while farther forward a troop of men carried the luggage aboard. Raucous gulls swooped in the sky.

Jakob was wearing a white hat with a broad brim, tipped far forward to shade his face, and a dark brown traveling suit. He carried a small leather case in one gloved hand.

"You've got your papers?" Kitty said.

"For the tenth time, yes." He was still a little tearful after the parting from his mother, and this made him irascible.

"It's not a long voyage," she said peaceably. "You'll be there tomorrow."

"I know." He tugged at the hat brim. "Think I'll pass through?"

"Oh yes. They're not looking for us, are they? The passport's only a precaution."

"Mmm. But with my face—"

"They won't give it a second look. Trust me."

"Okay. Are you sure you won't . . . ?"

"I can always follow on. Are you going to give that guy your case?"

"I suppose so."

"Go and do it, then. I'll wait." With only the briefest of hesitations, he moved away. Kitty watched him pass slowly through the hurrying crowds, and was pleased to see that no one so much as glanced at him. The ship's whistle blew, and somewhere nearby a bell rang. The quay was alive with activity now, with sailors, cargo men and merchants hurrying past, with final orders being given, letters and packets being exchanged. On the deck of the ferry, many of the embarkees were standing at the rail, faces shining with excitement, talking happily to one another in a dozen languages. Men and women from distant lands—from Europe, Africa, Byzantium, and the East . . . Kitty's heart beat fast at the thought, and it made her sigh. More than a little, she wished to join them. Well, perhaps she would in time. She had other things to do first.

On that terrible morning, they had fled, the two of them, to the Hyrnek factory, where Jakob's brothers concealed them in a disued room hidden behind one of the printing machines. There, amid the noise and fug and the stench of leather, Kitty's wounds were tended, and their strength revived. Meanwhile, the Hyrnek family prepared for the inevitable repercussions, for the searches and the fines. A day passed. The police did not arrive. Word came of the golem's march through London, of the downfall of Duvall, of the boy Mandrake's promotion. But of them—the fugitives—they heard nothing at all. There were no searches, no reprisals. Each morning, magicians' orders arrived at the factory as usual. It was most curious. Kitty and Jakob appeared to have been forgotten.

On the end of the second day, a council was held in the secret room. Despite the authorities' apparent indifference, the family considered it highly unsafe for Jakob and Kitty to remain in London. Jakob, in particular, with his distinctive appearance, was vulnerable. He could not remain in the factory forever, and sooner or later the magician Mandrake, or one of his associates or demons, would find him. He had to go somewhere safe. Mrs. Hyrnek expressed this opinion forcefully and at volume.

When she had subsided, her husband stood up; between puffs of his rowan-wood pipe, Mr. Hyrnek made a calm suggestion. The family's prowess at printing, he said, had already enabled them to bring down vengeance upon Tallow, doctoring his books so that his own spells brought about his destruction. It would be a simple matter now to forge certain documents, such as new identity papers, passports, and the like that would make it easy for both children to leave the country. They could go to the Continent, where other offshoots of the Hyrnek family—in Ostend, Brugges, or Basel for instance—would be happy to receive them.

This suggestion was greeted with general acclaim and Jakob accepted it at once: he had no wish to fall afoul of the magicians again. For her part, Kitty seemed distracted. "That's very kind, very kind of you," she said.

While the brothers set to forging the documents, and Mrs. Hyrnek and Jakob began preparing supplies for the voyage, Kitty remained in the room, lost in thought. After two days' solitary pondering she announced her decision: she would not be traveling to Europe.

The white hat with the broad brim came rapidly toward her through the crowd; Jakob was smiling now, lighter of step. "You gave him the case?" she said.

"Yes. And you were right—he didn't give me a second look." He glanced across at the gangway, then at his watch. "Look, I've got only five minutes. I'd better get on board."

"Yes. Well . . . see you, then."

"See you. . . . Look, Kitty—"

"Yes?"

"You *know* I'm grateful for what you did, rescuing me and all. But frankly . . . I also think you're an idiot."

"Oh, cheers."

"What are you doing staying here? The Council of Brugges is made up of commoners; magic hardly figures in the city. You can't imagine the freedoms, my cousin says—there're libraries, debating chambers, stuff right up your alley. No curfews—imagine that! The Empire keeps its distance, most of the time. It's a good place for business. And if you wanted to carry on with your"—he peered cautiously from side to side—"with your *you know*, my cousin reckons there are strong links to underground movements there, too. It would be far safer—"

"I know." Kitty shoved her hands into her pockets, blew out her cheeks. "You're quite right. All of you are quite right. But that's sort of the point. I think I need to be here, where the magic's happening, where the demons are."

"But why—"

"Don't get me wrong, I'm grateful for the new identity." She patted her jacket pocket, felt the papers crackle. "It's just, well, some things that demon Bartimaeus said have . . . set me thinking."

He shook his head. "This is what I can't fathom," he said. "You're going on the word of a demon—one that kidnapped me, threatened you—"

"I know! It's just he wasn't what I expected at all. He talked about the past, about patterns repeating themselves, about the rise and fall of the magicians through history. It happens,

Jakob, time and time again. No one manages to break out of the cycle—not commoners, not demons, not magicians. We're all stuck fast, trapped in a wheel of hate and fear—"

"Not me," he said firmly. "I'm getting out."

"You think Brugges is safe? Get real. 'The Empire keeps its distance, most of the time'—that's what you said. You're still part of it, like it or not. That's why I want to stay here, in London, where the information is. There are great libraries, Jakob, where the magicians store their historical records. Pennyfeather used to tell me about them. If I could get access, get a job there somehow . . . I could learn something—about demons, in particular." She shrugged. "I don't know enough yet, that's all."

He snorted. "Of course you don't. You're not a cursed magician."

"But from what Bartimaeus said, the magicians don't know much either. About demons. They just use them. That's the point. We—the Resistance—weren't getting anywhere. We were just as bad as the magicians, using magic without understanding it. I already knew that, really, and Bartimaeus kind of confirmed it. You should have heard him, Jakob—"

"Like I said, you're an idiot. Listen, that's my call." A deep siren sounded from somewhere up on the ferry; seagulls wheeled into the sky. He leaned forward, gave her a rapid hug. She kissed him on the cheek. "Don't get killed," he said. "Write to me. You've got the address."

"Sure."

"I'll see you in Brugges. Before the month is out."

She grinned. "We'll see."

She watched him trot down to the gangway, thrust his papers under the nose of an attendant, receive a cursory stamp on his passport, and clamber up on board. The canopy was removed, the gangway drawn back. Jakob took up position at the rail. He waved to her as the ship moved away. His face, like those of the other travelers, was aglow. Kitty smiled, rummaged in a pocket, and drew out a dirty handkerchief. She waved it until the ship banked and was lost from view around the curve of the Thames.

Then Kitty replaced the handkerchief in her pocket, turned, and set off up along the quay. Quite soon she was hidden by the crowd.

Don't miss the thrilling conclusion to

THE
BARTIMAEUS
TRILOGY
BOOK THREE

Ptolemy's Gate

With dawn, the first people returned to the little town. Hesitant, fearful, groping their way like blind men up the street, they began to inspect the damage wrought to their houses, shops, and gardens. A few Night Police came with them, ostentatiously flourishing Inferno sticks and other weapons, though the threat was long since gone.

I was disinclined to move. I spun a Concealment around the chunk of chimney where I sat and removed myself from the humans' sight. I watched them passing with a baleful eye.

My few hours' rest had done me little good. How could it? It had been two whole *years* since I'd been allowed to leave this cursed Earth; two full years since I'd last escaped the brainless thronging mass of sweet humanity. I needed more than a quiet kip on a chimney stack to deal with *that*, I can tell you. I needed to go home.

And if I didn't, I was going to die.

It is technically possible for a spirit to remain indefinitely on Earth, and many of us at one time or another have endured prolonged visits, usually courtesy of being forcibly trapped inside canopic jars, sandalwood boxes, or other arbitrary spaces chosen by our cruel masters.[1] Dreadful punishment though this is, it at least has the advantage of being safe and quiet. You aren't called upon to *do* anything, so your increasingly weakened essence is not immediately at risk. The main threat comes from the remorseless tedium, which can lead to insanity in the spirit in question.[2]

My current predicament was in stark contrast. Not for me the luxury of being hidden away in a cozy lamp or amulet. No—day in, day out, I was a djinni on the street, ducking, diving, taking risks, exposing myself to danger. And each day it became a little more difficult to survive.

For I was no longer the carefree Bartimaeus of old. My essence was raddled with Earth's corruption; my mind was bleary with the pain. I was slower, weaker, distracted from my tasks. I found it hard to change form. In battle my attacks were sputtering and weak—my Detonations had the explosive power of lemonade, my Convulsions trembled like jelly in a breeze. All my strength had gone. Where once, in the previous night's scrap,

---

[1] When goaded into invoking the spell of Indefinite Confinement, magicians usually compress the spirit into the first object they spy close at hand. I once cheeked a master a little too cleverly during his afternoon tea; before I knew it I was imprisoned inside a half-filled pot of strawberry jam and would have remained there possibly for all eternity had not his apprentice opened it by mistake at supper that same evening. Even so, my essence was infested with sticky little seeds for ages after.

[2] The afrit Honorius was a case in point: he went mad after a hundred years' confinement in a skeleton. A rather poor show; I like to think with my engaging personality I could keep myself entertained a *little* longer than that.

I would have sent that public convenience right back at the she-pig, adding a phone box and a bus stop for good measure, now I could do nothing to resist. I was vulnerable as a kitten. A few small buildings in the face, I could stand. But already I was practically at the mercy of second-rate fops such as Ascobol, a fool with no great history to speak of.[3] And if I met a foe with even a grain of power, my luck would surely end.

A weak djinni is a bad slave—bad twice over, since he is both ineffective *and* a laughingstock. It does a magician no favors to maintain one in the world. This is the reason why they usually allow us back to the Other Place on a temporary basis, to repair our essence and renew our strength. No master in his right mind would permit a djinni to deteriorate as far as I had done.

No master in his right mind . . . Well, that of course was the problem.

---

[3] It is a curious fact that, despite our fury at being summoned into this world, spirits such as I derive a good deal of retrospective satisfaction from our exploits. At the time, of course, we do our darnedest to avoid them, but afterward we often display a certain weary pride in the cleverest, bravest, or most jammy events on our C.V. Philosophers might speculate this is because we are essentially *defined* by our experiences in this world, since in the Other Place we are not so easily individualized. Thus, those with long and glittering careers (e.g. me) tend to look down on those (e.g. Ascobol) whose names have been unearthed more recently, and haven't amassed so many fine achievements. In Ascobol's case, I also disliked him for his silly falsetto voice, which ill becomes an eight-foot cyclops.

Look for the first book in the
thrilling and chilling

series

The Screaming Staircase
JONATHAN STROUD

Lockwood & Co.

BOOK ONE

The Screaming Staircase

Chapter 1

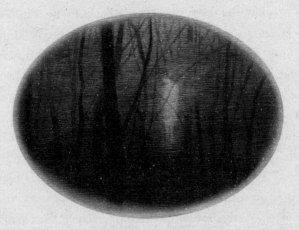

Of the first few hauntings I investigated with Lockwood & Co. I intend to say little, in part to protect the identity of the victims, in part because of the gruesome nature of the incidents, but mainly because, in a variety of ingenious ways, we succeeded in messing them all up. There, I've admitted it! Not a single one of those early cases ended as neatly as we'd have wished. Yes, the Mortlake Horror was driven out, but only as far as Richmond Park, where even now it stalks by night among the silent trees. Yes, both the Gray Specter of Aldgate and the entity known as the Clattering Bones were destroyed, but not before several further (and I now think unnecessary) deaths. And as for the creeping shadow that haunted young Mrs. Andrews, to the imperilment of her sanity and her hemline, wherever she may continue to wander in this world, poor thing, there it follows too. So it was not exactly an unblemished record that we took with us, Lockwood and I, when we walked up the path to 62 Sheen Road on that misty autumn afternoon and briskly rang the bell.

We stood on the doorstep with our backs to the muffled traffic, and Lockwood's gloved right hand clasped upon the bell pull. Deep in the house, the echoes faded. I gazed at the door, at the small sun blisters on the varnish and the scuffs on the letter box, at the four diamond panes of frosted glass that showed nothing beyond except for darkness. The porch had a forlorn and unused air, its corners choked with the same sodden beech leaves that littered the path and lawn.

"Okay," I said. "Remember our new rules. Don't blab about everything you see. Don't speculate openly about who killed who, how, or when. And, above all, don't impersonate the client. Please. It never goes down well."

"That's an awful lot of don'ts, Lucy," Lockwood said.

"I've plenty more."

"You know I've got an excellent ear for accents. I copy people without thinking."

"Fine, copy them quietly *after* the event. *Not* loudly, *not* in front of them, and *particularly* not when they're a six-foot-six Irish dockworker with a speech impediment, and we're a good half-mile from the public road."

"Yes, he was really quite nimble for his size," Lockwood said. "Still, the chase kept us fit. Sense anything?"

"Not yet. But I'm hardly likely to, out here. You?"

He let go of the bell pull and made some minor adjustment to the collar of his coat. "Oddly enough, I have. There was a death in the yard sometime in the last few hours. Under that laurel halfway up the path."

"I assume you're going to tell me it's only a smallish glow." My head was tilted to one side, my eyes half closed; I was listening to the silence of the house.

"Yes, about mouse-sized," Lockwood admitted. "Suppose it might have been a vole. I expect a cat got it, or something."

"So . . . possibly not part of our case, then, if it was a mouse?"

"Probably not."

Beyond the frosted panes, in the interior of the house, I spied a movement: something shifting in the hall's black depths. "Here we go," I said. "She's coming. Remember what I said."

Lockwood bent his knees and picked up the duffel bag beside his feet. We both moved back a little, preparing pleasant, respectful smiles.

We waited. Nothing happened. The door stayed shut.

There was no one there.

As Lockwood opened his mouth to speak, we heard footsteps behind us on the path.

"I'm so sorry!" The woman emerging from the mists had been walking slowly, but as we turned, she accelerated into a token little trot. "So sorry!" she repeated. "I was delayed. I didn't think you'd be so prompt."

She climbed the steps, a short, well-padded individual with a round face expanding into middle age. Her straight, ash-blond hair was pulled back in a no-nonsense manner by clips above her ears. She wore a long black skirt, a crisp white shirt, and an enormous wool cardigan with sagging pockets at the sides. She carried a thin folder in one hand.

"Mrs. Hope?" I said. "Good evening, madam. My name is Lucy Carlyle, and this is Anthony Lockwood, of Lockwood and Company. We've come about your call."

The woman halted on the topmost step but one, and regarded us with wide, gray eyes in which all the usual emotions figured. Distrust, resentment, uncertainty, and dread: they were all there. They come standard in our profession, so we didn't take it personally.

Her gaze darted back and forth between us, taking in our neat clothes and carefully brushed hair, the polished rapiers glittering at our belts, the heavy bags we carried. It lingered long on our faces. She made no move to go past us to the door of the house. Her free hand was thrust deep into the pocket of her cardigan, forcing the fabric down.

"Just the two of you?" she said at last.

"Just us," I said.

"You're very young."

Lockwood ignited his smile; its warmth lit up the evening. "That's the idea, Mrs. Hope. That's the way it has to be."

"Actually, I'm *not* Mrs. Hope." Her own wan smile, summoned in involuntary response to Lockwood's, flickered across her face and vanished, leaving anxiety behind. "I'm her daughter, Suzie Martin. I'm afraid Mother isn't coming."

"But we arranged to meet her," I said. "She was going to show us around the house."

"I know." The woman looked down at her smart black shoes. "I'm afraid she's no longer willing to set foot here. The circumstances of Father's death were horrible enough, but recently the nightly . . . *disturbances* have been getting too persistent. Last night was especially bad, and Mother decided she'd had enough. She's staying with me now. We'll have to sell, but obviously we can't do that until the house is made safe. . . ." Her eyes narrowed slightly. "Which is why you're here. . . . Excuse me, but shouldn't you have a supervisor? I thought an adult always had to be present in an investigation. Exactly how old *are* you?"

"Old enough and young enough," Lockwood said, smiling. "The perfect age."

"Strictly speaking, madam," I added, "the law states that an adult is only required if the operatives are undergoing training. It's true that some of the bigger agencies *always* use supervisors, but that's their private policy. We're fully qualified and independent, and *we* don't find it necessary."

"In our experience," Lockwood said sweetly, "adults just get in the way. But of course we *do* have our licenses here, if you'd like to see them."

The woman ran a hand across the smooth surface of her neat blond hair. "No, no . . . that won't be necessary. Since Mother clearly wanted you, I'm sure it will be fine. . . ." Her voice was neutral and uncertain. There was a brief silence.

"Thank you, madam." I glanced back toward the quiet, waiting door. "There's just one other thing. Is there someone else at home? When we rang the bell, I thought—"

Her eyes rose rapidly, met mine. "No. That's quite impossible. I have the only key."

"I see. I must've been mistaken."

"Well, I won't delay you," Mrs. Martin said. "Mother's filled out the form you sent her." She held out the manila folder. "She hopes it will be useful."

"I'm sure it will." Lockwood tucked it somewhere inside his coat. "Thank you very much. Well, we'd better get started. Tell your mother we'll be in touch in the morning."

The woman handed him a ring of keys. Somewhere on the road a car horn blared, to be answered by another. There was plenty of time until curfew, but night was falling and people were growing antsy. They wanted to get home. Soon there'd be nothing moving in the London streets but trails of mist and twisting moonbeams. Or nothing, at least, that any adult could clearly *see*.

Suzie Martin was conscious of this too. She raised her shoulders, pulled her cardigan tight. "Well, I'd better be going. I suppose I should wish you luck. . . ." She looked away. "So *very* young! How terrible that the world has come to this."

"Good night, Mrs. Martin," Lockwood said.

Without reply, she pattered down the steps. In a few seconds she had vanished among the mists and laurels in the direction of the road.

"She's not happy," I said. "I think we'll be off the case tomorrow morning."

"Better get it solved tonight, then," Lockwood said. "Ready?"

I patted the hilt of my rapier. "Ready."

He grinned at me, stepped up to the door and, with a magician's flourish, turned the key in the lock.

———

When entering a house occupied by a Visitor, it's always best to get in quick. That's one of the first rules you learn. Never hesitate, never linger on the threshold. Why? Because, for those few seconds, it's not too late. You stand there in the doorway with the fresh air on your back and the darkness up ahead, and you'd be an idiot if you didn't want to turn and run. And as soon as you acknowledge *that*, your willpower starts draining away through your boots, and the terror starts building in your chest, and bang, that's it—you're compromised before you begin. Lockwood and I both knew this, so we didn't hang around. We slipped straight through, put down our bags, and shut the door softly behind us. Then we stood quite still with our backs against it, watching and listening, side by side.

The hall of the house lately occupied by Mr. and Mrs. Hope was long and relatively narrow, though the high ceiling made it seem quite large. The floor was tiled in black and white marble squares, set diagonally, and the walls were palely papered. Halfway along, a steep staircase rose into shadows. The hall kinked around this to the left and continued into a void of black. Doorways opened on either side: gaping and choked in darkness.

All of which could have been nicely illuminated if we'd turned on the lights, of course. And there was a switch on the wall, right there. But we didn't attempt to use it. You see, a second rule you learn is this: electricity interferes. It dulls the senses and makes you weak and stupid. It's much better to watch and listen in the dark. It's good to have that fear.

We stood in silence, doing what we do. I listened; Lockwood

watched. It was cold in the house. The air had that musty, slightly sour smell you get in every unloved place.

I leaned in close to Lockwood. "No heating," I whispered.

"Mm-hm."

"Something else too, you think?"

"Mm-hm."

As my eyes grew used to the dark, I saw more details. Beneath the curl of the banister was a little polished table, on which sat a china bowl of potpourri. There were pictures on the wall, mostly faded posters of old-time musicals, and photographs of rolling hills and gentle seas. All pretty innocuous. In fact, it wasn't at all an ugly hallway; in bright sunlight it might have looked quite pleasant. But not so much now, with the last light from the door panes stretching out like skewed coffins on the floor in front of us; and with our shadows neatly framed inside them; and with the manner of old Mr. Hope's death in this very place hanging heavy on our minds.

I breathed hard to calm myself and shut out morbid thoughts. Then I closed my eyes against the taunting darkness and *listened*.

Listened . . .

Halls, landings, and staircases are the arteries and airways of any building. It's here that everything is channeled. You get echoes of things currently going on in all the connecting rooms. Sometimes you also get *other* noises that, strictly speaking, ought not to be there at all. Echoes of the past, echoes of hidden things . . .

This was one such time.

I opened my eyes, picked up my bag, and walked slowly down the hall toward the stairs. Lockwood was already standing by the little polished table beneath the banister. His face shone dimly in the light from the door. "Heard something?" he said.

"Yep."

"What?"

"A little knocking sound. Comes and goes. It's very faint, and I can't tell where it's coming from. But it'll get stronger—it's scarcely dark yet. What about you?"

He pointed at the bottom of the steps. "You remember what happened to Mr. Hope, of course?"

"Fell down the stairs and broke his neck."

"Exactly. Well, there's a tremendous residual death-glow right here, still lingering three months after he died. I should've brought my sunglasses, it's so bright. So what Mrs. Hope told George on the phone stacks up. Her husband tripped and tumbled down and hit the ground hard." He glanced up the shadowy stairwell. "Long, steep flight . . . Nasty way to go."

I bent low, squinting at the floor in the half-dark. "Yeah, look how the tiles have cracked. He must've fallen with tremendous f—"

Two sharp crashes sounded on the stairs. Air moved violently against my face. Before I could react, something large, soft, and horribly heavy landed precisely where I stood. The impact of it jarred my teeth.

I jumped back, ripping my rapier from my belt. I stood against the wall, weapon raised and shaking, heart clawing at my chest, eyes staring wildly side to side.

Nothing. The stairs were empty. No broken body sprawled lifeless on the floor.

Lockwood leaned casually against the banister. It was too dark to be certain, but I swear he'd raised an eyebrow. He hadn't heard a thing.

"You all right, Lucy?"

I breathed hard. "No. I just got the echo of Mr. Hope's last fall. It was very loud and very real. It was like he'd landed right on top of me. Don't laugh. It's not funny."

"Sorry. Well, *something's* stirring early tonight. It's going to get interesting later. What time is it?"

Having a watch with a luminous dial is my third recommended rule. It's best if it can also withstand sudden drops in temperature and strong ectoplasmic shock. "Not yet five," I said.

"Fine." Lockwood's teeth aren't quite as luminous as my watch, but when he grins, it's close. "Plenty of time for a cup of tea. Then we find ourselves a ghost."